The Marquis de Villemer

The Marquis de Villemer

George Sand

MINT EDITIONS

The Marquis de Villemer was first published in 1860.

This edition published by Mint Editions 2021.

ISBN 9781513279541 | E-ISBN 9781513284569

Published by Mint Editions®

 MINT
EDITIONS
minteditionbooks.com

Publishing Director: Jennifer Newens
Design & Production: Rachel Lopez Metzger
Translated from French by Ralph Keeler
Project Manager: Micaela Clark
Typesetting: Westchester Publishing Services

Contents

I

Letter to Madame Camille Heudebert

At D——, Via Blois

Do not worry, dear sister, for here I am, at Paris, without
accident or fatigue. I have slept a few hours, breakfasted
on a cup of coffee, made my toilet, and, in a moment, I am
going to take a carriage to Madame d'Arglade's, that she may
present me to Madame de Villemer. This evening I will write
you the result of the solemn interview, but I want first to mail
you these few words, that you may feel easy about my journey
and my health.

Take courage with me, my Camille; all will go well. God
does not abandon those who depend upon him, and who
do their best to second his tender providence. What has
been saddest for me in my resolution are your tears,—yours
and the dear little ones'; it is hard for me to restrain mine
when I think of them; but you *must* see it was absolutely
necessary. I could not sit with folded hands when you have
four children to rear. Since I have courage and health, and no
other claim upon me in this world than that of my tenderness
for you and for those poor angels, it was for me to go forth
and try to gain our livelihood. I will reach that end, be sure.
Sustain me instead of regretting me and making me weaker;
that is all I ask of you. And with this, my much-loved sister,
I embrace you and our dear children with all my heart. Do
not make them weep by speaking to them of me; but try,
nevertheless, not to let them forget me; that would pain me
beyond measure.

Caroline de Saint-Geneix
January 3, 1845

Second Letter.—To the Same

Victory, great victory! my good sister. I have just returned
from our great lady's, and—success unhoped for, as you
shall see. Since I have one more evening of liberty, and that

probably the last, I am going to profit by it in giving you an account of the interview. It will seem as if I were chatting with you again at the fireside, rocking Charley with one hand and amusing Lili with the other. Dear loves, what are they doing at this moment? They do not imagine that I am all alone in a melancholy room of a public house, for, in the fear of being troublesome to Madame d'Arglade, I put up at a little hotel; but I shall be very comfortable at the Marchioness's, and this lone evening is not a bad one for me to collect myself and think of you without interruption. I did well, besides, not to count too much upon the hospitality which was offered me, because Madame d'Arglade is absent, and so I had to introduce myself to Madame de Villemer.

You asked me to give you a description of her: she is about sixty years old, but she is infirm and seldom leaves her arm-chair; that and her suffering face make her look fifteen years older. She could never have been beautiful, or comely of form; yet her countenance is expressive and has a character of its own. She is very dark; her eyes are magnificent, just a little hard, but frank. Her nose is straight and too nearly approaches her mouth, which is not at all handsome. Her mouth is ordinarily scornful; still, her whole face gleams and mellows with a human sympathy when she smiles, and she smiles readily. My first impression agrees with my last. I believe this woman very good by principle rather than by impulse, and courageous rather than cheerful. She has intelligence and cultivation. In fine, she does not differ much from the description which Madame d'Arglade gave us of her.

She was alone when I was conducted into her apartment. Gracefully enough she made me sit down close to her, and here is a report of our conversation:—

"You have been highly recommended to me by Madame d'Arglade, whom I esteem very much indeed. I know that you belong to an excellent family, that you have talents and an honorable character, and that your life has been blameless. I have therefore the greatest wish that we may understand each other and agree. For that, there must be two things: one that my offer may seem satisfactory to you; the other that our views may not be too much opposed, as that would be the source of frequent misunderstandings. Let us deal with the first question. I offer you twelve hundred francs a year."

"So I have been told, Madame, and I have accepted."

"Have I not been told, too, that you would perhaps find that insufficient?"

"It is true, that is little for the needs of my situation; but Madame is the judge of her own affairs, and since I am here—"

"Speak frankly; you think that is not enough?"

"I cannot say that. It is probably more than my services are worth."

"I am far from saying so, and you—you say it from modesty; but you fear that will not be enough to keep you? Do not let it trouble you; I will take everything upon myself; you will have no expense here except for your toilet, and in that regard I make no requirement. And do you love dress?"

"Yes, Madame, very much; but I shall abstain from it, because in that matter you make no requirement."

The sincerity of my answer appeared to astonish the Marchioness. Perhaps I ought not to have spoken without restraint, as it is my habit to do. She took a little time to collect herself. Finally she began to smile and said, "Ah, so! why do you love dress? You are young, pretty, and poor; you have neither the need nor the right to bedizen yourself?"

"I have so little right to do it," I answered, "that I go simply clad, as you see."

"That is very well, but you are troubled because your toilet is not more elegant?"

"No, Madame, I am not troubled about it at all, since it must be so. I see that I spoke without reflection when I told you that I was fond of dress, and that has given you a poor idea of my understanding. I pray you to see nothing in that avowal but the effect of my sincerity. You questioned me concerning my tastes, and I answered as if I had the honor to be known to you; it was perhaps an impropriety, and I beg you to pardon it."

"That is to say," rejoined she, "if I knew you, I would be aware that you accept the necessities of your position without ill-temper and without murmuring?"

"Yes, Madame, that is it exactly."

"Well, your impropriety, if it is one at all, is far from displeasing me. I love sincerity above all things; I love it perhaps more than I do understanding, and I make an appeal to your entire frankness. Now what was it that persuaded you to accept such slight remuneration for coming here and keeping company with an infirm and perhaps tiresome old woman?"

"In the first place, Madame, I have been told that you are very intelligent and kind, and on that account I did not expect to find life tiresome with you; and then, even if I should have to endure a great deal, it is my duty to accept it all rather than to remain idle. My father having left us no fortune, my sister was at least well enough married, and I felt no scruples in living with her; but her husband, who had nothing but the salary of his place, recently died after a long and cruel illness, which had absorbed all our little savings. It therefore naturally falls upon me to support my sister and her four children."

"With twelve hundred francs!" cried the Marchioness. "No, that cannot be. Ah! Madame d'Arglade did not tell me that. She, without doubt, feared the distrust which misfortune inspires; but she was very much mistaken in my case; your self-devotion interests me, and, if we can agree in other respects, I hope to make you sensible of my regard. Trust in me; I will do my best."

"Ah! Madame," I replied, "whether I have the good fortune to suit you or not, let me thank you for this good prompting of your heart." And I kissed her hand impulsively, at which she did not seem displeased.

"Yet," continued she, after another silence, in which she appeared to distrust her own suggestion, "what if you are slightly frivolous and a little of a coquette."

"I am neither the one nor the other."

"I hope not. Yet you are very pretty. They did not tell me that either, and the more I look at you, the more I think you are even remarkably pretty. That troubles me a little, and I do not conceal it from you."

"Why, Madame?"

"Why? Yes, you are right. The ugly believe themselves

beautiful, and to the desire to please they add the faculty of making themselves ridiculous. You would better perhaps have the art of pleasing,—provided you do not abuse it. Well now, are you good enough girl and strong enough woman to give me a little account of your past life? Have you had some romance? Yes, you have,—have n't you? It is impossible that it could have been otherwise? You are twenty-two or twenty-three years old—"

"I am twenty-four, and I have had no other romance than the one of which I am going to tell you in two words. At seventeen I was sought in marriage by a person who pleased me, and who withdrew when he learned that my father had left more debts than capital. I was very much grieved, but I have forgotten it all, and I have sworn never to marry."

"Ah! that is spite, and not forgetfulness."

"No, Madame, that was an effort of the reason. Having nothing, but believing myself to be something, I did not wish to make a foolish marriage; and, far from having any spite, I have forgiven him who abandoned me. I forgave him especially the day when, seeing my sister and her four children in misery, I understood the sorrow of the father of a family who dies with the pain of knowing that he can leave nothing to his orphans."

"And you saw that ingrate again?"

"No, never. He is married, and I have ceased to think of him."

"And since then you have never thought of any other?"

"No, Madame."

"How have you done?"

"I do not know. I believe I have not had time to think of myself. When one is very poor, and does not want to give up to misery, the days are well filled out."

"But you have, nevertheless, been much sought after, pretty as you are,—have you not?"

"No, Madame, no one has troubled me in that way. I do not believe in persecutions which are not at all encouraged."

"I think as you do, and I am satisfied with your manner of answering. Do you, then, fear nothing for yourself in the future?"

"I fear nothing at all."

"And will not this solitude of the heart make you sad or sullen?"

"I do not foresee it in any way. I am naturally cheerful, and I have preserved my command over myself in the midst of the most cruel tests. I have no dream of love in my head; I am not romantic. If I ever change I shall be very much astonished. That, Madame, is all I can tell you about myself. Will you take me such as I represent myself with confidence, since I can after all but give myself out for what I know myself to be?"

"Yes, I take you for what you are,—an excellent young woman, full of frankness and good-will. It remains to be seen whether you really have the little attainments that I require."

"What must I do?"

"Talk, in the first place; and upon that point I am already satisfied. And then you must read, and play a little music."

"Try me right away; and if the little I can do suits you—"

"Yes, yes," she said, putting a book into my hands, "do read; I want to be enchanted with you."

At the end of a page she took the book away from me, with the remark that my reading was perfect. Then came the music. There was a piano in the room. She asked me if I could read at sight. As that is about all I can do, I could satisfy her again on that point. Finally she told me that, knowing my writing and my style of composition, from letters of mine which Madame d'Arglade had shown her, she considered that I would be an excellent secretary, and she dismissed me, giving me her hand, and saying many kind things to me. I asked her for one day—to-morrow—in order to see some people here with whom we are acquainted, and she has given orders that I should be installed Saturday.—

Dear sister, I have just been interrupted. What a pleasant surprise! It is a note from Madame de Villemer,—a note of three lines, which I transcribe for you:—

"Permit me, dear child, to send you a trifle on account, for your sister's children, and a little dress for yourself. As you are fond of dress we must humor the weaknesses of those we like.

It is arranged and understood that you are to have a hundred and fifty francs a month, and that I take upon myself to keep you in clothes."

How good and motherly that is,—is it not? I see that I shall love that woman with all my heart, and that I had not estimated her, at first sight, as highly as she deserved. She is more impulsive than I thought. The five hundred franc bill I enclose in this letter. Make haste! some wood in the cellar, some woollen petticoats for Lili, who needs them, and a chicken from time to time on that poor table. A little wine for you; your stomach is quite shattered, and it will take so little to restore it. The chimney must be repaired; it smokes atrociously: it is unbearable; it may weaken the children's eyes,—and those of my little girl are so beautiful!

Really, I am ashamed of the dress which is intended for me,—a dress of magnificent pearl-gray silk. Ah, how foolish I was to say that I liked to be well dressed! A dress for forty francs would have satisfied my ambition, and here I am attired in one worth two hundred, while my poor sister is repairing her rags. I do not know where to hide myself; but do not at least think that I am humiliated by receiving a present. I shall relieve my conscience of the burden of these kindnesses, my heart tells me. You see, Camille, everything succeeds with me as soon as I enter upon it. I light, the first thing, upon an excellent woman, I get more than I had agreed to take, and I am received and treated as a child whom it is desired to adopt and spoil. And then to think that you kept me back a whole six months, imposing an increase of privations upon yourself and tearing your hair at the idea of my working for you! Good sister, were you not then a bad mother? Ought not those dear treasures of children to have been considered above all things, and should they not have silenced even our own regard for each other? Ah! I was very much afraid of failure, nevertheless, I will confess to you now, when I took out of the house our last few louis for the expenses of my journey, at the risk of returning without having pleased this lady. God has been concerned in it, Camille; I prayed to him this morning with such confidence! I asked him so fervently to make me amiable, decorous, and persuasive. Now I am going to bed, for I am overcome with fatigue. I love you, my little sister, you know, more than anything else in the world, and much more than myself. Do not grieve about me then; I am just now the happiest girl that lives, and yet I am not with you and do not see our children as they sleep! You see, indeed, that there is no true happiness in selfishness, since, alone as I am, separated from all that I love, my heart beats with joy in spite of my tears, and I am going to thank God upon my knees before I fall asleep.

CAROLINE

While Mlle de Saint-Geneix was writing to her sister, the Marchioness de Villemer was talking with the youngest of her sons in her little drawing-room in the Faubourg Saint-Germain. The house was large and respectable; yet the Marchioness, formerly rich and now in very narrow circumstances,—we shall soon see why,—had of late occupied the second floor in order to turn the first to account.

"Well, dear mother," said the Marquis, "are you satisfied with your new companion? Your people have told me that she has arrived."

"My dear child," answered the Marchioness, "I have but one word to say of her, and that is that she has bewitched me."

"Really? Tell me about it."

"Upon my word, I am not too sure that I dare. I am afraid of turning your head in advance."

"Fear nothing," was the sorrowful reply of the Marquis, whom his mother had tried to win into a smile; "even if I were so easy to inflame, I know too well what I owe to the dignity of your house and to the repose of your life."

"Yes, yes, my friend; I know too that I can be at ease upon a question of honor and delicacy, when it is with you that I have to do; I can also tell you that the little D'Arglade has found for me a pearl, a diamond, and that, to commence with, this phoenix has led me into follies."

The Marchioness gave an account of her interview with Caroline, and described her thus: "She is neither tall nor short, she is well formed, has pretty little feet, the hands of a child, abundant light blond hair, a complexion of lilies and roses, perfect features, pearly teeth, a decided little nose, large sea-green eyes, which look straight at you unflinchingly, without dreaminess, without false timidity, with a candor and a confidence which please and engage; nothing of a provincial, she has manners which are excellent because they do not seem to be manners at all; much taste and gentility in the poverty of her attire; in a word, all that I feared and yet nothing that I feared, that is, beauty which inspired me with distrust and none of the affectations and pretensions which would have justified that distrust; and more, a voice and pronunciation which make real music of her reading, sterling talent as a musician, and, above all that, every indication of mind, sense, discretion, and good-nature: to such an extent that, interested and carried away by her devotion to a poor family to which I see plainly she is sacrificing herself, I forgot my projects of economy, and have engaged to give her the eyes out of my head."

"Has she been bargaining with you?" demanded the Marquis.

"Quite the contrary, she was satisfied to take what I had determined to give her."

"In that case you did well, mother, and I am glad that you have at last a companion worthy of you. You have kept too long that hungry and sleepy old maid who worried you, and when you have a chance to replace her by a treasure, you would do very wrong to count the cost."

"Yes," replied the Marchioness, "that's what your brother also says; neither he nor you care to count the cost, my dear children, and I fear I have been too hasty in the satisfaction which I have just given myself."

"That satisfaction was necessary to you," said the Marquis with spirit, "and you ought the less to reproach yourself with it since you have yielded to your need of performing a good action."

"I acknowledge it, but I was wrong perhaps," replied the Marchioness, with a careworn expression; "one has not always the right to be charitable."

"Ah! my mother," cried the son, with a mingling of indignation and sadness, "when you are forced to deny yourself the joy of giving alms, the injury that I have done will be very great!"

"The injury! you? what injury?" rejoined the mother, astonished and troubled; "you have never done an injury, my dear son."

"Pardon me," said the Marquis, greatly moved. "I was to blame the day I engaged, out of respect to you, to pay my brother's debts."

"Hush!" cried the Marchioness, turning pale. "Let us not speak of that, we would not understand each other." She extended her hands to the Marquis to lessen the involuntary bitterness of this answer. The Marquis kissed his mother's hands and retired shortly afterward.

The next day, Caroline de Saint-Geneix went out to mail with her own hands the registered letter which she sent to her sister, and to see some people from the remotest part of her province with whom she kept up her acquaintance. These were old friends of her family, whom she did not succeed in meeting, and she left her name without giving her address, as she no longer had a home which she could consider her own. She felt a species of sadness to think of herself thus lost and dependent in a strange house; but she did not indulge in long reflections upon her destiny. In addition to the fact that she refused once for all to nourish in herself the least unnerving melancholy, she was not at all a timid character, and any test, howsoever unpleasant, did not set her at variance with life. There was in her organization an astonishing vitality, an ardent activity, which was all the more remarkable because it arose from great tranquillity of mind and from a singular absence of thought about herself. This character, which is exceptional enough, will develop and explain itself as much as we can make it do so, by the events of the following narrative; but the reader must necessarily remember, what all the world knows, that no one can explain completely and set in an exact light the character of another. Every individual has in the depth of his being a mystery of power or of weakness which he himself can as little reveal as he can understand. Analysis should seem satisfactory when it comes near to truth, but it could not seize the truth in the fact without leaving some phase of the eternal problem of the soul incomplete or obscure.

II

It was with a mingled feeling of sadness and joy that Caroline, sometimes on foot and sometimes in an omnibus, traversed all alone the great city of Paris, where she had been reared in ease, and which she had left ruined and broken as to her future, in the very flower of her life. Let us recount in a few words, once for all, the grave, yet simple events of which she has given some outlines to the Marchioness de Villemer.

She was the daughter of a gentleman of Lower Brittany, settled in the neighborhood of Blois, and of a Mlle de Grajac, a native of Velay. Caroline hardly knew her mother. Madame de Saint-Geneix died the third year of her marriage in giving birth to Camille, having exacted a promise from Justine Lanion to spend several years with the motherless children.

Justine Lanion—Peyraque, by marriage—was a robust and honest peasant-woman of Velay, who consented to remain eight years with M. de Saint-Geneix. She had been Caroline's nurse, and had afterward returned to her own family, whence she was soon called back to give the milk of her second child to the second daughter of her "dear lady." Thanks to this faithful creature, Caroline and Camille knew the care and tenderness of a second mother; still, Justine could not forget her husband and her own children. She had, at last, to return to her province, and M. de Saint-Geneix took his daughters to Paris, where they were brought up in one of the convents then in fashion.

As he was not rich enough to live in Paris, he rented temporary apartments there, to which he went twice a year for the Easter Holidays and his daughters' vacations. These were also the worthy man's vacations. He practised economy the rest of the year that he might refuse nothing to his children in those days of patriarchal merry-making. Then their time was absorbed wholly in strolls, concerts, visiting the museums, excursions to the royal palaces or dinners, ruinous in their expense,—veritable pleasurings of a life, full of simple, paternal affection, indeed, but as imprudent as it well could be. The good man idolized his daughters, who were both very beautiful and as good as they were beautiful. It was a pleasant fancy with him to see them going out for a walk, dressed with perfect taste, looking fresher than their dresses and ribbons new from the shop; to display their beauty in the light and sunshine of Paris, that brilliant city, where he had few acquaintances, to be sure, but where the slightest notice of some casual passer-by seemed more important than any amount of provincial admiration. To make Parisians, real Parisian ladies, of these two charming girls was the dream of his life. He would have spent his whole fortune to accomplish this; and—he did so spend it.

This infatuated desire to taste the delights of life in Paris is a species of fatality which had, a few years ago, taken possession not only of the well-to-do people of the provinces, but of whole classes. Every great foreign nobleman, also, howsoever little his cultivation, rushed wildly to Paris, like a school-boy in vacation time, tore himself away from its attractions with bitter regret, and passed the rest of the year at home in devising measures to obtain the passport giving him leave to return. Even to-day, if it were not for the severity of laws which condemn Russians to Russia, and Poles to Poland, immense fortunes would vie with one another in their eagerness to come and be swallowed up in the pleasures of Paris.

The two young ladies each profited very differently by their elegant education. Camille, the younger and the prettier of the two,—which is saying a great deal,—entered heartily into the giddy tastes of her father, whom she resembled in face and in character. She was passionately fond of luxury, and it had never occurred to her that her life could ever become unhappy. Mild and loving, but not very intelligent, she became merely an accomplished young lady in the matters of style, dress, and manners. Returning to the convent at the close of her vacations, she passed three months languishing regretfully, the next three working a little in order to please her sister, who would otherwise find fault with her; and the rest of the term in dreaming about her father's return and the pleasures it would bring.

Caroline, on the other hand, was more like her mother, who had been a woman of seriousness and energy. Yet she was usually cheerful, and more demonstrative even than her sister in the hearty enjoyment of their freedom. She showed herself more eager to make the most of dress, of their walks and their sightseeing, but she relished all in a different way. She was far more intellectual than Camille, with no creative genius for Art indeed, but yet deeply sensitive to all its true manifestations. She was born appreciative; that is, she could express the unspoken thought of another with brilliancy and refinement. She repeated poetry or read music with a surprising mastery of both. She spoke little, but always well, yet with a strange precision, as if her ideas were all drawn from within. But whenever she received suggestions from outside sources,—from books, music, or the stage,—she gave the written thought a new radiance. She seemed to be the necessary instrument of genius; within the limits of interpretation, this gift of hers might have been genius itself, had it received its full development.

But this it never received. Caroline had commenced her education at ten years of age; at seventeen it was wholly broken off. This is the way it happened: M. de Saint-Geneix having an income of only twelve thousand francs, and yet dreaming of a future for his daughters worthy of their attractions, had entangled himself with pitiable ingenuousness in speculations which were to quadruple his property, and which engulfed it in instant ruin.

Very pale, and as if dazed by some powerful shock, he came one day to Paris for his daughters. He took them to his little manor-house with no explanation whatever, and complaining only of a slight fever. He lay there ill for three months, and then died of grief, confessing his ruin to his two future sons-in-law; for at the appearance of the young ladies at Blois, many suitors presented themselves, and two of them had been accepted.

The gentleman betrothed to Camille was a civil officer, a respectable man, who was sincerely fond of her, and married her in spite of everything. Caroline was engaged to a gentleman of property. He reasoned more selfishly, plead the opposition of his family, and withdrew his pretensions. Caroline was brave. Her weaker sister would have died of grief; but she was not the one deserted. Weakness exacts respect oftener than energy. Moral courage is something invisible, and it breaks down silently. Killing a soul too leaves no trace. Therefore the strong are always buffeted, and the weak are buoyed up always.

Fortunately for Caroline, her love had not been intense. Her heart, which was naturally affectionate, had begun to feel some confidence and sympathy; but the mysterious grief and the increasing illness of her father very soon took such strong possession of her mind that she could not permit herself to dwell much upon her own happiness. The love of a noble young woman is a flower which opens in the sunshine of hope; but all hopefulness on her own account was overshadowed by the feeling that her father's life was swiftly gliding away. She saw in her betrothed only a friend who would share with her the duty of weeping. Toward him she felt gratitude and esteem; but grief stood in the way of elation and enthusiasm. Passion had not had time to blossom.

Caroline was then rather bruised than broken by desertion. Her love for her father was so great, and she mourned him so deeply, that the ruin of her own future prospects seemed to her but a secondary grief. Though she was not at all indignant, yet she was sensible of the injury, and while she revenged herself only by forgetting, she preserved toward men a certain vague resentment, which kept her from believing in love and from listening to the flatteries addressed to her beauty up to the age at which we now find her, cured, courageous, and sincerely believing herself proof against all attraction.

It is unnecessary to recount the events of the years which we have just made her pass over. All the world knows that the loss of a fortune, small or great, does not become an accomplished fact visibly from one day to the next. Settlements with creditors are attempted, a belief that something may be saved from the wreck is entertained, a series of uncertainties is passed through, of astonishments, hopes deferred, up to the day when, seeing all efforts fruitless, the situation, good or bad, is finally accepted. Camille was prostrated by this disaster, in which, to the last moment, she refused to believe; but she was well married and did not suffer any real hardship. Caroline, with more foresight, was apparently less affected by the positive destitution which necessarily fell upon her. Her brother-in-law would not entertain the thought of their parting, and generously made her share the competence of his family; but she understood perfectly that her support was gone, and her pride increased on that account. Feeling that her sister lacked activity and a sense of order, and seeing moreover that she would be subject from year to year to the suffering and cares of maternity, Caroline became the housekeeper, the nurse of the children, in short, the first maid-servant of the little household, and into the austere duties of this self-sacrifice she contrived to work so much grace, good sense, and cheerfulness, that all was pleasant around her and she rendered more good offices than she received. Then came the illness of her brother-in-law, his death, the discovery of old debts which he had concealed, intending to pay them off, gradually and easily, out of his salary; in short, the embarrassment, anxiety, and trouble of Camille, and, at last, the utter despondency and misery of the young widow.

We have seen that, for some time, Caroline had been hesitating between the fear of leaving her sister alone and the desire to assist her by some direct effort. There was, indeed, one wealthy gentleman, neither young nor very gracious, who considered her a model housewife, and made her an offer of marriage. Caroline felt, at first vaguely but afterwards with sufficient clearness, that Camille wished her to sacrifice herself. She then determined that she would indeed make the sacrifice, but in a different way. She asked nothing better than to give up her freedom, her independence, her time, her life; but to demand the offering up of herself, soul and body, to procure a little more comfort for the family,—this was too much. She pardoned in the mother her selfishness as a sister, and without appearing to see it, she decided upon the course which we have seen her take. She left Camille in a poor little country home, rented in the neighborhood of Blois, and set out for Paris, where we know she was kindly welcomed by Madame de Villemer, whose history we have now also briefly to relate.

Every family has its sore spot, every fortune its open wound out of which its life-blood and the very security of its existence may ebb away. The noble family of Villemer had its skeleton in the wild misdoings of the eldest son of the Marchioness. The first husband of the Marchioness had been the Duke d'Aléria, a haughty Spaniard, with a terrible disposition, who had made her as unhappy as she could be, but who, after five stormy years, had left her an ample fortune, and a son handsome, good-humored, and intelligent, though destined to become thoroughly sceptical, royally prodigal, and miserably profligate.

Having married the Marquis de Villemer, and becoming a mother and widow for the second time, the Marchioness found in Urbain, her second son, a devoted, generous friend, as austere in his habits as his brother was corrupt, rich enough by his paternal inheritance to prevent him from grieving too much about his mother's ruin; for, at the time when we begin our history of these three people, the Marchioness had little or nothing left, thanks to the life which the young Duke had led.

At this period, the young Duke was a little over thirty-six years of age, and the Marquis nearly thirty-three. The Duchess d'Aléria, as will be seen, had lost little time in becoming the Marchioness de Villemer. No one had blamed her for this. She was passionately attached to her second husband. It is even said that she had loved him as far as she might, in all honor and innocence, before her first widowhood. The Marchioness had a generous nature and was somewhat excitable. And the premature death of this second husband made her almost insane for one or two years. She would not see any one, and even her own children became almost like strangers to her. Seeing this, the relatives of both her late husbands were disposed to set her aside and to take charge themselves of the education of her sons; but, at this idea, the Marchioness came to her senses. Nature made a great effort; her soul rose above its sorrow, her motherly feeling awoke, and the passionate crisis which made her cling to her two sons with tears and caresses, restored her power of reasoning and the control of her will. She remained an invalid, weak and prematurely old, a little peculiar in some respects, yet highly energetic in her conduct, exemplary in her affections, and truly noble in all her relations with the world. From this time forth, she began to attract notice by the brightness of her mind, which had been for a long time asleep as it were in the midst of her sorrow and her love, but which now, at last, showed itself in the form of courage.

What precedes has sufficiently established her position in this story. We will now leave Caroline de Saint-Geneix to estimate as she understands them the Marchioness and her two sons.

Letter to Madame Camille Heudebert

Paris, March 15, 1845

Yes, dear little sister, I am very well settled, as I have told you in my preceding letters. I have a pretty room, a good fire, a fine carriage, servants, and a well-furnished table. I have only to believe myself rich and a Marchioness, since, scarcely ever out of the presence of my old lady, I am necessarily a sharer in all the comforts of her life.

But you reproach me with writing very short letters. It is because, up to this time, I have had but a few moments to myself. In fact, the Marchioness, who, I believe, wished to put me a little to proof, appears now to be satisfied that I am quite sincerely devoted to her, and she permits me to leave her at midnight. So I can chat with you without having to sit up till four o'clock in the morning to do it, for the Marchioness receives till two, and she kept me an hour afterward to discuss the people whom we had just seen,—a task which, I will confess to you as I confessed to her, began to be very wearisome to me. She thought that I was, like her, a late riser. When she learned that I always awoke at six o'clock in the morning, and could not get asleep again, she generously respected that "provincial infirmity." So, morning or evening, I shall be hereafter at your service, dear Camille.

Yes, I love this old lady, and I love her a great deal. She has a great charm for me, and the influence which she exercises over my mind comes especially from the sincerity and purity of her own. She is not without prejudices, it is true, and she has many ideas which are not, and never will be, mine; but she holds to these honestly, without anything like hypocritical subterfuge, and the antipathies which she expresses are not at all formidable; for even in her prepossessions her perfect integrity is manifest.

And besides, during the three weeks in which I have seen the great world,—since the Marchioness, without giving formal parties, receives quite a number of visits every evening,—I have become aware of a general eclipse, of which, in the remoteness of my province, I never formed so complete an idea. I assure you that, with the best of manners and a certain air of superiority, people here are as nearly nonentities as they can possibly be. They no longer have opinions on anything; they find fault with everything, and know the remedy for nothing. They speak ill of everybody, and are nevertheless on the best terms with everybody. There is no indignation about it, just merely scandal. They are always predicting the greatest catastrophes, and they seem to enjoy the most profound security. In a word, they are as empty and shallow as fickleness, as weakness itself; and in the midst of these troubled spirits and of these threadbare convictions, I love this old Marchioness, so frank in her antipathies and so nobly inaccessible to compromise. I seem to see a personage of another century, a sort of female Duke de Saint-Simon, guarding the respect of rank as a religion, and understanding nothing of the power of money against which feeble or hypocritical protests are made around her.

And as far as I am concerned, you know the contempt of money goes a good way. Our misfortunes have not changed me, for I do not call by the name of money that sacred thing, the salary which I now earn here proudly and even with a little haughtiness. That is duty, a guaranty of honor. Luxury itself, when it is the continuation or the recompense of an elevated life, does not inspire me with the philosophic disdain which always conceals a trifle of envy; but wealth coveted, hunted up and down, bought at the price of ambitious marriages, by the unwinding of political conscience, by family intrigues about successions,—these are what justly wear the villanous name of money, and on that point I agree heartily with the Marchioness, who has no pardon for interested and ill-suited marriages, and for all other insipid things, whether private or public.

That is why the Marchioness without regret and without dread sees all that she possesses fall day by day into a gulf. I have already said something to you about that. I told you that the Duke d'Aléria, her elder son, ruined her, while the younger, the Marquis, the son of her last husband, came to her support with tender respect, and again placed her upon a very comfortable footing.

I must now speak of these two gentlemen, of whom I have yet told you but a few words. I have seen the Marquis from the first day of my installation here. Every morning from noon to one o'clock, and every evening from eleven till midnight, he passes with his mother. Besides, he dines with her quite frequently. I have therefore had time to observe him, and I imagine that I already know him tolerably well. He is a young man who appears to me to have had no youth. His health is delicate, and his mind, which is cultivated and elevated, is engaged in a struggle against some secret grief, or a natural tendency to sadness. He could not have an external appearance less striking at first sight, and exciting more sympathy in proportion to the degree in which his face reveals itself. He is neither tall nor short, neither handsome nor homely. There is nothing negligent or studied in his style of dress. He seems to have an instinctive aversion to everything which might draw attention to the person. Yet one sees very soon that he is no ordinary man. The few words which he says to you have a deep or delicate meaning, and his eyes, when they lose the perplexity of a certain shyness, are so handsome, so good, so intelligent, that I do not believe I ever met their equals.

His conduct toward his mother is admirable and paints him at full length. I saw him pay out several millions, all his personal fortune, to discharge the rash debts of the elder son, and he never frowned, never said a word, never showed any vexation or regret. The weaker she was toward this ungrateful and graceless son, the more tender and devoted and respectful was the Marquis. You see it is impossible not to esteem this man, and, as for me, I feel a sort of veneration for him.

His conversation, too, is very agreeable. He scarcely speaks at all in society; but in intimacy, when the first reserve is worn off, he talks charmingly. He is not only a cultivated man, he is a well of science. I believe he has read everything, for upon whatever subject you suggest, he is interesting, and proves that he has sounded it to the bottom. His conversation is so necessary to his mother, that when anything prevents his accustomed visit or lessens its duration, she is restless, and, as it were, out of her reckoning for the remainder of the day.

At first, as soon as I saw him come in the morning, I took it upon myself to retire, and I did so the more readily, seeing that this superior and therefore excessively modest man appeared embarrassed by my presence. It was doing me great honor, to be sure; but at the end of three or four days he had so far regained his tranquillity as to ask me very kindly why he put me to flight. I should not have believed myself authorised by that to restrain the confidential freedom of the son and mother; but she herself begged me to stay, even insisting upon it, and she afterward gave me with her habitual frankness her reason for so doing. And here is that reason, which is a little singular:—

"My son is of a melancholy spirit," she said; "that, however, is not my character. I am very much depressed or very animated, never dreamy, and dreaminess in others irritates me a little. In my son it troubles or afflicts me. I have never been able to resign myself to it. When we are alone together it requires constant effort on my part to keep him from falling into his reveries. When we are surrounded by fifteen or twenty persons of an evening, he gives himself up to his thoughts without restraint, and frequently maintains a complete reserve. To enjoy the full flavor of his mind, which is my peculiar pleasure and greatest happiness, nothing is more favorable than the presence of a third person, especially if that third person is one of merit. The Marquis then takes the trouble to be charming, at first out of politeness and then little by little out of a fastidious desire to please, though he may not suspect it himself. In fact, he is a man who needs to be drawn away from his own reflections, and he is so perfect to me that I have not the right or the wish to enter upon this contest openly, while the presence of a person, who even without saying anything is supposed to listen, forces him to exert himself; seeing that, if he fears to appear a pedant by speaking too much, he fears still more to appear affected when he forgets himself in thought. So, my dear, you will do us both a great service in not leaving us too much alone."

"Nevertheless, Madame," I answered, "if you should have private matters to speak about, how shall I know?"

Thereupon she promised that in such a case she would give me notice by asking me *if the clock is not slow.*

III

I go on with my letter which sleep forced me to leave off last night, and, as it is only nine o'clock and as I do not see the Marchioness before noon, I have all the intervening time to complete the details which will be necessary to post you as to my situation.

But it seems to me that I have described the Marquis to you sufficiently, and that you can now very well represent him to yourself. To answer all your questions, I am going to tell you how my days are passed.

The first fortnight was a little hard, I confess, now that I have obtained a very necessary modification of my duties. You know how much need I have of exercise, and how active I have been for the last six years; but here, alas! I have no house to keep in order and to run over from top to bottom a hundred times a day, no child to walk with and to make play, not even a dog with which I can run, under the pretext of amusing it. The Marchioness has a horror of animals; she goes out but once or twice a week to ride up and down the avenue of the Champs-Élysées. She calls that taking exercise. Infirm and unable to go up stairs, except with the aid of a servant's arm,—a thing dreadful enough to her, for she was once let fall in doing it,—she pays no visits, though she passes her life in receiving them. All the activity, all the vigor of her existence, is in her head, and much in her speech; she talks remarkably well and she knows it; but she is not on that account guilty of any weak vanity, and thinks less of making herself heard than of venting the ideas and sentiments which agitate her.

She has, you see, an energetic nature and a singular earnestness in her opinions of all things, even of those which seem to me of very little account. She could never be quite happy; she has been seeking to be so too long; and living with her incessantly is tiresome, in spite of the attraction which she exercises. Her hands are perfectly idle; nevertheless her sight is sharp and her fingers are still nimble, for she plays tolerably upon the piano; but she eschews everything that interferes with talking and no longer asks me to read or to play. She says that she holds my talents in reserve for the country, where she finds herself more alone and whither we are to go in two months. I look forward to this change with real pleasure, as here the life of the body is too much suppressed. And then the good Marchioness has the habit of living in a temperature of Senegal, besides covering herself with perfumes, and her apartment is filled with the most odorous of flowers; they are very beautiful to see, but in the absence of air, it is not so easy a thing to breathe.

Moreover I have to be idle, like her. I tried at first to embroider while with her; that, I saw very soon, disturbed her nerves. She asked me if I was working by the day, if there was any hurry for what I was doing, if it was very useful, and she interrupted a dozen times with no other motive than to see me stop the work which annoyed her. At last I had to abandon it altogether or it would have thrown her into a fit of illness. She was well pleased at this, and in order to insure herself against a renewal of the attempt on my part, she gave me a very frank exposition of her way of thinking in such matters. She holds that women who busy their hands and eyes with needlework put a great deal more of their minds into it than they are themselves willing to acknowledge. It is, according to her, a way of stultifying one's self in order to escape the tedium of existence. She does not understand it except in the hands of unhappy persons and of prisoners. And then she sweetened the draught for me by adding that this sort of work gave me the appearance of a lady's maid and that she wished me to be in the eyes of all her visitors her companion and her friend. So she puts me forward in conversation, referring to me frequently in order to force me to "show my intelligence,"—what I am especially careful not to do, for I feel that I have none at all when people are looking at me and listening to me.

I do my best, however, not to sit stolidly motionless, and I regret deeply that my old friend—since my friend she really is—does not consent to receive from me the most trifling service; she even rings for her maid to pick up her pocket-handkerchief, unless I hasten to seize it, and yet she reproaches me with devoting myself to her too much, not perceiving that I suffer for the want of something to which I can devote myself.

You may ask why, therefore, she has taken me into her service; I will tell you: she does not receive before four o'clock, and up to that time—that is, as soon as the Marquis leaves her—she hears the reading of the newspapers and attends to her correspondence; it is I, then, who read and write for her. Why she does not read and write herself, I am sure I do not know, for she is very able to do both. I think, however, I can see that she cannot endure solitude, and that the dread with which it inspires her cannot be counteracted by any occupation whatever. Certainly there is in her something strange which does not appear, but which exists in the secret places of her heart or head. Hers is perhaps a nature a little perverted by the relations it has been forced to sustain toward others. It is too late to teach her to be busy, and perhaps she cannot even think when she is alone.

It is certain that when I enter her apartment at the stroke of noon I find her very different from what I left her the night before in the midst of her drawing-room. She seems to grow ten years older every night. I know that her maids make a long toilet for her, during which she does not speak a single word to them, for she has a great contempt for people whose language is vulgar. She becomes so annoyed by the presence of these poor women (perhaps she has been sleepless, which also annoys her desperately), that she appears half dead and is frightfully pale when I first see her; but at the end of ten minutes this is no longer the case; she becomes thoroughly waked up, and by the time the Marquis arrives she has regained the ten years of the night.

Her correspondence, of which I ought to say nothing, although there is not the least secret about it, is by no means a necessity of her position or of her interests. It merely gratifies her need to talk with her absent friends. It is, she says, a manner of speaking, of exchanging ideas, which varies the only pleasure she knows, namely, that of being in continual communication with the minds of others.

So be it! but, for my part, that would not be my taste, if I were troubled with leisure. I would please myself only with those I loved, and certainly the Marchioness cannot love very much the forty or fifty persons to whom she writes, and the two or three hundred whom she receives every week.

My taste, however, does not come into the question, and I will not criticise her to whom I have given my liberty. That would be cowardly, for, after all, if I did not esteem or respect her, I should be free to betake myself elsewhere. Besides, supposing my respect and esteem are cumbered by the endurance of certain eccentricities,—as I might everywhere meet with eccentricities, and probably worse things,—I do not see why I should look with a magnifying-glass upon those which I want to put up with cheerfully and philosophically. Then, dear sister, if I have happened to blame or ridicule any one or anything here, take it as having escaped me inadvertently, and believe that with you I have not cared to restrain myself; for, be assured, nothing troubles me or gives me any real suffering.

The gist of all this is that in the soul of the Marchioness there is something strong, warm, and therefore sincere, which really attaches me to her and causes me to accept without the least repugnance the task of diverting her and keeping her cheerful. I know very well, whatever she may say, that I am something much worse than an attendant; I am a slave; but I am so by my own will, and therefore I feel in my conscience as free as the air. What is freer than the spirit of a captive, or of one proscribed for his faith?

I had not reflected upon all this when I left you, my sister; I believed that I would have to suffer a great deal. Well, I have reflected upon it now, and, save the want of exercise, which is altogether a physical matter, I have not suffered at all. That little suffering will be spared me hereafter; do not torment yourself about it. I was forced to acknowledge it to you. Henceforth I shall be permitted to go to sleep early enough, and I can walk in the garden of the hotel, which is not large, but in which I succeed in going a good way, while thinking of you and our wide fields. Then I imagine myself there, with you and the children around me,—a beautiful dream, which does me good.

But I perceive that I have told you nothing yet of the Duke; I now come to that subject.

It was no more than three days ago that I finally got sight of him. I will confess that I was not very impatient to see him. I could not help feeling a sort of horror of the man who has ruined his mother, and who, it is said, is adorned with every vice. Well, my surprise was very great, and if my aversion to his character abides, I am forced to say that his person is not, as I had pictured it, disagreeable to me.

In my dread I had endowed him with claws and horns. Nevertheless, you shall see how I approached this demon without recognizing him. I must tell you first that nothing could be more irregular than his relations with his mother. There are weeks, months even, in which he comes to see her almost every day; then he disappears, is not spoken of for months or weeks, and when he appears again there is no more explanation on one side or the other than if he had gone away the night before. I do not know yet how the Marchioness takes this. I have sometimes heard her mention her eldest son as calmly and respectfully as if she were speaking of the Marquis, and you may well suppose that I have never permitted myself to ask the least question upon a subject so delicate. She merely related once in my presence, but without any sort of comment, what I have just told you about the capricious irregularity of his visits.

I had indeed expected him sooner or later to make some sudden or mysterious appearance, but I was not thinking at all of him when, entering the drawing-room after dinner, as I usually do, to see that everything is arranged to suit the Marchioness, I did not notice a personage quietly installed there in a corner upon a small sofa. When the Marchioness has dined she returns to her apartment, where her maids ply her with a little white and rouge, and she remains there a quarter of an hour, while I inspect the lamps and flower-stands of the drawing-room. I was therefore absorbed in that grave duty, and profiting by the chance to give myself a little exercise, I moved to and fro very quickly, singing one of our home songs, when I found myself confronted by a pair of large blue eyes of unusual clearness. I bowed, asking pardon. The owner of the eyes arose, apologizing in turn, and, left to do the honors, but not knowing what to say to a new face which seemed to be asking me who I was, I chose the part of saying nothing at all.

The man having attained his feet, turned his back to the mantel-piece, and followed me with his eyes with an air of kindness rather than astonishment. He is tall, somewhat heavy-made, with a large face, and—what is most surprising—very attractive features. He could not have a sweeter, a more humane, even a more candid expression; the tone of his voice is subdued and tender, and there are in his pronunciation, as in his manners, the unmistakable marks of high-breeding. I will say even that there is a certain suavity in the slightest movements of this rattlesnake, and that his smile is like a child's.

Do you begin to understand something of the truth? For my part I was so far from suspecting it that I went nearer to the mantel-piece, feeling myself drawn thither, as it were, by the kindliness with which he regarded me, and I stood ready to reply in the most affable manner if he should feel inclined to speak to me. He appeared desirous to begin, and did so very frankly.

"Is Mlle Esther ill?" he asked in his soft voice and with a very polite intonation.

"Mlle Esther has not been here for two months," I answered. "I never knew her. It is I who have taken her place."

"O no!"

"Pardon me."

"Say that you have succeeded her! Spring does not take the place of winter; it causes it to be forgotten."

"Winter can nevertheless have good in it."

"O, you did not know Esther! She was sharp as the north-wind of December, and when she came near you you felt the approach of rheumatism!"

Then he went into a description of the poor Esther which was very lively, though not at all malicious, and it was altogether so droll that I could not restrain a burst of laughter.

"That's right!" he rejoined; "but do you laugh? Then we shall hear laughter here! I hope you laugh often?"

"Certainly, when there is a good occasion."

"There never was a good occasion for Esther. After all she was right: if she had laughed she would have shown her teeth. Ah! but do not hide yours. I have seen them, and yet I shall say nothing about them. I know nothing sillier than compliments. Would it be impertinent to ask your name? But no; do not tell me it. I guessed Esther's: I baptized her Rebecca. You see that I detected the race. I want to guess yours."

"Come, then, guess."

"Well, a very French name,—Louise, Blanche, Charlotte?"

"That's it; my name is Caroline."

"There! you see—and you come from one of the provinces?"

"From the country."

"But see! why have n't you red hands? Do you like it here in Paris?"

"No, not at all."

"I will lay a wager your relatives have compelled you—"

"No, no one has compelled me."

"But you find it tedious here? Confess now that you do."

"O no; I never find it tedious anywhere."

"You are no longer frank."

"I assure you I am."

"You are then very reasonable?"

"I pride myself on being so."

"And positive, perhaps?"

"No."

"Romantic, though?"

"Still less."

"What then?"

"Nothing."

"How nothing?"

"Nothing that merits the slightest attention. I can read, write, and reckon. I thrum a little on the piano. I am very obedient. I am conscientious in the discharge of my duties, and that is all it is important that I should be here."

"Well, now, you do not know yourself. Do you want me to tell you what you are? You are a person of intelligence and an excellent soul."

"You believe so?"

"I am sure of it. I see very quickly, and I judge tolerably well. And you? Do you form an idea of people at first sight?"

"O yes, more or less."

"Well, then, what do you think of me, for example?"

"Naturally I think of you what you think of me."

"Is that out of gratitude or of politeness?"

"No, it is from a sort of instinct."

"Indeed? I thank you for it. Now I will tell you what really gives me pleasure: not brightness of mind, by any means; almost everybody can have that; it can at least in a measure be acquired; but thorough goodness,—you do not think me very bad, do you? Then,—come, will you let me take your hand?"

"What for?"

"I will tell you directly. Do you refuse me? There is nothing more honest in the world than the sentiment which causes me to ask that favor of you."

There was something so true and so touching in the face and accent of this man, that, in spite of the strangeness of his demand and the still greater strangeness of my consent, I put my hand in his with confidence. He pressed it gently, detaining it but a second; but tears came to his eyes and he faltered as if with suffocation, "Thanks; take good care of my poor mother!"

And I, comprehending at last that this was the Duke d'Aléria, and that I had just been touching the hand of this soulless profligate, this undutiful son, this heartless brother, in a word this man without restraint or conscience, I felt my limbs giving way under me and I leaned upon the table, becoming so exceedingly pale that he noticed it, and made a movement toward sustaining me, while he exclaimed, "What! are you ill?"

But he paused when he perceived the dread and disgust with which he inspired me, or perhaps merely because his mother was just entering the room. She saw my trouble, and looked at the Duke as if to demand of him the cause. He answered only by kissing her hand in the most tender and respectful manner, and by asking the news about herself. I immediately retired, as much to collect myself as to leave them alone together.

When I re-entered the drawing-room several persons had arrived, and I entered into conversation with a certain Madame de D——, who is particularly kind to me, and who appears to be an excellent woman. She cannot, however, endure the Duke, and it is she who has told me all the evil I know of him. A feeling of reaction against the sympathy with which he had inspired me caused me, no doubt, to seek now the society of this lady.

"Well," she said, as if she had divined what was passing in me, while she regarded the Duke, then engaged in conversation not far from his mother, "you have at last seen him, the 'beloved child'? What have you to say of him?"

"He is amiable and handsome, and that is what in my eyes condemns him all the more."

"Yes, is it not so? His is certainly a fine organization, and it is incredible that he should be so well preserved and so intellectually bright after the life he has led; but do not go to trusting him. He is the most corrupt being that exists, and he is perfectly able to play the good apostle with you in order to compromise you."

"With me? O no! The humbleness of my position will preserve me from his attention."

"Not at all. You will see. I will not tell you that your merit raises you above your position, since that is evident to everybody; but to know that you are honest will be enough to inspire him with a desire to lead you astray."

"Do not attempt to frighten me; I would not stay here an hour, Madame, if I thought I were going to be insulted."

"No, no; that is not what you need apprehend. He is always gentlemanly in the society of gentle and pure people, and you will never have to guard yourself from any impropriety on his part. Quite the contrary; if you are not careful he will persuade you that he is a repentant angel, perhaps even a saint in disguise, and—you will be his dupe."

Madame de D—— said these last words in a compassionate tone which wounded me. I was going to reply, but I remembered what I had heard another old lady say, namely, that a daughter of Madame de D—— had been very much compromised by the Duke. The poor woman must suffer horribly at the sight of him, and I thus explain to myself how a person so indulgent toward all the world speaks of him with such bitterness; but I do not so easily explain to myself why, in spite of her repugnance at seeing him and hearing him named, she speaks of him to me with a sort of insistence every time she can get me aside. One would indeed think that I were destined to be taken in the snares of this Lovelace, and that she sought her revenge in disputing my poor soul with him.

A moment of reflection led me to regard her excessive fear as a trifle ridiculous, and wishing neither to make her angry with me nor to remind her of her own griefs, I have from that moment avoided speaking of her enemy. Besides, the Duke did not say another word to me that evening, and since that evening he has not made his appearance. If I am in any *danger* I have not perceived it yet; but you can be as much at rest on that subject as I am myself, for I have not the least fear of people whom I do not esteem.

In the rest of the letter Caroline treats of other persons and circumstances that had more or less excited her attention. As those details do not connect directly with our story, we suppress them now, though expecting our narrative to lead us back to them.

IV

About this time Caroline received a letter which touched her deeply, and which we will transcribe without giving the incorrect spelling and punctuation, that would indeed make it difficult to read.

My dear Caroline,—permit your poor nurse always to address you this way,—I have just learned from your elder sister, who has done me the favor of writing me, that you have left her house to become the companion of a lady in Paris. I cannot describe the pain it gives me to think that a person like you, born to ease, as I know, should be obliged to be subject to others, and when I think that it is all of your own good heart, and to help Camille and her children, the tears come to my eyes. My dear young lady, I have only one thing to say, and that is, thanks to the generosity of your parents, that I am not among the most unfortunate. My husband is pretty well off, and carries on besides a small business, which has enabled us to buy a house and a bit of land. My son is a soldier, and your foster-sister has married quite well. So if you should be in want of a few hundred francs some day or other, we should be happy to lend them to you, for any length of time and without interest. By accepting this offer, you will honor and please persons who have always loved you; for my husband esteems you very much, though he knows you only through me, and he often says to me, "She ought to come to us; we could keep her as long as she liked, and as she is strong and a good walker, we could show her our mountains. If she would, she might, too, be the school-mistress of our village; this would not bring her in much, to be sure; but then her expenses would be small, and it would amount, perhaps, to the same as her salary in Paris, where living is so dear." I tell you this just exactly as Peyraque says it, and if your own heart will say the same, we shall have a neat little room all ready for you, and a somewhat wild country to show you. You will not feel afraid,—for when you were a very little thing even, you were always wanting to climb everywhere, so that your poor papa would call you his little squirrel.

Remember then, if you are not comfortable where you are, dear Caroline of my heart, that in a little corner of what is to you an unknown country there are those who know you for the best soul in the wide world, and who pray for you every night and morning, asking the good God to bring you here to see us.

JUSTINE LANION
PEYRAQUE by marriage

LANTRIAC, NEAR LE PUY, HAUTE LOIRE

Caroline replied immediately, as follows:—

"My good Justine, my dear friend,—I wept while reading your letter. They were tears of joy and gratitude. How happy I am to find your friendship as tender as it was on the day when we parted from one another, fourteen years ago! That day lingers in my memory as one of the saddest in my whole life. I had learned to know no mother but you, and losing you was being left motherless for the second time. My good nurse, you loved me so much that for me you had almost forgotten your good husband and your dear children! But they recalled you, your first duty was to them, and I saw from all your letters that they were making you happy. It was they who paid you my debt, for I owed you a great deal; and I have often thought that, if there is anything good or reasonable in me, it is because I have been treated lovingly, gently, and reasonably by her whom my childish eyes first learned to know. Now you want to offer me your savings, you dear good soul! That is good and motherly, like you, and on the part of your husband, who does not know me, it is great and noble. I thank you tenderly, my kind friends, but I need nothing. I am well provided for where I am, and I am as happy as I can be away from my own dear family.

"I shall not give up the hope of going to see you, all the same. What you tell me about the neat little room and the fine wild country gives me a strong desire to know your village and your little household. I cannot say when, in the course of my life, I shall find a fortnight of liberty; but be assured that if I ever do find it, it shall be at the disposal of my darling nurse, whom I embrace with all my heart."

While Caroline was giving herself up to this frank outburst of feeling, the Duke, Gaëtan d'Aléria, in a splendid Turkish morning costume, was conversing with his brother, the Marquis, from whom he was receiving a morning call in his elegant apartments on the Rue de la Paix.

They had just been speaking of business matters, and a lively discussion had arisen between the two brothers. "No, my friend," said the Duke, in a firm tone, "I will be energetic this time: I refuse your signature; you shall not pay my debts!"

"I will pay them," rejoined the Marquis, in a tone just as resolute. "It must be done; I ought to do it. I had some hesitation, I will not deny, before knowing the sum-total, and your pride need not suffer from the scruples I felt. I was afraid of becoming involved beyond my ability; but I know now that there will be enough left to maintain our mother comfortably. I have, therefore, determined to save the honor of the family, and you cannot stand in the way."

"I do stand in the way: you do not owe me this sacrifice; we do not bear the same name."

"We are the sons of the same mother, and I do not want her to die of grief and shame at seeing you insolvent."

"I have no more desire for such a disgrace than my mother has. I will marry."

"For money? In my mother's eyes, and in mine, as well as in yours, my brother, that would be worse still,—you know it perfectly well!"

"Well, then, I will accept a place."

"Worse, still worse!"

"No, there is nothing worse for me than the pain of ruining you."

"I shall not be ruined."

"And may I not know the whole amount of my debts?"

"It is of no use; enough that you have pledged your word that there is none unknown to the notary, who has charge of the settlement. I have only requested you to be so good as to look over some of these papers to prove their correctness, if that be possible. You have verified them; that is enough, the rest does not concern you."

The Duke crumpled the papers angrily, and strode about the room, unable to find words for his mental distress. Then he lighted a cigar which he did not smoke, threw himself into an armchair and became very pale. The Marquis understood the suffering of his brother's pride, and perhaps of his conscience.

"Calm yourself," he said. "I sympathize with your sorrow; but it is a good sign, and I trust to the future. Forget this service, which I am doing for my mother rather than for you; but do not forget that whatever is left is henceforth hers. Consider that we may yet have the happiness of keeping her with us a long while, and that she needs not necessarily suffer. Farewell. I will see you again in an hour, to arrange the last details."

"Yes, yes, leave me alone," replied the Duke; "you see that I cannot say a word to you now."

As soon as the Marquis was gone the Duke rang, gave orders that no one should be admitted, and began to pace the room as before, with desperate agitation. In this hour, he was passing through the supreme and inevitable crisis of his destiny. In none of his other disasters had he seen so much of his own guilt or felt so much real concern.

Up to this time, in fact, he had squandered his own fortune with that hardy recklessness which arises from the sense of injuring no one but one's self. He had, so to speak, only made use of a right; then, half without his own knowledge, by encroaching upon his mother's capital, he had consumed it entirely, becoming gradually hardened to the disgrace of throwing upon his brother the duty of maintaining her from his own resources. Let us say all that we can in excuse of the Duke's conduct up to this period. He had been fearfully spoiled; in his mother's heart a very marked preference for him had existed; nature, too, had been partial to him; taller, stronger, more elegant, more brilliant, and apparently more active than his brother, and more demonstratively affectionate from childhood, he had seemed to every one the better endowed and the more amiable of the two. For a long while weakly and taciturn, the Marquis had shown no fondness for anything but study; and this taste, which in a plebeian would have seemed a great advantage, was considered eccentric in a man of rank. This tendency was therefore repressed rather than encouraged, and precisely on that account it became a passion,—an absorbing, pent-up passion, which developed in the young man's soul a quick, inward sensibility and an enthusiasm all the more ardent from having been restrained. The Marquis was far more affectionate than his brother, and yet passed for a man of cold nature, while the Duke, always kindly and communicative, without loving any one exclusively, had long passed for the very soul of warmth.

The Duke inherited from his father the impulsive temperament which had proved so delusive, and during his childhood the wild freedom of his ways had given the Marchioness some anxiety. We have mentioned already that after the death of her second husband she had been very much carried away by grief, and that for more than a year she had shrunk from seeing her children. When this moral disease gave place to natural feeling, her first effort was to clasp in her arms the son of the husband whom she had loved. But the child, surprised and perhaps terrified by the impetuosity of caresses which he had almost forgotten, burst into tears without knowing why. It may have been the vague, instinctive reproach of a nature chilled by neglect. The Duke, older than he by three years, but more easily diverted, perceived nothing of all this. He returned his mother's kisses, and the poor woman imagined that he inherited her own warm heart, while the Marquis, she thought, had the traits of his paternal grandfather, a man of letters, but not quite sane. So the Duke was secretly preferred, though not more kindly treated, for the Marchioness had a deep and almost religious sense of justice; but he was petted more, since he alone, she believed, appreciated the value of a caress.

Urbain (the Marquis) felt this partiality and suffered from it; but he never allowed himself to complain, and perhaps, already putting a just estimate upon his brother, he did not care to contend with him on such frivolous grounds.

In the course of time, the Marchioness found out that she had been greatly mistaken, and that sentiments should be judged by deeds rather than by words; but the habit of spoiling her prodigal son had now become fixed, and to this she soon added a tender pity for the bewildered perversity which seemed to be leading the wilful youth to his own destruction. This perversity, however, did not take its rise in an evil heart. Vanity at first, and dissipation afterward, then the loss of energy, and at last the tyranny of vice,—that, briefly, is the history of this man, charming without real refinement, good without grandeur of soul, sceptical without atheism. At the age when we are describing him, there was in him an awful void in the place where his conscience should have been, and yet it was a conscience rather absent than dead. There would sometimes be returns of it, and struggles with it, fewer and briefer indeed than they had been in his youth, but perhaps on that account all the more desperate; and the one which was going on within him at this time was so cruel that he laid his hand repeatedly upon one of his splendid weapons, as if he were haunted by the spectre of suicide; but he thought of his mother, pushed away the pistols and locked them up, putting both hands to his head, in the fear that he was becoming insane.

He had always looked upon money as nothing. His mother's noble disinterested theories on the subject had made the way of false reasoning easy to him. Nevertheless he understood that, in effecting his mother's ruin, he had overstepped his right. He was astounded; he had gone on up to the last, promising himself that he would stop before reaching his brother's fortune, and then he had seriously encroached upon it; but the truth is, that he had not done this knowingly; for, from motives of delicacy, the Marquis had kept no accounts with him in matters of detail, and would never have mentioned them at all, had it not been for the necessity of preserving by an appeal to his honor the little which was left. The Duke therefore did not feel himself guilty of deliberate selfishness, and had reproached Urbain warmly and sincerely for not having warned him sooner. He saw at last the abyss opened by his lawless and reckless conduct; he was bitterly ashamed of having injured his brother's prospects and of having no way to repair the harm, without infringing upon certain rigid principles established by his mother and his education.

Yet this error was less serious than that of having wronged his own mother; but it did not appear so to the Duke. It had always seemed to him that whatever belonged to his mother was his own, while in dealing with his brother his pride kept up the distinction of *meum* and *tuum*. Besides,—should it not be admitted?—while there was no wicked dislike between the two brothers so differently constituted, there was at least a want of confidence and sympathy. The life of the one was a continual protest against that of the other. Urbain had made a silent but powerful effort that the voice of nature within him might be also that of friendship. Gaëtan had made no such effort; trusting to the freedom from malice which characterized him, he had felt a liberty to rail at the austerity of the Marquis. They were then together most of the time, upon a footing of blame delicately restrained by the one, and of ridicule manifested in easy revolt by the other.

"Very well," exclaimed the Duke, seeing the Marquis return. "It is an accomplished fact then? I see by your face that you have been signing."

"Yes, brother," replied Urbain; "it is all arranged, and there is left for you besides an income of twelve thousand francs, which I did not allow them to use in the liquidation."

"Left for me?" rejoined Gaëtan, looking him in the face. "No! you are deceived, there is nothing left for me; but, after having cleared me of debt, you are yourself making me an allowance."

"Well, yes," replied the Marquis, "since you must also learn, sooner or later, that you are not at liberty to dispose of the principal."

The Duke, who had not yet decided upon anything, wrung his hands with violence and fell back upon his mute opposition. The Marquis made an effort to conquer his habitual reserve, seated himself near Gaëtan, and taking in his own the clenched hands which seemed hesitating to extend themselves to him, "My friend," said he, "you are too haughty with me. Would you not have done for me what I am doing for you?"

The Duke felt his pride breaking down. He burst into tears. "No!" said he, pressing his brother's hand feelingly, "I never should have known how to do it. I never could have done it, for my destiny is to injure others, and I shall never have the happiness of saving any one."

"You will at least admit that it is a happiness," replied Urbain. "Then consider yourself doing me a kindness, and give me back your friendship which seems to be vanishing under this grievance."

"Urbain," cried the Duke, "you speak of my friendship. Now would be the time to thank you with all manner of protestations, but I will not do it; I will never fall so low as to take refuge in hypocrisy. Do you know, brother, that I have never liked you very well?"

"I know it, and I account for it by our differing tastes and dispositions; but has not the time now come to like each other better?"

"Ah! it is an awful time for that,—the hour of your triumph and of my disgrace. Tell me that, but for my mother, you would have let me succumb. Yes, you must tell me that, and then I may forgive you for what you are doing."

"Have I not already said so?"

"Tell me so again! You hesitate? It is then a question of the family honor?"

"Yes, it is that precisely, the family honor is in question."

"And you do not expect me to love you to-day more than on any other day?"

"I know," rejoined the Marquis, sadly, "that personally I am not made to be loved."

The Duke felt himself completely conquered; he threw himself into his brother's arms. "Come!" he cried, "forgive me. You are a better man than I. I respect you, admire you, I almost worship you; I know, I feel that you are my best friend. My God! what is there that I can do for you? Do you love any woman? Shall I kill her husband? Do you want me to go to China and find some precious manuscript, in some pagoda, risking the *cangue*, and other pleasant things?"

"You think of nothing but a discharge of obligations, Gaëtan. If you would only love me a little, I should be already paid a hundred times over."

"Well, then, I do love you with all my heart," replied the Duke, embracing him violently; "and you see I am weeping like a child. Look here! Give me a little esteem in return; I will reform. I am still young. Why, the deuce take it all, at thirty-six one can't have been ruined altogether! A fellow is only a little used up. I will turn over a new leaf,— all the more because that is needed in my case. Well, then, so much the better! I will renew my youth, my health. I will go and pass the summer with you and my mother in the country; I will tell you stories; I will make you laugh again. Come! help me lay my plans, support me, lift me up, console me; for, after all, I don't know where I am, and I feel very unhappy."

The Marquis had already noticed, without appearing to do so, the disappearance of the weapons which had been in sight an hour before. He had also read in his brother's face the fearful crisis through which he had passed. He knew furthermore that Gaëtan's moral courage would only bear a certain amount of strain. "Dress yourself now," he said, "and come to breakfast with me. We will chat; we will build air-castles. Who knows but I may convince you that, in certain cases, we begin to be rich on the very day we become poor?"

V

The Marquis conducted his brother to the Bois de Boulogne, which at that period was not a splendid English garden, but a charming grove of dreamy shade. It was one of the first days of April; the weather was magnificent; the thickets were covered with violets, and a thousand foolish tomtits were chattering around the first buds, while the citron-hued butterflies of those early beautiful days seemed, by their form, their color, and their undecided flight, like new leaves fluttering gently in the wind.

The Marquis was ordinarily thought to take his meals at home. In reality, he did not take his meals at all, using those terms after the manner of generous livers. He had a few very simple dishes served up, and he swallowed them hastily, without raising his eyes from the book at his side. That frugal habit agreed very well with the rule of strict economy which he was now about to adopt; for, in order that his mother's table might continue to be carefully and abundantly served, it was necessary that his own should not in the future be allowed the least superfluity.

Not only anxious to conceal this fact from his brother, but fearing, also, to sadden him by the usual austerity of his mode of life, the Marquis led him to a pavilion in the Bois and ordered a comfortable repast, saying to himself that he would buy so many books the less, and frequent the public libraries by necessity, neither more nor less than a needy scholar. He felt himself in no way saddened or appalled by a succession of little sacrifices. He did not think even of his delicate health, which demanded a certain amount of comforts in his sedentary life. He was happy at having finally broken down the cold barrier between himself and Gaëtan, and also at the prospect of gaining his confidence and affection. The Duke, who was still pale and nervously thoughtful, began to yield himself up more and more to the influence of the spring air which entered freely through the open window. The meal restored the equilibrium of his faculties, for he was of a robust nature, that could not endure privation; and his mother, who had certain pretensions of alliance to the ex-royal family, was in the habit of saying, somewhat vainly, that the Duke had the fine appetite of the Bourbons.

In the course of an hour the Duke was charming in his manner toward his brother; that is, he was with him, for the first time in his life, as amiable and as much at his ease as he was with everybody else. These two men had sometimes perhaps divined more or less of each other, but a thorough understanding had never been reached; and, surely, they had never questioned each other openly. The Marquis had been restrained by discretion; the Duke by indifference. Now the Duke felt a real need to know the man who had just rescued his honor and made him certain of his future. He questioned the Marquis with a freedom which had never before had place between them.

"Explain your happiness to me," he said, "for you are really happy; at least, I have never heard you complain."

The Marquis made a reply which astonished him greatly. "I cannot explain to you my courage," he said, "except by my devotion to my mother and by my love for study, since, as for happiness, I never had it and never shall have it. That, perhaps, is not what I should say to allure you to a quiet and retired life; but I would commit a crime not to be sincere with you; and besides, I shall never make myself a pretender to virtue, though you have slightly accused me of that eccentricity."

"It is true; I was very wrong; I see it now. But how and why are you unhappy, my poor brother? Can you tell me?"

"I cannot tell you, but I will confide in you. I have loved!"

"You? you have loved a woman? When was that?"

"It is now a long time ago, and I loved her a long time."

"And you do not love her any more?"

"She is dead."

"She was a married woman?"

"Precisely, and her husband is yet living. You will permit me to conceal her name."

"There is no need whatever to mention that; but you will conquer this feeling, will you not?"

"I do not positively know. Up to the present time I have not succeeded at all."

"She has not been dead long?"

"Three years."

"She loved you then very much?"

"No."

"How, no?"

"She loved me as much as a woman can love who ought not and will not break with her husband."

"Bah! that's no reason; on the contrary, obstacles stimulate passion."

"And they wear it out. She was weary with deceiving, and consequently of suffering. It was only the fear of driving me to despair that hindered her from breaking with me. I was greatly wanting in courage. She died a suffering death,—and through my fault!"

"But no, O no! You imagine that to torment yourself."

"I imagine nothing, and my grief is without resource, as my fault is without excuse. You shall see. There came one of those paroxysms of passion in which we wish, in spite of God and men, to appropriate forever the object of our love. She bore me a son whom I saved, concealed, and who still lives; but she, not wishing to give a foothold to suspicion, made her appearance in society the day after her delivery. There she seemed still beautiful, and full of her wonted animation; she spoke and walked, notwithstanding the fever which was devouring her: twenty-four hours afterwards she was a corpse. Nothing was ever known. She passed for the most rigid person—"

"I know who it was,—Madame de G——."

"Yes, you alone in the whole world possess the secret."

"Ah! Do not be so sure. Does not our mother herself suspect it?"

"Our mother suspects nothing."

The Duke was silent for a moment, then he said with a sigh, "My poor brother, this child that is living, and that you probably cherish—"

"Certainly."

"And I have ruined him too."

"What matter? If he has the means of learning to work, of being a man, it will be all that I desire for him. I can never recognize him openly, and for some years I do not wish to have him near me. He is very frail; I am having him brought up in the country, at the house of some peasants. He must get the physical strength which I have always lacked, and whose absence has, perhaps, induced in me the want of moral force. Then, too, at the last hour, from an imprudent word of the physician, M. de G— gained a suspicion of the truth. It would not do to have about me a child whose age should coincide with the time which has intervened since that sad event. Do you not see, Gaëtan, I am not, I cannot be, happy!"

"Is it then that passion which keeps you from marrying!"

"I shall never marry; I have sworn it."

"Very well, now you must think of it."

"And *you* preach marriage to me!"

"Yes, indeed, why not? Marriage is not, as you suppose, the object of my scorn! I proclaimed that antipathy to relieve myself of the trouble of finding a wife at the age when I might have chosen one. Since I have been ruined the thing has become more conditional. My mother would never have allowed me to accept a fortune without a name, and having nothing now but my name, I can no longer aspire to anything but fortune. You know that, wholly detestable as I am, I have never wanted to wound my mother by going counter to her opinions. I have therefore seen my chances rapidly decrease, and at this moment I should put the worst sort of estimate upon any young lady or widow, whatsoever her wealth or birth, who would have me. I should persuade myself that, to accept a good-for-nothing like me, she must have some very dark motive. But, Urbain, your position is altogether different; I have lessened your fortune, perhaps made you poor. That, however, takes nothing from your personal merit; on the contrary, it should make it greater in the eyes of every one knowing the cause of your meagre fortune. It is nothing more than probable that some pure young woman, of noble family and with a fortune, should be inspired with esteem and affection for you. It seems to me even that all you will have to do is but to wish such a thing, and to show yourself."

"No, I do not know how to show myself, except to my own disadvantage. Society paralyzes me, and my reputation as a scholar injures more than it serves me. Society does not understand why a man born for society does not prefer it above all things. Besides, you see, I cannot want to love; my heart is too dark and heavy."

"Why, then, do you mourn so long a woman who did not know how to be happy with your affection?"

"Because I loved her. In her it was perhaps my own passion that I loved. I am not of those lively natures which bloom again at each new season. Things take a terrible hold of me."

"You read too much, you reflect too much."

"Perhaps I do; come to the country, brother, as you have promised to do; you shall assist me; you will benefit me greatly. Will you come? I have a real need of a friend, and I have none. A silent passion has absorbed my life; your affection will rejuvenate me."

The Duke was greatly moved by the frank and tender confidence of his brother. He had expected lessons, counsels, consolations, which would have made him play the part of the weak, in the presence of the strong man; on the contrary, it was of him that Urbain asked for strength and pity. Whether this came from an actual need of the Marquis or from an exalted delicacy, the Duke was too intelligent not to be struck by the change. He assured him, therefore, of a lively affection, a tender solicitude; and after having spent the whole afternoon talking and walking in the grove, the two brothers took a carriage and returned together to dine with their mother.

For some days the Marchioness had been secretly very ill at ease. She had feared the resistance of Urbain when he should learn the whole amount of his brother's debts. However great her esteem for her younger son, she had not foreseen to what lengths his disinterestedness would go. Not having received his usual visit on that morning, she became seriously troubled, when, just before the hour of dinner, she saw her two sons arrive. She observed in the face of each such a calm expression of confidence and affection as led her at first to divine what had passed between them; then, however, in the presence of a visitor who was slow to depart, she could not question them, and finally she received the dreadful impression that she had been deceived and that neither the one nor the other was fully aware of the situation.

But when they were at last at table, she remarked that they addressed each other in the familiar and endearing *thee* and *thou*, she understood all, and the presence of Caroline and the servants hindering her from expressing her emotion, she concealed her joy in an affectation of extreme cheerfulness, while great tears fell upon her faded cheeks. Caroline and the Marquis perceived these tears at the same moment, and her troubled look seemed to ask of him whether the Marchioness was concealing joy or suffering. The Marquis quieted her solicitude by the same means in which it had been conveyed; and the Duke, detecting this mute, rapid dialogue, smiled with a sort of good-natured malice. Neither Caroline nor the Marquis paid attention to this smile. There was too much good faith in their mutual sympathy. Caroline still held to her dislike and distrust of the Duke. She continued to grudge him the power of being so amiable and of appearing so good. She thought indeed that Madame de D—— had slightly exaggerated his waywardness; but feeling, in spite of herself, a vague fear, she avoided seeing him, and even in his presence forced herself to forget his face. When the dessert was brought in and the servants had retired, the conversation became a little more intimate. Caroline asked timidly of the Marchioness if she did not think the clock was slow.

"No, no, not yet, dear child," kindly replied the old lady.

Caroline understood that she was to remain till they left the table.

"So, my good friends," said the Marchioness, addressing her sons, "you breakfasted together in the Bois?"

"Like Orestes and Pylades," answered the Duke, "and you could n't imagine, dear mother, how fine it all was. And then I made a delightful discovery there, namely, that I have a charming brother. O, the word seems frivolous to you when applied to him; very well, I at least do not understand it in its trivial sense. The charm of the understanding is occasionally the charm of the heart, and my brother has them both."

The Marchioness smiled again, but she soon became thoughtful; a cloud passed athwart her mind. "Gaëtan should be pained to receive his brother's sacrifice," she thought; "he takes it too lightly; perhaps he has lost his pride. Heavens! that would be fatal to him."

Urbain saw this cloud and hastened to dissipate it. "For my part," he said, addressing his mother cheerfully and tenderly, "I will not say in return that my brother is more charming than I am, for that is too apparent; but I will say that I have also made a discovery, which is that he has admirable and serious depths in his nature, and an unalterable respect for all that is true. Yes," he added, in instinctive reply to the profoundly astonished look of Caroline, "there is in him a veritable candor which no one suspects, and which I have never before fully appreciated."

"My children," said the Marchioness, "it does me good to hear you speak thus of each other; you touch my pride in the most sensitive place, and I am really led to believe that you are both right."

"As far as it concerns me," rejoined the Duke, "you think so because you are the best of mothers; but you are blind. I am good for nothing at all, and the sad smile of Mlle de Saint-Geneix says plainly enough that you and my brother are both deceiving yourselves."

"What! I smiled!" cried Caroline, in stupefaction; "have I looked sad? I could take my oath that I have not raised my eyes from this decanter, and that I have been meditating profoundly upon the qualities of crown-glass."

"Do not fancy we believe," returned Gaëtan, "that your thoughts are always absorbed by household cares. I believe that they are frequently elevated far above the region of decanters, and that you judge of men and things from a very high stand-point."

"I allow myself to judge no one, your Grace."

"So much the worse for those who are not worth the exercise of your judgment. They could but gain by knowing it, however severe it might be. I myself, for instance, like to be judged by women. From their mouths I like a frank condemnation better than the silence of disdain or of mistrust. I regard women as the only beings really capable of appreciating our failings or our good qualities."

"But, Madame de Villemer," said Caroline to the Marchioness in a distressed manner which was sportively assumed, "please tell his Grace the Duke that I have not the honor of knowing him at all, and that I am not here to continue in my head the portraits of La Bruyère."

"Dear child," replied the Marchioness, "you are here to be a sort of adopted daughter, to whom everything is permitted, because we are aware of your fine discretion and your perfect modesty. Do not hesitate therefore to answer my son, and do not be disturbed by his friendly attempt to tease you. He knows as well as I do who you are, and he will never be wanting in the respect which is your due."

"This time, mother, I accept the compliment," said the Duke, in a tone of entire frankness. "I have the profoundest respect for every pure, generous, and devoted woman, and consequently for Mlle de Saint-Geneix in particular."

Caroline did not blush, or stammer the thanks of a prude governess. She looked the Duke squarely in the eyes, saw that he was not at all mocking her, and answered him with kindness,—

"Why, then, your Grace, having so generous an opinion of me, do you suppose that I permit myself to have a bad one of you?"

"O, I have my reasons," answered the Duke; "I will tell them to you when you know me better."

"Well, but why not now?" said the Marchioness; "it would be the preferable way."

"So be it," rejoined the Duke. "It is an anecdote. I will tell it. Day before yesterday I was alone in your drawing-room, waiting for you, mother mine. I was musing in a corner, and finding myself comfortably seated upon one of your little sofas,—I had that morning been training an unruly horse and was as tired as an ox,—I was meditating upon the destiny of cappadine seats in general, as Mlle de Saint-Geneix was just meditating upon that of crown-glass, and I said to myself, 'How astonished these sofas and easy-chairs would be to find themselves in a stable or in a cattle-shed! And how troubled those beautiful ladies in robes of satin who are coming here directly would certainly be, if in the place of these luxurious seats they should find nothing but litter!'"

"But your revery hasn't common sense in it," said the Marchioness, laughing.

"That's true," rejoined the Duke. "Those were the thoughts of a man slightly intoxicated."

"What do you say, my son?"

"Nothing very improper, dear mother. I came home hungry, weak, bruised, already intoxicated with the open air. You know that water does not agree with me. I cannot slake my thirst, and in making the attempt I got fuddled,—that's all. You know too that it lasts me but a quarter of an hour at most, and that I have sense enough to keep myself quiet the necessary time. That is why, instead of coming to kiss your hand during your dessert, I slipped into the drawing-room, there to recover my senses."

"Come, come," said the Marchioness, "slip over this confusion of your senses, and let us have the point of your story."

"But that's just what I am coming to," rejoined the Duke, "as you shall see."

As he took up again the thread of his discourse with more or less difficulty, Caroline could see that the Duke was in exactly the same state of mind as that of which he was telling, and that his mother's heady wines had probably for some moments been responsible for his prolixity. Very soon, however, he overcame the slight disorder of his ideas, and continued with a grace which was really perfect.

"I was a little absent-minded, I will confess, but not at all besotted. On the contrary, I had poetical visions. From the litter scattered on the floor by my imagination, I saw a thousand odd figures arise. They were all women, some attired as for an old-fashioned court ball, others as for a Flemish peasant festival; the former embarrassed by contact of their crinoline and laces with the fresh straw, which impeded their steps and wounded their feet; the latter in short dresses, shod in great wooden shoes, which tramped lustily over the litter, while their wearers laughed till their mouths were opened wellnigh from ear to ear, at the odd appearance of the others.

"With regard to this side of the picture, it was, as the canvases of Rubens have been called, the festival of flesh. Large hands, red cheeks, powerful shoulders, very prominent noses upon blooming faces, still with admirable eyes, and a sort of cappadine attraction like your sofas and easy-chairs, which had undergone this magic transformation. I cannot otherwise explain to myself the point of departure of my hallucination.

"These splendid, great strapping women abandoned themselves entirely to a light-hearted joy; jumped up a foot in the air and came down again, to make the pendants of the candelabra vibrate, some of them rolling upon the straw, and getting up again with empty wheat-ears tangled in their hair of reddened gold. Opposite these the princesses of the fan attempted a stately dance without being able to accomplish it. The straws arrayed themselves against their furbelows, the heat of the atmosphere caused the paint to fall off, the powder trickled down upon their shoulders, and left the meagreness of their visages confessed; a mortal anguish was depicted in their expressive eyes. Evidently they feared the shining of the sun upon their counterfeit charms, and saw with fury the reality of life ready to triumph over them."

"Well, well, my son," said the Marchioness, "where are you wandering, and what signifies all this? Have you undertaken the panegyric of viragos?"

"I have undertaken nothing at all," replied the Duke; "I relate; I am inventing nothing. I was under the empire of that vision, and I have no idea into what reflections it would have led me, if I had not heard a woman singing close by me—"

Gaëtan sang very pleasantly the rustic words of which he had faithfully retained the air, and Caroline began to laugh, remembering that she had sung that refrain of her province before perceiving the Duke in the drawing-room.

The Duke continued: "Then I arose, and my vision was completely dissipated. There was no more straw upon the floor; the plump chairs and sofas with wooden legs were no longer girls in wooden shoes from the poultry yard; the slender candelabra, with their bulging ornaments, were no longer thin women in hoop-petticoats. I was quite alone in the lighted apartment, and had completely come to my senses; but I heard the singing of a village air in a style altogether rustic and true and charming, with a freshness of voice, too, of which mine certainly can give you no idea. 'What!' cried I to myself, 'a peasant, a peasant girl in the drawing-room of my mother!' I kept still, hardly breathing, and the peasant girl appeared. She passed before me twice without seeing me, walking quickly and almost touching me with her dress of pearl-gray silk."

"Ah, that," said the Marchioness,—"that then was Caroline?"

"It was somebody unknown," rejoined the Duke; "a singular peasant girl, you will agree, for she was dressed like a modest person, and of the best society. About her head she wore nothing but the glory of her own yellow hair, and she showed neither her arms nor her shoulders; but I saw her neck of snow, and her nice little hand, and feet too, for she did not have on wooden shoes."

Caroline, a little annoyed at the description of her person by this veteran Lovelace, looked toward the Marquis as if in protest. She was surprised to find a certain anxiety expressed in his face, and he avoided her look with a slight contraction of his brows.

The Duke, from whom nothing escaped, proceeded: "This adorable apparition struck me all the more that it recalled to my eyes the two types of my dispelled vision; that is, she preserved all that made the merit of the one or the other: nobleness of bearing and freshness of manners, delicacy of features, and the glow of health. She was a queen and a shepherdess in the same person."

"That is a picture which does not flatter," said the Marchioness, "but which, exposed face to face with its original, lacks perhaps a lightness of touch. Ah, my son, may you not again be a little—over-excited?"

"You ordered me to speak," rejoined the Duke. "If I speak too much, make me keep still."

"No," was the quick remark of Caroline, who observed a queer, half-suspicious look upon the face of the Marquis, and who was anxious that nothing vague should be left about her first interview with the Duke. "I do not recognize the original of the picture, and I wait for his Grace the Duke to make her speak a little."

"I have a good memory and I shall invent nothing," rejoined he. "Carried away by a sudden, irresistible sympathy, I spoke to this young lady from the country. Her voice, her look, her neat, frank replies, her air of goodness, of real innocence,—the innocence of the heart,—won me to such a degree that I told her of my esteem and respect at the end of five minutes as if I had known her all my life, and I felt myself jealous of her esteem as if she had been my own sister. Is that the truth this time, Mlle de Saint-Geneix?"

"I know nothing of your private sentiments, your Grace," replied Caroline; "but you seemed to me so affable that it never crossed my mind you could be tender in your cups, and that I was very grateful for your kindness. I see now that I must put a lower estimate upon it, and that there was a trifle of irony in the whole."

"And in what do you see that, if you please?"

"In the exaggerated praise with which you seem to try to excite my vanity; but I protest against it, your Grace, and perhaps it would have been more generous in you not to have commenced the attack upon a person so inoffensive and of so humble a quality as I am."

"Come now," said the Duke, turning toward his brother, who appeared to be thinking upon an entirely different subject, and who, nevertheless, heard everything, as if in his own despite; "she persists in suspecting me and in regarding my respect as an injury. Come now, Marquis, you have been telling her naughty things of me?"

"That is not a habit of mine," answered the Marquis, with the gentleness of truth.

"Well, then," continued the Duke, "I know who has ruined me in the opinion of Mlle de Saint-Geneix. It is an old lady whose gray hairs are turning to a slaty blue, and whose hands are so thin that her rings have to be hunted up in the sweepings every morning. She talked about me to Mlle de Saint-Geneix for a quarter of an hour the other evening, and when I sought again the kindly look which had made my heart young, I did not find it, and I do not find it now. You see. Marquis, there is no other way. Ah! but why are you so silent? You commenced my eulogy, and Mlle de Saint-Geneix seems to have confidence in you. If you would just commence again."

"My children," said the Marchioness, "you can resume the discussion another time. I have to dress, and I want to say something to you before any one comes to interrupt us. The clock is perhaps a few minutes slow."

"I think, indeed, that it is very slow," observed Caroline, rising; and, leaving the Duke and the Marquis to help their mother to her apartment, the young lady went quickly to the drawing-room. She expected to find visitors there, for the dinner had been prolonged a little more than usual; but no one had yet arrived, and, instead of tripping lightly about, singing as she went, she seated herself thoughtfully by the fire.

VI

Caroline in her own despite commenced to find something galling in her situation. She had endeavored not to think at all about the species of domestic service which she had heroically accepted. No one, indeed, could have been less fitted for this complete surrender of the will. She felt shocked by the obstinate or affected attention paid her by the Duke d'Aléria, and she considered herself constrained to hide her impatience and disdain. "In my sister's house," she said to herself, "I should not be obliged to endure the compliments of this person. I should put an end to them with a single word. He would think me a prude, but that would make no difference. He would be sent off, and all would be said. Here I must be sprightly and polite, like a lady of society, look upon the light side of everything, see nothing offensive in the gallantry of a libertine. I must guess the science of the women who are broken in to this kind of life. If I am as brusk with him as my frankness would lead me to be, the Duke would get a spite at me; he would calumniate me to revenge himself, and perhaps to have me sent away. Sent away! Yes, in my position, one is liable to be surprised by any vile plot, and dismissed without more ceremony than is observed with the humblest servant. These are the dangers and the insults to which I am exposed. I did wrong to come here. Madame d'Arglade never told me about this Duke, and I have been believing in an impossibility."

Caroline was not of an irresolute spirit. From the moment that the thought of going away had occurred to her, she began to cast about in her mind for some other way of supporting her sister. She had received an advance from the Marchioness, and it was necessary to find elsewhere another advance by which to return it, if the conduct of the Duke should not permit of her remaining with his mother till the time paid for by the little sum sent to Camille had been duly served. Thus Caroline came to think of the few hundreds of francs offered her by her nurse, whose letter received that morning was yet in her pocket. She now read that artless and motherly letter again, and, thinking how great a benefaction can go with the unpretending charity of the poor, she felt herself once more deeply touched and she wept.

The Marquis entered and found her wiping her eyes. She folded up the letter again and put it unaffectedly back in her pocket, without attempting to conceal her emotion under an assumption of cheerfulness.

Nevertheless she remarked a shade of irony upon M. de Villemer's face, which usually was so kind. She looked at him as if asking whom he wanted to ridicule, and he, becoming slightly embarrassed, hesitated for words, and ended by saying quite simply, "You were weeping?"

"Yes," she replied, "but not from sorrow."

"You have received good news?"

"No, a proof of friendship."

"You ought to receive such things frequently."

"There are testimonies more or less sincere."

"You seem to be in a doubting mood to-day; you are not every day so mistrustful."

"No, not every day; I am not naturally distrustful. Are you, M. de Villemer?"

Urbain was always a little startled when questioned directly about himself. It cost him an effort to interrogate others, and to be questioned in return caused him a species of trouble.

"I," he answered, after a moment's hesitation,—"I do not know. I should be very much at a loss how to tell you what I am—at this moment especially."

"Yes, you appear to be preoccupied," rejoined Caroline; "do not make an effort to speak to me, M. de Villemer."

"Pardon me, I want—I would like to speak with you; but it is a very delicate matter. I do not know how to begin."

"Ah! indeed? You disquiet me a little. And yet it seems to me that it will be well for me to know what you are thinking about just now."

"Well—yes, you are right. Quick, then, for we may be interrupted at any moment. I shall not have to say much, I hope, to make you understand me. I love my brother; to-day especially I love him tenderly. I am certain of his sincerity; but his imagination is very lively,—you have just had evidence of that. In short, if he has been a little too persistent in his endeavor to change the unfavorable impression of him which perhaps you may not have at all, and which, in any case, he does not merit but to a certain degree, I would like to have you promise to speak of it to my mother and to my mother only. Do not think it strange or impertinent in me to volunteer my advice. I have such a desire to see my mother happy, and I see so clearly that you already contribute largely to her happiness, the society of an intelligent and worthy person is so necessary to her, and it would probably be so impossible for her to replace you, that I would, knowing you to be happy and satisfied in your position, like to believe that you will always be with her. And now you know the only thing upon which I have been preoccupied."

"I thank you for this explanation, M. de Villemer," replied Caroline, "and I will confess I expected that your integrity would some day consent to give it."

"My integrity? But my whole explanation consists in this: my brother is light-hearted, amiable, and if his gayety has become painful to you, my mother, able to restrain him and possessing in that respect an ascendency over him which I cannot have, would on the one hand know how to reassure you, and how on the other, to keep my brother's vivacity of speech within proper bounds."

"Yes, yes, we understand each other," rejoined Caroline; "but we are not quite of the same opinion as to the means of curing the—the amiable sportiveness of his Grace, the Duke. You think that Madame the Marchioness will be able to preserve me from it; and I believe that between an adored son and a tender mother no one can or ought to carry complaints. Before certain judges we are never right. I have been thinking exactly of this situation, and I foresaw with real sorrow that a moment might come when I should be compelled—"

"To go away from us, to leave my mother?" asked the Marquis, with a sudden eagerness, which he repressed immediately. "That was exactly what I feared. If that idea has already entered your mind, I am very much distressed; but I do not believe it is well founded. Be careful not to be unjust. My brother was very much excited today. A particular circumstance, a family matter having much to do with the feelings, had almost overcome him this morning. This evening he was happy, merry, and therefore impulsive. When you know him better—"

The bell was heard to ring. The Marquis started. Friends arrived. He was compelled to leave in suspense many things which he would have liked to say and not to say. He hastened to add, "Now, in the name of Heaven, in the name of my mother, do not be in a hurry to take a step which would be so sad, so grievous to her. If I dared, if I had the right, I would pray you to decide nothing without consulting me—"

"The respect to which your character gives you the right," replied Caroline, "gives you also the right to counsel me, and I do not hesitate to promise you what you have been kind enough to ask."

The Marquis had no time to express his gratitude. They were no longer alone in the drawing-room; but there was an extraordinary eloquence in his look, and Caroline found again in it the confidence and affection which had appeared under a cloud at the commencement of their interview. The eyes of the Marquis had that remarkable beauty which can spring only from an ardent soul joined to great purity of thought. They were the only expression of his inner nature which his timidity did not succeed in paralyzing. Caroline understood him now, and nothing confused, nothing troubled her in the language of those clear eyes which she questioned frequently as the keepers of her conscience and the guides of her conduct.

Caroline really had a veneration for this man, whose character every one appreciated, but whose intelligence and delicacy every one did not fathom or divine. In spite, however, of the satisfaction in which their conversation had just ended, she sought in going over it again to herself to understand it in all its bearings. She thought quickly, and, while going about the drawing-room to do the honors,—within the limits of the favor and reserve which had been imposed upon her, and whose exact lines she had easily observed from the first,—she demanded of herself why the Marquis had seemed to waver among two or three successive ideas in speaking to her. At first he had appeared disposed to reproach her for believing in the flatteries of the Duke, then he had given her a friendly warning against the continuance of these attacks, and finally, as soon as she had expressed her displeasure at them, he himself had hastened to allay it. She had never seen him irresolute, and, if his language was frequently timid, his convictions were never so. "It must be," she thought, "that in the first place he considered me imprudent, and his brother likely to take advantage of the fact; in the second place, it must be that I am really more necessary to his much-loved mother, already, than I could have believed. At all events, there is a hidden something in this which I cannot understand, and which I suppose he will explain to me hereafter. Whatever it may be, I am free. Five hundred francs will not bind me a day, an hour, in a humiliating position. I have not yet sent off my answer to Justine."

We see how far the honest, clear conscience of Mlle de Saint-Geneix was from seeking in the constrained silence of the Marquis an unbecoming sentiment or an instinct of jealousy. If the Marquis had been questioned at that moment, could he have answered with so much assurance, "With me it is only a respectful esteem and filial solicitude?"

At that moment, in point of fact, M. de Villemer was by no means pleased with his brother, and listened to him with an impatience which was painful enough. The Duke, having entered the drawing-room with his mother, had come and seated himself near him behind the piano, an isolated and protected place, which was a favorite with the Marquis; here then the Duke began the following conversation, speaking in a low voice but in a very lively manner:—

"Well," he said, "you saw her alone just now; did you speak to her of me?"

"But," replied M. de Villemer, "what singular persistency!"

"There is nothing singular about it," rejoined the Duke, as if he were continuing the details of a confidential disclosure already made. "I am struck, touched, taken. I am in love if you will. Yes, in love with her, upon my honor! It is no joke. Are you going to reproach me, when for the first time in my life I make you my confidant? Was that not agreed upon this morning? Did we not swear to tell each other everything, and to be each other's best friend? I asked you whether you had any feeling for Mlle de Saint-Geneix; you answered me 'No,' very seriously. Do not, therefore, think it extraordinary that I ask you to serve me with her."

"My friend," replied the Marquis, "I have done exactly the contrary of what you would have me to do. I told her to take nothing you said too seriously."

"Ah, traitor!" cried the Duke, with a gayety whose frankness was as a reparation for his former prejudices against his brother, "that is the way you serve your friends. Trust in Pylades! At the first call he resigns; he whistles at my dreams, and gives my hopes to the winds. But what do you suppose will become of me, if you abandon me in this fashion?"

"For that kind of service I have n't even common sense, you see very plainly."

"That's so; at the first difficulty you renounce it. Well, but I am maddened. I have driven from my heart all that is not you, and none but you shall hear of my new flames."

"With regard to the present one at least, will you pledge me your honor?"

"Ah! you are in great fear lest I compromise her?"

"That would give me serious pain."

"Bah! Come now, why?"

"Because she is proud, sensitive perhaps, and would leave my mother, who dotes upon her,—have you not observed that?"

"Yes, and it is that very thing which has turned my head. She must really be a girl of great cleverness and a deal of heart. Our mother has such perfect tact. This evening, in taking me to task a little for what she considered my attempt at teasing, she held the sugarplum very high, saying, 'Your conduct toward Caroline was neither proper nor agreeable. She is a person of whom you are not permitted to think.' The deuce! A fellow always has the right to dream; that certainly harms no one. But see though how pretty she is; how alive in the midst of all those plastered women! One can look at the contour of her face in the nearest and most trying light; one will not see there those dull, sticky lines which make the others look like plaster casts. It is true she is too pretty to be any one's young-lady companion. My mother can never keep her; every one will fall in love with her, and if she continues to be well-behaved some one will want to marry her."

"Then," rejoined the Marquis, "you cannot think of her."

"Why so, pray?" demanded the Duke. "Am I not to-day a poor devil with nothing in the world? Is she not of good birth? Is not her reputation spotless? I should like to know what my mother would find to say against it,—she who already calls the young lady her daughter, and who wishes us to respect her as if she were our own sister."

"You, sir, carry your enthusiasm or your joke to great lengths," said the Marquis, stunned by what he heard.

"Good," thought the Duke, "he has forgotten his brotherly *thee* and *thou*; he calls me 'you, sir.'"

And he continued to maintain with astonishing seriousness that he was quite capable of marrying Mlle de Saint-Geneix, if there were no other means of winning her. "I should prefer to run away with her," he added; "that would better accord with my usual way of doing things; but I no longer have the means with which to run away with her, and now my laundress herself would not trust herself to my hands. Besides, it is time to break with my entire past. I have said it to you, and it is done, because I have said it. Starting from to-day,—a complete reformation along the whole line. You are going to see a new man,—a man whom I myself do not know, and who indeed is going to astonish me; but that man, I feel now, is capable of all things, all, even to believe, to love, and to marry. So good evening, brother; those are my last words; if you do not repeat them to Mlle de Saint-Geneix, it is because you wish to do nothing to aid me in my conversion."

The Duke withdrew, leaving his brother stupefied,—divided between the necessity of believing him sincere in his momentary passion and the indignity of being solicited as an accomplice in a flagrant libertinism.

"But no," he said to himself, going to his own apartments; "that was all merely his gayety, his trifling, his folly,—or it was still the wine. Nevertheless, this morning in the grove he interrogated me about Caroline with a surprising insistence, and that, too, almost in the midst of my confidences concerning my past, which he received with genuine emotion, with tears in his eyes. What kind of a man then is this brother of mine? Not twelve hours ago, he thought of killing himself. He hated me, he detested himself. Then I believed I had won his heart. He sobbed in my arms. All day long it has been the extreme of impulse and devotion, winning tenderness and goodwill; and to-night I no longer know what it is. Has his reason received some shock in the uncurbed life which he has hitherto led, or did he indeed make sport of me all the fore part of the day? Am I the dupe of my need to love? Shall I have cause for bitter repentance, or have I in fact taken upon myself the task of caring for a diseased brain?"

In his fright the Marquis accepted this latter supposition as the less appalling; but another anguish was mingled with it. The Marquis felt himself bruised and irritated by a sentiment which he did not avow to himself, and to which he would not so much as give a name. He set himself to work and worked badly. He went to bed and slept still worse.

As for the Duke, he innocently rubbed his hands. "I have succeeded," said he to himself; "I have found the proper reaction against his despair. Poor, dear brother! I have turned his head, I have aroused his feelings, I have excited his jealousy. He is in love. He will be cured, and he will live. For passion there is no remedy but passion. It is not my mother who would have found that out, and if she is opposed to so humble a match, she will forgive me for making it on the day when she shall know that my brother would have died of his regrets and of his constancy."

The Duke was not perhaps mistaken, and a wiser man could have been less ingenious. He would have endeavored to lead the Marquis back to an interest in life through the love of letters, through filial affection, through reason and duty,—things which were all excellent, but which the invalid himself had long since vainly called to his aid. Now the Duke, from his point of view, imagined that he had rescued everything, and did not foresee that with an exclusive nature like his brother's, the remedy might soon become worse than the disease. The Duke, knowing human susceptibility through himself, believed in a general susceptibility in women, and admitted no exceptions. According to his ideas, Caroline would not make any struggle at all; he believed her already quite disposed to love the Marquis. "She is a good young woman," he said to himself; "not at all ambitious, and entirely disinterested. I judged her at the first glance, and my mother assures me that I am not mistaken. She will yield through her need to love some one, and through allurement, too, for my brother has great attractions for an intelligent woman. If she resists him awhile, it will be all the better; he will be so much the more attached to her. My mother will see nothing of this, and if she does see it, it will agitate her, it will occupy her too. She will be good, she will preach the requirements of caste, and yield to endearment. These little domestic emotions will rescue her from the tedium which is her greatest torment."

To these heartless calculations the Duke gave himself up with perfect candor. He grew tender himself over this sort of puerility which oftentimes characterizes corruption as an exhaustion. He laughed to himself as he regarded the beautiful victim already immolated, in imagination to his projects; and if any one had questioned him on the subject, he would have answered with a laugh, that he was in the act of arranging a romance after the manner of Florian, as a beginning to his contemplated life of sentiment and innocence.

He remained in the drawing-room the whole evening, and found the means to speak to Caroline without being overheard. "My mother has been scolding me," he said. "It appears that I have been absurd with you. I did not suspect such a thing, I assure you, for I really wanted to prove to you my respect. In a word, my mother has made me pledge my honor that I will not think of making love to you, and I pledged it without hesitation. Are you quieted now?"

"All the more that I have not thought of being disquieted."

"That's fortunate. Since my mother forced me into the rudeness of saying to a woman what we never say, even when we think it, let us be good friends like two well-meaning people as we are, and let us be frank with each other to commence with. Promise me, then, no longer to speak ill of me to my brother."

"No longer? When, pray, have I spoken ill of you to him?"

"You did not complain of my impertinence—there, this evening?"

"I said that I dreaded your raillery, and that, if it continued, I should go away; that is all."

"Indeed," thought the Duke, "they are already on better terms than I had hoped." He rejoined, "If you think of quitting my mother on my account, it will condemn me to go away from her myself."

"That could not be thought of. A son giving place to a stranger!"

"That nevertheless is what I have resolved to do, if I displease you and if I frighten you; but remain, and command me to be and do as you would wish. Ought I never to see you, never speak to you, not even salute you?"

"I exact no affectation in any sense whatever. You are too clever and experienced not to have understood that I am not skilled enough in the artifices of speech to sustain any assault against you."

"You are too modest; but since you do not wish that the prescribed forms of admiration should mingle with those of respect, and since the attention, which it is so difficult for you not to awaken, alarms and afflicts you, be at ease; I consider it said and done: you will have no further cause, of complaint in me. I swear it by all that a man can hold sacred,—by my mother!"

After having thus made reparation for his fault and reassured Caroline, whose going away would have foiled his plan, the Duke began to speak to her of Urbain with a veritable enthusiasm. Upon this point he was so thoroughly sincere, that Mlle de Saint-Geneix laid aside her prejudices. Her mind became calm again, and she hastened to write to Camille that everything was going well, that the Duke was much better than his reputation, and that, at all events, he had engaged upon his honor not to disturb her.

During the month succeeding that day Caroline saw very little of M. de Villemer. He was obliged to be occupied with the details of settling his brother's debts; then he absented himself. He told his mother that he was going to Normandy to see a certain historical castle whose plan was necessary for his work, and he set out in quite an opposite direction, confiding to the Duke alone that he was going in the strictest incognito to see his son.

As for the Duke himself, he was very busy with the change of his pecuniary position. He sold his horses, his furniture and personal property, discharged his lackeys, and came, at the request of his mother, to install himself provisionally, for economy's sake, in a suite of apartments between the ground floor and the first story of her hotel, which was going to be sold also, but with the reservation that the Marquis should remain for ten years the principal tenant, and that nothing should be changed in the apartments of his mother.

Urbain himself had ascended to the third story and piled up his books in a lodging more than modest, protesting that he had never been better off, and that he had a magnificent view of the Champs-Élysées. During his absence the preparations for the departure to the country were made, and Mlle de Saint-Geneix wrote to her sister: "I am counting the days which separate us from the blissful time when I can at last walk to my heart's content, and breathe a pure air. I have enough of flowers which faint and die upon the mantels; I am thirsty for those which bloom in the open fields."

VII

Letter From The Marquis de Villemer

To The Duke D'Aléria

Polignac, *via* Le Puy (Haute-Loire)
May 1, '45

The address I give you is a secret which I intrust to you, and which I am happy to intrust to you. If by any unforeseen accident I should chance to die, away from you, you would know that your first duty would be to send hither and see that the child was not neglected by the people in whose charge I have placed him. These people do not know who I am; they know neither my name nor my country; they are not aware even that the child is mine. That these precautions are necessary, I have already told you. M. de G— clings to suspicions which would naturally lead him to doubt the legitimacy of his daughter,—really his own, nevertheless. This fear was the torture of their unhappy mother, to whom I swore that the existence of Didier should be concealed until Laura's fortune had been assured. I have noticed more than once the uneasy curiosity with which my movements have been watched. I cannot therefore cloud them too much in mystery.

This is my reason for placing my son so far away from me and in a province where having no other interests of any kind, I run less risk than I should elsewhere of being betrayed through some accidental meeting. The people with whom I have to deal give me every possible guaranty of their honesty, goodwill, and discretion, in the single fact that they abstain from questioning or watching me. The nurse is the niece of Joseph, that good old servant whom we lost a year ago. It was he who recommended her to me; but she, too, is in complete ignorance regarding me. She knows me by the name of "Bernyer." The woman is young, healthy, and good-humored, a simple peasant, but comfortably provided for. I should fear that, in making her richer, I could not eradicate the parsimonious habits of the country, which, I perceive, are even more inveterate here than elsewhere; and I have held merely to this, that the poor child, while brought up in the true conditions of rustic development, should not have to suffer from an excess of these conditions; this excess having precisely the same effect upon children that lack of sunlight produces upon plants.

My hosts, for I am writing this in their house, are farmers, having charge of the enclosed grounds, within which rises, from a rocky platform, one of the rudest of mediæval fortresses, the cradle of that family whose last representatives played such an unhappy part in the recent vicissitudes of our monarchy. Their ancestors in this province played no less sad a one, and no less important to an age when the feudal system had made the part of king very insignificant. It is not without interest for the historical work upon which I am engaged, to gather up the traditions here and to study the look and character of the old manor and the surrounding country; so I have not absolutely deceived my mother in telling her that I was going to travel in "search of information."

There is really much to be learned here in the very heart of our beautiful France, which it is not fashionable to visit, and which consequently still hides its shrines of poetry and its mines of science in inaccessible nooks. Here is a country without roads, without guides, without any facilities for locomotion, where every discovery must be conquered at the price of danger or fatigue. The inhabitants know as little about it as strangers. Their purely rural lives confine their ideas of locality to a very limited horizon: on a stroll, then, it is impossible to get any information, if you do not know the names and relative situations of all the little straggling villages; indeed, without a very complete map to consult at every step, although I have been in this country three times in the two years of Didier's life here, I could find my way only in a straight line, a thing entirely out of the question over a soil cut up with deep ravines, crossed in every way by lofty walls of lava, and furrowed by numerous torrents.

But I need not go far to appreciate the wild and striking character of the landscape. Nothing, my friend, can give you an idea of this basin of Le Puy with its picturesque beauty, and I can think of no place more difficult to describe. It is not Switzerland, it is less terrible; it is not Italy, it is more lovely; it is Central France with all its Vesuviuses extinct and clothed with splendid vegetation; and yet it is neither Auvergne nor Limosin, with which you are familiar.

BUT I HAVE SAID ENOUGH to keep my promise and to give you some general idea of the country. My dear brother, you urged me to write a long letter, foreseeing that, in my lonely, sleepless hours, I should think too much about myself, my sad life, and my painful past, in the presence of this child who is sleeping yonder while I write! It is true that the sight of him reopens many wounds, and that it is doing me a kindness to compel me to forget myself while generalizing my impressions. And yet I find here powerful emotions, too, which are not without sweetness. Shall I close my letter before I have spoken of him? You see I hesitate; I fear I shall make you smile. You pretend to detest children. As for me, without feeling that repugnance I used formerly to shrink from coming in contact with these little beings, whose helpless candor had something appalling to my mind. To-day I am totally changed in this regard, and even if you should laugh at me, I must still open my heart to you without reserve. Yes, yes, my friend, I must do it. That you may know me thoroughly, I ought to conquer my sensitiveness.

Well, then, you must know I worship this child, and I see, that sooner or later, he will be my whole life and my whole aim. It is not duty alone that brings me to him, it is my own heart that cries out for him, when I have gone without seeing him for a certain length of time. He is comfortable here, he wants for nothing, he is growing strong, he is beloved. His adopted parents are excellent souls, and, as to caring for him properly, I can see that their hearts are in the matter as well as their interests. They live in a part of the manor-house which yet remains standing and which has been suitably restored. They are neat and painstaking people, and they are bringing up the child within these ruins, on the summit of the large rock, under a bright sky, and in a pure and bracing atmosphere. The woman has lived in Paris; she has correct ideas as to the amount of energy and also of humoring that it takes to manage a child more delicate, indeed, than her own children, but with as good a constitution; so I need not feel anxious about anything, but can await the age when it will become necessary to care for and form other material than the body. Well! I am ill at ease about him just as soon as I am away from him. His existence then often seems like an anxiety and a deep trouble in my life; but, when I see him again, all fears vanish and all bitterness is allayed. What shall I say then? I love him! I feel that he belongs to me and that I belong equally to him. I feel that he is mine, yes, mine, far more than his poor mother ever was; as his features and disposition become more marked, I seek vainly in him for something which may recall her to me, and this something does not seem to unfold. Contrary to the usual law which makes boys rather than girls inherit the traits of the mother, it is his father that this child will resemble, if he continues, henceforth, to develop in the way he seems to be doing now. He has already my indolence and the unconquerable timidity of my earliest years, which my mother so often tells me about, and my quick, impulsive moments of unreserved confidence, which made her, she says, forgive me and love me in spite of all. This year he has taken notice of my presence near him. He was afraid at first, but now he smiles and tries to talk. His smile and broken words make me tremble; and when he takes my hand to walk, a certain grateful feeling toward him, I cannot tell what, brings to my eyes tears which I conceal with difficulty.

But this is enough, I do not want to appear too much of a child myself: I have told you this that you may no longer wonder why I refuse to listen to your plans for me. My friend, you must never speak to me of love or marriage. I have not store of happiness enough to bestow any upon a being that would be new to my life. My life itself is hardly sufficient for my duties, as I see clearly in the affection I have for Didier, for my mother, and for you. With this thirst for study, which so often becomes a fever in me, what time should I have for enlivening the leisure hours of a young woman eager for happiness and gayety? No, no, do not think of it; and if the idea of such isolation is sometimes fearful at my age, help me to await the moment when it will be perfectly natural. This will be my task for several years to come. Your affection, as you know, will make them seem fewer and shorter. Keep it for me, indulgent to my faults, generous even toward my confidence.

P. S. I presume that my mother has left for Séval with Mlle de Saint-Geneix, and that you have accompanied them. If my mother is anxious about me, tell her you have heard from me and that I am still in Normandy.

VIII

T he same day on which the Marquis wrote to his brother Caroline wrote to her sister, and sketched, after her own manner, the country where she was.

Séval, near Chambon (Creuse), May 1, '45

At last, my sister, we are here, and it is a terrestrial paradise. The castle is old and small, but well arranged for comfort and picturesque enough. The park is sufficiently large, not any too well kept, and not in the English fashion—thank Heaven!—rich in fine old trees covered with ivy, and in grasses running wild. The country is delightful. We are still in Auvergne, in spite of the new boundaries, but very near to the old limits of La Marche, and within a league of a little city called Chambon, through which we passed on our way to the castle. This little town is very well situated. It is reached by a mountain ascent, or rather, through a cleft in a deep ravine; for mountain, properly speaking, there is none. Leaving behind the broad plains of thin, moist soil, covered with small trees and large bushes, you descend into a long, winding gorge, which in some places enlarges into a valley. In the bottom of this ravine, which soon divides into branches, flow rivers of pure crystal, not navigable, and rather torrents than rivers, although they only whirl along, boiling a little, but threatening no danger. As for myself, having never known anything but our great plains and wide, smooth rivers, I am somewhat inclined to look upon all here as either hill or abyss; but the Marchioness, who has seen the Alps and the Pyrenees, laughs at me, and pretends that all this is as insignificant as a table-cover. So I forbear to give you any enthusiastic description, lest I mislead your judgment; but the Marchioness, who cannot be accused of an undue love of nature, will never succeed in preventing me from being delighted with what I see.

It is a country of grasses and leafage, one continual cradle of verdure. The river, which descends the ravine, is called the Vouèze, and then, uniting with the Tarde at Chambon, it becomes the Char, which, again at the end of the first valley, is called the Cher, a stream that every one knows. For myself, I like the name Char (or car); it is excellent for a stream like this, which in reality rolls along at about the pace of a carriage well under way down a gentle slope, where there is nothing to make it jolt or jar unreasonably. The road also is straight and sanded like a garden walk, lined too with magnificent beeches, through which one can see outspread the natural meadows that are just now one carpet of flowers. O, these lovely meadows, my dear Camille! How little they resemble our artificial plains, where you always see the same plant on ground prepared in regular beds! Here you feel that you are walking over two or three layers of vegetation, of moss, reeds, iris, a thousand kinds of grasses, some of them pretty, and others prettier still, columbines, forget-me-nots, and I know not what! There is everything; and they all come of their own accord, and they come always! It is not necessary to turn over the ground once in every three or four years to expose the roots to the air and to begin over again the everlasting harrowing which our indolent soil seems to need. And then, here, some of the land is permitted to go to waste or poorly tilled, or so it seems; and in these abandoned nooks Nature heartily enjoys making herself wild and beautiful. She shoots forth at you great briers which seem inexhaustible and thistles that look like African plants, they flaunt such large coarse leaves, slashed and ragged, to be sure, but admirable in design and effect.

When we had crossed the valley,—I am speaking of yesterday,—we climbed a very rugged and precipitous ascent. The weather was damp, misty, charming. I asked leave to walk, and, at the height of five or six hundred feet, I could see the whole of this lovely ravine of verdure. The far-off trees were already crowding toward the brink of the water at my feet, while from point to point in the distance rustic mills and sluices filled the air with the muffled cadences of their sounds. Mingled with all this were the notes of a bagpipe from I know not where, and which kept repeating a simple but pleasing air, till I had heard more than enough of it. A peasant who was walking in front of me began to sing the words, following and carrying along the air, as if he wanted to help the musician through with it. The words, without rhyme or reason, seemed so curious that I will give them to you—

> *"Alas! how hard are the rocks!*
> *The sun melts them not,—*
> *The sun, nor yet the moon!*
> *The lad who would love*
> *Seeketh his pain."*

There is always something mysterious in peasant songs, and the music, as defective as the verses, is also mysterious, often sad and inducing revery. For myself, condemned as I am to do my dreaming at lightning speed, since my life does not belong to me, I was forcibly impressed by this couplet, and I asked myself many times why "the moon," at least, did not melt the rocks; did this mean that, by night as well as by day, the grief of the peasant lover is as heavy as his mountains?

On the top of this hill, which appropriately bristles with these large rocks, so cruelly hard,—the Marchioness says they are small as grains of sand, but then I never happened to see any such beautiful sand,—we entered upon a road narrower than the highway, and, after walking a little way amid enclosures of wooded grounds, we found ourselves at the entrance of the castle, which is entirely shaded by the trees, and not imposing in appearance; but on the other side it commands the whole beautiful ravine that we had just passed through. You can see the deep declivity, with its rocks and its bushes, the river too with its trees, its meadows, its mills, and the winding outlet through which it flows, between banks growing more and more narrow and precipitous. There is in the park a very pretty spring, which rises there, to fall in spray along the rocks. The garden is well in bloom. In the lower court there is a lot of animals which I am permitted to manage. I have a delightful room, very secluded, with the finest view of all; the library is the largest apartment in the house. The drawing-room of the Marchioness, in its furniture and arrangement, calls to mind the one in Paris; but it is larger, not so deadening to sound, and one can breathe in it. In short, I am well, I am content, I feel myself reviving; I rise at daybreak, and until the Marchioness appears, which, thank Heaven, is no earlier here than in Paris, I am going to belong to myself in a most agreeable fashion. O, how free I shall be to walk, and write to you, and think of you! Alas! if I only had one of the children here, Lili or Charley, what delightful and instructive walks we could take together! But it is in vain for me to fall in love with all the handsome darlings that I meet, for it does not last. A moment after I compare them with yours, and I feel that yours will have no serious rivals in my affections, and in the midst of my rejoicing at being in the country, comes the thought that I am farther from you than I was before!—and when shall I see you again?

"Alas! how hard are the rocks!" But it's of no use to struggle against all of those which cumber the lives of poor people like us. I must do my duty and become attached to the Marchioness. Loving her is not difficult. Every day she is more kind to me; she is really almost like a mother to me, and her fancy for petting and spoiling me makes me forget my real position. We expected to find the Marquis on our arrival, since he promised to meet his mother here. It cannot be long before he comes. As for the Duke, he will be here, I think, next week. Let us hope that he will be as civil to me in the country as he has been lately in Paris, and not oblige me to show my temper.

At another time Caroline reported to her sister the opinions of the Marchioness on country life.

"'My dear child,' said she to me not long since, 'in order to love the country one must love the earth stupidly, or nature unreasonably. There is no mean between brutal stupidity and enthusiastic folly. Now you know that if I have anything excitable or even sanguine in my composition, it is for the concerns of society rather than for what is governed by the laws of Nature, which are always the same. Those laws are the work of God, so they are good and beautiful. Man can change nothing in them. His control, his observation, his admiration, even his descriptive eloquence, add nothing at all to them. When you go into ecstasies over an apple-tree in bloom, I do not think you are wrong; I think, on the contrary, that you are very right, but it seems to me hardly worth while to praise the apple-tree which does not hear you, which does not bloom to please you, and which will bloom neither the more nor the less, if you say nothing to it. Be assured that when you exclaim, "How beautiful is the spring!" it is just the same as if you said, "The spring is the spring!" Well, then, yes, it is warm in summer because God has made the sun. The river is clear because it is running water, and it is running water because its bed is inclined. It is beautiful because there is in all this a great harmony; but if it had not this harmony, all the beauty would not exist.'

"Thus you see the Marchioness is nothing of an artist, and that she has arguments at her service for not understanding what she does not feel; but in this is she not like the rest of the world, and are we not all acting like her, with respect to any faculty we may happen to lack?

"As she was thus talking, seated on a garden bench much fatigued with the 'exercise' she had taken,—namely, a hundred paces on a sanded walk,—a peasant came to the garden gate to sell fish to the cook, who was bargaining with him. I recognized this peasant as the one who had walked before me on the day of our arrival, singing the song about the 'hard rocks.' 'What are you thinking of?' asked the Marchioness, who saw that I was observing him.

"'I am thinking,' I replied, 'of watching that stout fellow. It is no longer an apple-tree or a river, you see, and he has a peculiar countenance, with which I have been struck.'

"'How, pray?'

"'Why, if I were not afraid to repeat a modern word of which you seem to have a horror, I should say that this man has character.'

"'How do you know? Is it because he is obstinate about the price of his fish? Ah! that's it; but pardon me. Character! the word, you see, has become a pun in my mind. I have forgotten to think of it as used in literature—or art. A piece of dress goods, a bench, a kettle, have character now; that is to say, a kettle has the shape of a kettle, a bench looks like a bench, and dress goods have the effect of dress goods? Or is it the contrary, rather? Have dress goods the character of a cloud, a bench that of a table, and a kettle that of a well? I will never admit your word, I give you warning!'—and then she began to talk about the neighboring peasantry. 'They are not bad people,' said she; 'not so much given to cheating as to wheedling. They are eager for money, because they are in want of everything; but they allow themselves nothing from the money which they make. They hoard up to buy property, and, when the hour has come, they are intoxicated with the delight of acquisition, buy too largely, borrow at any price, and are ruined. Those who best understand their own interests become usurers and speculate on this rage for property, sure that the lands will return to them at a lower price, when the purchaser shall have become bankrupt. This is why some peasants climb up into the citizen class, while the greater number fall back lower than ever. It is the sad side of the natural law, for these people are governed by an instinct almost as fatal and blind as that which makes the apple-tree blossom. So the peasant interests me but little. I assist the lame and the half-witted, the widows and children, but the healthy ones are not to be interfered with. They are more headstrong than their mules.'

"'Then, Madame, what is there here to interest one?'

"'Nothing. We come here because the air is good, and because we can benefit our health and purse a little. And then it is the custom. Everybody leaves Paris at the earliest possible moment. One must go away when the others do.'"

"You see, dear Camille, by this specimen of our conversation, that the Marchioness looks gloomily upon the present age, and you can, too, by the same means, now form some idea of this 'talking life' of hers, which you said you could not understand. Upon every subject she has an intelligent criticism always ready, sometimes bright and good-natured, sometimes sharp and bitter. She has talked too much in the course of her life to be happy. Thinking of two or three or thirty people, continually, and without taking time to collect one's self, is, I believe, a great abuse. One ceases to question one's self, affirming always; for otherwise there could be no discussion, and all conversation would cease. Condemned to this exercise, I should give way to doubt or to disgust of my fellow-creatures, if I had not the long morning to recover myself and find my balance again. Although Madame de Villemer, by her wit and good-humor, throws every possible charm about this dry employment of our time, I long for the Marquis to come and take his share in this dawdling oratory."

The Marquis did really arrive in the course of a week or ten days, but he was worried and absent-minded, and Caroline noticed that he was peculiarly cold toward her. He plunged directly into his favorite pursuits, and no longer allowed himself to be seen at all till the hour of dinner. This peculiarity was the more evident to Mlle de Saint-Geneix, because the Marquis seemed to be making more effort than he had ever done before to stand his ground in discussions with his mother,—to the very great satisfaction of the latter, who feared nothing in the world but silence and wandering attention; so that Caroline, seeing herself no longer needed to spur on a lagging conversation, and getting the impression that she paralyzed the Marquis more than she assisted him, was less assiduous in profiting by his presence, and took it upon herself to withdraw early in the evening.

IX

When at the end of another week the Duke also arrived, he was surprised by this state of affairs. Deeply touched by his brother's letter from Polignac, but believing that he detected in him rather a struggle against himself than a resolution actually formed, his Grace had intentionally delayed his appearance, so as to give time to the isolation and freedom of the country to work upon the two hearts which he believed to have been moved by his words, and which he expected to find in accord. He had not foreseen the absence of coquetry or imagination on the part of Caroline, the real dismay, serious resistance, internal combat, on the part of the Marquis. "How is this now?" the Duke asked of himself, as he saw that even their friendly disposition one for the other seemed to have disappeared. "Is it a sense of morality that has so soon quenched the fire? Has my brother been making an abortive attempt? Is his access of sadness from fear or spite? Is the girl a prude? No. Ambitious? No. The Marquis will not know how to explain himself. Perhaps he has kept all the powers of his mind for his books, when he should have bestowed them in the service of his growing passion."

The Duke, nevertheless, did not hasten to discover the truth. He was the prey of conflicting resolutions. He had succeeded in gaining a thorough knowledge of the state of the Marquis's affairs. The income of the latter was barely thirty thousand francs, twelve thousand of which were given over as a pension to his spendthrift brother. The rest was applied almost entirely to the support and service of the Marchioness, and the Marquis himself lived in his own house without making any more expense there on his private account than if he had been an unobtrusive guest.

The Duke was wounded by this state of affairs, which he had brought about, and of which the Marquis did not appear to think at all. His Grace had endured his own ruin in the most brilliant manner. He had shown himself a veritable grandee, and if he had lost many companions of his pleasures, he had recognized many faithful friends. He had grown in the opinion of the world, and he was forgiven the trouble and scandal he had caused in more than one family, when he was seen to accept with courage and spirit the expiation of his wild and reckless life. He had thus undauntedly assumed the part which was hereafter proper for him; but there was a feeling of penitence which disturbed his mental balance, and about which he agitated himself with less clearness of sight and strength of resolution than he would have done if it had been a matter concerning only himself. Thoroughly sincere and well disposed in his lack of reason, he cast about him for the means of making his brother happy. Sometimes he persuaded himself that love should be introduced into Urbain's life of meditation and competence; at other times he thought it his duty to inspire the Marquis with ambition, dealing sharply with his repugnances and trying once more to suggest to him the idea of a great marriage.

This latter was also the dream of the Marchioness, one that had always been dear to her; and she now gave herself up to it more than ever, believing that her maternal enthusiasm at the generosity of the Marquis would be shared by some accomplished heiress. She confided to the Duke that she was in treaty with her friend, the Duchess de Dunières, about marrying the Marquis to a Xaintrailles, an orphan, very rich, and reputed beautiful, who was weary of her studies at the convent, and who nevertheless was very exacting as to merit and quality. From all indications the thing was possible, but it was necessary that Urbain should favor it, and he did not favor it, saying that he should never marry, if the occasion did not come to find him, and that he was the last man in the world to go and see an unknown woman with the intention of pleasing her.

"Try then, my son," said the Marchioness to the Duke, the day after his arrival, "to cure him of that wild timidity. As for me it is a sheer waste of words."

The Duke undertook the task, and found his brother uncertain, careless, not saying no, but refusing to take any step in the matter, and observing merely that it was necessary to wait for the chance which might lead him to meet the person; that, if she pleased him, he would *afterward* endeavor to learn whether she had no dislike for him. Nothing could be done just then, since they were in the country; there was no hurry about it; he was not more unhappy than usual, and he had a great deal of work to do.

The Marchioness grew impatient at this compromising with time, and continued to write, taking the Duke for secretary in this affair, which was not in Caroline's department.

The Duke seeing clearly that for six whole months this marriage would not advance one step, returned to the idea of bringing about a temporary diversion of his brother's mind by a country romance. The heroine was at hand, and she was charming. She was suffering perhaps a little from the very apparent coldness of M. de Villemer. The Duke devoted himself to learning the cause of this coldness. He failed utterly; the Marquis was inscrutable. His brother's questions seemed to astonish him.

The fact is that the idea of making love to Mlle de Saint-Geneix had never entered his mind. He would have made it a very grave case of conscience with himself, and he did not compound with his conscience. He had insensibly submitted to the strong and real attraction of Caroline, given himself up to it unreservedly; then his brother, in seeking to excite his jealousy, had caused him to discover a more pronounced inclination in this sympathy without a name. He had suffered terribly for some days. He had demanded of himself if he were free, and he considered himself placed between a mother who desired him to make an ambitious marriage, and a brother to whom he owed the wreck of his fortune. He had foreseen, besides, invincible resistance in the proud scruples of Mlle de Saint-Geneix. He already knew enough of her character to be certain that she would never consent to come between his mother and himself. Equally resolved not to commit the folly of being uselessly importunate, and to be guilty of the baseness of betraying the good faith of a fine soul, he worked and struggled to conquer himself, and appeared to have succeeded miraculously. He played his part so well that the Duke was deceived by it. Such courage and delicacy exceeded perhaps the notion which the latter had formed of a duty of this kind. "I have been mistaken," he thought, "my brother is absorbed in the study of history. It is of his book that I must speak to him."

Thereafter the Duke demanded of himself in what way he could employ his own imagination for the next six months of comparative inaction. Hunting, reading novels, talking with his mother, composing a few ballads,—these were hardly sufficient for so fantastic a spirit, and naturally he began to think of Caroline as the only person who could throw a little poetry and romance about his life. He had decided to pass the half of the year at Séval, and that was a noble resolution for a man who did not like the country except with a great establishment. He intended, by living on the most modest footing with his brother for six months of every year, to refuse six thousand francs of his yearly allowance; and if the Marquis should reject the proffered sacrifice, he purposed to employ that sum in restoring and repairing the manor-house;

but he must have a little flirtation to crown all this virtue, and there stopped the virtue of the brave Duke.

"How shall I do," said he to himself, "now that I have pledged my word to her, as well as to my mother, to have nothing of the kind to do with her! There is but one way, simpler perhaps than all the ordinary and worn-out ways: that is, to pay her little attentions, but with the appearance of entire disinterestedness; respect without gallantry, a friendly regard, perfectly frank, and which will inspire her with real confidence. Since, with all this I am in no way prevented from being as clever and gracious as I can be, and as perfectly amiable and devoted as I should be in showing my pretensions, it is very probable that she will be sensible of them, and that of her own accord she will relieve me little by little of my oath. A woman is always astonished that at the end of two or three months of affectionate intimacy one does not say a word of love to her. And then she will find it tedious here, too, since my brother's eyes speak to her no longer. Well, we will see. It will, indeed, be something quite new and spicy to conquer a heart which is held in alarm, without seeming to do it, and to bring about a capitulation without seeming to have been a besieger. I have seen this sort of artifice practised with coquettes and prudes; but I am curious to see how Mlle de Saint-Geneix, who is neither coquette nor prude, will undertake to bring about this evolution."

Thus occupied by a puerility of self-conceit, the Duke no longer gave way to tedium. He had never liked brutal debauch, and his dissoluteness had always preserved a certain stamp of elegance. He had used and abused so much of life that he was sufficiently used up himself to make self-restraint no very difficult matter. He had said he was not sorry to renew for himself his health and youth, and even at times he flattered himself that he had perhaps found again the youth of the heart, of which his manners and language had been able to keep up the appearance. From the fact that his brain was still busy upon a perverse romance, he concluded that he could still be romantic.

He manœuvred so skilfully that Mlle Saint-Geneix had the modesty to be completely deceived by his feigned honesty. Seeing that he never sought to be alone with her, she no longer avoided him. And while without losing her from his eyes, he brought about in the most natural and apparently the least foreseen ways occasions to meet her in her walks, he took his advantage of these meetings by appearing not at all desirous to prolong them, and by himself withdrawing with an air of discretion and just the shade of regret which reconciled amiable politeness with provoking indifference.

He employed all this art without Caroline's having the least suspicion of it. Her own frankness prevented her from divining a plan, of that nature. In the course of a week she was as much at her ease with him as if she had never mistrusted him, and she wrote to Madame Heudebert:—

"The Duke is greatly changed for the better since the family event which brought him to himself, or indeed he never merited the accusations of Madame de D——. The latter perhaps is the truth, for I cannot believe that a man of such refined manners and sentiments has ever desired to ruin a woman for the sole pleasure of having a victim to boast of. She (Madame de D——) maintained that he has done so with all his conquests, out of sheer libertinism and vanity. Libertinism—I am not too sure that I know what that is, in the life of a man of high rank. I have lived among virtuous people, and all I have seen of debauchery has been among poor laborers, who lose their reason in wine and beat their wives in paroxysms of mortal frenzy. If the vice of great lords consists in compromising the women of society, there must be many women of society who easily allow themselves to be compromised, since so great a number of victims has been attributed to the Duke d'Aléria. For my part, I do not see that he concerns himself with women at all, and I never hear him speak ill of any woman in particular. Quite the contrary, he praises virtue, and declares that he believes in it. He seems never to have had anything in the way of perfidy to reproach himself with, because he establishes a very marked difference between those who consent to be ruined and those who do not consent to it. I do not know if he is imposing upon me, but he would appear to have loved with respect and sincerity. Neither his mother nor his brother seems to doubt that, and I certainly like to believe that this is a sincere but inconstant nature, which it was necessary to be very credulous or very vain to have hoped to fix upon one object. That he has been liberal in excess, a gamester, forgetful of his duty to his family, intoxicated with luxury and with trivial pursuits unworthy of a serious man, I do not doubt, and it is in these things that I see the feebleness of his judgment and his vanity; but they are the faults and misfortunes of education and of a life which began in too much privilege. His class is not usually made aware of duty by necessity, being taught everything that is just the opposite of providence and economy. Did not our own poor father ruin himself too, and who would dare say he was to blame for it? As to foppishness or self-conceit in the Duke, after seeking for it patiently, I have not detected the least trace. His conduct here is as unaffected as that of a country squire. He goes in the plainest and cheapest attire, and wins all hearts by his good-nature and simplicity. He never makes the slightest allusion to his past triumphs, and he never boasts of any of his gifts, which are nevertheless real, for he is charmingly clever; he is always handsome, he sings delightfully, and even composes a little,— not very well but with a certain elegance. He talks marvellously well, though not very profoundly, for he has read or retained only things of a light nature; but he confesses this with candor, and serious topics are far from being displeasing to him, since he questions his brother on every subject and listens to him intelligently and respectfully.

"As regards the latter, he is always the same spotless mirror, the model of all the virtues, and modesty itself. He is very busy upon a great historical work of which his brother says marvellous things, and that does not astonish me. Nature would have been very illogical, if she had denied him the faculty of expressing the world of weighty ideas and true sentiments with which she has endowed his soul. He carries about with him a sort of religious meditation of his work which causes him to be more reserved with me, and more communicative with his mother and brother than he used to be. I rejoice for them, and, as to myself, I am not offended; it is very natural that he should not expect any light upon such grave subjects from me, and that he should be led to question persons who are more mature and who are better instructed in the science of human actions. At Paris he manifested a good deal of interest in me, especially the day when his brother thought himself at liberty to tease me; but because he has not since showed that particular interest, I have not come to the conclusion that it no longer exists, and that it may not on occasion be again apparent. There will be, however, no such future occasion, since the Duke has so thoroughly improved; but I shall not be the less grateful for being able to count upon so estimable a protector."

We see that, if Caroline was really affected by the change in the manner of M. de Villemer, she was so without knowing it herself, and without wanting to yield to a vague wound. Her woman's self-love did not enter into the question at all. She felt sure that she had done nothing to forfeit his esteem, and as she did not expect or desire anything more, she attributed everything to a worthy preoccupation.

Nevertheless, in spite of all her efforts, she began to feel that the time passed tediously with her. She was careful not to write this fact to her sister, who could have imparted no new courage, and whose letters were indeed always loving, yet full of condoling and complaints about her absence and the manner of her self-sacrifice. Caroline humored this tender and timid soul, for whom she had habitually exerted a maternal care, and whom she forced herself to sustain by appearing always as strong and as much at ease as the force of her character enabled her generally to be; but she had her hours of profound weariness, in which her heart was oppressed with a dread of being alone. Although she was more of a captive, more really subjected during a part of the day than she had ever been in her family, she had her mornings and the last hour of the night in which to taste the austerity of solitude and to question herself of her own destiny,—a dangerous liberty which she had never been allowed when she had four children and a necessitous household upon her hands. At times she took refuge in certain poetical musings and found in them an enchanting tenderness; at times, too, a bitterness without cause and without aim made nature hateful to her, her walks fatiguing, and sleep oppressive.

She struggled with herself courageously, but these attacks of melancholy did not escape the eager attention of the Duke d'Aléria. He remarked, on certain days, a bluish shade, which made her eyes look sunken, and a sort of involuntary resistance in the muscles of her face when she smiled. He thought that the hour was approaching, and he proceeded with the plan which he had adopted. He was more kind and more attentive, and when he saw that she recognized the change in his manner, he hastened to remind her delicately that love had nothing to do with it. This grand game, however, was all to no purpose. Caroline was so simple-natured that all skill of this kind could hardly fail to be lost on her. When the Duke surrounded her with delicate and charming attentions, she attributed them to his friendship, and when he endeavored to goad her on by withdrawing them she rejoiced the more that they sprang only from friendship. The Duke's self-esteem prevented him from seeing clearly in this second phase of his enterprise. Confidence had come; but, in reality, Caroline might open her eyes with no other pain than that of profound astonishment and a pitying disdain. The Duke hoped every returning day to see the growth of spite or impatience in her. He could, however, detect only a little sadness, for which he ingenuously gave himself the credit, and which was mildly pleasurable, though by no means satisfactory to him. "I would have believed her more sensitive," thought he; "there is a trifle of torpidity in her sorrow, and more mildness than warmth."

Gradually this mildness charmed him. He had never seen anything equal to this supposed resignation. He saw in it a hidden modesty, a hopelessness of pleasing, a tender submission, which deeply touched him. "She is good above all others," he said to himself again,—"good as an angel. One could be very happy with that woman, she would be so grateful and so little disposed to quarrel. Truly she does not know what it is to cause suffering; she keeps it all for herself."

By dint of waiting for his prey, the Duke found himself fascinated, and the feeling grew upon him. He was forced to acknowledge that he was ill at ease in her presence, and that his own cruelty troubled him a great deal. At the end of a month he began to lose patience, and to say to himself that he must hasten the catastrophe; but that all at once appeared to him extremely difficult. Caroline yet had too much virtue in his eyes, to permit him to forfeit his word, for in being abrupt he might lose everything.

Entering his mother's apartment one day, the Duke said, "I have just been greatly amusing myself riding one of your farm colts. He resembles a wild boar and a trotting errand-boy at the same time. He has fire and speed, and is very gentle besides. Mlle de Saint-Geneix might ride him if she happens to be fond of the exercise."

"I am very fond of it," she replied. "My father required it of me, and I was not grieved to satisfy him in that regard."

"Then I will wager you are an excellent rider?"

"No, I can sit upright and have a nimble hand, like all women."

"Like all women who ride well, for generally women are nervous and would like to lead men and horses after the same fashion; but that is not your character."

"As far as men are concerned, I know nothing at all about it. I have never attempted to lead any one."

"O, you will attempt that, too, some day?"

"It is not probable."

"No," said the Marchioness, "it is not probable. She does not wish to marry, and in her position she is greatly in the right."

"O, certainly," rejoined the Duke. "Marriage without fortune must be a hell!"

He looked at Caroline to see if she were moved by such a declaration. She was quite passive; she had renounced marriage sincerely and irrevocably.

GEORGE SAND

The Duke, wishing to judge whether she was armed against the idea of an irreparable fault, added, in order to compromise nothing too gravely, "Yes, it must be a hell except in the case of a great passion which gives the heroism to undergo everything."

Caroline was still just as calm and apparently a stranger to the question.

"Ah! my son, what nonsense are you preaching now? There are days when you talk like a child."

"But you know well enough that I am very much of a child," said the Duke; "and I hope to be so for a long time to come."

"It is being altogether too much so to rest the chances of happiness in misery," said the Marchioness, who courted discussion. "There is no such thing; misery kills all, even love."

"Is that your opinion, Mlle de Saint-Geneix?" rejoined the Duke.

"O, I have no opinion on the subject," she replied. "I know nothing of life beyond a certain limit, but I should be led in this instance to believe with your mother rather than with you. I have known misery, and if I have suffered it was in seeing its weight upon those whom I loved. There is no need, therefore, of extending and complicating one's life when it is already so perplexing. That would be to go in search of despair."

"Bless me! everything is relative," exclaimed the Duke. "That which is the misery of some is the opulence of others. Would you not be very rich with an income of twelve thousand francs?"

"Certainly," replied Caroline, without remembering and perhaps even without knowing that to be the exact amount of her questioner's yearly allowance.

"Well, then," continued the Duke, who endeavored to inspire a hope with one word that he might crush it with the next,—still intent upon his plan of agitating this placid or timid heart,—"if any one should offer you such a modest competence as that, together with a sincere love?"

"I could not accept," Caroline rejoined. "I have four children to support and rear; no husband would accept such a past as that."

"She is charming," cried the Marchioness; "she speaks of her past like a widow."

"Ah! I did not speak of the widow, my poor sister. With myself and an old woman-servant, who is attached to us, and who shall share the last morsel of bread in the house, we are seven, neither more nor less. Now do you know the young man to marry with his twelve thousand francs a year? I think decidedly he would make a very bad bargain."

Caroline always spoke of her situation with an unaffected cheerfulness, which showed the sincerity of her nature.

"Well, in point of fact, you are right," said the Duke. "You will get through life better all alone with your fine, brave spirit. I believe, indeed, that you and I are the only persons in the world who are really philosophers. I regard poverty as nothing when one is responsible only to his own free will, and I must say that I was never before so happy as I am now."

"So much the better, my son," said the Marchioness, with an almost imperceptible shade of reproach, which the Duke, however, perceived in an instant, for he hastened to add,—

"I shall be completely happy the day my brother makes the marriage in question, and he will make it, will he not, dear mother?"

Caroline was on the point of going to examine the clock.

"No, no, it is not slow; it is just right," said the Marchioness. "We have no secrets from you hereafter, dear little one, and you must know that I have to-day received good news relative to a great project which I have for my son. If I have not made use of your pretty hand in negotiating this matter, it is for reasons altogether different from that of distrust. Here, read us this letter, of which my elder son as yet knows nothing."

Caroline would have gladly refrained from looking thus in advance into the secrets of the family, and especially into those of the Marquis. She hesitated; "M. de Villemer is not here," she said; "I do not know that he, for his part, will approve of the entire confidence with which you honor me—"

"Yes, he will, certainly," answered the Marchioness. "If I had a doubt of it, I would not beg you to read it. Come, now begin, my dear."

There was nothing further to be said to the Marchioness. Caroline read as follows:—

"Yes, dear friend, it must and will succeed. True, the fortune of Mlle de X—— is upwards of four millions at least, but she knows it, and is no prouder on that account. On the contrary, after a new attempt on my part, she said to me no later than this morning, 'You are right, dear godmother; I have the power and the privilege to enrich a man of true merit. All you tell me of your friend's son gives me an exalted idea of him. Let me complete the time of my mourning at the convent, and I will consent to see him at your house the coming autumn.'

"It is well understood that in all this affair I have named no one, but your history and that of your two sons are so well known, that my dear Diana has divined. I did not think I ought to let pass the chance to make the excellent conduct of the Marquis do valuable service in the attainment of our object. The Duke, his brother, has himself proclaimed it everywhere, with a feeling which does him honor. Do not, therefore, prolong your retreat at Séval too far into the bad season. Diana must not see too much society before the interview. Society takes away, even from the most candid natures, that first freshness of faith and generosity, which I admire, and which I do my best to preserve in my noble godchild. You will continue my work, I know, when she is your daughter, my worthy friend. It is my most earnest wish to see your dear son recover the place in the world which is his due. To have lost it without a frown is fine in him, and the only finer thing which a person of lineage can do is to restore it to him. It is the duty of the daughters of gentle blood to give these grand examples of pride to the upstarts of the day, and as I am one of these daughters, I shall be satisfied with nothing short of success in this matter, putting all my heart in it, all my religion, all my devotion for you.

DUCHESS DE DUNIÈRES
née DE FONTARQUES

The Duke could have scrutinized Caroline after the reading of this letter, in which her voice never once grew weak: he would not have detected in her the least effort, the least personal feeling which was not in harmony with the satisfaction felt by himself; but he never thought of observing her! In presence of a family affair so important, poor Caroline held a place quite secondary and accidental in his mind, and he would have reproached himself for thinking of her at all, when he saw in the future of his brother the providential reparation of the evil which he had caused. "Yes," he cried, joyfully kissing the hands of his mother,—"yes, you will be happy again, and I shall cease to blush. My brother shall be the man, the head of the family. The whole world shall know his rare worth, for without fortune, in the eyes of the majority, talent and virtue are not sufficient. He will then be master of everything, this dear brother, glory, honor, credit, power, and all in spite of those little fine gentlemen of the citizen court, and without bending at all before the pretended necessities of politics. Mother, have you shown this letter to Urbain?"

"Yes, my son, to be sure."

"And he is satisfied? Things are already so far under way, the lady prepossessed in his favor, accepting in advance, and asking only to see him—"

"Yes, my friend, he has promised to allow himself to be introduced."

"Victory!" cried the Duke. "Then let us be gay, let us do something foolish! I want to jump up to the ceiling, I want to embrace some one, it makes no matter whom! Dear mamma, will you let me go and embrace my brother?"

"Yes, but do not congratulate him too much; he is startled at anything new, you understand?"

"O, never fear; I know him."

And the Duke, still very nimble in spite of his tendency to stoutness and the more or less damaged state of his joints, went out gambolling like a school-boy.

X

He found the Marquis absorbed in his work. "Do I disturb you? So much the worse!" cried the Duke. "I must embrace you. My mother has just read me the letter from the Duchess de Dunières."

"But, my friend, the marriage is not yet arranged," replied the Marquis, while he submitted to the fraternal hugging.

"It is arranged if you wish it, and you cannot be opposed to it."

"My friend, I might perhaps wish it ever so much. I would still have to be simply charming to sustain the brilliant reputation which that old Duchess has made for me, a great deal too much at your expense, I am inclined to think."

"The Duchess has done just right, except only that she has not said enough. I should like to go to her and let her know everything. He believes that he is not charming! See how little he knows himself!"

"I know myself too well," rejoined M. de Villemer; "I am not mistaken."

"The deuce take! Do you consider yourself a bear? You were attractive enough to Madame de G—, the most reserved person in the world."

"Ah! I pray you do not speak of her; you remind me of all I suffered before I could inspire her with confidence in me,—all I afterwards suffered lest that confidence should from moment to moment be withdrawn. Look here!" added the Marquis, slightly forgetting himself; "people who are subject to strong passion have no reason. You do not know that, for you attract at first sight, and besides you do not seek for an exclusive love which shall endure for a lifetime. I know but one word to say to a woman,—*I love*, and if she does not understand that my whole soul is in that word, I could never add another."

"Well, then, you will love Diana de Xaintrailles, and she will understand that supreme word of yours."

"But suppose I should not love her?"

"O my dear fellow, she is charming. I saw her when she was quite little; she was a very cherub."

"Every one, I know, calls her charming; but what if she does not please me? Do not tell me that it is not necessary to adore one's wife,—that it suffices to esteem her and know her to be agreeable. I do not want to argue on that subject; it would be throwing away time. Let us confine ourselves to the question of my pleasing her. If I do not love, I do not know how to make myself loved, and therefore I shall not marry."

"One would indeed think you expect and depend upon that!" exclaimed the Duke with real sorrow. "Ah! our poor mother, who is so happy in her hope! And I, who believed myself absolved by destiny! Urbain, must it be then that we are under a curse, all three of us?"

"No," replied the Marquis, deeply moved; "let us not despair. I am working to modify my timid, unsociable character. Upon honor, I am working with all my power for that end. I want to put an end to this agitated, sterile existence. Give me the summer to triumph over my memories, my doubts, my apprehensions; true, I want to make you happy, and God perhaps will come to my aid."

"Thank you, brother; you are the best of beings!" responded the Duke, embracing him again. And as the Marquis was much agitated, he led him forth to walk, in order to divert his mind from his work and to fortify him in his good intentions.

The Duke did then what Urbain had done to conquer him on the day of their first real intimacy. He represented himself weak and suffering as a means of restoring his brother's strength and courage. He gave vivid expression to his remorse and spoke feelingly of the need he had of moral support. "Two unhappy people can do nothing for each other," he said; "your melancholy has its fatal rebound on me, and overcomes me. The day when I see you happy, real energy and the joy of living will return to me."

Urbain, touched by these words, renewed his promise, and, as it cost him dearly, he forced it from his mind by leading his brother's talk to lively subjects; this did not take long, for the Duke required but little encouragement to return to the theme which had lately been absorbing so much of his time and thought.

"Come," he said, seeing his brother smile, "you will bring me happiness in everything. I am reminded now that for some days I have had a vexation intense enough in all conscience; it has made me sullen, awkward; my mind has been clouded; I could not see my way clearly. I have been frightfully stupid. I am sure that I shall now recover my faculties."

"Again some story of a woman?" asked the Marquis, mastering a vague and sudden uneasiness.

"And what would you want it to be? That little De Saint-Geneix occupies my mind more perhaps than she ought."

"It is exactly what she ought not to do," quickly replied the Marquis. "Have you not given your oath to our mother? She told me you had. Have you deceived mother?"

"No, not at all; but I should like very much to be compelled to deceive her."

"Compelled? I have no idea what you mean."

"Dear me! Well, this is just what I mean." And the Duke gave his brother a detailed account of how he had at first told a falsehood when he announced himself in love with Caroline, from the commendable motive of getting Urbain himself in love with her; how, seeing that he had not succeeded, he had conceived the plan of making her love him, without loving her; and how at last he had fallen sincerely in love with her himself, without a surety that his feeling was returned. Nevertheless, he added that he counted upon victory if he could only have the courage not to declare himself; and he said all this in terms so delicate or so ambiguous that the Marquis could not give him a moral lecture about it without making himself ridiculous. Then, when the latter, recovering from his stupefaction, attempted to speak of the repose of his mother and the dignity of their domestic life, not daring in his distress to say anything whatever of the respect due to Caroline, the Duke, becoming impressed with a sudden fear that his brother might think it his duty, to give her warning, swore that he would do nothing to tempt her, but that if of her own accord she threw herself bravely into his arms at any given moment, without conditions and without calculation, he was ready to marry her. Was he sincere then? Yes, probably, as he had always been, when eagerness had given the appearance of possibility to what passion had afterward caused him to evade.

As his brother spoke from a kind of conviction, the Marquis dared not express himself against this unlooked-for repetition of offence in the strange project. He knew that their mother did not expect to make an advantageous marriage for the one of her sons who no longer offered a guaranty of character, and the Duke proved to him by arguments cogent enough that he alone was the master of his future, to whom ambition was no longer permitted. "You see," he said, in conclusion, "that all this is very serious. I attempted once more to lay a snare, I will confess to you, but I did not expect to profit by it; it was merely a game without results. I was taken in my own net, and I suffer for it a great deal. I do not ask you to aid me, but I prohibit you in the name of our friendship from influencing any one about us; for, if you frighten

Mlle de Saint-Geneix, you will exasperate me perhaps, and I no longer answer for anything; or, if you succeed in making me renounce her, it is she who, exasperated, will perhaps commit some folly in the estimation of my mother. Since things are so situated that they can be cleared up only by some unforeseen circumstance, do not interfere in any way, and be certain that I shall conduct myself, come what may, in a manner to reassure your delicacy and to conflict neither with our mother's peace nor with the proprieties of the hospitality which you extend to me."

XI

During this conversation, so painful to the Marquis, Caroline was having a talk with the Marchioness, which, without disturbing her so much, was by no means cheering to her. The Marchioness, full of her project, showed her young favorite a depth of family ambition, which the latter had never suspected. What she had loved and admired in the Marchioness was the chivalrous disinterestedness and resignation to the loss of wealth and to the actual state of things which had struck her so forcibly; but now she was compelled to modify her impressions, and to recognize the fact that this unselfish philosophy was only a fine costume gracefully worn. The Marchioness, however, was not a hypocrite; a person as communicative as she was had little or no premeditation, good or bad; she yielded to the sway of the moment, and did not think herself illogical in saying that she would rather die of famine than see one of her sons do a mean thing to enrich himself, but that, nevertheless, dying of famine was very hard, that her own present condition was a life of privation, while that of the Marquis was a purgatory; and finally, that one cannot be happy unless, along with honor and the pride of a blameless conscience, one has an income of at least two hundred thousand francs.

Caroline ventured to make a few general objections, which the Marchioness quickly repulsed. "Should not," she asked, "the sons of great families lead those of all other classes of society? This is a religion which you ought to have,—you, who are of good family. You ought to understand that gentlefolks have demands upon them—demands legitimate or, perhaps, obligatory—for a very large liberality, and that the higher the position these persons hold, the more it is required of them to possess a fortune on a level with their natural elevation. I suffer bitterly, I assure you, when I see the Marquis settling accounts himself with his farmers, busying himself about certain inevitable wastings, and even, if necessary, descending to the details of my kitchen. To one knowing our distress, it seems admirable in him to be tormenting himself thus that I may want for nothing; but with those who have no correct idea of this, we must certainly pass for misers, and so fall to the level of the lower classes!"

"Since you suffer so much," said Caroline, "from what I have considered an easy life, a very honorable one, and even a very noble one,

God grant that this marriage may succeed, for you would have to renew your store of courage in case of any obstacle. Nevertheless, if I may be permitted to have an opinion—"

"One should always have opinions. Speak, my dear child."

"Well, then, I should say that it would be safest and wisest to accept the present state of affairs as quite endurable, without, on that account, giving up the marriage in question."

"And what signify disappointments, my poor little one? You fear that I shall have them? They do not kill, and hopes give us life. But why do you doubt the fulfilment of mine?"

"O, I do not doubt it," replied Caroline; "why should I have any doubts, if Mlle de Xaintrailles is as perfect as she is said to be?"

"She is perfect, as you can very well see, since she decides in favor of personal merit, contenting herself with her own wealth."

"That does not seem to me very difficult," thought Caroline; but she was not inclined to make any audible rejoinder, and the Marchioness proceeded: "Besides, she is a Xaintrailles! Only think, my dear, of the prestige of such a name! Do you not see that a person of that blood, if she is fine at all, cannot be so by halves? Come, you are not sufficiently convinced of the excellence that comes to us by descent. I believe I have noticed this in you before. You have, perhaps, philosophized a little too much about it. Distrust all these new ideas and the pretensions of these self-made gentlemen! They may say and do what they will, but a man of low origin will never be truly noble at heart; a sordid weight of prudence and parsimony will always cling to him, like a birth-mark, and stifle his finer impulses. You will never see him sacrifice his fortune and his life for an idea, for his religion, for his prince, or for his honorable name. He may do brilliant deeds from a love of glory; but there will always be a personal interest in it some way; so do not be at all deceived by it."

Caroline felt wounded at the infatuation which the Marchioness professed to feel for the patrician orders. She found means to change the subject of the conversation; but, while they were at dinner, she was absorbed in the idea that her old friend, her tender adopted mother, assigned her unceremoniously to a place among these second-class families. The Marchioness had thought that she might speak thus before a gentleman's daughter, having the feelings proper to her class and therefore imbued with good principles; but Caroline said to herself, and very reasonably, too, that her claims to nobility were slight, questionable, perhaps. Her ancestors, who were provincial magistrates, had been ennobled in the reign of Louis XIV; her father, without great presumption, had therefore assumed the title of knight. She saw plainly, then, that the disdain of the Marchioness for the lower classes was a question of degree, and that a girl who was poor and of the lesser nobility was, in her eyes, twice her inferior in all respects.

This discovery did not awaken a foolish sensitiveness in Mlle de Saint-Geneix, but her natural sense of justice revolted against a prejudice so solemnly imposed as a duty upon her belief. "So," said she to herself, "my life of misery, of self-sacrifice, of courage, and of cheerfulness withal, even my voluntary renunciation of all the joys of life, are nothing to the heroism of a Xaintrailles, who consents to be contented with two hundred thousand francs a year, that she may marry an accomplished man! It is because she is a Xaintrailles that her choice is sublime, and because I am only a Saint-Geneix, my sacrifice is a thing vulgar and obligatory!"

Caroline repelled these thoughts of wounded self-respect, but they traced a slight furrow on her expressive face, in passing. A beauty which is true and fresh can hide nothing. The Duke observed this trace of secret melancholy and ingenuously attributed it to himself. His delusion increased when he saw that in spite of her efforts to maintain her usual cheerfulness, Mlle de Saint-Geneix grew more and more thoughtful. The real cause was this: Caroline had, exactly as was her wont, addressed to the Marquis certain questions about the household accounts, and he, usually so polite, had compelled her to repeat them. She thought that he, too, must be absent-minded or ill at ease; but two or three times she met a glance from him, which was cold, haughty, almost contemptuous. Chilled with surprise and terror, she suddenly became dejected and was obliged to attribute her state of mind to a headache.

The Duke had a vague suspicion of the truth so far as his brother was concerned; but this suspicion was dissipated when he saw the latter suddenly recover his gayety. He did not imagine the alternations of depression and reaction through which this troubled soul was passing, and, thinking he might now with impunity bestow attention upon Caroline, "You are not well," said he, "I see that you are really suffering! Mother, do have a care; Mlle de Saint-Geneix has been looking pale for some time past."

"Do you think so?" asked the Marchioness, looking at Caroline with some interest. "Are you ill, my darling? Do not conceal it from me."

"I am remarkably well," said Caroline. "It is true that I feel to-day a somewhat unusual desire for fresh air and sunshine; but it is nothing at all."

"But it is something, though," returned the Marchioness, regarding her attentively, "and the Duke is right. You are very much changed. You must go take the fresh air at once, or retire to your room, perhaps. It is too warm here. I expect a whole company of neighbors this evening. I have no need of you; I give you a holiday."

"Do you know what will restore you!" asked the Duke of poor Caroline, now thoroughly vexed by the attention of which she was the object: "you ought to ride horseback. The little rustic quadruped that I told you about is gentle and strong. Would you like to try him!"

"All alone!" demanded the Marchioness; "and a horse not properly trained!"

"I am sure that Mlle Caroline would be amused," said the Duke. "She is brave, she is afraid of nothing, as I very well know. Besides, I will have an eye to her myself; I will answer for her."

He insisted so much, that the Marchioness asked Caroline if this horseback ride would be really to her taste.

"Yes," she replied, impelled by the necessity of escape from the oppression which was wellnigh crushing her. "I am just childish enough to be amused in that way; but some other day will do better. I have no wish to make a display of my riding before the people whom you expect, especially as my first appearance is likely to be very awkward."

"Well, then, you shall go into the park," said the Marchioness; "it is deeply shaded, so that no one can witness your first attempt; but I want somebody to follow you on horseback,—old André, for instance. He is a good squire, and has a staid nag, for which you can exchange yours, if he is too unruly."

"Yes, yes, that's it!" exclaimed the Duke. "André on old Blanche, that is perfect. I will superintend the start myself, and all will go well."

"But a side-saddle!" interposed the Marquis, apparently indifferent to this equestrian project.

"There is one; I saw it in the saddle-room," replied the Duke, quickly. "I will run and arrange all that."

"And a riding-habit!" said the Marchioness.

"The first long skirt will be sufficient," said Caroline, suddenly bent upon braving the hostile air of the Marquis and upon escaping from his presence. The Marchioness bade her make her preparations, and, leaning upon the arm of her second son, she went to meet her visitors as they arrived.

When Mlle de Saint-Geneix came down the winding staircase from her room in the little tower, she found the horse already saddled, and held by the Duke in person before the small arched door which looked out on the lawn. André was there also, mounted upon an old cabbage-carting nag of proverbial leanness and very miserably accoutred, for everything belonging to the stable was in complete disorder. Confined strictly to what was necessary, even necessary things had not as yet been put into order. The Marquis, more embarrassed in his circumstances than he was willing to confess, intrenched himself behind the habit of blaming his own negligence, while the Duke, suspecting the truth, had declared that, for his own part, he preferred hunting on foot, as a check to his tendency to corpulence.

To equip Jacquet (that was the name of the farm-colt, raised twelve hours ago to the dignity of saddle horse) had been no small undertaking, and André, bewildered by this sudden fancy, would not have been prompt in finding the side-saddle and putting it in a condition for use. The Duke had done everything himself, in a quarter of an hour, with the swiftness and skill of a practised hand. He was in a lively perspiration, and Caroline was confused enough to see him holding the stirrup for her, arranging the curb, and tightening the girths as if he had been a jockey by profession, laughing at the incongruity of things, and playing his part gayly, while he paid her all the hundred little attentions which a fraternal prudence could dictate.

When Mlle de Saint-Geneix had started off on a trot, after having thanked him cordially and begged him not to be anxious about her, the Duke dismissed André, nimbly mounted the beast of the cabbage cart, plunged the spurs into his sides, and resolutely followed Caroline into the shadows of the park.

"What! is that you?" said she to him, stopping after the first gallop. "You, your Grace the Duke, mounted in that fashion, and taking the trouble to escort me! No, that cannot be. I will not have it; let us go back again."

"Why, how so?" he asked. "Are you afraid to be alone with me now? Have we not met each other here in these avenues at all hours, and have I ever annoyed you with my eloquence?"

"No, certainly not," said Caroline, with entire confidence. "I have no such whims as that, you know very well; but that horse of yours,—it is a torture to you."

"Are you comfortable on yours?"

"Perfectly."

"In that case we could not be better suited. As for myself, I take great delight in riding this white nag. See! Don't I look as well as I should upon a blooded steed? Down with all prejudice; let us amuse ourselves with a gallop!"

"But what if this creature's legs should give out?"

"Bah! it will do well enough. And if it does break my neck, why, I shall have the extreme happiness of knowing that it happens in your service."

The Duke lanced this bit of flattery with a tone of gayety which could not alarm Caroline. They set out on a gallop and made the circuit of the park quite bravely. Jacquet behaved excellently, showing no vicious inclinations of any kind; besides, Mlle de Saint-Geneix was a good rider, and the Duke noticed that she was as graceful as she was skilful and self-possessed. She had improvised a long skirt by dexterously letting down a hem; she had thrown over her shoulders a jacket of white dimity, and her little straw gardening-hat on her blond curls, dishevelled by the race, was wonderfully becoming. Animated by the pleasure of the ride, she looked so remarkably beautiful that the Duke, following with his eye the elegant moulding of her form, and the brilliant smile which played about her candid mouth, felt himself dazzled by them. "The devil take the oath which I let them get from me so unsuspectingly!" said he to himself. "Who would have thought I should have so much trouble in keeping it?" But it was necessary that Caroline should be the first to betray herself, and the Duke led her slowly around the park again to let the horses breathe, but all to no purpose; she chatted with a witty freedom and general good-humor, which did not admit the idea of any painful agitation.

"O, so, that is it?" thought he, as they recommenced their gallop. "You imagine that I am going to dislocate my joints on this Apocalyptic beast to converse just as we should under the maternal eye? Some one else may try it for all me! I am going to sadden your tranquil gratitude by a retreat which will give you material for reflection."

"My dear friend," said he to Caroline,—he sometimes allowed himself to use this expression in a tone of easy good-nature,—"you are very sure of Jacquet now, are you not?"

"Perfectly sure."

"He is not at all inclined to shy, and is not hard-bitted?"

"Not at all."

"Very well, if you are willing, I will leave you to yourself, and send André in my place."

"Do so, do so by all means!" replied Caroline; quickly; "or don't send any one at all. I will go around the park once more, and then I will take the animal back to André. Really, I shall enjoy cantering alone, and it pains me to see you so frightfully jolted."

"O, it is not that," responded the Duke, resolved upon a bold stroke. "I'm not yet so old as to be afraid of a hard horse; but I remember that Madame d'Arglade is coming to-night."

"Not to-night; to-morrow."

"That is not certain," said the Duke, watching for the effect his words might produce.

"O, then, perhaps, you are better informed than I am."

"Perhaps, my dear friend! Madame d'Arglade—In fact, it is sufficient—"

"Ah! indeed?" replied Caroline, laughing. "I did not know. Go quickly, then; I shall escape, and—a thousand thanks again for your kindness."

She was about to start her horse, but the Duke detained her. "What I am doing now is not polite, to say the least of it."

"It is better than polite; it is very good of you."

"O, then you have had enough of my company?"

"That is not what I mean. I say that your impoliteness is a proof of your confidence in me, and that I take it as such."

"Do you think she is pretty,—Madame d'Arglade, I mean?"

"Very pretty."

"How old is she, precisely?"

"Very nearly my own age. We were together at the convent."

"I know it. Were you great friends?"

"No, not exactly; but she has shown much interest in me since my misfortunes."

"Yes, it was she who was the means of bringing you here. Why did you detest each other at the convent?"

"We did not detest each other; we were not very intimate,—that was all."

"And now?"

"Now she is kind to me, and consequently I like her."

"Then you like people who are kind to you?"

"Is not that natural?"

"Then you like me a little, for it seems to me that I am not unkind to you myself?"

"Certainly, you are excellent, and I like you very much."

"Just hear how she says that! I love my nurse dearly, but I love to ride on my rocking-horse better still! Come, tell me, you don't mean to prejudice your little friend D'Arglade against me, do you?"

"Prejudice her against you! There are some words in your vocabulary which do not get into mine."

"Yes, that is true, I beg pardon. It is because—you see, she is suspicious—she may question you. You will not fail to tell her that I have never made love to you?"

"O, as to that, count upon her knowing the truth," replied Caroline, starting. And the Duke heard her laugh as she rode off at full speed.

"There!" said he to himself, "I have lied, and it is trouble wasted. I have made a precious blunder, have n't I? She does n't love any one,—or else she has a little lover somewhere, in reserve against the day when a thousand crowns shall be forthcoming to set up housekeeping with. Poor girl! If I had them, I would give them to her! It's all the same; I have been ridiculous. Perhaps she saw it too. Perhaps she will laugh at me with her 'dear friend,' when she writes to him secretly, for she does write a great deal. If I did think so!—But I have given my word of honor."

The Duke withdrew, trying to laugh at himself, but annoyed at losing his game, and almost angry.

Just as he was leaving the wood, he saw a man gliding into it cautiously. The evening had come; he could distinguish nothing about this man except his furtive movements, in trying to penetrate the thicket. "Stop, stop," thought he, "this is perhaps the lover in question, coming to make a mysterious visit. By Jove! I will be satisfied on that point! I will know who it is!" He dismounted, gave a vigorous blow with his riding-whip to Blanche, who needed neither urging nor guiding to take the road to her stable, and stole away under the trees in the direction which Caroline had taken. It would have been almost impossible to find the man in the coppice, and besides there was the risk of giving him the alarm. To walk noiselessly in the dark shadows, along the walk, and to see how these two persons would meet and conduct themselves was, he considered, by far the surest course.

Caroline had already ceased thinking at all about the Duke. After having becomingly withdrawn to avoid disclosures hardly proper for her to hear, and which had astonished her coming from the lips of a man so well bred, she had brought the little horse down to a slow pace, lest she might come in contact with the boughs in the darkness. And, indeed, she felt inclined rather to think her own thoughts just then than to ride at greater speed. An absorbing anxiety weighed upon her mind. The attitude of the Marquis toward her was inexplicable and almost offensive. She searched for the cause of this in the most secret recesses of her conscience, and finding nothing there amiss, she reproached herself for thinking so much about it. He was perhaps subject to certain whims, like many people absorbed in great tasks; and after all, even if she had become displeasing to him, was he not about to be married, and would not the joy of the Marchioness be so complete that a poor young lady companion could leave her without ingratitude?

While she was thus thinking of her future, promising herself that she would speak about it to Madame d'Arglade, who would perhaps aid her in finding another situation, her horse was stopped suddenly, and she saw before her a man whose movements frightened her.

"Is it you, André?" asked she, as she perceived that her horse seemed to be obeying a well-known hand. And as there was no answer and she could distinguish nothing of the clothes worn by the person confronting her, she added, quickly and anxiously, "Is it you, your Grace the Duke? Why do you stop me?"

She received no reply; the man had disappeared; the horse was free. She was overcome by a vague fear, and, not daring to turn round, she urged Jacquet forward, and returned to the house on a gallop without seeing any one.

The Duke was ten paces off when this singular encounter took place. He saw nothing, but heard the frightened voice of Mlle de Saint-Geneix at the moment of the horse's sudden stop. He sprang forward, and finding himself face to face with an unknown person, he seized him by the collar, demanding, "Who are you?"

The unknown person struggled vigorously to escape from this investigation; but the Duke, who was a very powerful man, dragged his adversary out of the wood into the path. There, what was his ineffable surprise to recognize his brother?

"Heavens! Urbain," cried he, "did I not strike you? It seems to me that I did. But why didn't you answer me?"

"I don't know," replied M. de Villemer, much agitated. "I did not recognize your voice! Did you speak to me? Whom did you take me for, then?"

"For a robber, in sober earnest! Did you not frighten Mlle de Saint-Geneix just now?"

"I perhaps frightened her horse, unintentionally. Where is she?"

"Why, she was afraid and took to flight. Did you not hear her riding off toward the house?"

"And why should she have been afraid of me?" rejoined the Marquis, with singular bitterness. "I did not wish to offend her." And then, weary of deception, he added, "I merely wanted to speak to her!"

"About whom? About me?"

"Yes, perhaps. I wanted to know whether she loved you."

"And why did n't you speak to her?"

"I do not know. I could not say a word to her."

"Are you in pain?"

"Yes. I am ill, very ill, to-day."

"Let us go in, brother," said the Duke. "I see that you are in a fever, and the dew is falling."

"No matter!" said the Marquis, seating himself on a block at the edge of the walk. "I wish I was dead!"

"Urbain!" cried the Duke, a sudden light striking him at last; "it is you who are in love with Mlle de Saint-Geneix!"

"I in love with her? Is she not,—is she not yours?"

"Never, since you love her! On my part it was only a caprice, an idle, selfish vanity; but, as truly as I am my father's son, she has not the least inclination toward me; she has just simply understood nothing of my artifices; she is as pure, as free, and as proud as on the day she came among us."

"Why did you leave her alone in this wood after you had brought her out into it?"

"Ah! you suspect me after the solemn assertion that I have just made! Can it be that love is making you insane?"

"You have played with your promise about this young lady. For you, in questions of gallantry, oaths count nothing; I know that. If it were otherwise, would you and your fortunate compeers be able to persuade so many women? Do you not know how to slip away from all engagements? Was it honorable, this absurd manœuvring,—which may have been very skilfully done for aught I know about such games,—to draw her into your arms through fascination, through spite, through all the weak or bad impulses in woman's nature? Is there anything that you do respect! Is not virtue, in your eyes, an infirmity of which a poor

GEORGE SAND

innocent girl, helpless and inexperienced, must be cured? Is not the abyss into which you want to see her fling herself, in your opinion, the rational condition, fortunate or fatal, of a girl without a dowry and without an ancestry? See! did you not mock me this very morning, when you wished to persuade me that you would marry her! And this is what you said only a moment ago: 'It is you who are in love with her. For me, it was only a fancy, an idle, selfish vanity.' Come, it is frightful,—this libertine vanity of yours! It drags down into the mire all that comes near you! Your very gaze soils a woman, and it is too much for me already that this girl has undergone the insult of your thoughts. I love her no longer."

Having spoken thus to his brother for the first time in his life, the Marquis rose and strode away from him swiftly with a kind of gloomy hatred and with a curse seemingly irrevocable.

The Duke, beside himself, arose immediately to demand satisfaction. He even took a few steps in pursuit of his brother, then stopped abruptly and returned, throwing himself down on the spot which Urbain had just left. He was the victim of a terrible conflict; irritated, furious, he still felt that the person of the Marquis was sacred to him; he was not in the habit of rendering to himself a just account of his own faults, and yet in spite of himself, he felt none the less overwhelmed by the language of truth. He wrung his hands convulsively, and great tears of rage and grief flowed down his cheeks.

André came to find him, having been sent by his mother. The visitors were gone, but Madame d'Arglade had arrived. They were astonished not to see him. The Marchioness, knowing that he had ridden Blanche, was afraid that the unfortunate horse might have been crushed under him.

He followed the servant mechanically, and asked, just as he was going into the house, "Where is M. de Villemer?"

"In his room, your Grace. I saw him go in."

"And Mlle de Saint-Geneix?"

"She has also gone to her room; but Madame the Marchioness has informed her of the arrival of Madame d'Arglade, and she will come down again soon."

"Very good! Go tell M. de Villemer that I wish to speak with him. In ten minutes I will go up to his room."

XII

Madame d'Arglade was the wife of a great provincial dignitary. She had obtained an introduction to the Marchioness de Villemer at the South, when the latter was passing the summer there upon a large estate, since sold to pay the debts of her eldest son. Madame d'Arglade had that particular kind of narrow and persevering ambition of which certain wives of officials, small or great, furnish quite remarkable specimens. To rise in order to shine, and to shine in order to rise,—that was the sole thought, the sole dream, the sole talent, the sole principle of this little woman. Rich, and without an ancestry to boast of, she had bestowed her dowry upon a ruined noble to serve as security for a place in the department of finance, and to add splendor to her house; for she understood perfectly well that, in that condition of life, the best way to acquire a large fortune was to begin by having one suitable to her position and by spending it liberally. Plump, active, pretty, cool, and adroit, she considered a certain amount of coquetry as a duty of her station, and secretly prided herself upon the lofty science which consists in promising with the eyes but never with the pen or the lips, in making transient impressions, but calling forth no abiding attachments, and, lastly, in gaining her objects by surprise, without appearing to hold them, and never descending to ask for them, that she might find herself supported on all occasions by useful friends, she gathered them up everywhere, received every one with no great nicety of choice, with a well-acted good-nature or thoughtlessness, and, in fine, she penetrated skilfully into the most exclusive families and was not long in contriving to become indispensable to them.

It was thus that Madame d'Arglade had wormed herself into what was almost an intimacy with Madame de Villemer, in spite of the prejudice of that noble lady against her origin, her position, and the occupation of her husband; but Léonie d'Arglade paraded her own complete lack of political opinions, and dexterously went round begging pardon of every one for her utter incapacity and nothingness in this regard,—which was her expedient to shock no one, and to make people forget the compulsory zeal of her husband for the cause he served. She was gay, heedless, sometimes silly, laughing loudly at herself, but inwardly laughing at the simplicity of others, and managing to pass for the most ingenuous and disinterested creature in the world, while all her proceedings were based on calculation, and all her impulses were premeditated.

She had very well understood that a certain class of society, however divided in opinion it may be, is always held together by some indissoluble tie of kinship or expediency, and that, upon occasion, all its shades of difference are blended by one animating spirit of caste or of common interest. She was quite well aware, then, that she needed acquaintance with the Faubourg St. Germain, where her husband was not usually admitted, and, thanks to Madame de Villemer, whose good-nature she had adroitly captivated by her prattle and untiring "availability," she had gained a foothold in certain drawing-rooms, where she pleased people and passed for an amiable child of no great consequence.

This child was already twenty-eight years old and did not appear more than twenty-two or twenty-three, although balls were a little fatiguing to her; she had managed to preserve so much engaging sauciness and simplicity that no one perceived her growing a trifle too fleshy. She showed her little dazzling teeth when she smiled, lisped in her speech, and seemed intoxicated with dress and pleasure. In fine, no one suspected her and perhaps there was really nothing to dread in her, since her first interest was to appear good-natured and to make herself inoffensive; but it required great exertion in any one who did not want to find himself suddenly entangled with her.

It was in this way that, without being on her guard and all the while declaring that she would take no step to influence the ministry of the citizen king, Madame de Villemer had found herself inveigled into affecting more or less directly Léonie's withdrawal from her province. Thanks to Madame de Villemer and to the Duke d'Aléria, M. d'Arglade had just received an appointment in Paris, and his wife had written to the Marchioness:—

"Dear Madame, I owe to you my life; you are my guardian angel. I quit the South, and I shall only touch at Paris; for, before establishing myself there, before beginning to rejoice and amuse myself, before everything, in a word, I want to go and thank you and prostrate myself before you at Séval for twenty-four hours, and tell you during those twenty-four hours how much I love you and bless you.

"I will be with you on the 10th of June. Say to his Grace the Duke that it will be the 9th or the 11th, and that, in the mean time, I thank him for having been so kind to my husband, who is going to write him on his own account."

This pretended uncertainty as to the day of her arrival was, on the part of Madame d'Arglade, the graceful reception of a joke which the Duke had often made about the ignorance of days and hours that she always affected. The Duke, with all his cunning with regard to women, had been completely duped by Léonie. He thought her silly, and had a way of addressing her thus: "That's it! You are coming to see my mother to-day, Monday, Tuesday, or Sunday, the seventh, sixth, or fifth day of the month of November, September, or December, in your blue or gray or rose-colored dress, and you are going to honor us by supping, dining, or breakfasting with us, or with them, or with other people."

The Duke was not at all taken with her. She amused him, and the small talk and witticism which characterized his manner with her were merely as a mask for a sort of desultory groping about in the dark, which Madame d'Arglade pretended not to notice, but of which she knew very well how to keep clear.

When the Duke entered the presence of Madame d'Arglade and his mother, he was still much disturbed, and the change in his countenance struck the Marchioness. "Bless me!" cried she, "there has been some accident!"

"None at all, dear mother. Reassure yourself; everything has passed off finely. I have been a little cold, that is all."

He was really cold, although he had still on his brow the perspiration of vexation and anger. He drew near the fire which burned every evening, at all seasons of the year, in the drawing-room of the Marchioness; but, after a few moments, the habit of self-mastery, which is the whole science of fashionable life, and the brilliant pyrotechnics of Léonie's words and smiles, dispelled his bitterness.

Mlle de Saint-Geneix now came forward to embrace her old companion at the convent. "Ah! but you are pale too," said the Marchioness to Caroline. "You are concealing something from me! There has been some accident—I am sure of it—with those infernal beasts."

"No, Madame," replied Caroline, "none at all, I assure you, and, to relieve your anxiety, I will tell you everything: I have been very much frightened."

"Really? By what, pray?" asked the Duke; "it certainly was not by your horse?"

"Perhaps it was by you, your Grace. Come, was it you who stopped my horse for sport, while I was alone walking him slowly in the green avenue?"

"Well, yes, it was I," replied the Duke. "I wanted to see whether you were as brave as you seemed."

"And I was not. I ran like a terrified chicken."

"But you did not cry out, and you did not lose your presence of mind,—that's something."

They told Madame d'Arglade about the horseback ride. As was her custom, she pretended to take very little notice of what was said; but she lost not a word, and asked herself earnestly whether the Duke had deceived or wanted to deceive Caroline, and whether this combination might not be useful in some way at a future day. The Duke left the ladies together, and went up to his brother's room.

The reason why Caroline and Léonie were not intimate at the convent was the difference in their ages. Four years establish a very considerable barrier in youth. Caroline had not wished to tell the Duke the true reason, fearing to seem desirous to make her companion appear old, fully aware besides, that it is doing an ill-turn to most pretty women to recollect their ages too faithfully. It is also worth mention, that all the time Madame d'Arglade remained at Séval, she passed for the younger, and that Caroline, like a good girl, allowed this error of memory to go uncontradicted.

Caroline then, in reality, knew very little about her protectress; she had never met her since the time, when, as a child upon the benches of the "little class," she had seen Mlle Léonie Lecompte emerge from the convent, eager to marry some man of birth or position, regretting no one, but, already shrewd and calculating, bidding every one a tender farewell. Caroline and Camille de Saint-Geneix, at that period girls of gentle blood and comfortable fortune, might, she thought, be good acquaintances to find again at some future time. She wrote them, in a very compassionate tone, therefore, when she learned of their father's death. In her reply Caroline did not conceal the fact that she was left not only an orphan but penniless, Madame d'Arglade took good care not to desert her friend in her misfortunes. Other convent mates, of whom she saw more, had told her that both the Saint-Geneix were charming, and that, with her talents and beauty, Caroline would be sure to make a good match nevertheless,—the idle talk of inexperienced young women. Léonie thought, indeed, that they were mistaken; but she might try to marry off Caroline, and in that way find herself mixed up in confidential questions, and in intimate negotiations with divers families. From that time she thought of nothing but gaining many supporters, extending her relations everywhere, and obtaining the secrets of others while pretending to impart her own. She wanted to attract Caroline to her house in her province, offering her with a delicate grace, a refuge and a prospective home of her own. Caroline, touched by so much kindness, replied that she could not leave her sister, and did not wish to marry, but that if she should ever find herself painfully situated, she would appeal to Léonie's generous heart to seek out for her some modest employment.

From that time Léonie, always full of promises and praises, saw plainly that Caroline did not understand a life of expedients, and troubled herself no further about her, until some old friends, who perhaps pitied Caroline more sincerely, informed Léonie that she was seeking a place as governess in a quiet family, or as reader to some intelligent old lady. Léonie loved to use her influence, and always had something to ask for some one; it was an opportunity for her to get into notice, and to make herself agreeable. Finding herself in Paris at the time, she made greater haste than any one else did, and in her search fell upon the Marchioness de Villemer, who had just then dismissed her reader. She wanted an elderly lady. Madame d'Arglade expatiated on the disadvantages of old age, which had made Esther so crabbed. She also diminished as much as she could the youth and beauty of Caroline. She was a girl about thirty, pretty enough in other days, but who had suffered and must have faded. Then she wrote to Caroline to describe the Marchioness, urging her to come quickly, and offering to share her own temporary lodgings in Paris with her. We have seen that Caroline did not find her at home, but introduced herself to the Marchioness, astonished the latter with her beauty, and charmed her with her frankness, doing by the charm and ascendency of her appearance more than Léonie had ever hoped for her.

Upon seeing Léonie stout, flaunting, and shrewd, but having still preserved her girlish ways, and even exaggerated her childish lisping, Caroline was astonished and asked herself at first sight if all this was not affected; but she was soon to change her mind good-naturedly, and to share in the delusion of every one else. Madame d'Arglade was charmingly polite to her, and all the more so because she had already questioned the Marchioness about Mlle de Saint-Geneix, and knew her to be well anchored in the good graces of the old lady. Madame de Villemer declared her perfect in all respects, quick and discreet, frank and gentle, of unusual intelligence and the noblest character. She had warmly thanked Madame d'Arglade for having procured her this "pearl of the Orient," and Madame d'Arglade had said to herself, "Well and good! I see that Caroline can be useful to me; she is so already. It is always well not to despise or neglect any one." And she overwhelmed the young lady with caresses and flatteries, which seemed as unstudied as the affectionate rapture of a school-girl.

JUST BEFORE GOING TO HIS brother's room, the Duke, who was resolved upon a reconciliation, walked for five minutes on the lawn. Involuntary fits of wrath returned upon him, and he feared that he might not be master of himself, if the Marquis should renew his admonitions. At last he came to a decision, went up stairs, crossed a long vestibule, hearing his blood beat so loudly in his temples as to conceal the sound of his footsteps.

Urbain was alone at the farther end of the library, a long room in the ogive style, with slender arches, which his small lamp lighted but feebly. He was not reading; but hearing the approach of the Duke, he had placed a book before himself, ashamed of appearing unable to work.

The Duke stopped to look at him before saying a word. His dull paleness, and his eyes hollow with suffering, touched the Duke deeply. He was going to offer his hand, when the Marquis rose and said to him in a grave voice: "My brother, I offended you very much an hour ago. I was unjust probably, and, in any case, I had no right to remonstrate with you,—I who, having loved but one woman in my whole life, have yet been the guilty cause of her ruin and her death. I confess the absurdity, the harshness, the arrogance of my words, and I sincerely beg your pardon."

"Well, then, I thank you with all my heart," replied Gaëtan, taking him by both hands; "you are doing me a great kindness, for I had resolved to make an apology to you. The deuce take me, if I know what for! But I said to myself, that in wrestling with you under the trees, I must have excited your nerves. Perhaps I hurt you; my hand is heavy. Why didn't you speak to me? And then—and then—Come, I had been causing you much suffering, and perhaps for a long time, without knowing it; but I could not guess,—I ought to have suspected it, though, and I, too, sincerely beg your pardon for that, my poor brother. Ah! why did you lack confidence in me after what we had both solemnly promised?"

"Have confidence in you!" rejoined the Marquis; "do you not see that this is my greatest need, my keenest thirst, and that my wrath was only grief? I wept for it, this confidence that was put in question, I wept bitter tears for it. Give it back to me; I cannot do without it."

"What must I do? Tell me, do tell me! I am ready to go through fire and water! It is only the trial by water which I beg you to spare. What if I should be called upon to drink it!"

"Ah! you laugh at everything; do you not see that you do?"

"I laugh—I laugh—because it is my way of being pleased, and from the moment you love me again, the rest is nothing. And then what is there so very serious? You love this charming girl. You are not wrong. Do you wish me never to speak to her, and never to meet her, or never to look at her? It shall be done, I swear, it, and if this is not enough, I will set out to-morrow, or now, if you like, on Blanche. I don't see what worse thing I can do?"

"No, no, don't go away, don't desert me! Do you not see, Gaëtan, that I am dying?"

"My God! why do you say that?" cried the Duke, lifting up the shade of the lamp and looking his brother in the face; then he seized the hands of the Marquis, and, not finding the pulse readily, laid both his own on his brother's chest, and felt the disordered and uneven beating of the invalid's heart.

This disease had seriously threatened the life of the Marquis in his early youth. It had disappeared, leaving a delicate complexion, a great deal of nervous uneasiness, with sudden reactions of strength, but, on the whole, as great certitude of life as a hundred others have who are apparently more energetic and really less finely tempered, less sustained by a healthy will and the power of discrimination. This time, however, the old disease had reappeared, with violence enough to justify the alarm of Gaëtan and to produce in his brother the oppression and the awful sensations of a death-agony.

"Not a word to my mother!" said the Marquis, rising and going to open the window. "It is not to-morrow that I shall sink under this. I have some strength still; I do not give myself up yet. Where are you going?"

"Why, I am going to get a horse. I am going for a physician."

"Where? For whom? There is not one here who knows my constitution so well as not to run a risk of killing me, should he undertake my case in the name of his logic. If I should fail, take care not to leave me to any village Esculapius, and remember that bleeding will carry me off as the wind carries away an autumn leaf. I was doctored enough ten years ago to know what I need, and I am in the habit of taking care of myself. Come, do not doubt this," added he, showing the Duke some powders prepared in doses, from a drawer in his bureau. "Here are quieting and stimulating medicines, which I know how to use variously. I perfectly understand my disease and its treatment. Be sure that, if I can be cured, I shall be cured, and that, to this end, I shall do all that ought to be done by a man who knows the extent of his duties. Be calm. It was my duty to tell you what I am threatened with, so that you might thoroughly forgive in your heart my feverish anger. Keep my secret for me; we must not uselessly alarm our poor mother. If the time to prepare her should arrive, I shall feel it and will give you warning. Until then, be calm, I beg of you!"

"Calm! It is you who must be calm," retorted the Duke, "and here you are fighting with a passion! It is passion that has awakened this poor heart physically as well as morally. It is love, it is happiness, enthusiasm, tenderness, that you need. Well, nothing is lost then. Tell me, do you wish her to love you, this girl? She shall love you. What am I saying? She does love you, she has always loved you, from the very first day. Now I recall the whole. I see plainly. It is you—"

"Stop, stop!" said the Marquis, falling back into his arm-chair. "I cannot hear it; it stifles me."

But after a momentary silence, during which the Duke watched him with anxiety, he seemed better, and said with a smile, which restored to his expressive face all its youthful charm,—

"And yet what you said then was true! It is perhaps love. Perhaps it is nothing else. You have soothed me with an illusion, and I have given myself up to it like a child. Feel of my heart now; it is refreshed. The dream has passed over it like a cool breeze."

"Since you are feeling better," said the Duke, after making sure that he was really calm, "you ought to make the most of it and try to sleep. You do not sleep, and that is dreadful! In the morning, when I start for a hunt, I often see your lamp still burning."

"And yet, for many nights past, I have not been at work."

"Well, then, if it is sleeplessness, you shall not keep watch alone; I will answer for that. Let me see; you are going to lie down, to lie down on your bed."

"It is impossible."

"Yes, I see: you would suffocate. Well, you shall sit up and sleep. I will stay close by. I will talk to you about her until you no longer hear me."

The Duke conducted his brother to his room, placed him in a large arm-chair, took care of him as a mother would take care of her child, and seated himself near him, holding his hand in his own. Then all Urbain's natural kindliness returned, and he said, gratefully,—

"I have been hateful this evening. Tell me again that you forgive me."

"I do what is better: I love you," replied Gaëtan; "and I am not the only one, either. She is also thinking about you at this very hour."

"O Heaven! you are lying. You are lulling me with a celestial song; but you are lying. She loves no one; she will never love me!"

"Do you want me to go after her and tell her that you are seriously ill? I'll wager that in five minutes she would be here!"

"It is possible," replied the Marquis, with languid gentleness. "She is full of charity and devotedness; but it would be worse for me to ascertain that I had her pity—and nothing more."

"Bah! you know nothing about it. Pity is the beginning of love. Everything must begin with something which is not quite the middle or the end. If you would let yourself be guided by me, in a week you would see—"

"Ah! now you are doing me more harm still. If it were as easy as you think to win her love, I should not long for it so ardently."

"Very well. The illusion would be dispelled. You would regain your peace of mind. That would be something at least."

"It would be my death, Gaëtan," resumed the Marquis, growing animated and recovering strength in his voice. "How unhappy I am that you cannot understand me! But there is an abyss between us. Take care, my poor friend, with an imprudence, or a slight levity, or a mistaken devotedness, you can kill me as quickly as if you held a pistol to my head."

The Duke was very much puzzled. He found the situation simple enough, between two persons more or less attracted toward each other and separated only by scruples, which had little importance in his eyes; but in his opinion, Urbain was complicating this situation by whimsical delicacy. If Mlle de Saint-Geneix should accept him without really loving him, the Marquis felt that his own love for her would die, and in the loss of this love which was killing him, the thunderbolt would fall the quicker. This was a sort of blind alley which drove the Duke wellnigh to despair, but into which it was none the less necessary respectfully to follow his brother's wishes and ideas. By conversing longer with him, and sounding him to the very depths of his being, Gaëtan reached the conclusion that the only joy it was possible to give him would consist in aiding him to a knowledge of Caroline's affection and to a hope of its patient and delicate growth. So long as his imagination could wander through this garden of early emotions, romantic and pure, the Marquis was lulled by pleasant ideas and exquisite joys. As soon, however, as he saw the uncertain approach of the hour when he must decide upon his course and risk an avowal, he felt a dark presentiment of an inevitable disaster, and, unhappily for him, he was not mistaken. Caroline would refuse him and take to flight, or, if she should accept his hand, his aged mother would be driven to despair and perhaps sink under the loss of her illusions.

The Duke plunged deeply into these reflections, for Urbain began to drowse, after having made him promise that he would leave to get some rest himself as soon as he should see him fairly asleep. Gaëtan was vexed at finding no way to be of real service to him. He would have liked to tell Caroline the danger, to appeal to her kindliness and her esteem, asking her to humor the moral condition of the invalid, veiling the future to him, whatever it might be, and soothing him with vague hopes and fair dreams; but this would be pushing the poor girl down a very dangerous slope, and she was not so childish as not to understand that she would thus risk her reputation and probably her own peace of mind.

Destiny, which is very active in dramas of this kind, since it always meets with souls predisposed to yield to its action, did what the Duke dared not do.

XIII

Notwithstanding the promise made to his brother, to inform no one of his condition, the Duke could not quite make up his mind to assume the dangerous responsibility of absolute silence. He believed in a doctor, whoever he might be, in spite of his assertion that he did not believe in medicine, and he resolved to go to Chambon and make arrangements with a young man there who did not appear to him to be lacking either in knowledge or prudence, one day when he himself had consulted him about a slight indisposition. Under the seal of secrecy he would confide the situation of the Marquis to this young physician, and engage him to come to the manor-house the next day, under the pretext of selling a bit of prairie enclosed in the lands of Séval. Then he would bring about a chance for the doctor to see the patient, if only to observe his face and general symptoms, without giving any professional advice; a way of submitting this advice to M. de Villemer would be found, and perhaps he would consent to follow it. In a word the Duke, who could not endure to watch through the loneliness and silence of the night, felt the need of doing something to calm his own anxiety. He calculated that he could reach Chambon in a half-hour, and that an additional hour would give him time to rouse the physician, talk with him, and return. He could, he ought, to be back before his brother, who now seemed resting quietly, should awake from his first sleep.

The Duke withdrew noiselessly, left the house through the garden so as to be heard by no one, and descended quickly toward the bed of the river to a foot-bridge by the mill, and to a path which led him straight to the town. By taking a horse and following the road, he would have made a noise and gained very little time. The Marquis, however, did not sleep so soundly as not to hear him leave the room; but, knowing nothing of his project, and not wishing to hinder his brother from going to rest, he had pretended to be unconscious of everything.

It was then a little after midnight. Madame d'Arglade, after having taken her leave of the Marchioness, had followed Caroline to her room to have a little more talk with her. "Well now, pretty dear," she said, "are you really as well satisfied in this house as you say? Be frank with me, if anything troubles you here. Ah, bless me! there is always some little thing in the way. Take advantage of my presence now to confide it to me. I have some influence with the Marchioness, without having sought for it, to be sure; but she likes silly heads, and then I, who am naturally of a happy disposition, and never need anything for myself,—I have the right to serve my friends unhesitatingly."

"You are very good," replied Caroline; "but here everybody is good to me, too, and if I had anything to complain of I should speak of it quite freely."

"That's right, thank you," exclaimed Léonie, taking the promise as made to herself. "Well, now, how about the Duke? Has he never teased you, the handsome Duke?"

"Very little, and that is all over with now."

"Indeed, you give me pleasure by saying that. Do you know that after having written to you to engage you for this place I felt a certain remorse of conscience? I had never spoken to you of this great conqueror."

"It is true you seemed to have a fear of speaking to me about him."

"A fear! no, I had entirely forgotten him; I am so giddy-headed! I said to myself, 'Heavens! I hope that Mlle de Saint-Geneix will not be annoyed by his artifices!' for he has his artifices and with everybody."

"He has had none with me, I am thankful to be able to say."

"Then all is well," replied Léonie, who did not believe a word of what she heard. She changed the subject to that of dress, and all at once she exclaimed, "O, bless me! how sleepy I am becoming! It must be on account of the journey. Till to-morrow, then, dear Caroline. Are you an early riser?"

"Yes; are you?"

"Alas! not much of a one; but when I do get my eyes open, say, between ten and eleven, I shall find you in your room,—shall I not?"

She retired, resolved to get up early in the morning, wander about everywhere as if by chance, and obtain a stealthy knowledge of all the most intimate details of the family affairs, Caroline followed her to install her in her apartment, and returned to her own little room, which was some distance from that of the Marquis, but whose casements, looking out on the lawn, were almost opposite to his.

Before going to rest, she put in order certain books and papers, for she studied a great deal, and with a genuine relish; she heard it strike one o'clock in the morning, and went to shut her blinds before disrobing. At that moment she heard a sharp stroke against the glass of the opposite casement, and her eyes, following the direction of the sound, saw a pane fall rattling from the lighted window of the Marquis. Astonished by this accident, and by the silence which followed, Caroline listened attentively. No one stirred; no one had heard it. Gradually, confused sounds reached her, feeble plaints at first, and then stifled cries and a species of rattle. "Some one is assassinating the Marquis," was her first thought, for the sinister murmurs came evidently from his room. What should she do? Call, find some one, tell the Duke who lodged still farther away?—all that would take too much time, and, besides, under the oppression of such a warning there must be no indecision. Caroline measured the distance with her eye: there were twenty paces to go across the grass. If malefactors had penetrated to M. de Villemer's room it must have been by the stairs of the Griffin turret which was opposite to that of the Fox. These two cages with stairways in them bore the names of the emblems rudely sculptured on the tympans of their portals. The stairs of the Fox led away on this side from Caroline's room. No one else could arrive on the scene so soon as she could, and her solitary approach might cause the assassins to release the Marquis. In the Griffin turret there was besides the rope of a little alarm bell. She said all this to herself while running, and by the time she had finished saying it, she had reached this door, which she found open. The Duke had gone out there, intending to return in the same way without causing the hinges to creak, and thinking nothing about robbers, an unknown class in that country.

Caroline, however, all the more confirmed in the imaginary construction she had put upon the matter, bounded up the spiral stairway of stone. Hearing nothing at all there, she advanced along the passage, and stopped hesitating, before the door of the Marquis's apartment. She ventured to knock, but received no answer. There were certainly no assassins near her, yet what were the cries which she had heard? An accident of some kind, but undoubtedly a serious one, and one which made immediate assistance necessary. She pushed open the door, that was not even latched, and found M. de Villemer extended upon the floor, near the window which he had not had strength enough to open, and of which he had broken the glass to gain air, feeling himself overwhelmed by a sudden strangling.

The Marquis had not fainted. He had had the terrors of death; he now felt the return of his breathing and of life. As he had his face turned towards the window, he did not see Caroline enter, but he heard her, and thinking it was the Duke, "Do not be alarmed," he said, in a feeble voice; "it is passing off. Aid me to rise, I have no longer the strength."

Caroline rushed forward and raised him up with the energy of an overexcited will. It was only when he found himself again in his chair that he recognized her, or thought he recognized her, for his sight, still dim, was crossed by blue waves, and his limbs were so cold and rigid that they were insensible to the touch of the arms and dress of Caroline.

"Heaven! is it a dream?" he said, with a sort of wildness. "You! is it you?"

"Yes, certainly it is I," she answered; "I heard you groan. What is the matter? What shall I do? Call your brother, must I not? But I dare not leave you again. How do you feel? What has happened to you?"

"My brother," rejoined the Marquis, rousing himself enough to recover his memory. "Ah! it was he who led you here. Where is he?"

"He is not about; he knows nothing of this."

"You have not seen him?"

"No, I will go and have him called."

"Ah! do not leave me."

"Well, then, I will not; but to aid you—"

"Nothing, nothing! I know what it is; it is nothing. Do not be alarmed; you see I am quiet. And—you are here!—and you knew nothing?"

"Nothing in the world. For some days I have found you changed—I thought, indeed, that you were ill, but I dared not be anxious—"

"And now at this moment—did I call you?—What—what did I say?"

"Nothing. You broke this window-pane in falling perhaps. Has it not wounded you?"

And Caroline, approaching the light, took up and examined the hands of the Marquis. The right one was quite badly cut: she washed away the blood, adroitly removed the particles of glass, and dressed the wound. Urbain submitted, regarding her with the mingled astonishment and tenderness of a man who, picked up on the battle-field, discovers himself in friendly hands. He repeated feebly, "My brother, then, has told you nothing,—is it true?"

She did not at all understand this question, which seemed to have gained the fixedness of a diseased fancy, and to banish it she recounted to him, while binding up his hand, that she had believed him in the hands of assassins. "It was absurd, to be sure," she said, forcing herself to be cheerful; "but how could I help it? That fear took possession of me, and I ran hither, as to a fire, without informing any one."

"And if that had been really the case, you were coming here to expose yourself to danger?"

"Upon my word, I never thought of myself; I thought only of you and your mother. Nonsense! I would have helped you to defend yourself; I don't know how, or with what, but I would have found something; I would have made a diversion at any rate. There, your wound is dressed, and it will be nothing; but the other, what is the nature of it? You do not wish to tell me? Your friends must nevertheless know how to help you; your brother—"

"Yes, yes, the Duke knows all, my mother nothing."

"I understand you do not wish—I will tell her nothing; but you will permit me to be anxious; to try and find with the Duke what ought to be done to relieve you. I will not be troublesome. I know how one should be with those who suffer. I was the nurse of my poor father and of my sister's husband. See now, do not take it ill that I came here unwittingly and without reflection. You could have arisen from the floor yourself, I know very well; but it is a sad thing to suffer alone. You smile? Come, M. de Villemer, it seems to me that you are a little better. O, how much I want you to be!"

"I am in heaven," replied the Marquis, and, as he had no idea of the hour, "Stay a while longer," he said. "My brother watched with me a little this evening; he will return."

Caroline did not allow herself to make any objection; she simply did not consider at all what the Duke might think when he found her there, or what the servants would say if they saw her going back to her room; in the presence of a friend in danger, the possibility of any insulting suspicion had not even occurred to her. She remained.

The Marquis wished to say more to her, but had not the strength. "Do not speak," she said. "Try to sleep; I solemnly promise that I will not leave you."

"What? You want me to sleep? But I cannot. When I fall asleep I strangle."

"And yet you are overcome with fatigue; your eyes close in your own despite. Well, now you must obey nature. If you have another severe attack I will help you to bear it; I shall be here."

The confidence and good-will of Caroline had a magical effect upon the invalid. He fell asleep and rested peacefully till day. Caroline had seated herself near a table, and knew now the nature of his malady and how to care for it, for upon that table she had found a diagnosis of the case with simple, intelligible rules for its treatment signed by one of the first physicians of France. The Marquis, to relieve his brother from any anxiety he might have as to his manner of treating himself, had shown him that document invested with the authority of a great name, and the document had remained there under the hand, under the eyes of Caroline, who studied it very carefully. She perceived that the Marquis had been, since she had known him, living under a regimen quite opposed to the one there prescribed: he took no exercise, he ate stintingly, and went with too little sleep. She did not know but that this relapse would be mortal; but if it were not, she resolved to be on her guard in the future and to be bold enough to watch over his health, even if he still had that gloomy, cold manner toward her which she now attributed to an anguish altogether physical.

The Duke returned before sunrise. He had not found the physician; he had to go and look for him at Évaux. Before starting thither, he wanted to see his brother. The dawn was streaking the horizon with its first lines of white when he noiselessly regained the apartment of the Marquis. The latter was then sleeping so soundly that he did not hear the ascending footsteps, and Caroline could go out to meet the Duke upon the stairway, so that he should utter no exclamation of surprise at sight of her. His surprise was indeed great when he saw her coming down toward him with her finger to her lips. He understood nothing of what had passed. He thought that the Marquis had concealed the truth from him, that she was aware of his love, his sorrow, and that she had come to console him.

"Ah! my dear friend," taking her hands, "be at ease; he has confided all to me. You have come, you are good, you will save him;" and he carried Caroline's hands to his lips with genuine affection.

"But," said she, slightly astonished, "knowing him to be so ill, why did you leave him to-night? And since you counted upon my care for him, why did you not tell me it was needed?"

"What, then, has happened?" asked the Duke, who perceived that they did not understand each other. She told him briefly what had occurred, and as, absorbed by what he was hearing, he conducted her back across the grass-plot to the stairs of the Fox turret, Madame d'Arglade, who was already upon her feet behind the casement of her window, saw them pass, talking in a low voice with an air of mysterious intimacy. They stopped before the door, and stood talking awhile longer. The Duke gave Mlle de Saint-Geneix an account of his attempt to bring a physician to see his brother, and Caroline dissuaded him from that design. She believed that the directions she had read would be sufficient, and that it would be highly imprudent to adopt a new treatment when they were aware that the first one had been attended with beneficial results. The Duke readily promised her to conform to this advice, and consequently to have confidence in it. Madame d'Arglade saw them take each other by the hand at parting, and the Duke, retracing his steps, ascend the stairs of the Griffin turret.

"Very well, I have seen enough," thought Léonie; "and I have n't to run about in the dew, which I don't like to do at all; I can lie abed the whole forenoon." And in getting herself to sleep again; "That Caroline!" she said to herself, "I see plainly that she lied. How probable it is that the Duke would allow her to go free! But I will keep it, this fine secret of hers, and if ever I have need of her, she will of course have to do as I wish."

Caroline retired quickly, that she might get quickly to sleep, so as to return to the service of her patient.

At eight o'clock she was up and looked through her window. The Duke was at that of his brother. He made her a sign that he would go through the halls and meet her in the library. She went thither immediately from her side of the house, and there she learned that the Marquis was remarkably well. He had just awakened, and he had said, "Heavens, what a miracle! This is my first sleep after a whole week of this suffering, and I no longer feel any pain; I breathe freely; it seems to me that I am cured. It is to her that I owe it all!"—"and it is the truth, my dear friend," added the Duke; "it is you who have saved him, and who will preserve him for us, if you have pity upon us."

The Duke had resolved to say nothing; he had sworn it to his brother; but, although thinking himself very discreet, he had let the truth escape him in his own despite. That truth darted through the mind of Caroline ike a flash of lightning. "What is it that your Grace says?" cried she. "Who am I, and how am I here to have such an influence?"

The Duke himself was frightened by the frightened look of Caroline. "Come, in whom are you disappointed?" he said, resuming the mask of his tranquil smile. "What is that you have got into your head now? Do you not see that I worship my brother, that I am in great fear of losing him, and that, because of the assistance you were to him last night, I speak to you as if you were my sister? I am very much embarrassed; I lose my senses, do you see? Urbain is killing himself with work. My influence over him is not sufficient; he does not want me to inform our mother of the return of his old disorder. Informing her would be

GEORGE SAND

indeed to agitate her dangerously; infirm as she is, she would be always with him to watch. At the end of two nights she would succumb to her exertions. It remains for us two, therefore, to save my brother, without seeming to do so, without taking the lackeys and chambermaids into our confidence. That sort of people will always talk. Come, are you a woman of heart and head as I have persuaded myself that you are? Will you, can you, dare you, seriously, aid me to nurse him in secret, and watch alternately with me for several evenings, several nights if necessary, never leaving him alone an hour, so that even for an hour he cannot betake himself again to his accursed old books! He needs nothing, I feel sure, but absolute repose of mind, sufficient sleep, a little walking, and that he should try to eat. To bring these things about, it requires the despotic authority—yes, the despotic authority of some one who is not afraid to go counter to his will—of some devoted heart not easily moved or harshly immovable, or unseasonably distrustful,—some one who will bear with his whims if he should have any, and with the impulsive excesses of his gratitude if such should escape him,—a serious friend, in a word, who shall have such delicate, intelligent charity for him as will make him accept and perhaps love his yoke. Well, now, Caroline, you are the only one here who can be that person. My brother has great esteem, profound respect, and, I believe, even a sincere friendship for you. Try to govern him a week, a fortnight, a month perhaps, for if he could get up to-day he would be here this evening turning over the leaves of his books and taking notes; if he sleeps again to-night he will believe himself through with the whole thing, and will not go to bed at all the next night. You see what task we ought to impose upon ourselves. As for my part, I am resolved upon it, entirely devoted to it, but by myself alone I can do nothing. I shall weary him, he will allow no one but me to see him, and his impatience will neutralize the effect of my care. With you,—a woman, a voluntary guardian, generous, firm and tender, patient and resolute, as women only know how to be,—I will answer for it that he will submit without ill-will, and later, when all the paroxysms of his disorder are passed, he will bless you for having thwarted him."

This insidious explanation of the case entirely dissipated the vague and sudden suspicion of Caroline. "Yes, yes," she answered, with decision, "I will be that guardian. Count upon me; I thank you for having chosen me, and do not think better of me on that account. I am used to nursing; it costs me neither effort nor fatigue. Your brother is to me, as to you, so worthy of respect and so superior to every one we know that it is a happiness and honor to serve him. Let us, therefore, understand each other, so that we can share this good task without arousing suspicion of any one around us here as to his real state. To begin with, you install yourself in his room to-night."

"He will not allow that."

"Well, then, his breathing can be heard from here. There is a large sofa on which one can sleep quite comfortably, muffled in a cloak. You and I can pass the night here alternately, till a change is brought about."

"Very well."

"You must make him rise early, so that he will get the habit of sleeping at night; and you must bring him to breakfast with us."

"If you will make him promise to do these things."

"I will try. It is absolutely necessary that he should eat oftener than once in twenty-four hours. We will make him walk or simply seat himself with us in the open air till noon. That is the hour of his visit and yours to the Marchioness. I work with her till five o'clock; then I dress—"

"That will not take you an hour. Will you not come and pay him a short visit in the library? I shall be there."

"Yes, so I will; we will all dine together. We will keep him in the drawing-room till ten o'clock. Then you will follow him."

"All this is perfect, but when my mother has visitors she will leave us at liberty, and you can then easily come here and talk with us an hour or two?"

"No, not to talk," replied Caroline. "I will come and read to him a little, for you can well imagine he will not pass all this time without wishing to interest himself in something, and I will read to him in a way to quiet him and dispose him to sleep. So, it is agreed. Only to-day we shall be very much hindered by Madame d'Arglade."

"To-day I take everything upon myself, and Madame d'Arglade leaves to-morrow at daylight; then my brother is saved, and you are an angel!"

GEORGE SAND

XIV

B eing informed by his brother of all these arrangements, the Marquis submitted with gratitude. He was extremely weak, and recovering apparently from a dangerous crisis, which had not wholly exhausted him, but had broken him down morally almost as much as a long illness would have done. He could struggle against his love no longer; and having ceased to feel the dangerous storms of passion, thanks to this prostration, he gave himself up to the pleasure of being tenderly cared for. The Duke would not permit him to question the future. "You cannot come to any decision in your present state," Gaëtan would say to his brother. "You have n't the free use of your will: without health there can be no moral clear-sightedness. Let us cure you, and then you will see plainly that, with your health, you have also regained the strength necessary to resist your love, or to deal with the scruples it causes. In the mean time I don't see what you can have on your conscience, for Mlle de Saint-Geneix suspects nothing, and after all is only doing what a sister would do in her place."

This compromise quieted all the invalid's uneasiness. He arose and went to see his mother a few moments, making her believe that a slight indisposition was responsible for the change in his countenance. He asked to be excused from returning till the next day, and so for twenty-four hours, that is, until after the departure of Madame d'Arglade, he could give himself up to almost absolute repose.

Throughout the day there subsisted between the Duke and Caroline an air of mutual intelligence and an exchange of glances which had for their subject only the Marquis and his health, but which completely deluded Léonie. She went away perfectly sure of her facts, but without saying anything to the Marchioness which could lead that old lady to suppose her possessed of any penetration whatever.

At the close of the week M. de Villemer was much better. Every symptom of aneurism had passed away, and under rational treatment he even regained a certain glow of health, as well as a mental serenity, to which he had long been a stranger. No one for ten years had taken care of him with the assiduity, the devotedness, the evenness of temper, the unheard-of charm, with which Mlle de Saint-Geneix contrived to surround him: we might even say he had never met with attentions at once so sensible and so tender, for his mother, aside from her lack of active physical strength, had shown herself excitable and over-anxious in the care she had lavished on him when his life had before been threatened. She had, indeed, at this time some suspicion of a relapse, when she saw her son more frequently with her, and consequently less devoted to his work; but when this idea occurred the crisis had already passed: the good understanding between the Duke and Caroline as to the need of tranquillity, the absolute ignorance of the servants, few in numbers and therefore very busy, and the serenity of the Marquis himself, all tended to reassure her; and at the close of a fortnight she even observed that her son was regaining an air of youth and health at which she could but rejoice.

The condition of the Marquis had been carefully concealed from Madame d'Arglade. The Duke would in no wise give up the great marriage projected for his brother. He thought Léonie was a foolish chatterbox, and did not care to have it understood in society that his brother's health, at any moment, might give serious cause for alarm. The Duke had thoroughly warned Caroline on this point. He was playing with her, in the interests of his brother as he understood them, the double game of preparing her as far as possible, and little by little, for the exercise of an unlimited devotion; and to this end, he thought best to remind her, now and then, that the future well-being of the family rested entirely on the famous marriage. Caroline, then, had no chance to forget this; and relying on the integrity of the two brothers, on her own ideas of duty and the unselfishness of her heart, she walked resolutely toward an abyss which might have engulfed her. And thus the Duke, naturally kind, and animated by the best intentions toward his brother, was coolly working out the misery of a poor girl whose personal merit made her worthy of the highest places of happiness and consideration.

Fortunately for Mlle de Saint-Geneix, although the conscience of the Marquis was somewhat stupefied, it was not wholly asleep. Besides, his passion was made up of enthusiasm and sincere affection. He insisted that the Duke should be with them almost always, and in his abrupt sincerity he came near releasing Caroline from her attendance altogether, promising not to begin work again without her permission. The moment came even when he did give her this promise to induce her to cease her watch in the library; he had found her there more than once, a guardian, gently and gayly "savage," over the books and portfolios, placed, she said, under interdict till further orders; but the

GEORGE SAND

Duke counteracted the effect of this "imprudence" on his brother's part, by telling Caroline, in a very low voice, that she must not trust a promise, given in good faith to be sure, but which Urbain would not have it in his power to keep. "You don't know how absent-minded he is," said the Duke; "when an idea takes hold of him it masters him, and makes him forget all his promises. I have found him myself, more than twenty times, searching over these bookshelves while my back was turned, and when I called out, 'Here, here, you marauder!' he seemed startled out of a revery and looked at me with an air of great surprise."

So Caroline did not relax her watchfulness. The library was much farther from her room than from that of the Marquis; but yet so near the centre of the house that the constant presence of the young lady reader in this room devoted to study was not likely to strike the servants as anything remarkable. They saw her there often, sometimes alone, sometimes with the Duke or the Marquis, more frequently with both, although the Duke had a thousand pretexts for leaving her alone with his brother; but even then the doors always open, the book often in Caroline's hands, the evident interest with which she was reading, and lastly, more than all this, the real truth of the situation,—truth, which has more power than the best-planned deception,—removed every pretext and even every desire for malicious comment.

In this state of things Caroline was really happy, and often recurred to it in after years as the most delightful phase of her life. She had suffered from Urbain's coldness, but now she found him showing an unhoped-for kindness and a disposition to trust her again. As soon as all fears for his health were dispelled, a bond was established between them, which, for Caroline, had not a single doubt or apprehension. The Marquis enjoyed her reading exceedingly, and before long he even consented to let her help him with his work. She conducted investigations for him and took notes, which she classified in the very spirit he desired,—a spirit she seemed to divine wonderfully. In short, she rendered his studies so pleasant, and relieved him so cleverly from the dry and disagreeable portions, that he could once more betake himself to writing without pain or fatigue.

The Marquis certainly needed a secretary far more than his mother did; but he had never been able to endure this interposition between himself and the objects of his researches. He saw very soon, however, that Caroline never led him off into ideas foreign to his own, but kept him from straying away himself into useless speculations and reveries.

She had a remarkable clearness of judgment, joined with a faculty rarely possessed by women, namely, that of order in the sequence of thought. She could remain absorbed in any pursuit a long while, without fatigue or faltering. The Marquis made a discovery,—one that was destined to direct his future. He found himself in presence of a superior mind, not creative, indeed, but analytic in the highest degree,—just the organization he needed to give balance and scope to his own intellect.

Let us say, once for all, that M. de Villemer was a man of very sound understanding; but he had not found as yet, and was still awaiting, the crisis of its development. Hence the slow and painful progress of his work. He thought and wrote rapidly; but his conscientiousness, as a philosopher and moralist, was always putting fresh obstacles in the way of his enthusiasm as an historian. He was the victim of his own scruples, like certain devotees, sincere but morbid, who always imagine they have failed to tell their confessor the whole truth. He wanted to confess to the human race the truth about social science; and did not sufficiently admit that this science of truths and facts is, largely, a relative one, determined by the age in which one lives. He could not decide on his course. He strove to discover the meaning of facts long buried among the arcana of the past, and after he had, with great labor, caught a few traces of these, he was surprised to find them often contradictory, and in alarm would doubt his own discernment or his own impartiality, would suspend judgment, laying aside his work, and for weeks and months would be the prey of terrible uncertainties and misgivings.

Caroline, without knowing his book, which was still only half written, and which he concealed with a morbid timidity, soon divined the cause of his mental uneasiness from his conversation, and especially his remarks while she was reading aloud. She volunteered a few off-hand reflections of extreme simplicity, but so plainly just and right as to be unanswerable. She was not perplexed by a little blot on a grand life or a tiny glimmer of reason in an age of delirium. She thought the past must be viewed just as we look at paintings, from the distance required by the eye of each in order to take in the whole; and that, as the great masters have done in composing their pictures, we must learn to sacrifice the petty details, which sometimes really destroy the harmony of nature, and even her logic. She called attention to the fact that we notice on a landscape, at every step, strange effects of light and shade, and the multitude will say, "How could a painter render that?" and the painter would reply, "By not rendering it at all."

She admitted that the historian is fettered more than the artist to accuracy in matters of fact, but she denied that there could be progress on any different principles in either case. The past and even the present of individual or collective life, according to her, take color and meaning only from their general tenor and results.

She ventured on these suggestions, cautiously putting them in the form of questions; without being positive, and as if willing to suppress them in case they were not approved; but M. de Villemer was struck with them, because he felt she had given expression to a certainty, an inward faith, and that if she consented to keep silence, she would still remain none the less convinced. He struggled a little, nevertheless, laying before her a number of facts which had delayed and troubled him. She passed judgment on them in one word, with the strong, good sense of a fresh mind and a pure heart, and he soon exclaimed with a glance at the Duke, "She finds the truth because she has it within her, and that is the first condition of clear insight. Never will the troubled conscience, never will the perverted mind, comprehend history."

"Perhaps," said she, "that is why history should not be too much made up from memoirs, for these are nearly always the work of prejudice or passions of the moment. It is the fashion now to dig these out with great care, bringing forward many trifling facts not generally known, and which do not deserve to be known."

"Yes, you are right," replied the Marquis; "if the historian, instead of standing firm in his belief and worship of lofty things, lets himself be misled and distracted by trivial ones, truth loses all that reality usurps."

If we relate these bits of conversation, perhaps a little out of the usual color of a romance, it is because they are necessary to explain the seriousness and apparent calmness of the relations that were growing up between the scholar and the humble lady-reader in the castle of Séval, in spite of the pains the Duke was taking to leave them as much as possible to the tender influences of youth and love. The Marquis felt that he belonged to Caroline, not only through his enthusiasm, his dreams, his need of throwing a kind of ideal about grace and beauty, but through his reason, his judgment, and through his present certainty that he had met that ideal. Henceforth Caroline was safe; she commanded respect by the weight of her character, and the Marquis stood in no further fear of losing control of his own impulses.

The Duke was at first astonished by this unlooked-for result of their intimacy. His brother was cured, he was happy, he seemed to have conquered love by the very power of love itself; but the Duke was intelligent and he understood. He was even seized himself with a serious deference for Caroline. He took an interest in her reading, and soon, instead of falling asleep under the first few pages, he wanted to read in his turn and give them his impressions. He had no convictions, but, in the artist spirit, allowed himself to be moved and borne along by those of others. He had read but little on serious subjects, in the course of his life, but he had admirably retained all kinds of dates and proper names. So that he had in his fine memory, as one might say, a sort of network with large meshes to which the loose lines of his brother's studies could be tied. That is, he was a stranger to nothing except the logical and profound meanings of historical events. He did not lack prejudices; but excellence of style had a power over him which put them to silence, and before an eloquent page, whether of Bossuet or Rousseau, he felt the same enthusiasm.

Thus he also found himself pleasantly initiated into the pursuits of the Marquis and the society of Mlle de Saint-Geneix. What was really very good in him is that, from the day he first became aware of his brother's affection for Caroline, she ceased to be a woman in his eyes. He had nevertheless felt some emotion for several days in her presence, and the truth had come upon him unexpectedly in an hour of feverish spite. From day to day he abjured every evil thought, and, touched by seeing that the Marquis, after a terrible attack of jealousy, had restored to him his entire confidence, he knew, for the first time in his life, what it was to feel a true and worthy friendship for a pretty woman.

In the month of July Caroline wrote to her sister thus:—

"Be easy about me, dear Camille, it is some time since I ceased to watch the invalid, for the invalid has never before been so well; but I have always kept up the practice of rising at day-break in the summer season, and every morning I have several hours I can devote to the work he is kindly permitting me to share with him. Just now he is himself sleeping a good sound sleep, for he retires at ten o'clock, and I am allowed here to do the same, and I often have precious intervals of freedom even in the daytime. Our proximity to the baths of Évaux and the road to Vichy brings us visitors at the very hours when in Paris the Marchioness used to shut herself up; she says this disturbs and wearies her, and yet, all the while, she is delighted! The great correspondence suffers under it, but even the correspondence itself has diminished, since the marriage of the Marquis was projected. This scheme so absorbs Madame de

Villemer, that she cannot help confiding it or hinting something about it to all her old friends; after which she will reflect seriously, admitting the imprudence of saying much about it, and that she ought not to rely on the discretion of so many people; and then we throw into the fire the letters she has just dictated. This it is that leads her to say so often: 'Bah! let us stop writing, I would rather say nothing at all than not to mention things that interest me.'

"When she has visitors she makes a sign that I may go and join the Marquis, for she knows now that I am taking notes for him. Since his illness is over, I thought there ought to be no mystery made about so simple a thing, and she is quite willing to have me relieve her son from any wearisome portions of his work. She is very curious to know what this book so carefully concealed can possibly be; but there is no danger, of my betraying anything, for I don't know a single word in it. I only know that just now we are deep in the history of France, and more especially in the age of Richelieu; but what I need not mention to any one here is, that I anticipate a great divergence in opinion between the son and the mother on a host of grave matters.

"Do not blame me for having taken on myself a double task, and for having gained, as you put it, two masters in the place of one. With the Marchioness the task is sacred, and I have an affectionate pleasure in it; with her son the task is agreeable, and I put into it that kind of veneration of which I have often told you. I enjoy the idea of having contributed to his recovery, of having managed to take care of him without making him impatient, of having gently persuaded him to live a little more as people ought to live in order to be well. I have even taken advantage of his passion for study by telling him that his genius will feel the effects of disease, and that I have no faith in the intellectual clearness of fever. You have no idea how good he has been to me, how patiently he has taken rebuke, and how he has even let himself be scolded by this young-lady sister of yours; how he has thanked me for my interest in him, and submitted to all my prescriptions. It has gone so far that at table, even, he consults me with his eyes as to what he shall eat, and when we go out for a walk he has no more mind of his own than a child as to the little journey which the Duke and I insist on making him take. He has a charming disposition, and every day I discover some new trait in his character. I did think he was a little whimsical and decidedly obstinate; but, poor fellow! it was the crisis that was threatening his life. He has, on the contrary, a gentleness and evenness of temper which is beyond everything; and the charm of familiar intercourse with him resembles nothing so much as the beauty, of the waters flowing through our valley, always limpid, always plentiful, borne along in a strong and even current, never ruffled or capricious. And to follow out this comparison, I might say that his mind has also flowery banks and oases of verdure where one can pause and dream delightfully, for he is full of poetry; and I always wonder how he has ever subjected the warmth of his imagination to the rigid demands of history.

"What is more, he pretends that all this is a discovery of mine, and that he is just beginning to perceive it himself. The other day we were looking at the beautiful pastures full of sheep and goats in a ravine crossing that of the Char. At the farther end of this sharp cut, there is a casing of rugged rocks, and some of their notches rise so far above the plateau that, in comparison with the lower level, it is really a mountain; and these beautiful rocks of lilac-gray form a crest, sufficiently imposing to conceal the flat country that lies behind, so you cannot see from here the upper part of the plateau, and you might imagine yourself in some nook of Switzerland. At least, this is what M. de Villemer tells me, to console me for the way in which the Marchioness scouts my admiration. 'Don't worry about that,' said he, 'and don't think it necessary to have seen many sublime things in order to have the conception and the sensation of sublimity. There is grandeur everywhere for those who carry this faculty within themselves; it is not an illusion which they cherish either; it is a revelation of what really exists in nature in a manner more or less pronounced. For dull senses, there must be coarse signs of the power and dimensions of things. This is why many people who go to Scotland, looking for the pictures described by Walter Scott, cannot find them, and pretend that the poet has overpraised his country. His pictures are there, nevertheless, I am very sure, and if you should go there, you would find them at once.'

"I confessed to him that real immensity tempted me greatly; that I often saw, in dreams, inaccessible mountains and giddy abysses; that, before an engraving representing the furious waterfalls in Sweden or the bergs that stray from Arctic seas, I have been carried away with wild imaginations of independence, and that there is no tale of distant explorations with enough of suffering and danger in it to take away my regret at not having shared them.

"'And yet,' said he, 'before a charming little landscape like this you seemed happy and really satisfied a moment ago. Do you then really feel more in need of emotions and surprises than of tenderness and safety? See how beautiful it is, this stillness! How this hour of reflected lights, barred across with lengthening shadows, this water, in spray which seems caressing the sides of the rock, this motionless leafage looking as if it were silently drinking in the gold of the last sunbeams, how truly indeed is all this serene and thoughtful solemnity the expression of the beautiful and good in nature! I never used to know all this myself. It has not impressed me strongly until lately. I have always been living in the midst of dust and death, or among abstractions. I used, indeed, to dream over the pictures of history, the phantasmagoria of the past. I have sometimes seen the fleet of Cleopatra sailing to the verge of the horizon; in the silence of the night I have thought I heard the warlike trumpets of Roncesvalles; but it was the dominion of a dream, and the reality did not speak to me. But when I saw you gazing at the horizon without saying a word, with an air of content that was like nothing else in the world, I asked myself what could be the secret of your joy; and, if I must tell you all, your selfish patient was a little jealous of everything that charmed you. He set himself perturbedly to work at gazing too, when he settled the point at once; for he felt that he loved what you loved.'

"You understand perfectly, my dear little sister, that in talking to me thus the Marquis told an audacious falsehood, for one can but see from all his remarks, and his manner of making them, that he has the true artist enthusiasm for nature, as well as for all else that is lovely; but he is so grateful to me, and so full of honest kindliness, that he misrepresents things in perfect good faith, and imagines himself indebted to me for something new in his intellectual life."

XV

O ne morning the Marquis, writing at the large table in the library, while Caroline at the other end was turning over some maps, laid down his pen and said to her with emotion,—

"Mlle de Saint-Geneix, I remember that you have sometimes expressed a good-natured wish to know about this work of mine, and I thought I could never make up my mind to satisfy you; but now,—yes, now, I feel that submitting it to you will give me pleasure. This book is your work much more than it is mine, after all; because I did not believe in it, and you have led me to respect the impulse which prompted it. By restoring my faith in my task, you have enabled me to carry it further in one month than I had done for ten years before. You are also the cause why I shall certainly finish a thing which I should, perhaps, have been always recommencing until my last hour. Besides, it was near at hand, this last hour! I felt it coming quickly, and I hastened, the prey of despair, for I could see nothing advancing but the close of my life. You ordered me to live, and I have lived; to be calm, and I am at peace; to believe in God, and in myself, and I do so believe. Since I now have faith in my thought you must also give me faith in my power to express it, for although I do not hold to style more than is reasonable, yet I consider it necessary to give weight and attractiveness to truth. Here, my friend, read!"

"Yes," replied Caroline, eagerly; "you see that I do not hesitate, that I do not refuse; and this is neither prudent nor modest on my part. Very well, I am not disturbed by that! I am so sure of your talent, that I stand in no fear of the fact that I shall have to be sincere, and I believe so thoroughly in the harmony of our opinions, that I even flatter myself I shall comprehend what, under other circumstances, would be beyond my reach."

But, as she was about to take the manuscript, Caroline hesitated before accepting so especial a mark of confidence, and inquired whether the excellent Duke was not also to be a sharer in this gratification.

"No," replied the Marquis, "my brother will not come to-day. I have seized upon a time when he is away hunting. I do not wish him to know about my work before it is finished; he would not comprehend it. His hereditary prejudices would stand in the way. To be sure he thinks he has a few 'advanced ideas' as he calls them, and he knows that I go

GEORGE SAND

farther than he; but he does not suspect how far I have strayed from the road in which my education placed me. My rebellion against these things of the past would put him in consternation, and this might disturb me before the close of my work. But you yourself,—perhaps you are going to be a little uneasy?"

"I have reached no decision myself," replied Caroline, "and very probably I shall adopt your opinions when I understand them exactly. Sit down now; I will read aloud for your benefit as well as my own. I want you to hear yourself speak. I think this must be a good way of rereading one's work."

Caroline read that morning a half-volume, resuming the employment the next day and the day after. In three days, she had made the Marquis listen to a summary of his studies for many years. She followed his handwriting as easily as print, although it was somewhat blind; and as she read aloud with admirable clearness, intelligence, and simplicity, growing animated and conscious of her own emotion when the narration rose to the lyric passages in the epic construction of the history, the author felt himself enlightened at once by a very sun of certainty formed of all the scattered rays by which his meditations had been penetrated.

The picture was fine, of beautiful originality, bearing the stamp of real greatness. Under the simple and mysterious heading, "The History of Titles," he raised a whole series of bold questions, which aimed at nothing less than rendering universal, without restrictions and forever, the thought of the revolutionary night, August 4, 1789. This son of a noble house with ancient privileges, brought up in the pride of family and in the disdain of commoners, introduced before our modern civilization a written accusation of the nobility, along with documents to sustain his case, the proofs of their usurpations, their outrages, or their crimes, and pronounced sentence of forfeiture against them in the name of logic and justice, in the name of the human conscience, and, more than all, in the name of simple, scriptural Christianity. He boldly attacked the compromise of eighteen centuries, which would ally the equality revealed by the apostles to the arrangements of civil and theocratical hierarchies. Admitting in all classes none but political and executive hierarchies, that is to say, official positions, held as proofs of personal courage and social activity, or in a word, of any real services rendered, he pursued the privilege of birth as far as into the present state of public opinion and even as far as its final influences; tracing with a firm hand the history of the spoliations and usurpations of power from the creation of the feudal nobility down to the present time. It was reconstructing the history of France from a special point of view, under the sway of one idea,—a distinct, absolute, inflexible, indignant idea, springing from that religious feeling, which aristocracy cannot attack, without itself committing suicide, invoking, as it does, the divine right for the support of its own institution.

We will say no more about the data of this book, even a criticism of which would be foreign to our subject. Whatever judgment might be passed on the convictions of the author, it was impossible not to recognize in him a splendid talent, joined to the knowledge and strong good faith which mark a mind of the first rank. His style especially was magnificent, of a copiousness and richness which the modest brevity of the Marquis in social life would never have led one to suspect; though, even in his book, he gave small space to discussions. After having stated his premises and the motives of his investigation in a few pages of warm and severe criticism, he passed on with eloquent clearness to the facts themselves and classified them historically. His narrations, teeming as they did with color, had the interest of a drama or a romance, even when, rummaging among obscure family archives, he revealed the horrors of feudal times, with the sufferings and degradation of the lower classes. An enthusiast, but making no apologies for the fact, he deeply felt all offences against justice, against modesty, against love, and in many pages his soul, in its passion for truth, justice, and beauty, would reveal itself entirely in bursts of excited eloquence. More than once Caroline felt the tears come to her eyes, and laid aside the book to recover her composure.

Caroline made no objections. It is not for the simple narrator to say that she should have made them or that there were really none to make; it is necessary to relate merely that she found no objections to offer; so great was her admiration of his ability and her esteem for the man himself. The Marquis de Villemer became in her eyes a person so completely superior to all she had ever met, that she then and there formed the purpose of devoting herself to him unreservedly and for her whole life.

When we say "unreservedly" we are mindful that there was very certainly one exception which would not have been agreed to thus, had it presented itself to her mind; but it did not present itself. In such a man there was nothing to disturb the serenity of her enthusiasm. And yet we should not dare to affirm that, from this time onward, her enthusiasm did not unconsciously include love as one of the elements indispensable to its fulness; but love had not been its point of departure. The Marquis had never until now revealed all the attractiveness of his intellect or of his person; he had been constrained, agitated, and out of health. Caroline did not, at first, perceive the change in him, that was taking place in such a gradual way, for he grew eloquent, young, and handsome, day by day, and hour by hour; recovering his health, his confidence in himself, the certainty of his own power, and the charm happiness gives to a noble face which has been veiled by doubt.

When she began to account for all these delightful transformations, she had already felt their effects without her own knowledge, and the autumn had come. They were about returning to Paris, and Madame de Villemer, under the sway of a fixed idea, would say every day to her young companion, "In three weeks, in a fortnight, in a week, the 'famous' interview of my son with Mlle de Xaintrailles will take place."

Caroline then felt a fearful anguish in the depths of her heart, a consternation, a terror, and an overmastering revelation of a kind of attachment which she did not yet confess even to herself. She had so fully accepted the vague and still distant prospect of this marriage that she had never been willing to ask herself whether it would give her pain. It was for her a thing inevitable, like old age or death; but one does not really accept, old age or death until either arrives, and Caroline felt that she was growing weak and that she should die at the thought of this absolute separation, so near at hand.

She had ended by believing with the Marchioness that the scheme could not fail. She had never dared to question the Marquis; besides the Duke had forbidden this, in the name of the friendship she felt for the family. According to him, the Marquis would never come to a decision as long as he was tormented about it, and the Duke well knew that the least anxiety on Caroline's part would overthrow all his brother's designs.

The Duke, after having sincerely admired the purity of their relations, began to grow anxious about it. "This is becoming," said he to himself "an attachment so serious that one cannot foresee its results. Shall we believe that his tender respect for her has killed his love? No, no, such respect in a case like this is love with redoubled power."

The Duke was not mistaken. The Marquis was not at all concerned at the prospect of a marriage which he had now determined not to contract. He was only troubled about the change which a residence in

Paris would for a time effect in his relations with Mlle de Saint-Geneix, in their free intimacy, in their common studies, in that continuous security which could not be found elsewhere. He mentioned this to her with great sadness. She felt the same regret, and attributed her own inward sorrow to her love for the country and to the breaking up of a life so sweet and noble.

She, however, experienced a charming surprise on her arrival in Paris. She found her sister there awaiting her with the children, and learned that Camille was going to be near her. She was to live at Étampes in a little house, half city and half country residence, pretty, new, in a good atmosphere, with the enjoyment besides of a considerable garden. She would be only an hour's ride by rail from Paris. She had placed Lili at school, having obtained a scholarship for her in a Parisian convent. Caroline would be able to see her every week. Finally a scholarship had also been promised her for little Charles, in a college when he should be old enough to enter.

"You fill me with surprise and delight!" cried Caroline, embracing her sister; "but who has worked all these miracles?"

"You," replied Camille, "you alone; it is always you."

"No, indeed. I had hopes of obtaining these scholarships, that is, of procuring them some day or other, through Léonie, who is so obliging; but I did not hope for such prompt success."

"O no!" replied Madame Heudebert, "this did not come from Léonie; it came from some one here."

"Impossible! I have never said a word about it to the Marchioness. Knowing how much she is at variance with 'the powers that be,' I should not have dared—"

"Some one has dared to approach the ministry, and this some one—he does not wish to be named; he has acted in secrecy, and yet I shall betray him because it is impossible for me to keep a secret from you—this some one is the Marquis de Villemer."

"Ah! Then you wrote to ask him—"

"Not at all. It was he who wrote to me, inquiring about my situation and my claims with a kindness, a propriety, a delicacy,—yes, Caroline, you were quite right in esteeming a character like his. But stop, I have brought his letters. I wish you would read them." Caroline read the letters, and saw that, beginning from the day when she had taken care of M. de Villemer, he had been bestowing attentions upon her family, with a lively and constant interest. He had anticipated her secret wishes, he had concerned himself about the education of the children. He had taken prompt and sure measures by letter, without even offering to take them; confining himself to asking Camille for the necessary information as to the services of her husband in his department. He had announced his success, refusing to be thanked, and saying that his debt of gratitude to Mlle de Saint-Geneix was far from being paid. This good news had reached Camille during the slow journey with post-horses which Caroline was taking with the Marchioness, for the old lady had a fear and horror of coaches and railways.

As to the house at Étampes, this was also the idea and proposition of the Marquis. There was, he said, a little estate, bringing in nothing, which had been left him by an aged relative, and he begged Madame Heudebert to do him the favor of living there. She had accepted this offer, saying that she would take upon herself all the expense of repairs; but she had found the little house in excellent condition, furnished, and even provided with fuel, wine, and vegetables for more than a year. When she inquired about the rent of the person charged by the Marquis with these details, he replied that his orders were to receive no money, that it was too slight a matter, and that the Marquis had never proposed to rent the house of his aged cousin to strangers.

Though Caroline was deeply moved by these favors from her friend, and pleased to see the lot of her family so much improved, she felt, nevertheless, a sorrow at heart. It seemed as if this was a kind of farewell from him whose life was to be parted forever from her own, and, as it were, an account settled by his gratitude. She drove back this sorrow, however, and passed her mornings for several days in walking out with her sister and the children, in buying the outfit of the little school-girl, and finally in establishing her at the convent. The Marchioness wished to see Madame Heudebert, and the pretty Elizabeth who was going to lose at the convent her soft pet name of Lili. She was pleasant to Caroline's sister, and did not let the child depart without a pretty present: she wished to give Caroline two days of freedom with her family, so that she might have ample time to bid them good by and conduct them to the station again. She even rode herself to the convent to recommend Elizabeth Heudebert as under her special protection.

Camille had also seen the Marquis and the Duke at their mother's; she had only ventured to present Lili to her benefactor, the other children not being old enough; but M. de Villemer wanted to see them all; he went to call upon Madame Heudebert at the hotel where she had taken lodgings, and found Caroline in the midst of the children, by whom she was almost worshipped. She found him, for his part, not in a revery, but apparently absorbed in the contemplation of the cares and caresses that she gave them. He looked at each child with tender attention, and spoke to them all, like a man in whom the paternal sentiment is already well developed. Caroline, ignorant that he really was a father, imagined, with a sigh, that he was thinking of future family joys.

The following day, after she had seen her sister safely in the railway carriage which was to carry her back to Étampes, Caroline felt herself horribly alone, and, for the first time, the marriage of the Marquis presented itself to her mind as an irreparable disaster in her own life. She left the platform quickly to hide her tears; but in the court she came directly upon M. de Villemer. "What!" said he, offering her his arm. "You are weeping. That is just what I was expecting; and I was anxious to come to this place, where pretexts for the public are not wanting, to sustain you a little in this sorrow which is so natural, and to remind you that you still have sincere friends here."

"What! did you come here on my account?" replied Caroline, wiping away her tears. "I am ashamed of this momentary weakness. It is ingratitude to you who have loaded my relatives with favors, who have established them near me, and whom I ought to bless with joy instead of feeling the slight pain of a separation which cannot last very long. My sister will often return to see her daughter, and I shall see her myself oftener still. No, no, I have no cause for grief; on the contrary, I am very happy,—thanks to you for it!"

"Then why do you still weep?" said the Marquis, as he led her back to the carriage he had brought for her: "come, you are a little nervous, are you not? but it troubles me. Let us go back to the platform as if we were in search of some one. I shall not leave you in tears. It is the first time I have seen you weeping, and it hurts me. Stop, we are only a few steps from the Jardin des Plantes; at eight in the morning there is no risk of meeting any one we know. Besides, with that mantle and veil, no one will recognize you. It is pleasant enough; will you come and look at the 'Swiss Valley'? We will try to imagine ourselves in the country again, and when I leave you, I shall be sure—at least, I hope, that you will not be ill."

There was so much friendly solicitude in the tone of the Marquis, that Caroline did not think of refusing his offer. "Who knows," thought she, "that he does not wish to bid me a brotherly adieu before entering upon his new existence? It is, indeed, a thing which is allowable for us to do,—which perhaps we ought to do. He has never yet spoken to me of his marriage; it would be strange if he did not speak to me about it, and if I were not prepared and willing to hear him."

XVI

The Marquis made a sign for the coachman to follow them, and conducted Caroline on foot, chatting pleasantly with her about her sister and the children; but, neither during this short walk, nor on the shaded avenues of the "Swiss Valley" in the Jardin des Plantes, did he say one word about himself. It was only when he stopped with her under the pendent boughs of Jussieu's cedar, just as they were on the point of returning, that he said, smiling, and in the most indifferent tone, "Do you know that my official presentation to Mlle de Xaintrailles takes place to-day?"

It seemed to the Marquis that he felt Caroline's arm trembling as it rested on his own; but she replied, with sincerity and resolution, "No, I did not know that it was to-day."

"If I speak to you at all about this," he resumed, "it is only because I know my mother and my brother have kept you informed of this fine project. I have never talked with you about it myself; it was not worth while."

"Then you thought that I would not be interested in your happiness?"

"My happiness! How can it be in the hands of a lady I do not know? And you, my friend, how can you speak so,—you who know me?"

"Then I will say the happiness of your mother,—since that depends upon this marriage."

"O, that is another matter," replied M. de Villemer, quickly. "Shall we rest a moment on this seat, and while we are alone here will you let me talk a little about my position?"

They seated themselves. "You will not be cold?" continued the Marquis, wrapping the folds of Caroline's mantle around her.

"No, and you?"

"O, as for me, my health is robust now, thanks to you, and that is why they think seriously of making me the head of a family of my own. It is a happiness which I do not need so much as they suppose. There are already children in the world that one loves,—just as you love those of your sister! But let us pass that over and suppose that I really dream of descendants in a long line. You understand that I do not hold to this as a point of family pride; you know my ideas about nobility; they are not precisely those of the people around me. Unfortunately for the people around me, I cannot change in this regard; it no longer depends upon myself."

"I know that," replied Mlle de Saint-Geneix, "but your heart is too comprehensive not to long after the warmest and holiest affections of life."

"Suppose all that you please in that respect," replied the Marquis, "and then understand that the choice of the mother of my children is the most important affair of my life. Well, then, this great transaction, this sacred choice, do you think any one else could attend to it in my place? Do you admit that even my excellent mother can wake up some morning and say, 'There is in society a young lady, whose name is illustrious and whose fortune is large, and who is to be the wife of my son, because my friends and I consider the match advantageous and proper? My son does not know her, but no matter! Perhaps she will not please him at all; perhaps he will displease her as much; no matter again! It would please my eldest son, my friend the duchess, and all those who frequent my little drawing-room. My son must be unnatural if he does not sacrifice his repugnance to this fancy. And if Mlle de Xaintrailles should think of such a thing as not calling him perfect, she will be no longer worthy of the name she bears!' You see plainly, my friend, that all this is absurd, and I am astonished that you have taken it seriously for one moment."

Caroline struggled in vain against the inexpressible joy which this assurance caused her; but she quickly remembered all the Duke had said, and all that duty required her to say herself.

"You astonish me too," rejoined she. "Did you not promise your mother and your brother to see Mlle de Xaintrailles at the appointed time?"

"And so I shall see her this evening; it is an interview arranged in such a way as to appear accidental, and one which does not bind me in ny respect."

"That is an evasion which I cannot admit in a conscience like that of the Marquis de Villemer. You have passed your word that you will do your best toward recognizing the merit of this person, and making her appreciate yours."

"O, I ask nothing better than to do my best in that direction," replied the Marquis, with so merry and winning a laugh that Caroline was dazzled by the look he fixed upon her.

"Then you are making light of your mother's wishes?" resumed she, arming herself with all her reserve of resistance; "I never would have believed you capable of that."

"No, no, I am not, indeed," replied M. de Villemer, recovering his seriousness. "When they exacted this promise from me I did not laugh,

I assure you. I was in deep sorrow and seriously ill; I felt myself dying, and I thought my heart was already dead. I yielded to tender and cruel persuasions, in the hope that they would let me die in peace; but I have been recalled, my friend; I have taken a new lease of life; I feel myself full of youth again, and of the future. Love is astir within me, like the sap in this great tree; yes, love,—that is, faith, strength, a sense of my immortal being, which I must account for to God, and not to human prejudice. I will be happy in my own way; I will live, and I will not marry unless I can love with my whole soul!

"Do not tell me," continued he, without giving Caroline time to reply, "that I have other duties in opposition to this. I am not a weak, irresolute man. I am not satisfied with words consecrated by usage, and I do not propose to become the slave and the victim of ambitious chimeras. My mother desires to recover our wealth! She is at fault in that. Her true happiness and her true glory are in having renounced it all to save her eldest son. She is richer now—since I have arranged for her support at the price of nearly all I have left—than she was ten years ago, submitting with terror to a doubtful situation, and one which she believed must grow worse. See, then, if I have not done for her all that I could do! I have certain strong opinions, the fruit of the study and thought of my whole life. I have held them in silence. I have suffered terribly from griefs which she has never suspected. I have been in real torture from my own heart, and I have spared her the pain of seeing my agony. I have even suffered at her hands and have never complained. Have I not seen, from childhood, that she had an irresistible preference for my brother, and did I not know, besides, that she thought this due to the oldest and most highly titled of her sons? I have conquered the vexation of this wound, and when my brother at last permitted me to love him, I did love him devotedly; but before that time how many secret affronts and bitter jests I have brooked from him, and from my mother too, in league with him against the seriousness of my thought and life! I bore them no ill-will for this; I understood their mistakes and prejudices; but without knowing it, they did me much harm.

"In the midst of so many vexations, only one thing could tempt a solitary man like me,—the glory of letters. I felt within me a certain fire, an impulse towards the beautiful, which might draw around me manifold sympathies. I saw that this glory would wound my mother in her beliefs, and I determined to keep the most strict incognito, that the paternity of my work might not even be suspected. You alone, you only

　　　　　　　　　　　　GEORGE SAND

in the whole world, have been intrusted with a secret which is never to be disclosed. I will not add, during my mother's lifetime, for I have a horror of these mental reservations, these parricidal schemes, which seem like calling death down upon those whom we ought to love better than ourselves. I have said 'never' in this matter, so as never to entertain the idea of any state of things in which a personal gratification could lessen my grief at losing my mother."

"Very well! in all this, I like you as much as I admire you," replied Mlle de Saint-Geneix; "but it strikes me, that with respect to your marriage, it can all be arranged as it ought, with due regard to your own wishes and to those of your family. Since they say that Mlle de Xaintrailles is entirely worthy of you, why, at the moment of assuring yourself of this, do you say beforehand that it is neither possible nor probable! This is where I do not comprehend you at all, and where I doubt if you have any serious or respectable reasons that I could be brought to accept."

Caroline spoke with a decision which at once changed the resolution of the Marquis. He was on the point of opening his heart to her at all hazards; he had felt himself guided onward by a glimmer of hope, of which she had now deprived him, and he became sad, and seemingly quite overcome.

"Well, you see," resumed she, "you can find no answer to this."

"You are not wrong," said he; "I had no right to tell you that I should certainly be indifferent to Mlle de Xaintrailles. I know it myself; but you cannot be a judge of the secret reasons that give me this certainty. Let us say no more about her. I expect you to be thoroughly convinced of my independence and clear conscience in this matter. I would not have a thought like this remaining in your mind, M. de Villemer is to marry for money, for position, and for a name. O my friend, never believe that of me, I beg of you. To fall so low in your esteem would be a punishment which I have not merited through any fault, by any wrong against you or against my family. I expect, likewise, that you will not reproach me, if I should happen to find myself obliged openly to oppose my mother's wishes with regard to my marriage. I have felt it my duty to tell you all that justifies me in a pretended eccentricity. Be so good as to absolve me beforehand if, sooner or later, I have to show her and my brother that I will give them my blood, my life, my last franc and even my honor, if need be, but not my moral freedom, not my truth to myself. No, never! These are my own, these are the only possessions I reserve, for they come from God, and man has no claim upon them."

As he spoke thus, the Marquis laid his hand upon his heart with a forcible pressure. His face, at once energetic and charming, expressed his enthusiastic faith. Caroline, bewildered, was afraid of having understood aright and yet equally afraid lest she might have deceived herself; but what mattered that which, thus against her will, passed in her mind? She must pretend not to suppose that the Marquis could ever think of her. She had great courage and invincible pride. She answered that it was not for her to decide upon the future: but that, for her own part, she had loved her father so much that she would have sacrificed her own heart even, if, by a complete renunciation of herself, she could have prolonged his life. "Take care," said she with spirit, "whatever you may decide upon to-day or afterward, always remember this; that when beloved parents are no more, all that we might have done to render their lives longer or happier will come before us with terrible eloquence. The slightest short-coming then assumes enormous proportions; and there will never be a moment of peace or happiness for one who, even while using all his rightful freedom, gains the memory of having seriously grieved a mother who is no more."

The Marquis pressed Caroline's hand silently and convulsively; she had hurt him deeply, for she had spoken the truth.

She rose, and he conducted her to the carriage again. "Be content," said he, breaking the silence as he was about leaving her. "I will never openly wound my mother. Pray for me, that I may have eloquence to convince her when the time comes. If I do not succeed—Well, what is that to you? It will be so much the worse for me."

He flung the address to the coachman and disappeared.

XVII

It was no longer possible for Caroline to feel a doubt of the sentiment she had inspired. To avoid responding to it, she had but one line of defence, which was to act either as if she had never suspected it, or as if she did not suppose the Marquis would dare to speak of it a second time to her, even indirectly. She resolved to discourage him so completely that he would never recur to the subject, and not to remain alone with him long enough for him to lose his natural timidity under the impulse of increasing emotion.

When she had thus marked out her course of conduct, she hoped to be at peace; but, after all, she had to give way to natural feelings, and sob as if her heart would break. She wisely yielded to this grief, saying to herself, that, since it must be so, it was better for her to suffer from a momentary weakness than to struggle against herself too much. She well knew that in a direct contest our instinctive self-love awakes, in spite of us, and leads us to seek some side issue, some compromise with the austerity of duty or destiny. She refused, then, to dream or reflect; it was better for her to hide her head and weep.

She did not see M. de Villemer again until evening, just as the ordinary visitors of the family were taking leave; he came in with the Duke, both of them in evening dress. They had just returned from the residence of the Duchess de Dunières.

Caroline would have retired immediately. The Marchioness detained her, saying, "O, so much the worse, my dear, you will have to sit up a little later this evening. It's worth while though; we are going to hear what has happened."

Before long the explanation was forthcoming. The Duke had an undefined look as of astonishment; but the countenance of the Marquis was open and calm. "Mother," said he, "I have seen Mlle de Xaintrailles. She is beautiful, amiable, full of attractions; I can't imagine any sentiments which she might not inspire in the man who has the good fortune to please her; but I have had no such good fortune. She would n't look at me twice,—so entirely did the first glance suffice for her to pass judgment on me."

And as the Marchioness was silent in utter consternation, the Marquis took her hands, adding, as he kissed them, "But this need n't affect you the least in the world. On the contrary, I have come back full of dreams and plans and hopes. There is in the air—O, I felt it at once—quite another marriage than this, and one which will give you infinitely more pleasure!"

Caroline felt herself dying and reviving by turns at every word she heard; but she also knew the eyes of the Duke were fastened upon her, and she said to herself that perhaps the Marquis was stealthily watching her, between each of his phrases. So she kept her countenance. It was plain that she had wept; but her sister's departure might be the only cause. She had acknowledged it, and the Marquis had himself witnessed her tears on that occasion.

"Come, my son," said the Marchioness, "don't keep me in suspense, and if you are talking seriously—"

"No, no," said the Duke, mincing gracefully, "it is n't serious."

"But, indeed, it is," cried Urbain, who was unusually gay; "it's on the programme for the most plausible and delightful thing in the world!"

"It's singular enough, at least—and spicy enough," rejoined the Duke.

"Come now, do stop your riddles," cried the Marchioness.

"Well, let us have it," said the Duke to his brother with a smile.

"I propose to do that; I ask nothing better," replied the Marquis; "it's quite a story, and I must proceed with it in order. Imagine, my dear mamma, our arrival at the Duchess's, both as fine as you see us now,— no, finer still, for there was on our faces that air of conquest which suits my brother so well, and which I attempted for the first time, but with no success at all, as you shall see."

"That means," rejoined the Duke, "that you had an air of prodigious abstraction, and began operations by looking at a portrait of Anne of Austria, lately placed in the drawing-room of the Duchess, instead of looking at Mlle de Xaintrailles."

"Ah!" said the Marchioness, sighing, "it was very lovely then, this portrait?"

"Very lovely," replied Urbain. "You will say it was no time for me to be noticing this; but you are going to see how fortunate it was, after all, that it happened. Mlle Diana was seated by the corner of the mantel; with Mlle de Dunières and two or three other young ladies of haughty ancestry more or less English. While my distracted eyes are hanging upon the plump countenance of our late queen, Gaëtan, thinking me close at his heels, goes directly, in his capacity of elder brother, to salute first the Duchess, then her daughter and the whole juvenile group, singling out at once, with an eagle eye, the beautiful

Diana, whom he had n't seen since she was five years old. Having promenaded his bewitching smile into this privileged corner, and traversed the other groups with that meek and triumphant elegance which belongs to him alone, he returns to me, just as I am beginning my evolution toward the Duchess, and says in an angry tone though in a low voice, 'Come on! what are you about there?' I dart forward, I salute the Duchess in my turn, I try to look at my betrothed; she had her back turned to me squarely. An evil omen! I retreat to the mantel-piece, in order to display all my advantages. The Duchess addresses some conversation to me, charitably bent on giving me a chance to shine. And I—why, I was ready to talk like a book; but it was all for nothing; Mlle de Xaintrailles never looked at me and listened still less; she was whispering to her young companions. At last she turns round and darts at me a glance full of wonder and most decidedly cool. I am introduced to her neighbor, Mlle de Dunières, a young girl slightly deformed, but brilliant intellectually it seemed to me, and who was very evidently nudging her friend with her elbow; but all in vain, and I return to my rostrum, that is, to the mantel-piece, without having called up the faintest blush. I do not lose my self-possession, but, resuming conversation with the Duke, I go on making some very judicious remarks about the session of the Chambers, when, all at once, I hear the music of charming bursts of laughter, poorly suppressed, from the young ladies in the corner. Probably they found me stupid. I am not confounded, however; I continue; and after having properly shown the fluency of my elocution, I inquire about the historical portrait, to the great satisfaction of the Duke de Dunières, who thinks of nothing but having his picture appreciated. While he is leading me toward it to examine it and admire the beauty of its execution, my brother quietly takes my place and on my return I find him installed between the arm-chair of the Duchess and that of her daughter, close by Mlle Diana, in the midst of the group, joining in the chat of the young ladies."

"Is this true, my son?" asked the Marchioness of the Duke, with anxiety.

"It is quite true," replied the Duke, ingenuously. "I laid siege to the fortress; I took a position. I expected Urbain to manœuvre so as to come to my support; but no, the traitor leaves me alone exposed to the fire, and you see I have to get off as I can. What took place meanwhile? He is going to tell you."

"Alas! I know more than enough," said the Marchioness, in despair; "he was thinking of something else."

"Pardon me, mamma," replied the Marquis, "I had no wish to do so and no time either, for the Duchess, leaving Gaëtan engaged with the young ladies, took me aside, and, laughing in spite of herself, said these memorable words, which I report *verbatim*: 'My dear Marquis, what has taken place here this evening is like a scene in a comedy. Just imagine to yourself that the young person—whom it is useless to name—takes you for your brother, and consequently persists in taking your brother for you. We tell her she is mistaken, but all in vain; she will have it that we are deceiving her, that she is not to be taken in so—and—must I tell you the whole?'

"'Yes, certainly, Madame de Dunières; you are too much my mother's friend to let me sail on a false course!'

"'Yes, yes, that's it! I ought not to leave you on the wrong track, I should be really distressed at that, and you must know at once how matters stand. They find the Duke charming, and you—'

"'And me absurd? Come! be frank clear to the end.'

"'You! You are not thought of at all, you are not seen, you are nothing, no one is heard but the Duke! If I did n't know you were very fond of your brother, I should never tell you this—'

"I reassured the Duchess so earnestly, I expressed so much joy over the idea that my brother was preferred to me, that she replied, 'Well done! why, here we are in a romance! When it is known the Duke is the one who pleases, don't you expect a great outcry?'

"'Why, who will make it? You, Madame de Dunières?'

"'Perhaps so, but it's certain *she* will! Well, now, all this must be explained. Come with me and see what is going on; we cannot part on the strength of a *quid pro quo.*'

"'No, no,' I said to the Duchess, 'you must listen to me first. Here I have a cause to plead which is a hundred times dearer than my own. You have said something that alarms me, at which I feel a real concern, and I beg you will take it back. You seem disposed to decide against my brother in case your amiable god-daughter should pardon him for not being the Marquis. As I am sure, now, that she will pardon him without difficulty, if she has not done so already, I want to understand your objections to him, in order to do battle against them. My brother has, on his father's side, a descent far more illustrious than my own; he has all the traits of a true gentleman, and all the attractions of an agreeable man; as for me, I am not a man of the world, and, if I must avow all, I have some tendency toward being a liberal.'

"The Duchess made a gesture of horror; then she began to laugh, thinking I was in jest."

"Knowing you were in jest, my son!" interposed the Marchioness, in a tone of reproach.

"Good or poor," rejoined the Marquis, "the joke had no ill effect. The Duchess let me set off my brother's merits, agreed with me that a man of rank, who has never forfeited his honor, has a right to ruin himself financially, that a life of pleasure has always been well received in high circles, when there is wisdom enough to leave it behind in season, to accept poverty nobly, and to show one's self superior to one's follies. Finally, I appealed to the friendship of the Duchess for you, to the desire she had felt for an alliance with you on the part of her god-daughter, and I had the good fortune to be so persuasive that she promised not to influence the choice of Mlle de Xaintrailles."

"Ah! my son, what have you done?" cried the Marchioness, trembling. "I recognize your good heart in it all, but it is a dream! A girl brought up in a convent will certainly be afraid of a conquering hero like this vain fellow. She would never dare to trust him."

"Stop, mother," resumed the Marquis, "I have n't finished my story. When we returned to the young ladies, Mile. Diana was calling my brother 'Your Grace,' as boldly as you please. She was talking and laughing with him, and I was allowed to aid him in shining before her. However, he had no great need of me. She drew him out brilliantly herself, and I found she was n't sorry to show us in her replies that she was quite witty, and that mirth suited her excellently."

"The fact is," said the Duke, carried away by an irresistible infatuation, "she is bewitching, this little Diana, whom I have seen playing with her dolls! I reminded her of it, for I did n't wish to impose upon her as to my age—"

"And to this," continued the Marquis, "I added that you were fibbing to her, that it was I who had seen the doll, and that you were a child in the cradle then; but Mlle Diana would n't let me suppose that she saw in me the material for a Duke. 'No, no, monsieur, the Marquis,' said she, laughing, 'your brother here is thirty-six years old, I know all about it.' And this was said with a tone, with an air—"

"That drove me distracted, I admit it," said the Duke, rising and tossing his mother's spectacles up to the ceiling, catching them again adroitly; "but, see, all this is folly! Mlle Diana is an artless and adorable little coquette—a thorough school-girl, a little wild over her approaching entrance into society, preparing herself in the retirement of her family circle to keep all heads turned, until at last her own is turned also; but it's too soon now! To-morrow morning, after she has thought it over—And then they will tell her such naughty things about me!"

"To-morrow night you will see her again," said the Marquis, "so you can counteract the evil influences, if any such are near her, and I don't believe there will be. Don't make yourself more interesting than you really are, brother mine! Besides, the Duchess is on your side, and she did n't let you go without saying, '*Come again soon. We are at home every evening: we don't go into society till after Advent*,'—which means, in good plain French: 'There is still a whole month before my daughter and god-daughter will see the gay world. It is for you to please before they are intoxicated with dress and balls. We receive but few young people now, and it only remains for you to be the youngest, that is, the most eager and the most fortunate.'"

"Bless me, bless me!" said the Marchioness, "I feel myself in a dream. My poor Duke! And I never so much as thought of you. Why, I—I imagined you had won so many women that you would never find one simple enough, generous enough; wise enough, after all; for here you are, reformed, and I dare say you will make the Duchess d'Aléria perfectly happy."

"I can answer for that, mother," cried the Duke. "What has made me bad is suspicion, experience of coquettes and ambitious women; but a charming young girl, a child of sixteen, who is willing to trust me, ruined as I am—but I should become a child again myself! And you would be very happy too, would n't you? And you, Urbain, who were so afraid you would have to marry?"

"Has he taken a vow of celibacy, then?" asked the Marchioness, looking at the Marquis with tenderness.

"Not at all," replied Urbain, with some spirit, "but you see there has been no time lost, as my elder brother still makes such fine conquests! If you will give me a few months more for reflection—"

"Yes, yes, indeed! there is no real haste," rejoined the Marchioness; "and since we have such good fortune, I trust in the future—and in you, my excellent friend!"

She embraced her two sons, evidently intoxicated with joy and hope. She addressed her children in the most familiar and affectionate way,

GEORGE SAND

and also embraced Caroline, exclaiming, "You good pretty little blonde! you must rejoice too!"

Caroline had more disposition to rejoice than she cared to admit, even to herself. Overcome with fatigue after the excitement of the day, she slept delightfully; with the assurance that the crisis had been postponed, and that some time, at least, must elapse before she would see the final and irrevocable obstacle of marriage come between herself and M. de Villemer.

XVIII

The Marchioness slept little. Her impatience for the morrow almost stifled her. Want of sleep took away her spirits. She viewed everything on its dark side, and expected to find the whole a delusion; but when Caroline brought in her correspondence, there was a letter from the Duchess that transported her with joy. "My friend," said Madame de Dunières, "here is a change of scene like those at the opera. It is the case of your eldest son that demands attention. I talked with Diana when she awoke this morning. I did not asperse the Duke, but my religion obliged me not to hide from her any of the truth. She replied that I had said all this before, in speaking of the Marquis, that I had nothing to tell her which she had not already considered, and that on mature reflection, she had become equally interested in the two brothers, whose friendship was such a beautiful thing, and that, in thinking over the position of the Duke, she had found it more meritorious to have borne the burden of gratitude nobly than to have rendered a service exacted by duty." She added that, "Since I had counselled her to bestow happiness and wealth on some worthy man, she felt herself drawn toward him who pleased her best. In fine, the irresistible graces of your good-for-nothing son have done the rest. And then I must not be mistaken about Diana. She judges that the title of Duchess will suit her queenly figure best: she is inclined to be fond of society; and when, not long ago, some one, I know not who, told her that the Marquis did not like it at all, I saw she was uneasy, though I did not know the reason. Now she has confessed all. She has said to me that as a brother the Marquis would be all she could desire, but that as a husband the Duke would show her the gayest life. In short, my dear, she seems so determined that I have only to serve you all I can in this unforeseen contingency as I should have done in the other case.

"I will bring my daughter to you to-morrow morning, and as Diana will be with us, you can see her without appearing to suspect anything; but you will succeed in charming her completely, I am very sure."

While the Marchioness and the Duke were giving themselves up to their happiness, Caroline was left a little more alone; for the son and the mother held long conversations every day in which her presence was naturally undesired, and during which she practised music or wrote her own letters in the drawing-room, always deserted until five o'clock.

There she disturbed no one, and held herself in readiness to answer the least summons of the Marchioness.

One day the Marquis came in with a book, and seating himself at the same table where she was writing, with an air strangely calm and resolved, asked her permission to work in this room, where it was easier to breathe than in his little chamber. "That is, on condition," said he, "that I don't drive you away, for I see quite clearly that you have avoided me for some days past; don't deny it!" added he, seeing she was about to reply. "You have reasons for this which I respect, but which are not well grounded. In speaking of myself as I ventured to do at the Jardin des Plantes I startled the delicacy of your conscience. You thought I was going to make you my confidante in some personal project likely to disturb the peace of my family, and you were unwilling to become even a passive accomplice in my rebellion."

"Exactly so," replied Caroline, "you have divined my feeling perfectly."

"Now let my words become as if they had never been said," continued Urbain, calmly and with a firmness that commanded, respect; "I will not tell you to forget them, but do not dwell on them in any way, I beg, and never fear my bringing your attachment for my mother into collision with the generous friendship you have deigned to accord me."

Caroline felt constrained to yield to the power of this frankness. She did not comprehend all that was passing through the mind of the Marquis, all that was suppressed behind his words. She thought she must have been mistaken, that she had felt too much alarm at a fancy he had already conquered. In her own mind she accepted her friend's promise as a formal reparation for having caused her a moment of troubled thought, and thenceforth she found anew the full charm and security of friendship.

They saw each other, then, every day, and even sometimes for long hours together, in the drawing-room, almost under the eyes of the Marchioness, who rejoiced to see that Caroline continued to aid the Marquis in his labors. In fact, she assisted him now only with her memory: having arranged his documents in the country, he wrote his third and last volume with admirable swiftness and readiness. Caroline's presence gave him enthusiasm and inspiration. By her side, he no longer suffered from doubt or weariness. She had become so indispensable to him that he confessed his lack of interest in anything when alone. He was pleased to have her talk to him even in the midst of his work. Far from disturbing him this dearly loved voice preserved the harmony of his thought and the elevation of his style. He challenged her to disturb him, he begged her to read music at the piano, without fear of causing him the least annoyance. On the contrary, all that made him sensible of her presence fell on his soul like a pleasant warmth; for she was to him, not another person moving about near him, but his own mind which he could see and feel alive before him.

Her respect for his work, over which she was enthusiastic, bound Caroline to a certain respect for him personally. She made it a sacred duty, as it were, not, in any way, to disturb the balance needful to a mind so finely organized. She refused to think of herself any longer. She no longer asked herself whether she was not running some risk on her own score, or whether, at a given time, she would be strong enough to give up this intimacy which was becoming the groundwork of her own life.

The matrimonial alliance between the Duke d'Aléria and Mlle de Xaintrailles progressed with encouraging rapidity. The beautiful Diana was seriously in love and would not hear a word against Gaëtan. The Duchess de Dunières, having herself made a love-match with a veteran lady-killer, who had reformed on the strength of it and now rendered her perfectly happy, took the part of her god-daughter, and pleaded her cause so well that her guardians and the legal advisers of the family had to give way before the known will of the heiress.

The latter told her betrothed, even before he had expressed any wish to this effect, that she intended to pay off his indebtedness to the Marquis, and the Marquis had to accept the promise of a reparation which this high-minded young girl made one condition of the marriage. All the Marquis could obtain was that they should not restore to him the share in his mother's property which he had resigned when Madame de Villemer had been obliged to pay the debts of her eldest son for the first time. According to the Marquis, his mother had a right to dispose of her own fortune during her lifetime; and he regarded himself as entirely indemnified since the Marchioness was to live henceforth at the Hôtel de Xaintrailles and in the castles of her daughter-in-law, far more splendid than the little manor of Séval and much nearer Paris, thus living no longer at his expense.

In these family arrangements all parties showed the most exquisite delicacy and the most honorable generosity. Caroline directed the attention of the Marquis to this fact in order to make him insist, in his book, upon certain just reservations in favor of families where the true idea of nobility still served as the basis of real virtues.

In fact, here each one did his duty: Mlle de Xaintrailles would have no marriage-contract which, in protecting her fortune from her husband's lavish expenditures, should contain any clauses likely to wound his pride; while the Duke, on the other hand, insisted that the right of dowry should bind the wings of his magnificent improvidence. So it was specified with considerable flourish in the document that this stipulation was introduced at the request of the future bridegroom, and in compliance with his express wishes.

Everything being thus settled, the Marchioness found herself a sharer in a most generous style of living; and although she had declared herself satisfied with a simple promise and willing to rely on the discretion of her children, a very handsome income had been secured to her by the same contract in which the future bride had done so many other liberal and considerate things; the Marquis, on his side, became repossessed of capital enough to represent an ample competence. It is needless to state that he took the recovery of this fortune as calmly as he had borne the loss of it.

While the outfit of the bride was preparing, the Duke busied himself about his presents for her, the funds for their purchase having been forced upon his acceptance by his brother, as a wedding gift. What an affair it was for the Duke to choose diamonds and laces and cashmeres! He understood the lofty science of the toilet better than the most accomplished woman. He hardly found time to eat, passing his days in waiting upon his betrothed, consulting jewellers, merchants, and embroiderers, and telling his mother, who was equally excited over it all, the thousand incidents and even the surprising dramas connected with his marvellous acquisitions. Into the midst of all this heavy fire, in which Caroline and Urbain took only a modest share, Madame d'Arglade glided, as if in her own despite.

A great event had overturned Léonie's way of life and all her plans. At the beginning of the winter, her husband, twenty years her senior and for some time past an invalid, had succumbed to a chronic disease, leaving his affairs complicated enough; though she came out of her embarrassments in triumphant style, thanks to a lucky stroke at the Bourse, for she had gambled in stocks a long time without the knowledge of M. d'Arglade, and had at last laid hands on a fortunate number in the great lottery. So she found herself a widow, still young and handsome, and richer than she had ever been before, all which did not hinder her shedding so many and such big tears that people said of her with admiration, "This poor little woman was really attached to her duty, in spite of her frivolous ways! Certainly M. d'Arglade was not a husband to go distracted over, but she has such a warm heart that she is inconsolable." And thus she was pitied, and many took pains to amuse her: the Marchioness, seriously interested, insisted that she should come and pass her solitary afternoons with her. Nothing was more proper; it was not going into company, for the Marchioness received no visitors until four or five o'clock; it was not even going out, for Léonie could come in a cab without much of a toilet, and as if incognito. Léonie allowed herself to be consoled and amused by watching the preparations for the wedding, and sometimes the Duke would succeed in making her laugh outright; which did very well, because, passing from one kind of nervous excitement to another, she would immediately begin to sob, hiding her face in her handkerchief and saying, "How cruel you are to make me laugh! It does me so much harm."

Through all her despair, Léonie was contriving to win the intimate confidence of the Marchioness so as insensibly to supplant Caroline, who did not perceive this, and was a thousand leagues from suspecting her designs. Now Léonie's main project was this:—

As she saw the health of her disagreeable husband becoming impaired and her own private purse filling out round, Madame d'Arglade asked herself what kind of a successor she should give him, and, as she had not yet been confidentially informed of the marriage already arranged with Mlle de Xaintrailles, she had resolved to confer the right to the vacant living upon the Duke d'Aléria. She thought him "ineligible," on the conditions of fortune united to youth and rank, and said to herself, not without logic and plausibility, that the widow of a respectable and wealthy gentleman, without children, was the best match to which a penniless prodigal, reduced to going on foot and reckoning up accounts with his body-servant, could possibly aspire. Léonie then had no doubt of her success, and while busying herself with much skill in the investment of her capital she said to herself in supreme calm, "Now all is finished, I have plenty of money, I will speculate no more, I will intrigue no more. My ambition, satiated in this direction, must change its object. I must efface the birth-mark of plebeianism, which still incommodes me in society. I must have a title. That of Duchess is well worth the trouble of some thought!"

She had indeed thought of it in time, but M. d'Arglade died too late. She had scarcely laid aside her first mourning crapes, when, on her earliest visit to the Marchioness, she learned that she must think of it no longer.

Léonie then turned her batteries on the Marquis de Villemer. This was less brilliant and more difficult, but still it was satisfactory as a title, and, from her point of view, not impossible. The Marchioness was extremely anxious about her son's bachelor state, the prospect of which as a permanency seemed to have new charms for him in his negligence. She opened her heart to Madame d'Arglade. "He really frightens me," said she, "with his tranquil air. I fear he may have some prejudice—I know not what—against marriage, perhaps against women in general. He is more than timid, he is unsociable, and yet he is charming when you succeed in winning him into familiarity. He needs to meet some woman who will fall in love with him herself first, and then have courage enough to make him love her in return."

Léonie profited by these revelations. "Ah! yes," replied she, giddily, "he needs a wife of higher position than mine, one who is not the widow of the best of men; but somebody who would still have my age, my wealth, and my disposition."

"Your disposition is too impulsive for a man so reserved, my darling."

"And that is why a person of my character would save him. You know about extremes. If I could love any one, which now, alas! is totally impossible, I should certainly fancy a man who is serious and cold. Dear me! Alas! was not that the temperament of my poor husband? Well, his gravity tempered my vivacity, and my liveliness let sunshine into his melancholy. That was his way of putting it, and how often he would mention it! He had never been in love before he met me, and he also had precisely this distaste for marriage. The first time he saw me, he was a little afraid of my frivolity; but all at once he saw that I was necessary to his life, because this apparent thoughtlessness, which you know does n't hinder one from having a good heart, passed into his soul like a light, like a balm. These were his very words, poor dear man! There! stop! let us not talk about people who marry. It makes me feel too keenly that I am alone forever!"

Léonie found means to touch upon the subject so often and under so many different forms, with so much tact under an air of innocence, with so many civilities clothed in apparent indifference, that the idea entered the mind of the Marchioness almost without her being conscious of it, and when Madame d'Arglade saw she was not disposed to reject it absolutely in the proper time and place, she began a direct attack on M.

de Villemer with the same cunning, the same charming heedlessness, the same silence of conjugal despair, the same frank insinuations, bringing about the whole and carrying it on before the eyes of Caroline, about whom she did not trouble herself at all.

But the chatter of Madame d'Arglade was disagreeable to the Marquis; and, if she had never found this out, it was only because she had never provoked him into taking any notice of her whatever. Far from being the inexperienced savage he was supposed to be, he had a very fine tact with regard to women; so, at the first assault which Léonie made, he understood her designs, perceived all her intrigues, and made her feel this so thoroughly that she was wounded to the very heart.

From that time she opened her eyes, and, in a thousand delicate indications detected the boundless love Mlle de Saint-Geneix had inspired in the Marquis. She rejoiced over this greatly: she thought it was in her power to revenge herself, and she waited for the right moment.

The marriage of the Duke was appointed for one of the first days of January; but there were so many outcries in certain rigid drawing-rooms of the Faubourg Saint-Germain against the readiness with which the Duchess de Dunières had welcomed the suit of this great sinner, that she determined to avoid the reproach of undue precipitation by delaying the happiness of the young pair for three months, and introducing her god-daughter into society. This postponement did not alarm the Duke, but vexed the Marchioness exceedingly, for she was eager to open a really grand drawing-room, on her own responsibility, with a charming daughter-in-law, who would attract young faces around her. Madame d'Arglade, under pretext of business, became less assiduous in her visits, and Caroline resumed her duties.

She was much less impatient than the Marchioness to live at the Hôtel de Xaintrailles and to change her habits. The Marquis had not decided to accept an apartment at his brother's, and did not explain his own personal plans. Caroline was alarmed at this, and yet she saw, in his indifference to being under the same roof with her, one proof of the calm regard she had exacted from him; but she had now reached that stage of affection when logic is often found at fault in the depths of the heart. She silently enjoyed her last happy days, and when spring came, for the first time in her life, she regretted winter.

Mlle de Xaintrailles had taken Mlle de Saint-Geneix into high favor, and even into a close friendship; while, on the contrary, she felt a decided dislike for Madame d'Arglade, whom she met occasionally of a morning at the house of her future mother-in-law, where she herself made no formal visits, but only came with Madame and Mlle de Dunières at hours when none but intimate friends were received. Léonie pretended not to see this slight haughtiness in the beautiful Diana. She thought she had a hold on her happiness also, and that she could revenge herself upon her and upon Caroline at one and the same time.

She was not invited to the wedding festivities; her mourning, of course, preventing her appearance there. However, from regard to the Marchioness, toward whom Diana showed herself really perfect, a few brief words of regret, as to this deprivation, were said to her. That was all. Caroline, on the other hand, was chosen as a bridesmaid, and loaded with gifts, by the future Duchess d'Aléria.

At last the great day arrived, and for the first time, after many years of sorrow and misery, Mlle de Saint-Geneix, dressed in elegant taste, and even with a certain richness, through the gifts of the bride, appeared in all the splendor of her beauty and grace. She created a lively sensation, and every one inquired where this delightful unknown could have come from. Diana replied, "She is a friend of mine, a very superior person who is under the care of my mother-in-law, and whom I am delighted to see established so near me."

The Marquis danced with the bride and also with Mlle de Dunières, in order that he might afterwards dance with Mlle de Saint-Geneix. Caroline was so astonished at this that she could not help saying to him in a low voice, and with a smile, "How is this? After having stood by each other through the establishment of allodial rule and the enfranchisement of the lower classes, now we are going to dance a contra-dance!"

"Yes," he replied, quickly, "and this will go much better, for I shall feel your hand in mine."

It was the first time the Marquis had openly shown Caroline an emotion in which the senses had any part. Now she was sensible of his trembling hand and his eager eyes. She was frightened; but reminded herself that he had seemed to be in love with her once before and had triumphed over the ill-advised thought. With a man so pure and of such high morality ought she to feel afraid, even if he did forget himself for an instant! And besides, had she not herself experienced this vague intoxication of love even when her will was strong enough to subdue it at once! She could not help being aware of her own extraordinary beauty, for every eye told her of it. She eclipsed the bride herself in her diamonds, with her seventeen years, and her fine smile of fond triumph. The dowagers said to the Duchess de Dunières, "That poor orphan you have there is too pretty: it is disquieting!" The sons of the Duchess herself, young men of dignity and great promise, looked at Mlle de Saint-Geneix in a way that justified the apprehensions of these experienced matrons. The Duke, touched by seeing that his generous wife had not thought of harboring the slightest jealous suspicion, and also appreciating Caroline's considerate attitude toward him, showed her especial attention. The Marchioness, not to spoil this delightful day, made a point of treating her more maternally than ever, and of dispelling every shadow of servitude. In short, she was in one of those moments of life, when, in spite of fortune's caprices, the power which intelligence, honor, and beauty naturally exert seem to reclaim its rights and to reconquer its place in the world.

But if Caroline read her triumph on all faces, it was especially in the eyes of M. de Villemer that she could assure herself of it. She also noticed how this mysterious man had altered since that first day when he had appeared so timid, so self-absorbed, as if obstinately bent on remaining in obscurity. He was now as elegant in his manners as his elder brother, with more true grace and real distinction; for the Duke, in spite of his great knowledge of demeanor, had a little of that bearing, a shade too fine and slightly theatrical, which is characteristic of the Spanish race. The Marquis was of the French type in all its unaffected ease, in all its amiable kindliness, in that particular charm which does not impress but wins. He danced, that is, he walked through the contradance more simply than any one else; but the purity of his life had imparted to his motions, his countenance, his whole being, a perfume, as one might say, of extraordinary youth. He seemed, this evening, to be ten years younger than his brother, and a certain indescribable glow of hope gave his face the brightness of a beautiful life just commencing.

XIX

At midnight, the newly married couple having discreetly disappeared, the Marchioness signified to her son that she was tired and would like to withdraw. "Give me your arm, dear child," said she, when he came to her side; "let us not disturb Caroline, who is dancing; I will leave her under the protection of Madame de D——."

And as the Marquis was helping her through the corridor leading to her own room on the lower floor,—they had been considerate enough to humor her distrust of staircases, "My dear son," she said, "you will no longer have the trouble of carrying on your arm your poor little bundle of a mother. You did it very often when you were with us at the other house, and with you I did not seem afraid; but it pained me to give you the trouble."

"And I—I shall regret that lost pleasure," said Urbain.

"How elegant and aristocratic this reception is!" resumed the Marchioness, having at last reached her apartment; "and this Caroline who is its queen! I am astonished at the beauty and grace the little creature has."

"Mother," said the Marquis, "are you really very tired just now? and if I should ask fifteen minutes' conversation with you—"

"Let us talk, my son, by all means!" cried the Marchioness. "I was tired only because I could not talk with those I love. And then I was afraid of seeming ridiculous, in case I said too much about my happiness. Let us speak of it, let us speak of your brother, and of yourself as well! Come, will you not bring a second day like this into my life?"

"Dear mother," said the Marquis, kneeling before her and taking both her hands in his, "it depends upon you alone whether I, too, shall soon have my day of supreme joy."

"Ah! what do you say? Truly? Tell me quickly then!"

"Yes, I will speak. This is the moment I was waiting for; I have held myself in reserve, and turned all my longings toward this blessed hour, when my brother, reconciled to God, to truth, and to himself, could take a wife worthy to be your daughter. And when such a moment came I intended to say this: Mother, I also can present you with a second daughter, more lovely than the first and no less pure. For a year, for more than a year, I have devotedly loved a most perfect being. She has suspected this perhaps, but she does not know it; I have so much respect and esteem for her that without your consent I well knew I should never gain her own. Besides, she gave me to understand this sharply one day, one single day, when my secret came near escaping me in spite of myself, four months ago, and I have since kept strict silence in her presence and in yours. It was my duty not to plunge you into anxieties which, thank God! no longer exist. Your fate, my brother's, and my own are henceforth secure. Now, comfortably rich, I may properly refuse to enlarge my fortune, and I can marry according to my inclinations. You have a sacrifice to make for me nevertheless; but your motherly love will not refuse, for it involves the happiness of my whole life. This lady belongs to an honorable family; you made sure of this yourself before you admitted her to intimacy with you; but she does not belong to one of those ancient and illustrious lines, for which you have a preference that I do not mean to oppose. I said you would have to make a sacrifice for me; will you do it? Do you love me enough? Yes, mother, yes, your heart, which I can feel beating, will yield without regret, in its vast maternal tenderness, to the prayer of a son who worships you."

"Ah, bless me! you are speaking of Caroline," cried the Marchioness, trembling. "Stop, stop, my son! The shock is rude, and I was not prepared for it."

"O, do not say that!" resumed the Marquis, warmly; "if the shock is too rude, I do not want you to bear it. I will give it all up; I will never marry—"

"Never marry! Why, that would be worse still! Come, come, do let me know where I am! It is, perhaps, easier to bear than it seems. It is not so much her birth. Her father was knighted: that's nothing very great; but if that was really all! There is this poverty which has fallen upon her. You may tell me that but for you I should have fallen into it myself; but I should have died, while she—she has courage to work for a living, and to accept a kind of domestic service—"

"Heavens!" cried the Marquis, "would you make a blemish of what is the crowning merit of her life?"

"No, no, not I," returned the Marchioness, eagerly, "quite the contrary; but the world is so—"

"So unjust and so blind!"

"That is true too, and I was wrong to let it influence me. Come! we are in the midst of love-matches, so I have only one more objection to make. Caroline is twenty-five years old—"

"And I am now over thirty-four myself."

"It is not that. She is young enough, if her heart is as pure, as unsophisticated as your own; but she has been in love before."

"No. I know her whole life. I have conversed with her sister; she was to have married, but she has never really loved."

"Still, between this projected marriage and the time when she came to us some years must have elapsed—"

"I have inquired about this. I know her life day by day and almost hour by hour. If I tell you that Mlle de Saint-Geneix is worthy of you and of me, it is because I know it. A foolish passion has not blinded me. No, a serious love based upon reflection, upon comparison with all other women, upon certainty, has given me strength to keep silence and to wait, wishing to convince you on good grounds."

The Marquis talked with his mother some time longer, and he triumphed. He used all the eloquence of passion, and all that filial tenderness of which he had given so many proofs. His mother was touched and yielded.

"Well, now," cried the Marquis, "will you let me call her here on your behalf? Are you willing that, for the first time,—in your presence, at your feet,—I should tell her that I love her? See, I yet dare not tell her alone! One cold look, one word of distrust, would break my heart. Here, in your presence, I can speak, I will convince her."

"My son," said the Marchioness, "you have my promise. And you see," added she, taking him in her feeble arms, "if I have not given it with very impulsive joy, it is at least with tenderness unlimited and unalloyed. I ask, I exact one single thing; that is, that you will take twenty-four hours to reflect upon your position. It is new, for here you are in possession of my consent, which you thought more than doubtful an hour ago. Up to that time you believed yourself parted from Mlle de Saint-Geneix by obstacles that you did not think of overcoming so easily, perhaps, and this may have given illusive strength to your feelings for her. Don't shake your head! What do you know about it yourself? Besides, what I ask is a very little thing,—twenty-four hours without speaking to her, that is all. For myself, I feel the need of accepting completely before God the decision I have just reached; that my face, my agitation, my tears, may not lead Caroline to suspect that it has cost me something—"

"O yes, you are right," exclaimed the Marquis. "If she suspected that, she never would let me speak to her. To-morrow, then, dear mother. Twenty-four hours, did you say? It is very long! And then,—it is one o'clock in the morning. Will you be up again to-morrow night?"

"Yes, for we have a concert to-morrow at the apartments of the young Duchess. You see why we must sleep to-night. Are you going back to the ball-room?"

"Ah! please let me: she is there still, and she is so lovely with her white dress and the pearls. I have not looked at her enough, really. I did not dare—now only shall I truly see her."

"Well! make this sacrifice for me in your turn, not to look at her again,—not to speak to her before to-morrow evening. Promise me, as you have no idea of sleeping, to think of her, of me, and of yourself, all alone, for a few hours, and then again to-morrow morning. You are not to come here before dinner-time. You must not; promise me!"

The Marquis promised and kept his word; but the solitude, the darkness, the pain of not seeing Caroline, and of leaving her surrounded by the notice and homage of others, only increased his impatience, only fed the fire of his passion. Besides, his mother's precautions, although wise in themselves, were of no use to a man who had been reflecting and deciding so long.

Caroline was surprised not to see the Marquis reappear, and was one of the first to withdraw,—trying to persuade herself she had not been mistaken in thinking he would soon recover his self-control. She was, as will be seen, far from suspecting the truth.

Madame d'Arglade had her spies at this ball, and among others a man who desired to marry her, a secretary of legation, who, the next morning, reported to her the great success of the "young lady companion." The devotion of the Marquis had not escaped malevolent eyes, and the diplomatic apprentice had even scented out an interesting conversation between the Marquis and his mother, as they left the room together.

Léonie listened to this report with apparent indifference; but she said to herself it was time to act, and at noon she was inquiring for the Marchioness at the very moment Caroline appeared.

"One minute, my dear friend," said she to Mlle de Saint-Geneix, "let me go in before you do; it is an urgent matter,—a kindness to be done for some poor people who wish to remain unknown."

Once alone with the Marchioness, she apologized for coming to speak about the poor in these days of rejoicing. "They are, on the contrary, the days of the poor," replied the generous lady; "speak. One of my great joys now will be that I can do more good than I could awhile ago."

Léonie had her pretext all prepared. When she had presented her request, and put the Marchioness down on her subscription-list, she pretended that she was in haste to go, so as to be invited to stay a little while. It is useless to relate the skilful turns and tricks by which she maliciously contrived to reach the interesting point of the conversation. These mean-spirited attacks, unhappily too common, will be remembered by all those who have ever felt their cruel effects; and they are very few who have been forgotten by calumny.

They naturally spoke of Gaëtan's happiness and about the perfections of the young Duchess. "What I love most in her," said Léonie, "is that she isn't jealous of any one, not even of—Oh! beg pardon, the name was just going to escape me."

She returned to this subject several times, refusing to mention the name until the Marchioness began to grow uneasy. At last it did escape her, and the name was that of Caroline.

She hastened to take it back, to say her tongue had tripped; but in ten minutes the blow had been dealt by a sure hand, and the Marchioness had drawn from her a solemn asseveration that she had seen, with her own eyes seen, at Séval, the Duke conducting Caroline back to her room at daybreak, and holding both her hands in his, talking to her eagerly, for three good minutes, at the foot of the Renard stairway.

Upon this she made the Marchioness, whose word she knew was sacred, promise not to betray her, not to make her enemies,—because so far she had never had any; saying she was in despair at the persistence which had drawn this disclosure from her, that she would have done better to disobey the Marchioness outright, that at heart she really loved Caroline, and that, after all, since she had answered for her character, it was, perhaps, her duty to confess that she had been mistaken.

"Bah!" exclaimed the Marchioness thoroughly mistress of herself, "all this is not so serious. She may have been very good otherwise, and yet have been impressed by this irresistible Duke. He is so skilful! Have no fear. I am to know nothing of this, and I will act at the proper time and place, if need be, without its appearing at all."

When Caroline entered just as Léonie was going, the latter extended her hand with a good-natured air, telling her that the news of her triumph the evening before had reached her even, and that she offered her congratulations.

Caroline found the Marchioness so pale as to arouse her anxiety, and on asking the cause she received a very cool reply. "It is the fatigue of all this festivity," said the Marchioness; "it is nothing. Be so good as to read me my letters."

While Caroline was reading Madame de Villemer did not listen. She was thinking of what she was going to do. She was concealing deep indignation against the young girl, a violent grief at the blow she would have to inflict on the Marquis; and with this maternal sorrow mingled the involuntary satisfaction of a titled lady at being released from a promise which had cost her much, and to which, for twelve hours, she had not recurred without a shudder.

When she had reached her decision, she interrupted the reading harshly, saying, in an icy tone, "That is enough, Mlle de Saint-Geneix. I want to speak with you seriously. One of my sons, I need not say which, seems lately to have entertained sentiments for you which you surely have not encouraged?"

Caroline turned as pale as the Marchioness; but, strong in her own conscience, she replied without hesitation, "I am ignorant of what you assert, Madame. Neither of your sons has ever expressed to me any sentiments at which I could be seriously alarmed."

The Marchioness took this reply for an audacious falsehood. She flung at the poor girl one contemptuous look, and for a moment was silent; then she resumed, "I shall not speak of the Duke; it is entirely useless to defend yourself on this point."

"I have no complaint to make of him or of his brother," replied Caroline.

"I suppose not!" said the Marchioness, with a withering smile; "but as for me, I should have good cause for complaint if you had the presumption—"

Caroline interrupted the Marchioness with a violence she could not control. "I have shown no presumption," cried she, "and no one in the world has a right to speak to me as if I were to blame, or even ridiculous—Pardon, Madame," added she, seeing the Marchioness almost frightened by her excitement; "I have interrupted you. I have spoken rudely. Forgive me. I love you,—I love you so that I would give you my life willingly. You see why your suspicion hurts me so that I lose my temper. But I ought to control myself; I will control myself! I see there is some misunderstanding between us. Be so good as to explain—or question me. I will answer with all the calmness in my power."

"My dear Caroline," said the Marchioness, more gently, "I do not question you. I warn you. It is not my intention to condemn you or sadden you with useless questions. You were mistress of your own heart—"

"No, Madame, I was not."

"Indeed! Very well, the truth comes out in spite of you," said the Marchioness, with a return of her ironical disdain.

"No, a hundred times no!" rejoined Caroline, indignantly. "That is not what I mean. Knowing that a thousand duties, some more serious than others, forbade me to dispose of it, I have given it to no one."

The Marchioness looked at Caroline with astonishment. "How well she understands lying!" thought Madame de Villemer. Then she said to herself that, so far as the Duke was concerned, this poor girl was not obliged to betray herself; that the feeling she had entertained for him ought to be regarded just as if it had never been, since, after all, she had made him no trouble and claimed no rights detrimental to his marriage.

This idea, which had but just occurred to her, suddenly mollified the rancor of the Marchioness; and when she saw her silence was wounding Caroline, whose eyes were full of scalding tears, she returned to her friendship for her, and even to a new kind of esteem.

"My dear little one," said she, extending her hands to her, "forgive me! I have hurt your feelings; I have explained myself wretchedly. Let us even admit I was unjust for a moment. In point of fact I understand you better than you think, and I appreciate your conduct. You are unselfish, prudent, generous, and wise. If you have chanced—to think more of certain attentions than was for your own happiness, it is none the less certain you have always stood ready to make sacrifices on occasion, and you would be ready to do the same again; it is so, is it not?"

Caroline did not comprehend, and could not comprehend that in all this there was an allusion to Gaëtan's marriage. She thought only his brother's case was called in question; and as she had never relaxed her self-control for a moment, she felt as if the Marchioness had no right to pry into the painful secrets of her heart. "I have never had any sacrifice to make," replied she, haughtily. "If you have orders for me give them, Madame, and do not think it any merit on my part to obey you."

"You mean to say, and you do say, my dear, that you have never responded to the sentiments of the Marquis?"

"I have never known them."

"You had never suspected them?"

"No, Madame; and I do not believe in them! Who could have made you suppose the contrary? Certainly not the Marquis himself."

"Well, pardon me, but it was he. You see what confidence I have in you. I tell you the truth. I trust to your generosity without hesitation. My son loves you and thinks he may have won your love in return."

"Monsieur the Marquis is strangely mistaken," replied Caroline, wounded by an avowal which, presented thus, was almost an offence.

"Ah! you are telling the truth now, I see that," cried the Marchioness, deceived by the pride of Mlle de Saint-Geneix; and wishing to control her by means of her self-respect, the old lady kissed her on the forehead. "Thank you, my dear child," said she, "you restore me to life. You are sincere; you are too noble to punish my doubts by trifling with my peace. Very well; now let me tell my son Urbain that he has been only dreaming, that this marriage is impossible, not through my opposition, but through yours."

This imprudent request enlightened Caroline. She understood the admirable delicacy which had led the Marquis to consult his mother before declaring his feelings to her; but she was not deluded by this discovery, for she saw how much the Marchioness disliked the idea of their marriage. She attributed this severity to the ambition of Madame de Villemer, which she had known perfectly and feared for a long time. She was very far from thinking that, after having yielded the point with a good grace, the Marchioness was now withdrawing her consent because she believed in the stain of a fault. "Madame de Villemer," replied she, with a certain severity, "you are never wrong in the eyes of your son. I understand that; and I fear no reproaches from him, if, on my own part, I decline the honor he would do me. Over and above this you can tell him what you think best; I shall not be here to contradict you."

"What! do you want to leave me?" cried Madame de Villemer, alarmed at a conclusion which she did not expect so suddenly, although she had secretly desired it. "No, no, that is impossible! It would ruin everything. My son loves you with an earnestness,—whose future consequences I do not fear, if you will help me to contend against them, but whose violence at the first moment I do fear. Stop! He would follow you, perhaps; he is eloquent, he would triumph over your resistance, he would bring you back, and I should be forced to tell him—what I never want to tell him."

"You will never have to say 'No' to him!" replied Caroline, still under a delusion, and nowise suspecting this menace of her pretended misconduct hanging over her head; "it is I who should tell him, is it not? Well then I will write to him, and my letter shall pass through your hands."

"But his grief—his anger, perhaps—have you thought of that?"

"Madame, let me go away!" replied Caroline, desperately, for the thought of this grief touched her heart. "I did not come here to suffer in this way. I was brought here without even being told that you had sons. Let me leave you without trouble as well as without blame. I will never see M. de Villemer again; this is all I can promise. If he should follow me—"

"Do not doubt that he will! For Heaven's sake, speak lower! What if any one should hear you! In case he should follow you, what would you do?"

"I shall go where he cannot follow me. Permit me to arrange this according to my own judgment. In an hour I will return to take leave of you, Madame de Villemer."

XX

M lle de Saint-Geneix went out with such energetic resolution
that Madame de Villemer dared not say another word to detain
her. She saw that Caroline was irritated and hurt. She blamed herself
for having made it too evident that "she knew all," while the poor
woman actually knew nothing, for she did not perceive Caroline's real
affection.

So far was she from this that she tried to persuade herself Caroline
had always loved the Duke, that she had sacrificed herself to his
happiness, or that, perhaps, like a practical girl, she was counting upon
the return of his friendship after the honeymoon of his marriage. "In
the latter case," thought the Marchioness, "it would be dangerous to let
her remain in the house. Some time or other it would bring unhappiness
into my young household; but it is too soon to have her go away—and
so abruptly: the Marquis would be almost insane. She will grow calm,
lay her plans, and whenever she returns with them I will persuade her
to accommodate herself to mine."

For an hour, then, the Marchioness was engaged upon her own
plans. She would see her son again that evening, as had been agreed,
and would tell him that she had sounded Caroline's inclinations, and
found her very cold toward him. For several days she would avoid
the decisive explanation. She would gain time, she would induce
Caroline herself to discourage him, but gently and with prudence.
In a word she was planning to control the fates, when she saw the
hour had passed and Caroline had failed to come. She inquired
for her. She was told that Mlle de Saint-Geneix had gone away
in a hackney-coach with a very small bundle, leaving behind the
following letter:—

Madame de Villemer

"I have just received the sad news that one of my sister's
children is seriously ill. Pardon me for hastening to her at
once without having asked your leave; you have visitors.
Besides, I know how kind you are; you will surely give me
twenty-four hours. I shall be back by to-morrow evening.
Receive the assurance of my tender and profound regard.

Caroline

"Well now, that is admirable!" said the Marchioness to herself after a moment of surprise and fright. "She enters into my ideas; she has enabled me to win the first evening, the hardest of all certainly. By promising to come back to-morrow night she keeps my son from rushing away to Étampes. To-morrow probably she will have a new pretext for not returning—But I would rather not know what she means to do. I shall then be sure that the Marquis will never get the truth from me."

Nevertheless, the evening came too soon for her comfort. Her fears increased as she saw the hour approaching when they would have to dine together.

If Caroline had really fled a little farther than Étampes, it was necessary to gain time. She then decided upon telling an untruth. She never spoke to her son until they were just seating themselves at table, contriving to keep herself surrounded by others. It was a great dinner, very ceremonious; but unable to bear the anxious gaze which he fastened upon her, before taking her seat she said to the young Duchess, in such a way as to be overheard by the Marquis, "Mlle de Saint-Geneix will not come to dinner. She has a little niece ill at the convent, and has asked leave to go and see her."

Immediately after dinner the Marquis, tortured with anxiety, tried to speak to his mother. She avoided him again; but, seeing him preparing to go out, she made signs for him to come near and whispered to him: "She has n't gone to the convent, but to Étampes."

"Then why did n't you tell us so awhile ago?"

"I was mistaken. I had scarcely read the note, which was just given me this evening. It is not the little girl who is mentioned, but another of the children; however, she will return to-morrow morning. Come! there is nothing alarming in this. Be careful, my son, your bewildered face astonishes every one. There are ill-disposed persons everywhere: what if some one should happen to think and say that you were envious of your brother's happiness! It is known that at first it was you—"

"Ah! mother, that is the very thing! You are keeping something from me. It is Caroline who is ill. She is here, I am sure of it. Let me inquire on your behalf—"

"Do you want to compromise her, then? That would be no way to prepossess her in your favor."

"She is not well disposed toward me, then? Mother, you have spoken to her."

"No, I have n't seen her; she went away this morning."

"You said the note came this evening."

"I received it—some time, I can't tell when; but these questions are not very amiable, my son. Pray be calm; we are observed."

The poor mother did not know how to tell a lie. Her son's anguish pierced her to the heart. She struggled for an hour against the sight. Every time he approached a door, she followed him with a glance which plainly told of her fear that he would go: their eyes would meet, and the Marquis would remain, as if held by his mother's anxiety. She could not bear this long. She was broken down by the fatigue of the emotions she had endured for twenty-four hours; by the excitement of the festivity which, for several days, she had been trying to enliven with all her cleverness; and above all, by the violent effort she had made since dinner, to appear calm. She had herself conducted back to her own apartment, and there fainted in the arms of the Marquis, who had followed her.

Urbain lavished the most tender care on his mother, reproaching himself a thousand times for having agitated her; assuring her that he was composed, that he would not ask another question until she had recovered. He watched over her the whole night. The next day, finding her perfectly well, he ventured upon a few timid questions. She showed him Caroline's note, and he waited patiently until evening. The evening brought a fresh note, dated at Étampes. The child was better, but still so poorly that Madame Heudebert desired to keep Caroline twenty-four hours longer.

The Marquis promised to be patient for twenty-four hours more; but the next day, deceiving his mother with the pretence of going to ride with his brother and sister, he set out for Étampes.

There he learned that Caroline had really been with her sister, but had just set out again for Paris. They must have passed each other on the way. It occurred to the Marquis that on his arrival, which was evidently anticipated, one of the children was kept out of sight, and silence enjoined upon the others. He inquired after the little invalid, and asked to see him. Camille replied that he was asleep and she was afraid to wake him. M. de Villemer dared not urge the matter, and returned to Paris seriously doubting Madame Heudebert's sincerity, and wholly unable to explain her embarrassed and absent-minded ways.

He hastened to his mother's; but Caroline had not made her reappearance; she was perhaps at the convent. He went there to wait for her before the iron grate, and at the close of an hour he made up his mind to ask for her in the name of Madame de Villemer. He was told that she had not been seen there for the last five days. He returned a second time to the Hôtel de Xaintrailles; he awaited the evening; his mother still seemed ill, and he controlled himself. But on the morrow his courage finally broke down, and he sobbed at her feet, begging her to restore Caroline, whom he still believed hidden in the convent by her orders.

Madame de Villemer really knew nothing further about it. She began to share her son's uneasiness. However, Caroline had taken with her only a very small bundle of clothing; she could have had but little money, for she was in the habit of sending it all, as soon as she received it, to her family. She had left her jewels and her books behind; so she could not be very far off.

While the Marquis was returning to the convent with a letter from his mother, who, overcome by his grief, was now really anxious to have him find Caroline again,—the young lady, wrapped up and veiled to her chin, was alighting from a diligence just arrived from Brioude, and, carrying her own bundle, was making her way alone along the picturesque boulevard of the town of Le Puy in Velay, toward the station of another little stage-coach, which was just then setting out for Issingeaux.

No one saw her face or thought of troubling himself to do so. She asked no questions, and seemed thoroughly acquainted with the country, its customs, and its localities.

Nevertheless, she was there for the first time; but, resolute, active, and cautious, she had before leaving Paris bought a guide-book, with a plan of the town and the surrounding country, which she had carefully studied on the way. She then got into the diligence for Issingeaux, telling the driver she would stop at Brives, that is, at about a league from Le Puy. There she alighted at the bridge of the Loire, and disappeared, without asking her way of any one. She knew she had to follow the Loire until it met the Gâgne; then, directing her course toward the Red Rock, again follow the bed of the torrent flowing at its foot until she reached the first village. There could be no possible mistake. There were about three leagues to be traversed on foot in a wilderness, and it was midnight; but the road was smooth, and the moon came out clearly in a beautiful half-globe from among the great white clouds, driven back to the horizon by the winds of May.

Where, then, was Mlle de Saint-Geneix going in this fashion, in the depths of the night and the wilds of the mountain, through a bewildering country? Has it been forgotten that she had here, in the village of Lantriac, devoted friends and the safest of all retreats? Her nurse, the good-wife Peyraque, formerly Justine Lanion, had written her a second letter, about six weeks before, and Caroline, remembering with certainty that she had never mentioned to the Marquis or to any one of the family these letters, or these people, or this country, had accepted the stern suggestion of going there for a month or so, thus making sure that all traces of herself would be entirely lost. Thence arose her precautions against being recognized on the way, and against exciting chance curiosity by asking questions.

She had gone to Étampes to embrace her sister, and, after having told her all and intrusted her with all, except the secret feelings which disturbed her, she had burned her ships behind her by leaving a letter which, at the end of the week, was to be forwarded to Madame de Villemer. In this letter she announced that she had gone abroad, pretending to have found employment there, and begging that no anxiety should be felt on her account.

Cumbered with her bundle, she was planning to leave it at the first house where she could effect an entrance, when she became aware of a train of ox-teams coming behind her. She waited for it. A family of teamsters, young and old, with a woman holding a child asleep under her cape, were transporting some great hewn logs,—intended to serve as carpenters' timber,—by means of a pair of solid little wheels, bound with ropes to each end of the log. There were six of these logs, each drawn by a yoke of oxen with a driver walking beside them. It was a caravan, which occupied a long space on the road.

"Providence," thought Caroline, "always helps those who rely upon it. Here are carriages to choose from if I am weary."

She spoke to the first teamster. He shook his head: he understood only the dialect of the country. The second stopped, made her repeat her words, then shrugged his shoulders and resumed his walk: he understood no better than the first. A third made signs for her to address his wife, who was seated on one of the logs, her feet supported by a rope. Caroline asked her, as she walked along, if they were going in the direction of Laussonne. She did not wish to mention the name of Lantriac, which was nearer, on the same road. The woman replied in French of very harsh accent, that they were going to Laussonne, and that it was "far off,—yes, indeed!"

"Will you let me fasten my bundle to one of these logs?"

The woman shook her head.

"Is this a refusal?" returned Caroline. "I do not ask it for nothing; I will pay you."

The same response came. In Caroline's speech the mountaineer had understood only the name of Laussonne.

Caroline knew nothing of the dialect of the Cévennes. It had formed no part of the early education she had received from her nurse. The music of Justine's accent, however, had lingered in her memory, and she caught at the bright idea of imitating it, which she succeeded in doing so well that the ears of the peasant woman opened at once. She understood French measured out in this way, and even spoke it herself quite readily.

"Sit down there, behind, on the next log," said she, "and give your bundle to my husband. Come! we ask nothing for this, my daughter."

Caroline thanked her and took a seat upon the log. The peasant made her a stirrup like that which held up the feet of his wife, and the rustic procession went on its way but slightly delayed by the ceremony. The husband, who walked close at hand, made no attempt to talk. The Cévenol is grave, and if he is ever curious, he will not deign to let the fact appear. He contents himself with listening afterward to the comments of the women, who ask information boldly; but the logs were long, and Caroline was too far from the female mountaineer to be in danger of any cross-questioning.

She thus passed at no great distance the Red Rock, which she mistook at first for an enormous ruined tower; but she recalled the stories of Justine about this curiosity of her country, and recognized the strange dike, the indestructible volcanic monument, through whose pale shadow cast by the moon she was now journeying.

The narrow, winding road rose above the torrent little by little, growing so contracted that Caroline was frightened to see her feet hanging in space over these awful depths. The wheels cut down into the earth soaked by the rains on the extreme edge of the dizzy slope; but the little oxen never swerved in the least; the driver kept on singing, standing a little way off when he could find no comfortable place near his log, and the nurse had a fashion of swaying back and forth that seemed to mask a vain struggle with sleep.

"Bless me!" cried Caroline to the husband, "have you no fear for your wife and child?"

He understood the gesture, if not the words, and called out to his wife not to drop the little one, then launched forth anew in a dismal air, which resembled a religious chant.

Caroline soon became used to the dizziness; she would not be tempted into turning her back to the precipice, as the peasant motioned for her to do. The country was so fine and so strange, the splendor of the moon made it look so terrible, that she was unwilling to lose anything of the novel spectacle. In the angles of the ascent, when the oxen had turned the fore wheels, and the log still held the hind wheels to their former course until they threatened to go over the brink, the astonished traveller unconsciously stiffened herself up a little on her stirrup of rope. Then the driver would speak to his oxen in a calm and gentle tone, and his voice, which seemed to adapt their docile steps to the least unevenness of the ground, reassured Caroline as if it had been the voice of a mysterious spirit shaping her destiny.

"And yet why should I be afraid?" she asked herself. "Why should I cling to a life which will be henceforth full of dread?—to a succession of days which in prospect are a hundred times more frightful than death! If I fell into this chasm, I should be instantly crushed. And even if I suffered an hour or two before my death, what would that be compared with the years of sorrow, loneliness, and perhaps despair, which await me!"

We see that Caroline at last had owned to her love and her grief. Their full extent she had not yet measured, and, as she thought about that instinctive love of life which had just made her shudder, bold as she was by nature, she tried to persuade herself that it was a presentiment,—a celestial promise of speedy relief. "Who knows! Perhaps I shall forget sooner than I think. Have I any right to wish for death! Can I even afford to give way to grief, and waste my strength! Can my sister and her children do without me? Do I want them to live on the charity of those who have driven me away? Must I not soon go to work again, and, in order to work, shall I not be obliged to forget everything that is not work?"

And then she was troubled even by her own courage. "What," she said to herself again,—"what if this were only a snare of hope!" Some of M. de Villemer's words came back to her, and certain phrases in his book that showed a wonderful amount of energy, penetration, and perseverance. Would such a man give up a plan he was bent upon, allowing himself to be deceived by stratagem, and would he not have in its highest power that divining sense which is a part of love!

"I have acted to no purpose; he will find me again, if he tries to find me. It is useless for me to have come here, though I am a hundred and fifty leagues off, and though it seems impossible for any one to think of my being here rather than elsewhere; for he will have that gift of second sight, if he loves me with all his strength. So it would be childish to run away and hide, if this were the whole of my defensive resistance. My heart must take up arms against him, and at any moment, no matter when, I must stand ready to face him, and say to him, 'Suffer in vain or die if need be; I do not love you!'"

As she said this, Caroline was seized by a sudden impulse to lean forward, quit the stirrup, and let herself fall into the abyss. At last, fatigue overcame her excitement; the road, which still led upward, was not so steep, and had turned away from the cleft of the ravine, leaving all danger behind. Their slow progress, the monotonous swaying of the log, and the regular grinding of the yokes against the pole, had a quieting effect upon her. She watched the rocks as they passed slowly before her, under their fantastic lights, and the tree-tops, whose budding leafage resembled transparent clouds. It became quite cold as they rose above the valleys, and the keen air was benumbing. The torrent vanished into the depths, but its strong, fresh voice filled the night with wild harmonies. Caroline felt her eyelids growing heavy. Judging it could not be far from Lantriac, and not wanting to be carried to Laussonne, she jumped to the ground and walked on to rouse herself.

She knew Lantriac was in a mountain gorge and that she would be very near it when she had lost sight of the torrent of the Gâgne. At the end of a half-hour's walk, in fact, she saw the outlines of houses above the rocks, reclaimed her bundle, made the peasant take some money, though not without difficulty, evaded the curiosity of his wife, and stayed behind to let them pass through the village, exposed to the barking of the dogs and disturbing the rest of the villagers whom she hoped to find sound asleep again on her own arrival.

But nothing disturbs the sleep of the dwellers in a Velay hamlet, and nothing awakens their dogs. The procession of timber went along; the teamsters still singing, the wheels rumbling heavily over the blocks of lava which, under pretext of paving the streets, in these inhospitable villages, form a system of defence far more impassably sure than the perilous roads by which you arrive.

Caroline, noticing the deep silence which followed upon the noise of the wheels, ventured resolutely into the narrow and almost perpendicular street which was supposed to continue the highway. Here her knowledge of the place came to a sudden stop. Justine had never described the position of her house. The traveller, wishing to glide in quietly and arrange with the family to keep her incognito, resolved to avoid knocking anywhere or waking any one, and to wait for day, which could not be long in dawning. She laid her bundle down beside her on a wooden bench, and took her seat under the pent-house of the first cottage she came to. She gazed at the queer fantastic picture made by the roofs, brought into uneven and hard relief against the white clouds of the sky. The moon passed into the narrow zone left open between the neighboring pent-houses. The basin of a little fountain caught the clear moonlight in full, and a quarter of its circle sparkled under the fall of a slender spray of water from the rock. The peaceful aspect and continuous measured sound of this silvery water soon lulled our exhausted traveller to sleep.

"Here is certainly a change within three days," said she to herself, placing her bundle so as to make it a rest for her weary head. "Only last Thursday, nevertheless, Mlle de Saint-Geneix, in a dress of tulle, her neck and arms loaded with rare pearls, and her hair full of camellias, was dancing with the Marquis de Villemer, under the light of countless tapers, in one of the richest of Parisian drawing-rooms. What would M. de Villemer say now if he could see this pretended queen of the ball-room, wrapped in coarse woollen, lying at the door of a shed, her feet almost in the flowing water and her hands stiff with the cold? Happily the moon is beautiful,—and here it is striking two o'clock! Well, there is an hour more to be spent here, and since sleep will come whether or no, why, then, let it be welcome."

XXI

At daybreak Mlle de Saint-Geneix was awakened by the hens clucking and scratching around her. She rose and walked on, looking at the doors of the houses as they opened one by one, and saying to herself with reason that in a hamlet so small and stowed so close among the rocks, she could not stray far without finding the face she sought.

But here a difficulty presented itself. Was she sure of recognizing this nurse, whom she had never seen since she was ten years old? She had Justine's voice and accent in her memory far more clearly than her face. She followed the ups and downs of the road as far as the last house behind the rock, and there she saw written on the door "Peyraque Lanion." A horseshoe nailed over this sign indicated his occupation of farrier.

Justine had risen first, as was her custom, while the closed calico curtains of the bed shaded the last nap of M. Peyraque. The principal apartment on this ground-floor showed the comfort of a well-to-do household, and the mark of this easy competence consisted particularly in the garniture of the ceiling; which was trellised with racks of monumental supplies of vegetables and divers rural commodities; but the strict cleanliness, a rare deviation from the customs of the country, removed everything which might offend the eye or the sense of smell.

Justine was lighting her fire, and preparing to make the soup her husband was to find smoking hot on his awakening, when she saw Mlle de Saint-Geneix come in with her hood on, carrying her bundle. She cast a look of perplexity upon the stranger, and said at last, "What have you to sell?"

Caroline, hearing Peyraque snore behind his curtain, put her finger to her lips and threw her hood back on her shoulders. Justine stood still an instant, suppressed a cry of joy, and opened her stout arms with rapture. She had recognized her child. "Come, come!" said she, leading her toward a little break-neck staircase at the farther end of the entry, "your room is all ready. We have been hoping for you every day this year." And she called to her husband, "Get up, Peyraque, at once, and shut the door. Here is news, O, such good news!"

The little chamber, whitewashed and furnished in rustic fashion, was, like the lower room, of irreproachable neatness. The view was magnificent; and blossoming fruit-trees came up to the level of the window. "It is a paradise!" exclaimed Caroline to the good woman. "It only needs a little fire, which you are going to make for me. I am cold and hungry, but happy to see you and be with you. I must tell you something, first of all. I don't want it known here who I am. My reasons are good ones, and you shall know them; they will meet your approval. Let us begin by agreeing on our facts; you have lived at Brioude?"

"Yes; I was in service there before I was married."

"Brioude is a long way from here. Is there any one from that country in Lantriac?"

"No one; and strangers never come. There is no road except for ox-carts."

"I saw that myself. Then you can pass me off for some one you knew at Brioude?"

"Very easily,—the daughter of my old mistress."

"No; I'm not to be a young lady."

"But she was not a young lady; she was a little tradeswoman."

"That's it; but I must have an occupation."

"Wait a minute!—that's easy enough. Be a pedler of small wares, like the one I am speaking of."

"But then I shall have to sell something."

"I'll see to that. Besides, you are supposed to have made your rounds, and I shall have detained you here as a matter of friendship; for you are going to stay?"

"A month, at least."

"You must stay always. We will find you something to do, never fear. But, let's see; what shall be your name?"

"Charlette; you called me that when I was a little thing; so it will not give you any trouble. I am supposed to be a widow, and you must say 'thou' to me."

"Just as I used to. Good! it is agreed. But how will you dress, my dear Charlette?"

"Like this. You see it's not luxurious."

"It's not very rich, to be sure; though it will pass; but this lovely blond hair of yours will attract the eye; and a city bonnet will be a wonder."

"I thought of that; so I bought at Brioude one of the head-dresses worn there. I have it in my travelling-bag, and I'm going to don my costume at once for fear of a surprise."

"Then I'll go at once and get you some breakfast. You will eat with Peyraque, I take it?"

"And with you, I hope. To-morrow I mean to help you about the house and in the kitchen."

"O, you may pretend to do that! I don't want you to spoil those little hands I used to take such care of. Now I'm going to see if Peyraque is up, and let him know what has been agreed upon; then you must tell us why there is need of all this mystery."

While talking, Justine had kindled the wood already in the fireplace. She had filled the pitchers with pure cold water, which had trickled from the rock, coming through an earthen pipe to the toilet-table of her little chamber, and then down into the kitchen sink. This was an invention of Peyraque's, who prided himself oh having ideas of his own.

Half an hour afterward Caroline, whose simple attire marked no particular station, put up her fine hair under the little head-dress from Brioude, less scantily contrived, and more prettily curved than the round dish-cover—which, like it, is of black felt trimmed with velvet—worn by the women of Velay. It was all in vain; she was still charming in spite of the weariness that dimmed the large eyes "green like the sea," formerly so bepraised by the Marchioness.

The soup of rice and potatoes was quickly served in a small room where Peyraque at odd moments did a little carpenter-work. The good man thought this an unsuitable reception, and wanted to sweep away the shavings. "On the contrary," said his wife, spreading the chips and sawdust over the floor, "you don't understand at all! She will think it a pretty carpet. O you don't know her yet! She is a daughter of the good Providence, this one is!"

Caroline made acquaintance with Peyraque by embracing him. He was a man of about sixty years, still very robust though thin, of medium height, and plain-featured, like most of the mountaineers in this region; but that his austere and even stern countenance bore the stamp of integrity was evident at the first glance. His rare smile was remarkably genial. You saw in it real affection and sincerity, which were all the more unmistakable from the fact that they were never lavished demonstratively.

Justine also had rigid features, and a blunt way of speaking. She was a strong generous character. An earnest Roman Catholic, she respected the silence of her husband who was of Protestant descent, nominally converted indeed, but a free-thinker if there ever was one. Caroline knew these circumstances and was touched to see the delicate respect which this superior woman knew how to weave into her love for her husband. It must be remembered that Mlle de Saint-Geneix, the daughter of a very weak man, and the sister of an inefficient woman, owed the great courage she possessed first to her mother, who was of Cévenol parentage, and afterward to the ideas Justine had given her in early life. She perceived this very clearly when she found herself seated between this old couple whose precise language and notions caused her neither fear nor surprise. It seemed as if the milk of her mountain nurse had passed into her whole being, and as if she were there in the presence of types with which she had already been made familiar in some previous existence.

"My friends," said she, when Justine had brought her the cream of the dessert, while Peyraque washed down his soup with a draught of hot wine, followed up before long with a draught of black coffee, "I promised to tell you my story and here it is in few words. One of the sons of my old lady had some idea of marrying me."

"Ah, indeed! that might well be," said Justine.

"You are right, because our characters and ideas are alike. Any one ought to have foreseen that, and I myself first of all."

"And the mother, too!" said Peyraque.

"Well, no one seems to have thought of it; and the son surprised and even angered the mother when he told her he loved me."

"And you?" asked Justine.

"I—I—why he never told me of it at all; and, as I knew I was not noble enough or wealthy enough for him, I should never have allowed him to think of it."

"Yes, that's right!" returned Peyraque.

"And it's true!" added Justine.

"Then I saw I could not stay a day longer, and at the first angry word from the mother I went away without seeing the son again; but the son would have hurried after me if I had remained with my sister. The Marchioness wanted me to stay a little to have an explanation with him, to tell him I did not love him—"

"That is what ought to have been done, perhaps," said Peyraque.

Caroline was forcibly impressed by the austere logic of the peasant. "Yes, unquestionably," thought she, "my courage ought to have been pushed thus far."

And, as she still kept silence, the nurse, enlightened by the penetration of a loving heart, said to her husband, sharply, "Stop talking there, you! How you run on! How do you know she did n't love him, this poor child?"

"Ah! that, that is another thing," replied Peyraque, bowing his serious, thoughtful head, which now looked nobler for the sense of delicate pity expressed upon his face.

Caroline was touched in an unspeakable degree by the straightforwardness of this simple friendship, which with one word touched the sorest spot in her wound. What she had not had strength or confidence to tell her sister, she was impelled not to disguise from these hearts, so thoroughly true and so able to read her own. "Well, my friends, you are right," said she, taking their hands. "I should not perhaps have been able to lie to you, for, in spite of myself, I—I do love him!"

Hardly had she spoken the words, when she was seized with terror, and looked around as if Urbain might have been there to hear them; then she burst into tears at the thought that he never would hear them.

"Courage, my daughter, the Lord will aid you," exclaimed Peyraque, rising.

"And we will aid you, too," said Justine, embracing her. "We will hide you, we will love you, we will pray for you!"

She led her back to her room, undressed her, and made her lie down, with motherly care that she should be warm and not see the sun shining in too early on her bed. Then she went down to apprise her neighbors of the arrival from Brioude of a person named Charlette, to answer all their questions, mentioning her paleness and her beauty that these might not strike them too forcibly. She took pains to tell them also that the speech of Brioude was not at all like that of the mountains, so Charlette would be unable to talk with them. "Ah! the poor creature," replied the gossips. "She will find it very dull and tiresome with us!"

A week later, after having informed her sister, in the proper time and place, of her safe arrival, Caroline gave her some detailed account of her new mode of life. It must not be forgotten that, hiding her actual sorrow, she was trying to reassure her sister, and to divert her own thoughts by affecting an independence far from being so complete or so real as it seemed.

"You can form no idea of the care they take of me, these Peyraques. Justine is always the same noble woman, with a heart like an angel's, whom you know, and whom our father could not bear to see going away from us. So it is saying more than a little to declare that her husband is worthy of her. He has even more intelligence, although he is slower of comprehension; but what he does understand is as if engraved on marble without spot or blemish. I assure you I am not weary a single moment with them. I could be alone much more than I am, for my little room is free from all intrusion of servants, and I can dream without being disturbed; but I rarely feel the need of this: I am contented among these worthy people, I am conscious of being loved.

"They have, besides, something of intellectual life, like most of the people here. They inquire about things in the world without; and it is astonishing to find in a kind of blind alley, among such wild mountains, a peasantry with so many notions foreign to their own necessities and habits. Their children, their neighbors, and their friends impress me as active, intelligent, and honest, while Peyraque tells me it is the same in villages farther still from all civilization.

"As an offset to this, the dwellers in the little groups of cottages scattered over the mountain, those who are only peasants, shepherds, or laborers, live in an apathy beyond all comprehension. The other day I asked a woman the name of a river which formed a magnificent cascade not more than a hundred paces from her house. 'That is water,' she replied. 'But the water has a name, has n't it?' 'I will ask my husband; I don't know myself; we women always call all the rivers water.'

"The husband knew enough to tell me the names of the torrent and the cascade; but when I asked for those of the mountains on the horizon, he said he knew nothing about them, he had never been there. 'But you must have heard that those are the Cévennes?'

"'Perhaps so! The Mézenc and the Gerbier de Joncs [sheaf or stack of reeds] are over there, but I don't know which they are.'

"I pointed them out to him; they are easily recognized,—Mézenc, the loftiest of the peaks, and the Gerbier, an elegant cone, which holds in its crater reeds and swamp-grasses. Only, the good man would not even look. It was all precisely the same to him. He showed me the 'grottos of the ancient savages,' that is, a kind of Gallic or Celtic village hollowed out of the rock, with the same precautions that beasts of the wilderness use to conceal their dens; for you can examine this rock and follow it without discovering anything unusual unless you know the path which penetrates this labyrinth and its habitations. Ah, my dear Camille, am I not here a little like those 'ancient savages,' who, for fear of intrusion, hid themselves in caves and sought their peace in forgetfulness of the whole world?

"At all events, the inhabitants of La Roche impress me as being the direct descendants of those poor Celts, hidden in their rock, and, as it were, bound to it. I looked at the woman, with bare legs and dull eyes, who conducted us into the grottos, and asked myself whether three or four thousand years had really passed away since her ancestors took root in these stones.

"You see I go out, for prudence does not require the in-door life, which you feared for me. On the contrary, having nothing to read here, I feel the need of strolling about, and my movements surprise the good people of Lantriac much less than a mysterious retreat would do. I run no risk of meeting strangers. You saw me set out in clothing that would not attract attention in the least. Besides, I have a black felt hat, larger than those worn here, which shades my face quite nicely. In case of need, too, I can conceal it entirely under the brown hood I brought with me, which the capricious weather gives me an excuse for wearing in my walks. I am not just like the women of the country; but there is nothing in my appearance to create a sensation in the places where I go.

"Then, too, I have a pretext for going out, which accounts for everything. Justine has a little trade in small wares and gives me charge of a box whose contents I offer for sale, while Peyraque, who is a farrier, busies himself with visiting sick animals. This enables me to go into the houses and observe the manners and customs of the country. I sell but little, for the women are so absorbed in their lace-making that they never mend for their husbands, their children, or themselves. Here is the triumph of rags worn with pride. Their devotion to their one occupation is so passionate as to exclude all material well-being and all cleanliness even, as a profane superfluity. Avarice finds its account in this, and vanity also, for if Justine gave me jewelry to sell I should soon have customers more eager for that than for linen and shoes.

"They produce all those marvellous black and white laces, which you have seen Justine make at our house. It is wonderful to see, here among the mountains, this fairy-like work coming from the hands of these poor creatures, and the trifling sum they realize shocks the traveller. They would cheerfully give you for twenty sous what they ask twenty francs for in Paris, if they were allowed to trade with the consumer; but this is strictly forbidden. Under the pretext of having furnished silk, thread, and patterns, the dealer monopolizes and sets a price on their work. In vain you offer to supply the peasant-woman with materials and pay her well. The poor woman sighs, looks at the money, shakes her head, and replies that she will not risk losing the patronage of 'her master' in order to profit by the liberality of a person who will not employ her permanently, and whom she may possibly never see again. And then all these women are pious, or pretend to be so. Those who are sincere have sworn by the Virgin and the saints not to sell to individuals, and one is forced to honor their respect for a promise given. Those who make religion a regular profession (and I see there are more such than one would suppose) are conscious of being always under the hand and beneath the eye of the priests, nuns, monks, and seminarists, with whom this country is literally sown and covered even in the most uninhabitable places. The convents have the work done; and here, as elsewhere, under conditions of trade still more lucrative than those of the dealers. You can see, in the vestibules of the churches even, the women from the village in a sort of community, sitting in a circle, making their bobbins fly as they murmur litanies or chant offices in Latin; which does not, however, prevent them from gazing curiously at the passers-by and exchanging remarks, while they reply *ora pro nobis* to the gray, black, or blue sister who oversees the work and the psalmody.

"These women are generally kind and hospitable. Their children interest me, and when I find those who are ill, I am glad to be able to point out the more simple attentions that should be given them. There is either great ignorance or great indifference on this point. Maternity here is rather passionate than tender. It is as if they told you that children are created for the single purpose of learning how to suffer.

"Peyraque's business, as his services are much in demand, leads us into some almost inaccessible places on the mountain, giving me a chance to see the finest landscapes in the world, for this wonderful country is like a dream,—and my own life is a strange dream also, is it not?

"Our fashion of going in search of adventures is quite primitive. Peyraque has a little cart, which he is pleased to denominate a carriage, because it has an awning of canvas, which somewhat ambitiously pretends to shelter us. He harnesses to this vehicle now an intrepid little mule, and now a pony, spirited but gentle, all skin and bone like its owner, but like him, too, never flinching at anything. So, while Justine's eldest son, just returned from the regiment, where he has been shoeing artillery horses, continues his trade under the paternal roof, his father and I wander over hill and vale without regard to the weather. Justine pretends this does me so much good that I must stay with her 'always,'

GEORGE SAND

and vows she will find some way for me to earn our livelihood without humiliating myself to serve any great lady.

"Alas! I never felt humiliated so long as I knew I was loved; and then I loved so sincerely in return! Do you know it saddens me no longer to receive a blessing every morning from that poor old Marchioness, and not only so, but I am quite uneasy, alarmed about her even, as if I felt she could not live without me? God grant she may soon forget me, that my place may already have been filled by one less fatal than I to her peace. But will she be cared for, morally speaking, as I cared for her? Will her fanciful whims be understood, the dulness of her leisure hours charmed away, or her children spoken of as she loves to hear them spoken of? On my arrival here, I drank in the free air with long breaths; I gazed at this grand, rugged scenery which I had felt so strong a wish to know. I said to myself, 'Here I am then free! I shall go where I please; I will talk as little as I please; I shall no longer write the same letter ten times a day to ten different people; I shall not live in a hot-house; I shall not breathe the sharp perfumes of flowers distilled by chemical processes, or of plants half dead on the windowsills; I shall drink from the breeze hawthorn and wild thyme in their real fragrance.' Yes, I said all this to myself, and I could not rejoice. I saw my poor friend sad and lonely, perhaps weeping for having made me weep so much!

"But she chose this, and to all appearance, it was necessary. I have no right to blame her for a moment of unjust anger. The mother thought only of her son, and such a son well deserves all a mother's sacrifice. Perhaps she calls me hard and ungrateful for not falling in with her plans, and I often ask myself if I ought not to have fallen in with them; but I always answer that the end would not have been attained. The Marquis de V—— is not one of those men who can be sent off with a few commonplaces of cool disdain. Besides, you have no right to act thus toward one who, far from declaring his passion, has surrounded you with respect and delicate affection. In vain I seek some language, half cold, half tender, which I might have used in telling him that I hold his mother's happiness and his own equally sacred: I do not find in myself the requisite tact or skill. Either the real friendship I have for him would have deceived him as to my feelings, leading him to think I was sacrificing myself to a sense of duty, or my firmness would have offended him, as if I were parading a virtue whose aid he has never given me occasion to invoke. No, no! it could not be, it ought not to be.

"I have an impression that the Marchioness hinted that I might tell him I had an engagement, another love. For Heaven's sake, let her invent all she will now! Let her sacrifice my life and that which I hold still more sacred, if need be. I have left the field clear: but, for my own part, I could never have improvised a romance for the occasion. And would he have been duped by it?

"Camille, you will see him, you have doubtless already seen him again since that first visit, when you admitted it was hard for you to play your part. You say it made you very unhappy to see him; he was almost distracted—He is certainly calm now. He has so much moral strength, he will understand so well that I must never see him again? However, be on your guard! He is very keen. Tell him my nature is a cold one—no, not that; he would n't believe it. But speak of my invincible pride. That is true; yes, I am proud, I feel it! And if I were not, should I deserve his affection?

"Perhaps it would have been liked if I had become really unworthy of his regard,—not the mother; not she! no, never! She is too upright, too pious, too pure in heart; but the Duke, I mean. Now, I can recall a number of things which I did not understand, and they appear in a new light. The Duke is excellent; he worships his brother. I believe his wife, who is an angel, will purify his life and thoughts; but at Séval, when he told me to save his brother at any cost,—I think of it now, and I blush to think of it!

"Ah, that I might be allowed to disappear, that I might be allowed to forget all! For a year I believed myself calm, worthy, happy. One day, one hour has spoiled the whole. With one word, Madame de Villemer has poisoned all the memories I had hoped to carry away unsoiled,— memories which now I dare not dwell upon. In truth, Camille, you were right in saying, as you sometimes did, that one should not be too ingenuous, that I ventured out into life too quixotically. This will serve me as a lesson, and I will renounce friendship as well as love. I ask myself why I should not from this time onward break off all relations with a world so full of dangers and snares, why I should not accept my misery more bravely indeed than I have done. I could create some resources in this province even, remote as it is in point of civilization. I could not be a school-mistress, as Justine imagined last year; the clergy have usurped everything here, and the good sisters would not let me teach, even in Lantriac; but in a city I could find pupils, or I could become a book-keeper in some mercantile house.

"First of all, I must make sure of being forgotten there; but when this oblivion is complete, I must indeed take thought for our children, and I dwell upon this a little in advance. After all, be at ease. I will find something. I shall manage to conquer the malicious fates. I do not sleep, I cannot falter; you know this perfectly. You have enough to live on for two months more, and I need absolutely nothing here. Do not worry, let us always trust the good God, as you, for your part, must trust the sister who loves you."

XXII

Caroline had reason to be alarmed by the inquiries M. de Villemer was making at her sister's. He had already returned twice to Étampes, and, fully aware that delicacy forbade anything like a system of cross-questioning, he confined himself to watching the demeanor of Camille, and drawing his own inferences from her silent evasions. Thenceforth he might take it for granted that Madame Heudebert knew her sister's hiding-place and that Caroline's disappearance gave her no real uneasiness. Camille held in reserve the letter which said Caroline had found employment away from France, and did not produce it. She saw such anguish and distress in the features of the Marquis, which were already much changed, that she dared not inflict this last blow on the benefactor, the protector of her children. Besides Madame Heudebert did not share all Caroline's scruples or comprehend all her pride. She had not ventured to blame her, in this regard; but she herself would not have held it so great a crime to brave the displeasure of the Marchioness a little, and become her daughter-in-law notwithstanding. "Since the intentions of the Marquis were so serious," thought she, "and his mother loves him so that she dares not oppose him openly, and, finally, since he is of age and master of his own fortune, I don't see why Caroline could not have used her influence over the old lady, her powers of persuasion, and the evidence of her own worth, and so led her gently to admit the propriety of the marriage.—There! poor Caroline, with all her valiant devotedness, is too romantic, and will go away and kill herself in order to support us; while, with a little patient tact, she might be happy and make us all happy too."

Here is another common-sense opinion which may be set over against that of Peyraque and Justine. Of these two lines of reasoning the reader is free to adopt the one that he prefers; but the narrator must, of necessity, hold an opinion also, and he avows a little partiality for that of Caroline.

The Marquis perceived that Madame Heudebert made, now and then, some timid allusions to the state of things, and felt sure she knew the whole. He threw himself on her mercy a little more than he had done hitherto; and Camille, encouraged, asked him, with a sufficient want of tact, whether, in case the Marchioness proved inexorable, he was fully resolved to make Caroline an offer of his hand.

She seemed on the point of betraying her sister's secret, if the Marquis would pledge his word of honor.

The Marquis replied without hesitation: "If I was sure of being loved, if the happiness of Mlle de Saint-Geneix depended on my courage, I would contrive to do away with my mother's prejudices, at any cost; but you give me no encouragement. Only give me that, and you will see!"

"I give you encouragement!" exclaimed Camille, amazed and confused. She hesitated to reply. She had indeed divined Caroline's secret; but the latter had always guarded it proudly, not by falsehood, but by never allowing herself to be questioned, and Madame Heudebert had not the daring to inflict a severe wound on her sister's dignity, by taking it upon herself to compromise her. "That is something I am no wiser about than you," said she. "Caroline has a strong character,—one which I cannot always fathom."

"And this strength of hers is so great," said the Marquis, "that she would never accept my name without my mother's sincere benediction. This I know better even than you do. So tell me nothing; it is for me alone to act. I ask of you only one thing more, and that is to let me watch over you and your children until something new shall occur, and even— yes, I will venture to say it—I am haunted by the fear that Mlle da Saint-Geneix may find herself without resources, exposed to privations which it makes me shudder to think of. Spare me this dread. Let me leave you a sum which you can return, if there is no use for it, but which, in case of need, you will remit to her as coming from yourself.'

"O, that is quite impossible," replied Camille: "she would divine the source, and never forgive me for having taken it!"

"I see you are really afraid of her."

"Just as I am of all that commands respect."

"Then we feel alike," replied the Marquis as he took leave. "I am so thoroughly afraid of her that I dare not seek her any farther, and yet I must find her again or die."

Shortly afterward the Marquis drew an explanation from his mother, which was painful enough to both of them. Although he saw her suffering, sad, regretting Caroline a hundred times more than she admitted, and although he had resolved to await a more propitious moment for his inquiries, the explanation came, in his own despite and in despite of the Marchioness, through the fatality of circumstances. The anxiety of the situation was too intense; it could not be prolonged. Madame de Villemer confessed that she had conceived a sudden prejudice against the character of Mlle de Saint-Geneix, and that at the very moment of fulfilling her promise she had let Caroline feel the exceeding pain it caused her. Gradually, under the eager questioning of the Marquis, the conversation grew more animated, and Madame de Villemer, pushed to extremity, allowed the accusation against Caroline to escape her. The unfortunate girl had committed a fault pardonable in the eyes of the Marchioness when acting as her friend and guardian, but one which made it quite out of the question even to think of receiving her as a daughter.

Before this result of calumny the Marquis did not flinch one instant. "It is an infamous lie," he cried, beside himself,—"a base lie! And you could believe it? Then it must have been very artful and very audacious. Mother, you must tell me all, for I am not disposed to be taken in so myself."

"No, my son, I shall tell you no more," replied Madame de Villemer firmly; "and every word you add to those you have just uttered, I shall consider a breach of filial affection and respect."

So the Marchioness remained impenetrable; she had promised not to betray Léonie; and, besides, nothing in the world would tempt her to sow the seeds of discord between her two sons. The Duke had so often told her, in Urbain's presence, that he had never sought or obtained a single kind look from Caroline! This, in the opinion of the Marchioness, was a falsehood the Marquis would never pardon. She knew, now, that he had taken the Duke into his confidence, and that Gaëtan, touched by his grief, had persuaded his wife into taking measures for seeking Caroline in all the Parisian convents. "He does not speak," said the Marchioness to herself; "he will not dissuade his wife and brother from this folly, when he ought, at the very least, to have confessed the past to the Marquis, in order to cure him of it. It is too late now to risk such avowals. I cannot do it without leading my two sons to kill each other after having loved so warmly."

Meanwhile Caroline wrote her sister as follows:—

"You feel alarmed because I am in so uneven and rocky a region, and ask what can be fine enough to make one run the risk of being killed at every step. First of all, there is really no danger here for me under the guidance of this good Peyraque. The roads, that would be actually frightful, and, as I think, impassable for carriages like those with which we are familiar, are just large enough for the little carts of this region. Then, too, Peyraque is very prudent. When he cannot measure with his eye just precisely the space he needs, he has a method of ascertaining it, which made me laugh heartily the first time I saw him put it in practice. He trusts me with the reins, jumps to the ground himself, takes his whip, which has the exact size of his cart marked with a little notch on its stock, and, advancing a few paces on the road, he proceeds to measure the width of the passage between the rock and the precipice,—sometimes between one precipice on the right and another on the left. If the road has a centimetre more than is needful he comes back triumphant, and we go quickly by. If we have no such centimetre in which to disport ourselves, he makes me alight, while he leads the horse by the bridle, dragging on the carriage. When we find two little walls hemming in a foot-path, we place one wheel on either wall and the horse in the pathway. I assure you one soon becomes accustomed to all this, and already I think no more about it. The horses here have no vicious tricks, and are not inclined to shy; they know the danger as well as we, and accidents are no more frequent in this country than they are on the plains. I certainly exaggerated the danger of these jaunts in my first letters; it was from vanity, or a lingering fear, of which I am wholly cured now that I feel it was groundless.

"As to the beauty of Velay, I could never describe it for you. I did not dream there could be, here in the heart of France, a country so strange and so imposing. It is far more lovely than Auvergne, through which I passed on my way hither. The city of Le Puy is probably unique in point of location; it is perched upon masses of lava that seem to spring up from its very heart and form a part of its architecture. These lava pyramids are indeed the edifices of giants; but those which man has placed on their sides, and often on their summits, have certainly been inspired by the grandeur and wildness of the spot.

"The cathedral is admirable, in the Romanesque style, of the same color as the rocks, but slightly enlivened by the blue and white mosaics on the pediments of its façade. It is placed so as to seem colossal, for, to reach it, you must climb a mountain of dizzy steps. The interior is sublime in its elegant strength and solemn dimness. I never understood the terrors of the Middle Ages, or felt them, so to speak, as I did under these bare, black pillars, beneath these storm-laden domes. There was a furious tempest while I was there. The flashes sent their infernal lights across the splendid windows that strew the walls and pavements with jewels. The thunders seemed rolling forth from the sanctuary itself. It was Jehovah in all his wrath; but it gave me no alarm. The true God, whom we love to-day, has no menaces for the weak. I prayed there with a perfect faith, and felt it had done me good. As for these beautiful temples of the faith in ages both rude and stern, it is clear they are the expression of the one grand word, 'mystery,' whose veil it was forbidden to lift. If M. de Villemer had been there he would have said—

"But a course of history and religious philosophy is not to the point now. The ideas of M. de Villemer are no longer the book from which I may study the past or learn to anticipate the future.

"You see, thanks to good Peyraque and his desire to show me the marvels of Velay, thanks also to my impenetrable hood, I have ventured into the city and its suburbs. The city is everywhere picturesque; it is still a mediæval town, closely studded with churches and convents. The cathedral is flanked by a whole world of ancient structures, where, under mysterious arcades, and in the turns and twists of the rock they stand on, you can see cloisters, gardens, staircases, and mute shadows gliding by, hidden beneath veil and cassock. A strange silence reigns there, and a certain odor of the past, I know not what, which makes one shiver with fear, not of our God, the source of all confidence and spiritual freedom, but of everything that, in the name of God, breaks up forever the ties and duties of our common humanity. In our convent, I remember a religious life seemed cheerful; here, it is sombre enough to make one tremble.

"From the cathedral you must keep going down hill for an hour to reach the Faubourg d'Aiguilhe, where another monument rears its head, which is natural and historic, at one and the same time, and, indeed, the most curious thing in the world. It is a volcanic sugar-loaf three hundred feet in height, which you mount by a spiral stairway until you reach a Byzantine chapel, necessarily quite small, but charming, and built, it is said, on the site and from the fragments of a temple to Diana.

"A legend is current here, which struck me forcibly. A young girl, a Christian virgin, pursued by some miscreant, flung herself to escape him down from the top of the terrace; she arose at once; she was unharmed. The miracle was noised abroad. She was declared a saint. Pride grew strong in her heart; she promised to hurl herself down again, to show she was under the protection of angels; but this time Heaven deserted her, and she was crushed like a vain silly creature as she was.

"Pride! yes, God leaves the proud to themselves, and without him what can they do? But do not tell me that I am proud. No, it is not pride.

I have no desire to prove anything to any one. I ask to be forgotten, and that there should be no suffering on my account.

"There is near Le Puy, forming a part of its magnificent landscape, a village that also crowns one of those singular, isolated rocks, which break through the soil here at every step. It is called Espaly, and this rock also bears up the ruins of a feudal castle and of Celtic grottos. One of these caves is inhabited by two persons, aged and poor, whose squalid misery is heart-rending. This couple live here in the solid rock, with a single hole for chimney and window. At night they block up the door, in winter with straw; in summer, with the old woman's petticoat. A small, rude bed without coverlids or mattress, two stools, a little iron lamp, a spinning-wheel, and two or three earthen pots,—these are all the furniture.

"Nevertheless, only a few paces from them there is a vast and splendid house belonging to the Jesuits and named the Paradise. At the foot of the rock flows a brook which brings down precious stones in its sand. The old woman sold me for twenty sous a handful of garnets, sapphires, and jacinths, which I am keeping for Lili. The stones are too small to have any actual value, but there must be a precious deposit somewhere among these rocks. The Jesuit fathers will find it, perhaps; I don't expect to make the discovery myself, however; so I must think about procuring some work. Peyraque has an idea which he has enlarged upon for the last few days, and which was suggested to him by this very rock of Espaly; I will tell you how.

"While strolling about over this rock, I was taken with one of my sudden fancies for a little child, playing in the lap of a pretty woman from the village, who was strong and cheerful. This child, you see, I can compare with no one but our Charley, for inspiring affection. He does not look like Charley, but has the same demure playfulness, and the shy caresses which make one his willing slave. When I called upon Peyraque to admire him, remarking how clean he was kept, and that his mother made no lace, but seemed wholly taken up with him, as if she knew she had a treasure there, Peyraque at once replied, 'You have come nearer the truth than you thought. This child is a treasure for Dame Roqueberte. If you ask who he is, she will tell you it is the child of a sister she has in Clermont; but this is not true: the little one has been placed in her charge by a gentleman whom no one knows, who pays her for rearing it, who pays her, besides, for taking great care of it, as if it were the son of a prince. So you see this woman is well dressed and does not work. She was in easy circumstances before. Her husband has charge of the castle of Polignac, whose great tower, and in fact all the ruined portion, you can see over yonder, on a rock larger and loftier than that of Espaly; that is where she lives, and, if you meet her here, it is because now she has such fine chances for pleasure strolls. The real mother of the little one must be dead, for she has never been heard of; but the father comes to see it, leaves money, and stipulates that it shall not be allowed to want for anything.'

"You see, dear sister, this is a romance. That is partly what attracted me perhaps, since, according to your ideas, I am quite romantic. Certainly this little boy has something about him which captivates the imagination. He is not strong; they say when he first came here he had hardly life enough to breathe; but now he is quite blooming, and the mountain air agrees with him so well that his father, who came here at about this time last year to take him away, decided to leave him a year longer, in order to have him regain his strength completely. The little creature has an angelic face, dreamy eyes, with a far-off look in them, strange in a child of his age, and there is a wondrous grace in all his ways.

"Peyraque, seeing me so bewitched, scratched his head with an air of profundity and continued, 'Well, tell me, then, since you are fond of little children, why, instead of making it your occupation to read aloud, which must be wearisome, do you not find a little pupil like that, whom you could educate at your sister's with the other children? This would leave you in your own home and to your own ways.'

"'You forget, my good Peyraque, that perhaps it will be long before I can go to my sister.'

"'Well, then, your sister might come and live here, or else you could stay with us for a year or two; my wife would aid you in taking care of the child, and you would only have the trouble of watching over him and teaching him.—Stop! I have an idea of my own about this child, since he pleases you so that you are doting on him already. His father will come after him one of these days. Suppose I should tell him about you?'

"'Then you are acquainted with him!'

"'I acted as driver for him once, and carried him to the mountain in my carriage. He seems a fine man, but too young to take upon himself the bringing up of a child of three years. He will have to place it in charge of some woman, and he cannot leave it any longer with the Roqueberts, for they are not capable of teaching what a young gentleman like him ought to know. This would be your own task, especially, and the father would never find so good a mother for his child. Hope, hope! (which signifies wait!) I will keep watch at Polignac, and as soon as this father arrives, I will manage to talk with him in the proper way.'

"I let good Peyraque cultivate this project, and Justine also, but I have no faith in it myself, for the mysterious personage expected will ask questions I am unwilling to have answered, unless I am quite sure he knows none of the people, either intimately or remotely, from whom my place of retreat must be concealed. And how could I make sure of that? Peyraque's idea is, nevertheless, in itself a good one. To educate some child at home for a few years would please me infinitely better than going into a strange family again. I would rather take a girl than a boy, as she would be left with me a longer time; but there will be little room for choice, for these children hidden away by their parents are not easy to find. And there must needs be the most perfect confidence in me. I must be well recommended. Madame d'Arglade, who knows all the secrets of fashionable life, could find for me a chance like this; but I would rather not apply to her: without intending to do so, she might bring upon me some fresh misfortune."

XXIII

A few days later Caroline wrote again to her sister.

"Here I have been for five days past, in one of the most imposing ruined castles left from feudal times, on the summit of a great, black lava boulder, like those I told you about in connection with Le Puy and Espaly. You will think my position has changed, and my dream has become reality. No: I am certainly near little Didier, but I have taken it upon myself to watch over him, for his father or protector has not yet appeared. Now see what has happened.

"I felt a wish to see the child again, besides a slight wish to learn more about him; and lastly I had a desire to examine closely this castle of Polignac, which looks from afar like a city of giants, on a rock from the infernal depths. It is the strongest mediæval fortress in the country; it was the nest of that terrible race of vultures under whose ravages Velay, Forez, and Auvergne have trembled. The ancient lords of Polignac have left everywhere throughout these provinces mementos and traditions worthy of the legends about the ogre and Blue-Beard. These feudal tyrants robbed travellers, pillaged churches, murdered the monks, carried off women, set fire to villages, and this, too, from father to son, through long centuries. The Marquis de Villemer worked out of these facts one of the most remarkable chapters of his book; drawing the conclusion that the descendants of this family though innocent, assuredly, of the crimes of their ancestors, seem, by their misfortunes, to have been expiating the triumphs of barbarism.

"Their citadel was impregnable. The rock is sliced down perpendicularly on all sides. The village forms a group below on the little hill which supports the block of lava. It is some distance from Lantriac. The insuperable ravines here make all distances great. Having started early, however, we arrived last Tuesday toward noon, and our little horse carried us to the foot of the postern. Peyraque left me there, in order to take care of our animal, and to look at some others, for he has quite a reputation in veterinary science, and wherever he goes, practice of this kind always comes to him.

"I found a little girl ten years of age to open the door for me; but when I asked to see Dame Roqueberte, the child told me with tears

198   GEORGE SAND

that her mother was dying. I hurried to where she lives,—a part of the castle still standing, in good repair,—and I found her the victim of a brain-fever. Little Didier was playing about the room with another of this poor woman's children; the latter child was quite happy, comprehending nothing, although the elder; while Didier, between smiles and tears, was looking toward the bedside with as much anxiety as a little creature of three years could be expected to show. When he caught sight of me, he came to me at once, and without coquetting before embracing me, as he did the first time, he clung to my dress, pulling me with his little hands, and saying 'mamma,' in a voice so plaintive and gentle that my whole heart was won by it. He was certainly telling me about the strange condition of his adopted mother. I drew near the bed. Dame Roqueberte could not speak; she knew no one. Her husband came in after a moment and began to be alarmed, for she had been in this state only a few hours. I told him it was time to send for a physician and a woman to take care of his wife, which he did at once; and as I could not be sure that it was not typhoid fever, I sent the children out of the room, warning the husband that it might be dangerous to leave them there.

"When the physician came at the expiration of two hours, he approved what I had done, observing that the disease had not yet defined itself and that the children must be placed in some other house. This change I undertook to make with the help of Peyraque, for the husband had quite lost his senses, and thought of nothing but having candles burnt in the village church and prayers mumbled in Latin which he could not understand, but which seemed to him of more efficacy than the doctor's prescriptions.

"When he had calmed down a little it was already four o'clock; and it was necessary for Peyraque to set out again with me, that the night might not overtake us in the ravine of the Gâgne. There was no moon for the moment, and a storm was impending. Then poor Roquebert began to lament, saying that he was ruined unless some one would take care of the children, and especially of 'the child,' meaning by that Didier,—the hen with the golden eggs for his household. Special care was needful for him; he was not strong like the children of the country, and besides he was 'curious,' he wanted to go everywhere, and these ruins are a labyrinth of precipices, where a young gentleman of this adventurous temper must not be lost sight of a single moment. He dared not trust him with any one. The money this little one had brought into his house had made others envious, he had enemies; what did I know about it? In short, Peyraque said to me in a low voice, 'Come, your good heart and my own bright ideas are at one in this matter. Remain here; I see they have the wherewith to lodge you comfortably; I will come back to-morrow to see how the case stands, and take you home if there is no further need of you.'

"I confess I desired this decision; it seemed as if it were a duty as well as a privilege to watch over the child. Peyraque returned the next day, and as I saw that Dame Roqueberte, though out of danger, would not be able to sit up for some days, I consented to remain, telling Peyraque not to come after me till the end of the week.

"I am very comfortable here, in a vast room, which is, I believe, an old hall for the guards, that has been divided into several portions for the use of the farmers. The beds, though very rustic, are clean, and the housekeeping I attend to myself. I have the three children at my side all the time. The little girl does the cooking while I superintend; I see to the attendance which must be given the mother; I wash and dress Didier myself. He is clothed like the others, in a little blue blouse, but with more care, especially since I have made it my concern,—and I am so fond of him that I dread the moment when I shall have to leave him. You know my passion for children,—that is, for some children; this one is certainly well born. Charley would be as jealous of him as a tiger. Because, you see, this Didier is surely the son of a superior man or woman. He is of high, fine descent, morally speaking; his face is of a somewhat dull whiteness with little flushes of color like those on standard roses. He has brown eyes of admirable shape and expression, and a forest of black hair, half inclined to curl, which is fine and soft as silk. His little hands are perfect, and he never soils them. He does not dig in the earth, and never touches anything: he passes his life in looking at things. I am sure he has thoughts beyond his years which he cannot express, or rather, a series of dreams, charming and divine, that cannot be translated into human language; yet he talks very fluently for one of his age, both in French and patois. He has caught the accent of the country, but makes it very sweet by his infantile lisp. He has the prettiest reasons in the world for doing as he pleases, and what he pleases is to be out of doors, climbing over the ruins, or crawling into their crevices; once there, he sits down, gazing at the tiny flowers, and especially at the insects, without touching them, but following all their motions, apparently interested in these living marvels, while the other children think only of crushing and destroying them.

"I have tried to give him his first notions in reading, being persuaded (contrary to the father's opinion perhaps) that the earlier you begin with children the more you spare them the heavy strain on the attention, so painful when their strength and activity have found greater development. I have tested his intelligence and curiosity; they are unusual, and with our wonderful method, which succeeded so well with your children, I am sure I could teach him to read in a month.

"And then this child is all soul, and his self-will melts into boundless affection. Our fondness is growing too fast really, and I ask myself how we are ever going to part.

"Besides, although I miss my Justine and Peyraque, I enjoy myself exceedingly among these magnificent ruins, commanding as they do one of the loveliest spots on earth. The air is so pure that the white stones, mixed with rough fragments of lava, are as bright as if just from a quarry. And then the interior of this immense castle is stored with very curious things.

"You must know that the Polignac family pretend to a descent from Apollo or his priests in a direct line; and that tradition consecrates the existence here of a temple to this god,—a temple of which some fragments yet remain. As for myself, I think there is no doubt of it, and that just to see these fragments is enough. The question to decide is whether the inscriptions and carvings were brought here to decorate the castle according to Renaissance usage, or whether the castle was built upon these vestiges. Dame Roqueberte tells me the scientific men of the country have been disputing over it for fifty years, and for my own part I agree with those who think the curbstone of the well was the mouthpiece of the god's oracles. The orifice of this immense well, with which another and a smaller well grotesquely communicates, was closed by a colossal head of noble outline, whose perforated mouth gave forth the subterranean voice of the priestess. Why not? Those who say it was only the mask of a fountain are no surer. The head has been preserved from destruction in the lower story of a little tower, along with a pile of stone bullets found in the well. I have amused myself by taking a sketch of it, which I send you in this letter, with a portrait of my little Didier at its foot, lying sound asleep at full length upon the temple of the god. It does not look like him, to be sure; but it will give you an idea of the fantastic and charming picture which I have had before my eyes for the last fifteen minutes.

"As for other matters, I do not read at all here. I have not Peyraque's eight or ten stray volumes and his big old Protestant Bible. I no longer try to improve myself; I hardly think of it even. I mend the clothing of my Didier, following him step by step; I dream, I am sad, but not rebellious, and not given to wondering any further about a state of things to which I ought to submit,—and I am in good health, which is the most important thing.

"Good old Peyraque comes in, bringing your letter. Ah! my sister, do not give up weakly, or I shall be in despair. You say *he* is pale, already ill; and this gave you so much pain that you came near betraying me. Camille, if you have not strength enough to see a courageous man suffer, and if you do not understand that my courage alone can support his, I will set out again; I will go farther away still, and you shall not know where I am. Consider yourself notified, that the day I see the mark of a strange foot upon the sand of my island, I shall disappear so entirely that—"

CAROLINE LEFT THE SENTENCE UNFINISHED; Peyraque, who had just given her Madame Heudebert's letter, came back saying, "Here is the *gentleman* coming."

"Who? what?" cried Caroline, rising and evidently quite troubled. "What gentleman?"

"The father of the unknown child,—M. Bernyer he calls himself."

"Then you know his name? No one here knew it or would tell it."

"On my word, I am not very curious; but he threw his valise on a bench at Roquebert's door, and my eye happened to fall upon it, so I read."

"Bernyer! I don't know any such person; perhaps I might show myself without getting into difficulty."

"Why, certainly you must see him, to tell him about the little one; now is the time."

Roquebert came in, however, and defeated Peyraque's design. M. Bernyer was asking for his son; but, according to his custom, he had gone into a room, reserved for him especially, and did not wish, just then, to see any one not of the family.

"It is all the same," added Roquebert. "I will tell him how you took care of my wife and the little boy, and he will certainly give me something good to repay you with. Otherwise I will do it myself, out of my own pocket. Be easy about that."

He took the child in his arms and went out, closing the door behind him, as if to shut out even a curious look from following him into the passage leading to the stranger's room.

"Well, let us set out," said Caroline, whose eyes were full of tears at the thought that she would probably never see Didier again.

"No," replied Peyraque, "let us wait a little and see what the gentleman will think, when he knows you have stayed here five days to take care of his child."

"But don't you see, my friend, that Roquebert will take care not to tell him? He will never dare to own that, during his wife's illness, he knew of nothing better than trusting the child to a stranger. And beside, is he not anxious to keep Didier a year longer, which would be very feasible? Will he let us give the father a hint that the child would not only be better cared for, with us, but also educated as he needs to be at his age? No, no. Dame Roqueberte herself, in spite of the care I have given her, will say that no one knows me, that perhaps I am only an adventuress; and while seeking gratitude and confidence, we shall look as if we were intriguing to get the few sous which have been offered us already."

"But when we refuse them it will be seen who we are. I am known myself; it is understood that Samuel Peyraque has never lied or held out his hand for money."

"This stranger knows nothing of all that, and he will inquire of the Roqueberts only because he knows nobody else. Let me set out quickly, my dear friend; I suffer every minute I stay here."

"Just as you like," said Peyraque. "I have not unharnessed, and we can let the horse rest at Le Puy; but nevertheless, if you would trust me, we should remain here one or two hours. Going thither from here, we would naturally meet on the way; the child would come to you and ask for you himself, he is so fond of you already. Look here now! If the gentleman should see you only one minute, I am sure he would say, 'Here is a person who is like no one else: I must speak to her.' And when he had talked with you—"

Arguing in this way, Peyraque followed Caroline, who had gathered up her clothing and was turning her steps toward the castle gate, quite determined to start. Passing before the bench where the stranger's valise was still lying beside his travelling-cloak, she read the name which Peyraque had reported faithfully; but at the same time she made a gesture of surprise and hurried along with unusual agitation.

"What is it now? asked the good man, taking the reins.

"Nothing,—a fancy!" replied Caroline, when they were out of the enclosure. "I imagined I recognized the hand of the person who wrote the name of Bernyer on that valise."

"Bah! it was written just like print."

"That is true; I am silly! Never mind; let us go on, my good Peyraque."

Caroline was absorbed in thought all the way. She accounted for the singular emotion which the sight of this disguised handwriting had caused her by what she had just experienced in reading her sister's letter;

but she had a new anxiety. M. de Villemer had never told her that he had seen the castle of Polignac with his own eyes, but he had given a fine description of it, and an accurate one, in his book; he had taken it as an example of the strength of feudal restorations in the Middle Ages, and Caroline knew he often travelled into the provinces, in order to get a distinct impression of historic places. She searched all the recesses of her memory to find what could not possibly be there, to see if the Marquis had not accidentally chanced to tell her that he had visited Polignac. "No," replied she to herself, "if he had said so, I should have been impressed by it on account of the names Lantriac and Le Puy, which Justine had mentioned." Then she tried to remember whether, in connection with Polignac, she had not spoken of Lantriac and Justine; but she had never mentioned either of them to him, she was quite sure; so she grew calmer.

Yet she was agitated and thoughtful. Why had she taken such a fancy to this unknown child? What was the peculiarity in his eyes, his attitude, and his smile? Was it that he looked like the Marquis? In the idea which had so suddenly presented itself, of educating a little child and wishing for this one, might there not have been a vague instinct more powerful than chance or Peyraque's instigations?

With all this uneasiness there came, too, in Caroline's despite, the secret torment of a confused jealousy. "He has a son, then, a child of love?" said she to herself. "He must, then, have loved some woman passionately before he knew me, for frivolous adventures are incompatible with his exclusive nature, and there has been an important mystery in his past life! The mother is still living perhaps. Why is she supposed to be dead?"

Advancing among these feverish speculations, she recalled the words of the Marquis under the cedar in the Jardin des Plantes, and the struggle she had caught a glimpse of between his filial duty and some other duty, some other love, of which she herself might not be the object after all. Who knew whether the old Marchioness had not been equally at fault, whether the Marquis had told his mother the name of the person he wanted to marry; in short, whether she herself and Madame de Villemer had not both missed the truth?

Thus working herself into an involuntary excitement, Caroline strove in vain to feel reconciled to her fate. She loved, and for her the stronger feeling now was the fear rather than the hope of not being loved in return.

"What is the trouble?" asked Peyraque, who had learned to read her anxieties in her face.

She replied by overwhelming him with questions about this M. Bernyer whom he had seen once. Peyraque had a keen eye and a memory; but, habitually thoughtful and reserved, he bestowed his attention only on people who especially interested him. He drew, then, a picture of this pretended Bernyer so vague and incomplete that Caroline made no progress. She slept poorly that night, but toward morning she grew calm, and awoke saying to herself that there had been no common sense in her excitement of the day before.

Peyraque, having to go his rounds, could not linger till her awakening. He came in at nightfall. His air was triumphant.

"Our affair is working well," said he. "M. Bernyer will come here to-morrow, and you may rest easy; he is an Englishman, a sailor. You don't know any such person, do you?"

"No, not at all," replied Caroline. "You saw him again, then?"

"No, he had just gone out; but I saw Dame Roqueberte, who is better and begins to have her senses. She told me the little one cried last night, and before he fell asleep asked over and again for his Charlette. The father inquired who she was. It seems that Roquebert had no great wish to speak of you; but his wife, who is a good Christian, and the little girl, who is fond of you too, said you were an angel from heaven, and the gentleman replied he would like to thank you, and make you some recompense. He asked where you lived; he has never been at our house, but remembered me perfectly, and said he would come and see us soon. He promised the child this, and even that he would bring you back, in order to make him go to sleep."

"In all this," said Caroline, "I see only one thing, and that is, this stranger is coming to offer me money."

"Well, let him do it; so much the better! It will be an opportunity to show him you are not what he thinks. You will see one another, you will converse; he will find you are an educated young lady, above what he supposes you are, and I will tell him your history, because this history of yours does you credit."

"No, no," replied Caroline, quickly. "What! shall I intrust my secret to a stranger, after so many precautions to conceal my name and position?"

"But since you do not know him?" said Justine. "If you are agreed on the matter of the child, he should be intrusted with the whole. Having his secret, we can afford to give him ours. He would have no inducement to betray it."

"Justine!" cried Mlle de Saint-Geneix, who was near a window that faced the street. "Listen! Heaven! not another word. There he is, certainly, this M. Bernyer. He is coming here, and it is—yes, I was sure—it is he! It is M. de Villemer! O my friends, hide me! Tell him I am gone, that I am not coming back!—If he sees me, if he speaks to me,—can't you feel that I am lost?"

XXIV

Justine followed Caroline, who had escaped to her own room, and made signs to Peyraque that he should receive the Marquis and be self-possessed.

Peyraque was equal to the emergency. He received M. de Villemer with the calm dignity of a man who has the most rigid ideas of duty. It was no longer a question of putting him in communication with the pretended Charlette; it was necessary to get him away before any suspicions arose in his mind, or, in case they had already arisen, to dispel them at once. From the first words of the Marquis, Peyraque saw that he suspected nothing. Desirous to set out again in a few days with his son, whom he intended to keep nearer to himself in future, he had made the most of a fine morning to come on foot and repay this debt of gratitude to some generous stranger. He had not supposed the distance so great, and was, therefore, a little late in arriving. He confessed he was somewhat tired, and, in point of fact, his face betrayed both weariness and suffering.

Peyraque hastened to offer him food and drink, the duties of hospitality preceding everything else. He called Justine, who had, by this time, regained her composure; and they waited upon M. de Villemer, who, catching at this opportunity of rewarding his entertainers generously, accepted their services with a good grace. He learned with regret that Charlette had gone away; but there was no reason why he should ask many questions about her. He thought of leaving a present for her, which Justine, in a low tone, advised her husband to accept, that he might not be surprised at anything. Caroline would readily find a chance to send it back. Peyraque did not see the necessity; his pride revolted at the idea of seeming to accept money on her account.

Caroline, in her little chamber, overheard this strife on a point of delicacy. The voice of the Marquis sent shudders through her. She dared not stir. It seemed as if M. de Villemer would recognize her footfall through the flooring. He, for his part, hoping to find a way of discharging his obligations under some different form, pretended and really tried to eat a little; and after this inquired whether he could hire a horse to return with. The night was dark and the rain came on again. Peyraque agreed to carry him back and went out to get his wagon ready; but first, he climbed up softly to Caroline's room. "This poor gentleman makes me uneasy," said he in a low voice. "He is very ill, that I am sure of. You can see drops of sweat on his forehead, and yet he creeps up to the fire like a man with a fever-chill. He could not swallow two morsels, and when he breathes hard it seems to affect his heart like a spasm, for he puts his hand there, smiling bravely all the while, but afterwards carrying it to his head, as one does in severe pain.

"Heavens!" exclaimed Caroline, in alarm, "when he is ill it is so dangerous! You must not carry him back to-night; your wagon is not easy, and then the bad roads and the cold, and this rain and his fever! No, no, he must stay here to-night. But where, pray? He would rather sleep out of doors than at the inn, which is so untidy. There is only one way. Keep him from going, keep him here. Give him my room. I will gather up my things; it will not take long, and I will go to your daughter-in-law's."

"With my son's wife or in the village, you will be too near. If he should happen to be a little worse in the night you would come in spite of yourself, to take care of him."

"That is true. What shall I do?"

"Do you want me to say? Well, you have courage and health: I will take you to Laussonne, where you can pass the night with my sister-in-law; it is as neat there as it is here, and to-morrow, after he goes, I will come for you."

"Yes, you are right," said Caroline, doing up her bundle hastily. "Make him agree to stay, and tell your son, as you go by, to harness Mignon."

"No, not Mignon! he has been travelling all day. We must take the mule."

Peyraque, having given his orders, returned to tell the Marquis the rain had set in for the whole evening, which was indeed true; and, giving Justine a significant glance, he urged him to stay so cordially that M. de Villemer consented. "You are right, my friends," said he, with his heart-broken smile; "I am somewhat ill, and I am one of those who have no right to wish for death."

"No one has that right," replied Peyraque; "but you will not be dangerously sick here with us, I assure you. My wife will take good care of you. The chamber up above is very clean and warm, and if you get worse you have only to knock lightly, just once; we shall hear it."

Justine went up stairs to prepare his room and embrace poor Caroline, who was really dismayed. "What!" said Caroline, speaking very low; "I know he is sick and I am going to desert him in this way. No. I was mad! I will stay."

"But that is just what Peyraque will never let you do," replied Justine. "Peyraque is stern; but what would you! Perhaps he is right. If you take pity on one another now, you will never be able to part again. And then—for myself I am sure you would never do anything wrong, but the mother—And then, think what other people might say!"

Caroline would not listen; Peyraque went up stairs, took her hand with an air of authority, and made her come down. She had put her poor heart under the guidance of this Protestant of the Cévennes; there was no longer any way of drawing back.

He led her out to the carriage and put in her bundle. At this moment Caroline, who had really lost her senses, escaped from his grasp, darted into the house through the kitchen-door, and caught sight of M. de Villemer, who was seated with his back toward her. She went no farther; her reason returned. And then his appearance reassured her a little. He had not that bruised, broken-down aspect she had seen him wear on the night of his former attack. He was sitting before the fire, reading in Peyraque's Bible. The little iron lamp hanging from the mantel-piece threw its light on his black hair, wavy like his son's, and partly also on his clear, strong forehead. M. de Villemer was doubtless suffering much, but he still wished to live; he had not lost hope.

"Here I am," said Caroline, returning to Peyraque. "He did n't see me, and I have seen him! I am more at ease. Let us start; but you must promise on your honor," added she, as she drew near the step of the carriage, "that if he is taken to-night with suffocation you will come for me at whatever damage to your horse. It must be done, do you see? No one else knows what this sick man needs in way of care—and you—you would see him die in your own house, and you would have it on your conscience forever!"

Peyraque promised, and they set out. The weather was dreadful, and the road frightful; but Peyraque knew every one of its holes and its stones. Besides, the distance was short. He left Caroline at the house of his sister-in-law, and had reached home again by eleven o'clock.

The Marquis was feeling better; he had gone to lie down after having chatted with Justine in such a friendly way that she was delighted. "Do you see, Peyraque, this man," said she, "he has a good heart like hers—I can understand it perfectly myself—"

"Stop talking now," said Peyraque, who knew the thinness of the flooring; "if he is asleep, we ought to sleep too."

At Lantriac the night passed in absolute quiet. The Marquis actually rested, and at two o'clock awoke, having shaken off the fever. He felt imbued with a pleasant calm, such as he had not known for a long time, and he attributed this to some sweet dream that he had forgotten, though its impression remained. Unwilling to awaken his hosts, he kept still, gazing at the four walls of the little chamber, brightly lighted by his lamp, and grasping the facts of his position more positively than he had done before since Caroline's departure. He had debated a thousand extreme measures; then he had said to himself that his first duty was to his son; and the sight of this child had given him the force of will he needed to resist the physical disease which now began to threaten him anew. Within twenty-four hours he had fixed upon a definite plan. He would take Didier to Madame Heudebert, leaving with her a letter for Caroline, and then quit France for some time, so that Mlle de Saint-Geneix, reassured by his absence, might return to be near her sister at Étampes. In the course of a few quiet weeks, the Marchioness would perhaps get further information, or perhaps her secret would be discovered by the Duke, who had sworn he would draw it from her by surprise. If the Duke failed, Urbain was not at the end of his resources. He would come back quietly to the castle of Mauveroche, where his mother, was to pass the summer with her daughter-in-law, and he would not let Caroline know of his return until he had cleared her in his mother's estimation, and thus again smoothed away every difficulty.

The most important and the most urgent thing, then, was to draw Mlle de Saint-Geneix from her mysterious hiding-place. The Marquis still thought she was in some Parisian convent. He found himself compelled to stay a few days longer in Polignac to make sure of Dame Roqueberte's complete recovery, before grieving her by taking away his son, and this delay had fretted him more than anything else. To cheat his impatience, he asked himself why he should not write to Madame Heudebert at once and to Caroline also, that they might be prepared to rejoin each other after his departure for a foreign land. By this means he would perhaps gain a few days. He could mail the letter at once, as he would pass through Le Puy on his return to Polignac.

What gave him the idea of writing from Lantriac was, mainly, the sight of the little bureau, where Caroline had left pens, some ink in a cup, and a few stray sheets of paper. These objects, on which his gaze fastened mechanically, seemed inviting him to follow his inspiration. He rose noiselessly, put the lamp on the table, and wrote to Caroline.

"My friend, my sister, you will not desert an unhappy man, who, for a year past, has centred in you the hopes of his life. Caroline, do not mistake my meaning. I have a favor to ask of you which you cannot refuse. I am going away.

"I have a son who has no mother. I love him devotedly; I intrust him to you. Come back!—As for myself, I go to England. You shall never see me again, if you have lost faith in me,—but that is impossible. When have I been unworthy of your esteem? Caroline—"

The Marquis stopped abruptly. An object of little importance had caught his eye. The ordinary paper, the steel pens, had no peculiarities; but one black bead lay on the table between his hand and the inkstand, a trifle insignificant in itself, but one bringing with it a whole world of memories. It was a bit of jet, cut and perforated in a certain unusual fashion. It was part of a valueless bracelet Caroline had worn at Séval; which he easily recognized because she used to take it off whenever she wrote, and he had himself formed a habit of toying with this bracelet while talking to her. He had handled it a hundred times, and one day she had said to him, "Pray don't break it, it is all I have left from my mother's jewel-box." He had looked at it respectfully, and held it lovingly in his hands. Just as she was on the point of quitting her little room in Lantriac, Caroline, in her precipitation, had broken this bracelet; she had picked up the beads hastily, leaving behind but this one.

This black bead reversed all the ideas of the Marquis; but what kind of dreaming was this? These cut jets might be an industrial product of the country he was then in. Nevertheless he sat motionless, absorbed in new surmises. He breathed and questioned the vague perfume of the room. He looked everywhere without moving from his chair. There was nothing on the walls, nothing on the table, nothing on the mantel. Finally he became aware of some bits of paper in the fireplace, which were not completely charred. He bent over the ashes, searched minutely, and found one single fragment of an address, only two syllables of which were legible: one, written by hand, was the last in the word Lantriac, the other, "am," forming part of the postmark. The postmark was that of Étampes, the handwriting that of Madame Heudebert. There could be no longer a doubt: Charlette was no one but Caroline, and perhaps she had never gone away, perhaps she was still in the house.

From that moment, the Marquis had the cunning, the watchfulness, the coolness, and the keen perception of a savage. He discovered the pipe from the little spring leading down to the sink below. The pipe itself was stopped up, but there was more than one fissure in the plaster which surrounded it. He put his ear down to it closely, and caught Peyraque's long, even breathing as he lay yet asleep.

Not a word, though spoken ever so low, could then escape him. In a few moments he distinctly heard Justine rise, uttering the words, "Come, get up, Peyraque; perhaps poor Caroline has not been sleeping so well as we have!"

"A night is a night," said Peyraque; "besides, I can't go for her till after he has gone away."

Justine listened and replied, "He does n't stir, but he said he should get up at daybreak. Daylight is n't far off now; he means to go away without taking anything, he said so."

"It is all the same," rejoined Peyraque, who had now risen, and whose voice was even more audible, though he spoke quite low; "I don't want him to set out on foot; it is too far. The lad shall saddle my horse, and when I have seen him fairly off, I will start for Laussonne."

M. de Villemer had made sure. He stirred a little to show he was up, and went down stairs after having slipped his purse into the bureau-drawer. He seemed very impatient to get back to Polignac, and declaring he felt perfectly strong, obstinately refused the horse. It would have been an encumbrance in the war of observation he was about to wage. He shook hands cordially with his entertainers and set out; but, on the borders of the village, having inquired about the road of a passer-by, he changed his course, plunging into a by-way that led to Laussonne.

He thought he could arrive there in advance of Peyraque, wait for him stealthily, and see him take Caroline back. When he had made sure of her return to Lantriac, he would lay his plans further. Until then, being quite aware she was trying to escape him, he would not risk losing track of her again. But Peyraque was very expeditious; Mignon travelled fast in spite of the roads which grew worse and worse, forming one unbroken ascent in the direction of Laussonne, and crossing more than one mountain declivity. The by-path cut off the angles of the main road but slightly, and the Marquis was distanced by the rustic equipage. He saw it pass and recognized Peyraque, who, for his part, thought he distinguished, in the morning fog, a man who was not in peasant garb, and who quickly retreated behind an embanking wall of rough stones.

Peyraque was suspicious. "Very likely," thought he, "he has been fooling us, or he has found out something. Well! if it is he, and if he is no more of an invalid than that, I will cure him of trying to follow a mountain horse on foot."

He urged Mignon forward, and arrived at Laussonne with the first rays of the sun. Caroline, in deadly anxiety, after a cruelly sleepless night, came out to meet him.

"All is going well," said he. "I was mistaken yesterday; he is not so very ill, for he slept well and would return on foot."

"So he is gone?" replied Caroline, climbing to her seat by Peyraque. "He never suspected anything, then? And I shall never see him again? Well, so much the better!" and she burst into tears under her hood, which she pulled over her face in vain. Peyraque heard her sob as if her heart would break.

"So you are the one going to be sick now?" said he, in a tone of paternal severity. "Come, be reasonable, or your Peyraque will never believe you when you tell him you are a Christian."

"So long as I do not weep before him, can you not excuse one moment of weakness in me? But what are you doing? Why are we going on toward Laussonne?"

Peyraque thought he again caught sight of the Marquis still creeping onward. "You must excuse me," said he, "but I have an errand to do in the village. It is quite near."

He entered the village, shrewdly thinking that the Marquis would still keep himself in sight at a distance. He went up the street and exchanged a few words with one of the townspeople. Pretexts could not fail to be at hand. Then, returning to Caroline, he said, "You see, my daughter, you have too much on your mind. I want to revive your spirits; you know an excursion always does you good. Would you like to have me take you on one—O, a very pleasant one!"

"If you have business anywhere, I don't want to incommode you. I will go wherever you like."

"I shall have to go to the foot of Mézenc, to the village of Estables. It is a beautiful place really, and you have been longing to see the grandest of the Cévennes."

"You said it would be hard travelling over there until after next month."

"Bless me! Why, the weather is cloudy, to be sure, and perhaps the roads are a little damaged. I have n't passed over them since last year; but they have been worked upon, as I have heard, and besides you know with me there is no danger."

"I assure you I am in no mood to worry about danger. Let us set out."

Peyraque hurried on his horse, which soon crossed the boundaries of Laussonne and bravely descended the rocky hill, climbing the other slope again without delay, and even more rapidly. When they had reached the top, Peyraque turned round, saw no one in the paths behind him, and looked at the road ahead, which was taking on a discouraging aspect. "You are going to see a wilderness," said he; "but that need n't annoy you, need it?"

"No, no," replied she; "when we are desperate we cease to be annoyed."

Peyraque went on, not without warning his companion repeatedly that the sun might not be disposed to shine, that they had four leagues to go, and that perhaps Mézenc would be under a fog. All this had little interest for Caroline, who did not guess the hesitation of her old friend or his qualms of conscience.

They traversed a mountain wooded with pines, and cut into by a vast glade,—the result of an ancient felling of the trees,—which opened a gigantic avenue, where the road, from a distance, looked like a highway for a hundred chariots abreast; but when the little carriage had ventured in, it was a frightful task to get over the ground, rain-soaked and hollowed out into deep ruts in a thousand places. Further on, it was worse still; the turf was strewed with blocks of lava, which left boggy places between them; and when they found traces of the travelled road again, they had to turn aside for monstrous piles of flints and pebbles, to stop altogether before deep cuts or trenches, to seek the old road among twenty others that lost themselves in the morass. The horse performed prodigies of courage, and Peyraque miracles of skill and judgment.

At the expiration of two hours, they had accomplished only two leagues, and were in open country on an interminable plateau, at an elevation of fifteen hundred metres. Except the breaks here and there in the road, nothing could be distinguished. The sun had disappeared; a thick mist enshrouded everything, and nothing can paint the feeling of bitter desolation which fell upon Caroline. Peyraque himself lost courage and kept silence. The obstructed road, which, he had been forced to leave one side did not reappear, and for the last fifteen minutes they had been pacing over a spongy turf, broken up by the hoofs of cattle in search of pasturage, but no longer bearing any traces of wheels. The horse stopped, bathed in sweat; he thus gave warning that he had never been over this ground before.

Peyraque alighted, sinking almost knee deep in the boggy soil, and tried to find where he was. It was out of the question. The mountains and ravines were only one plain of white vapor.

"Have we lost our way?" asked Caroline with cool indifference.

At this point the wind made a little opening in the fog, and they saw in the distance fantastic horizons empurpled by the sun; but the mist closed in again so quickly that Peyraque could not determine his position from this isolated peak in the distant circle of mountains. However, they heard a confused barking and then voices, though they could not distinguish the dogs till they were quite upon them. These dogs were the advance-guard of a caravan of men and mules carrying vegetables and leather bottles. They were mountaineers who had been down to the plains to exchange the cheese and butter of their cows for the fruits and vegetables of the level country. They accosted Peyraque, who asked information. They told him that he had done very wrong to think of going with a carriage to Estables at this season, that it could not be done, and that he would have to return. Peyraque showed some obstinacy, and asked if he was still far from the village. They guided him into the road again, telling him he had work before him for an hour and a half; but as their animals were loaded and warm, and they themselves in haste to arrive, these mountaineers offered no assistance, and disappeared, with a laugh at the little carriage. Caroline saw them rapidly vanish into the fog like shadows.

It was absolutely necessary to let the horse breathe, for a fresh effort to regain the solid road had exhausted him. "What comforts me," said Peyraque, really moved, "is that you don't complain of anything! It is very cold, nevertheless, and I'm sure the dampness has gone through your cloak."

Caroline replied only by a shiver.

A new shadow had just passed along the side of the road; it was M. de Villemer. He pretended not to see the carriage, although he did see it perfectly; but he chose to seem unconscious that it held any one he knew. He advanced with extraordinary energy, affecting an air of indifference.

"It is he! I saw him," said Caroline to Peyraque. "He goes wherever we go."

"Well, let him go on, and we will turn back."

"No, I cannot, I will not! He will die after such a walk. He will never reach Estables. Let us follow him."

This time Caroline's terror was so commanding that Peyraque obeyed. They came up with M. de Villemer, who moved aside to let them pass, without stopping or looking up. He would be neither intrusive nor rebellious, but he would know, he would follow to the death.

Unfortunately he was at the end of his strength. The difficulty of this walk, which from Lantriac had been a continual ascent and, for the last two leagues, one chaos of stones and peaty turf, had started on him a profuse perspiration which he could feel freezing in the blast of a sharp wind that had suddenly veered to the east. He lost his breath, and was forced to stop.

Caroline turned her head toward him, and was on the point of crying out. Peyraque seized her arm. "Courage, my daughter," he said, with his stern religious fervor. "The Lord requires it at your hands." And she felt herself overborne by the strong faith of the peasant.

"What do you want to do for him?" resumed Peyraque, as he still drove on. "He has had strength to come so far, he will have enough to go the rest of the way. A man does not die from the effects of a walk. He will rest at Estables. And if he is sick,—I shall be there."

"But he is following me! You see I shall have to speak to him there or elsewhere."

"Why should he follow you? He does not suspect you are here even. So many travellers want to see Mézenc."

"In such weather as this?"

"The sun rose brightly, and we ourselves started to see Mézenc."

The Marquis saw Caroline hesitate and submit. This was the final blow. No sooner had he seen himself left behind than he felt he could go no farther. He sank down on a stone, his eyes fixed on the black speck slowly vanishing from his sight, for the wind had risen suddenly and was violently scattering the fog, in whose stead there now came light flurries of snow and sleet. "So she would have me know nothing more of her?" said he to himself, as he felt his strength failing. "She flees from hope, she has lost faith. Then she never loved me!"

And he lay down to die.

XXV

W e must hasten, we must hasten!" said Peyraque, at the close of another half-hour, as he saw the snow deepening. "Here is something worse than fog. When this begins to fall it soon piles up in the road higher than your head."

This imprudent admission set Caroline in open rebellion; she wanted to jump from the carriage, fully determined to walk back to the place where she had met M. de Villemer.

Peyraque dissuaded her from this; but finally had to yield and return, in spite of the ever-increasing danger and the difficulties of a still slower progress over the half-league they had so painfully traversed since losing sight of the Marquis.

It was in vain for them to search by simply looking for him. In one hour the snow in large, spreading flakes had buried up the ground and its ruggedness. It was impossible for them to tell whether they had not passed by the place they wanted to explore. Caroline uttered groans, inaudible to herself, finding no words at her command but the faint outcry, "My God, my God!" Peyraque no longer strove to quiet her, and only encouraged her by telling her to look carefully.

Suddenly the horse stopped. "It must be we have found the road again here," said Peyraque. "Mignon remembers."

"Then we have come too far," replied Caroline.

"But we have met no one," returned Peyraque. "This gentleman, seeing the storm coming on, has gone back to Laussonne, and we, who are nearer Estables, are running a great risk in staying here, unless it stops snowing. I give you warning."

"Go on, go on, Peyraque!" cried Caroline, leaping into the snow. "For my part, I shall stay here till I find him."

Peyraque made no reply. He alighted and began searching, but without the least hope. There was already half a foot of snow, and the wind, drifting it into every hollow, would soon bury up a corpse.

Caroline walked on at random, gliding forward like a spirit, so great was her excitement. She was already at some little distance from the carriage when she heard the horse snort loudly as he put down his head. She thought he was dying, and, watching him with real distress, saw him scenting out something in front of him in a strange way. It was a revelation; she darted forward and perceived a gloved hand, apparently belonging to one dead, which the breath of the horse, melting the snow over it, had brought to light. The body extended beneath was the obstacle which the animal had refused to tread under foot. Peyraque came running at Caroline's call, and, extricating M. de Villemer, put him in the carriage, where Mlle de Saint-Geneix held him up and tried to warm him in her arms.

Peyraque took the bridle and walked on again in the direction of Mézenc. He knew perfectly there was not a moment to lose, but went on without knowing where to set foot; and he soon disappeared in a ravine which he was unable to clear. The horse stopped of his own accord; Peyraque got up again, but, on trying to make him back, found the wheels caught in some unseen obstacle. Besides, the horse was at the end of his strength. Peyraque treated him harshly, but all to no purpose; he struck his pony for the first time in his life; he pulled on the bridle till the creature's mouth bled. The poor animal turned upon him with a glance of almost human intelligence, as if to say, "I have done all I could; I can do nothing more to save you."

"Must we then perish here?" said Peyraque, disheartened, as he watched the snow falling in inexorable whirls. The plateau had become a Siberian waste, beyond which Mézenc alone showed his livid head between the gusts of wind. Not a tree, not a roof, not a rock for shelter. Peyraque knew there was nothing to be done.

"Let us hope," said he, which, in these Southern forms of speech, simply means, "Let us wait."

It soon occurred to him, however, that he would gain the next fifteen minutes, even if they should be the last of life. He took a small board from his little carriage, and fought with the drifting snow, which threatened to bury up both horse and vehicle. Incessantly for ten minutes he worked like a wrestler at this task of clearing away, saying to himself that perhaps it was all useless, but that he would defend himself and Caroline to the last breath.

At the expiration of the ten minutes he thanked God the snow grew lighter; the wind abated; the fog, which was far less dangerous, strove to reappear. He slackened his work without giving it over. At last he saw something like a pale streak of light breaking through the depths of the sky; it was a promise of fair weather.

So far he had not spoken a word or uttered an oath. If Caroline had been fated to perish there, she would not have suspected it till the last moment. Yet he looked at her and found her so pale and her glance so wild that he was alarmed.

"Well, well!" said he, "what is the trouble? There is no more danger; this will be nothing."

"O, nothing, is it?" she replied, with a bitter smile, pointing to Urbain, stretched out on the seat of the little vehicle, his face livid with the cold, his large eyes wide open and glazed, like those of a corpse.

Peyraque looked around him again. It was hopeless to expect human aid. He sprang into the carriage, seized M. de Villemer firmly in his arms, rubbed him vigorously, bruised him in his iron hands, trying to impart to him the warmth of his own old blood reanimated by exercise and a strong will; but it was all in vain. With the effects of the cold were united those of a nervous crisis peculiar to the organization of the Marquis.

"He is not dead, though," said Peyraque. "I feel that; I am sure of it. If I only had something to make a fire with! But I can't make one of stones."

"We might burn the carriage, at all events," cried Caroline.

"That is an idea,—yes, but after that?"

"After that perhaps the Lord will send help. Don't you see the first thing is to prevent death from laying hold of us here?"

Peyraque saw Caroline so pale and the blue lines so defined under her eyes that he began to think she felt herself dying also. He hesitated no longer, but risked all to save all. He unharnessed the pony, which, like the horses of the Cossacks, at once rolled in the snow to rest himself. Taking the awning from his carriage and placing it on the ground, Peyraque carried M. de Villemer, still frozen and motionless, to it; then, drawing from his boxes a few handfuls of hay, some old papers, and fragments of matting, he put the whole under the vehicle and struck fire with the flint and steel with which he was accustomed to light his pipe. Breaking up with his farrier's tools the boards and planks of his poor little carriage, he succeeded in a few moments in kindling them into a blaze and into brands. He demolished and broke in pieces as fast as the fire burned. The snow no longer fell, and M. de Villemer, lying within a semicircle of blazing wreck, began to gaze in a stupor at the strange scene, which he took for a dream.

"He is saved, saved! Do you hear, Peyraque?" cried Caroline, who saw the Marquis making an attempt to rise. "A hundred blessings on your head! You have saved him!"

The Marquis heard Caroline's voice close by him, but, still thinking it some hallucination, made no effort to look at her. He did not comprehend what was taking place till he felt on his hands the distracted pressure of Caroline's lips. Then he thought he must be dying, as she no longer avoided him, and, trying to smile, he bade her adieu in a faint voice.

"No, no; not adieu!" she replied, covering his forehead with kisses; "you must live. I will have it so! I love you!"

A slight flush came over the livid face, but no words could express his joy. The Marquis still feared it might be all a dream; yet he was plainly reviving. The warmth had concentrated under the carriage-top which served him as a shelter. He was as comfortable as he could possibly be made there, lying on the cloaks of Caroline and Peyraque.

"But we must go on, nevertheless," thought the latter, and his unquiet eyes questioned the brightening horizon. The cold was severe, the fire was going out for want of fuel, and the invalid surely could not walk to Estables. And was Caroline herself equal to such an attempt? To mount them both on the horse was the only expedient; but would the exhausted animal have strength to carry them? No matter, it would have to be tried; and, first of all, they must give the horse some oats. Peyraque looked, but found none; the fire had consumed the little bag as well as the box in which it was stored.

An exclamation from Caroline revived his hopes. She showed him a light vapor on the rising ground which sheltered them. He ran in that direction, and saw below him an ox-cart, painfully approaching, the driver smoking in order to keep warm.

"You see now," said Caroline, when the cart had nearly reached them, "the Lord has helped us!"

M. de Villemer was still so weak that he had to be lifted into the cart, which, fortunately, was loaded with straw; and in this Peyraque buried him up, after a fashion. Caroline placed herself near him. Peyraque bestrode his pony, leaving the wreck of his poor carriage behind, and in an hour they had finally reached the village of Estables.

Peyraque went disdainfully by the inn of a certain giantess with bare legs and a golden necklace, a veritable tardigrade of peculiar repulsiveness. He knew the Marquis would find no zealous attention there. He conducted him, to the house of a peasant whom he knew. The people crowded around the invalid, overwhelming him with questions, and friendly proffers which he did not understand. Peyraque, with an air of authority, dismissed all who could be of no service, gave his orders, and went to work himself. In a few minutes the fire was blazing, and hot wine was foaming in the kettle. M. de Villemer, stretched on a thick bed of straw and dry turf, saw Caroline on her knees beside him, busily engaged in protecting his clothes from the fire and caring for him with a mother's tenderness. She was uneasy about the terrible drink which Peyraque was brewing for him with strong spices; but the Marquis had confidence in the experience of the mountaineer. He made a sign that he would obey him, and Caroline, with trembling hand, put the cup to his lips. He was soon able to speak, thank his new hosts, and tell Peyraque, pressing his hand warmly, that he would like to be alone with him and Caroline.

It was no easy thing to induce the family to forsake their own roof for several hours. Places of shelter are rare under this inclement sky, and the flocks, the sole dependence of the Cévenois, are lodged in a way to leave no room for the inhabitants. Those living here, in particular, have a reputation for rudeness and lack of hospitality which dates from the murder of the mathematician sent by Cassini to measure the height of Mézenc, and who was taken for a sorcerer. They have greatly improved, and now show themselves more civil; but their habits of life are those of the lowest poverty, and yet they are given to trading, raise magnificent cattle, and are as well provided as possible with commodities for barter. Still, the severity of the climate and the isolation of their rough dwelling-place have passed into their dispositions as well as into their blood.

The room which, with the stable, comprised the whole interior of the house, was given up at last to Peyraque and his friends. It was quite small, and hardly richer than the Celtic grotto of the old woman at Espaly. The smoke poured out partly through the chimney and partly, also, through a gaping hole in the wall on one side. Two beds, shaped like boxes, gave lodgings at night, in some incomprehensible way, to a family of six persons. The bare rock formed the floor; and on one side the cows, goats, sheep, and hens took their comfort.

Peyraque spread clean straw around everywhere, brought in a supply of wood, rummaged in the cupboard, found some bread, and urged Caroline to eat and rest. The Marquis, with a look, begged her to think of herself, for she dared not leave him a minute, and still held his hands in hers. He wanted to speak; he was able to speak now, and yet he was afraid to say a word. He feared she would go away from him as soon as she saw he knew himself beloved; and then Peyraque puzzled him cruelly. He did not comprehend in the least the part played by this rustic Providence which, in its watch over Caroline, had shown itself so obstinate and so merciless toward him; but which was now beginning to regard him with unbounded solicitude and devotion. At last Peyraque went out. He could not forget his poor horse,—his faithful companion,—which he blamed himself for having treated so brutally, and which, on his arrival, he had been forced to intrust to the care of strangers.

"Caroline," said the Marquis, having seated himself on a stool, and still leaning on her arm, "I had many things to tell you, but I have not my reason,—no, really, I have n't the use of it, and I'm afraid to talk in my delirium. Forgive me, I am so happy,—happy to see you, to feel you near me, now I have come back again from the verge of death. But I cannot trouble you any more. Heavens! what a burden I have been on your life! It shall be so no longer; this is only an accident,—a foolish, imprudent act on my part; but how could I consent to lose you again? You do not know, you never will know,—no, you have no idea, you don't comprehend what you are to me; and perhaps you don't care ever to comprehend it! To-morrow, perhaps, you will shun me again. And why, pray? Here, read!" he added, searching for and then handing her the crumpled page of the letter begun at Lantriac that very morning; "it maybe illegible now; the rain and the snow—"

"No," said Caroline, leaning toward the fire, "I can see, I read perfectly, and—I understand. I knew before. I guessed; and I accept. It was the wish of my heart,—the dream of my life. My heart and my life, do they not both belong to you?"

"Alas! no, not yet; but if you would believe in me—"

"Don't tire yourself by talking, trying to convince me," said Caroline, with something imperious in her warmth. "I believe in you, but not in my own destiny. Well! I accept it, such as you make it for me. Good or ill, it shall be dear to me, since I can accept no other. Now listen, listen to me! Perhaps I have only an instant to tell you this in. I don't know what events your conscience and mine will have to meet; I know your mother to be inexorable. I have felt the chill of her contempt; and we have nothing to hope from God if we break her heart. We must submit, then, and that forever. You yourself have said that to form any scheme of being happy upon the loss of a mother is placing the dream of happiness among the most criminal of thoughts, and such happiness would be under the ban of a hundred curses; we ourselves should curse it in our hearts."

"Why do you remind me of all this?" asked the Marquis, sorrowfully; "do you think I have forgotten? But you believe a change in my mother to be impossible; and I see from this that you would not have me try to bring it about, and that pity alone—"

"You see nothing at all," cried Caroline, putting her hand on his mouth; "you see nothing, if you don't see that I love you."

"O Heaven!" said the Marquis, sinking to her feet; "say that again! It seems like a dream. This is the first time you have said it. I have thought I divined it, but I dare not believe it now. Tell me so again,—tell me, and then let me die!"

"Yes; I love you more than my own life," she replied, pressing to her heart the noble brow, seat of a soul so brave and true; "I love you more than my pride, more than my pride of womanhood. I have denied it to myself this long time; I have denied it in my prayers to God, and I lied to God and to myself! At last I understood, and I fled through a cowardly weakness. I felt all was lost, and so it is. Well, what matters it, after all? It only involves myself. While I cherished the hope of learning to forget, I could struggle; but you love me too well,—I see that now,— and you will die, if I forsake you. I thought you were dead a few hours ago, and then I saw clearly into our lives; I had killed you! I might have saved you,—you, the noblest and best of beings,—but I made you the victim of my vain self-respect. And what am I to let you die so, when all that is not your regard is nothing to me? No, no! I have resisted long enough. I have been proud enough, cruel enough, and you have suffered too much from my wrong-doing. I love you, do you hear? I will not become your wife, because that would be to plunge you into bitter remorse, into a woe beyond remedy; but I will be your friend, your servant, a mother to your child, your faithful companion. The purity of our lives may be misunderstood; I shall be mistaken for Didier's actual mother perhaps. Well, I consent even to that. I accept the scorn I have dreaded; and it seems to me drinking of this cup, poured out by you, will give me a new life."

"O noble heart! as pure as heaven!" cried the Marquis. "I accept, for my part, this divine sacrifice. Pray do not scorn me for that! You make me feel worthy of it, and I will soon put an end to it. Yes, yes! I shall work miracles. I feel strong enough now. My mother will yield without a regret. In my heart I feel now the faith and the power that shall persuade her to it. But even if the whole world should rise up to condemn you,—do you see?—you, my sister and my daughter, my pure-minded companion, my dearest friend,—you will only stand the higher in my regard. I shall only be more and more proud of you. What is the world, what is public opinion, to a man who has penetrated the social life of past ages and that of the present as well, fathoming the mysteries of their selfishness and the nothingness of their deceit? Such a man knows full well that, at all times, by the side of one poor truth which floats safely, a thousand truths go under with the mark of infamy upon them. He well knows that the best and most unselfish spirits have walked in the footprints of their Lord, on a thorny path, where wounds and insults fall like rain. Well, we will walk there, if need be; love will keep us from feeling these base attacks. Yes, I can answer for that, at least, and this is what I can swear in defiance of all threats from that destiny the world would make for us: you shall be loved, and you shall be happy! You knew me well, cruel one, shutting your eyes as you ran away. You knew perfectly that my whole life, my whole soul is love and nothing else. You knew perfectly that, if I have sometimes been eager in pursuit of truth, it was from love of her alone; and not for the vain glory of proclaiming her in person. I am not myself a scholar; I am not an author. I am an unknown soldier, who, of my own free will, avoid the noise and smoke of the conflict, fighting unsupported and in the background, not through lack of courage, but that my mother and brother may not be wounded in the struggle. I have accepted this obscure position without a pang to my vanity. I felt that my heart stood in need, not of praise, but of love. All the ambition of my fellows, all their immoderate vanities, their thirst for power, their needs of luxury, their continual hunger for notoriety,—what did all these matter to me? I could not be amused with toys like these. I was myself only a poor, single-hearted man, enamored of an ideal,—an ingenuous child, if you will, seeking love and feeling it alive within him long before meeting her who was to develop its power. I kept silence, knowing I should have to bear raillery,—a thing indifferent, as far as I am concerned personally, but one which would have pained me as an outrage to my inmost, sacred religion. Once, only once in my life,—I should like to tell you this, Caroline,—I have loved—"

"Don't tell me!" cried she, "I don't want to know."

"Nevertheless, you ought to know all. She was good and gentle, and, in recalling her, I can without an effort respect and bless her in her tomb; but she could not love me. It was the fault of her destiny, and not her own. There is not a reproach in my heart for her; there are many for myself. I have hated myself bitterly, and done heavy penance for having yielded to a passion which was never encouraged or really shared. I was only reconciled to life when I saw life blooming into its fairest and purest form in you. I then understood why I was born in tears, why I had been fated to love, and condemned to love too early,—with sorrow, and in sin,—because I sought the one dream and aim of my life too eagerly. And now I feel restored forever and saved. I feel that my character will regain its balance, my youth its hopes, my heart its natural sustenance. Have faith in me,—you whom Heaven has sent me! You know for a certainty that we are made for each other. You have felt a thousand times, in spite of yourself that we had but one mind and one thought; that we loved the same principles, the same art, the same names, the same people, and the same things without influencing each other, except to strengthen and develop what was already there,—to make the germs of our deepest feelings bud and blossom. Do you remember, Caroline, do you remember Séval? And our sunny hours in the valley? And the hours of delicious coolness beneath the arches of the library, where, with lovely vases of flowers, you paid festive honors to this deep, mysterious union of our souls? Was it not an indissoluble marriage which our hands consecrated every morning in their pure touch of greeting! Did not our first glance every single day give us to each other, and that for all time? And can all this be lost utterly, flown forever? Did you yourself believe for one instant that this man could live without you, deprived of air and sunlight,—that he would consent to fall back into darkness again? No, no! you never believed it. He would have followed you to the end of the earth; he would have gone through fire and water and ice to rejoin you. And if you had left me to die in the snow to-day, can't you feel that my spirit set free would have still, like a desperate spectre, pursued you through the mountain storm?"

"Listen to him, just listen!" said Caroline to Peyraque, who had come in and was stupidly looking at the Marquis, now seemingly transfigured by passion; "hear what he says, and do not wonder if I love him better than myself. Do not be frightened, do not worry, do not go away, pitying us. Stay with us and see how happy we are. The presence of a good old man like you will not trouble us. Perhaps you will not understand us,—you who would listen to nothing beyond a certain duty, which I understood yesterday, but no longer admit to-day; yet, against your will even, you will love me again and give me your blessing, for you will feel the rightful authority of this man, who is more to me than all other men, and to whom God has given only the words of truth. Yes, I love him.—I love you, you whom I came near losing to-day, and I will never leave you again. I will follow you everywhere; your child shall be mine, as your country is my country, your faith my faith. There is no higher honor in this world, there is no other virtue before God, than loving you, serving you, and comforting you."

M. de Villemer stood there, radiant with a pure joy, which dazzled Caroline, but did not frighten her. In this hour of enthusiasm there was not even the memory of a trouble. He pressed her to his heart with that sacred paternal feeling which belonged to his nature, and which arose from an instinctive idea of protection,—the rightful authority of a high intelligence over a noble heart, of a superior mind over another mind raised by its love to the same level.

They did not ask themselves whether this lofty rapture would endure always. It must be said, to their praise, that they felt the infinite tenderness of friendship,—enthusiastic, it is true, but deep and sincere,—rather than any other intoxication; and that the aim of their future was, at this moment, defined and summed up in their minds in this one resolution,—never to forsake each other.

XXVI

At about four o'clock, while the brightening skies permitted Peyraque to make preparations for their return, by hiring another cart well provided with straw and blankets, together with oxen and a skilful teamster, so as to reach Laussonne before evening, the young and beautiful Duchess d'Aléria, robed in moire, her arms loaded with cameos, came into the apartment of her mother-in-law at the castle of Mauveroche, in Limousin, leaving her husband and Madame d'Arglade chatting with apparent friendliness in a magnificent drawing-room.

Diana had an air of joyful triumph, which struck the Marchioness.

"Well, what is it, my beauty?" asked the old lady. "What has happened! Has my other son returned!"

"He will come soon," replied the Duchess. "You have the promise of it, and, you know, we feel no uneasiness on his account. His brother knows where he is, and declares we shall see him again by the end of the week. So you find me excessively gay,—excessively happy, even—This little Madame d'Arglade is delightful. Dear mamma, she is the source of all my happiness."

"O, you are jesting, little masquerader! You can't endure her. Why have you brought her here? I did n't request it. No one can amuse me but you."

"And I undertake it more bravely than ever," replied Diana, with a bewitching smile, "and this very D'Arglade whom I adore is going to furnish me with weapons against your wretched melancholy. Listen, dear, good mamma. At last we have got her awful secret, though not without trouble, by any means. For three days we have been manœuvring round her,—the Duke and I,—overpowering her with our mutual trust, our surrender of ourselves to happiness, our most graceful tenderness. At last, the estimable woman, who is n't our dupe, and whom our aggravating mockeries drove to extremity, has given me to understand that Caroline had for an accomplice in her great fault—O, you know whom. She has told you. I pretended not to understand; it was a little thrust right into my heart,—no, a deep thrust, I must tell the truth,—but I hastened to find my dear Duke, and flung it squarely in his face. 'Is it true, you dreadful man, that you have been in love with Mlle de Saint-Geneix!' The Duke sprang like a cat,—no, like a leopard whose paw has been trodden on. 'There! I was sure of it,' said he, roaring; 'it is our good Léonie who has invented that.' And then he began to talk of killing her, so I had to quiet him and tell him I did n't believe it, which was n't quite true; I did believe it a little bit. And this son of yours, who is n't dull,—he perceived that, and he flung himself at my feet, and he swore—O! but he did swear by all that I believe and love, by the true God, and then by you, that it was an infamous lie; and now I am as sure of this as I am that I came into the world for nothing else but just to love his Grace the Duke."

The Duchess had a childish lisp, as natural as Madame d'Arglade's was affected, and she united with this a tone of resolute sincerity that made her perfectly charming. The Marchioness had no time to wonder over what she heard, for the Duke came in as triumphant as his wife.

"There!" cried he. "God be praised, you will never see that viper again! She has called for her carriage; she is going off furious, but with no poison in her fangs. I can answer for that. Mother, my poor mother, how you have been deceived. I can appreciate your suffering. And you would n't say a word, not even to me, who could in a breath—But I have confessed her, this odious woman, who would have brought despair into my household, if Diana were not an angel from heaven, against whom the Powers of Darkness will never prevail. Well, mother, be a little vexed with us all; it will do you good. Madame d'Arglade saw,—did she not?—with her own two eyes, saw Mlle de Saint-Geneix leaning on my arm and crossing the lawn of Séval at daybreak! She saw me speak to her affectionately and shake hands with her? Well, she didn't see the whole, for I kissed her hands one after the other, and what she did n't overhear I'm going to tell you, for I remember as well as if it happened yesterday,—I was excited enough for that. I said to her, 'My brother has been at the point of death to-night, and you have saved him. Pity him, still keep him under your care, help me to hide his illness from our mother, and, thanks to you, he will not die.' That is what I said, I swear it before Heaven, and this is what had taken place."

The Duke recounted the whole, and, going into the matter more thoroughly still, even confessed his false notions about Caroline and his fruitless manœuvring which she had not even perceived. He described the outburst of jealousy against him on the part of the Marquis; their disagreement for one hour; their passionate reconciliation; the confession of the one, the solemn oaths of the other; the discovery he made at that moment of his brother's alarming condition; his own imprudence in leaving him, thinking him asleep and comfortable; the broken window-pane, the cries Caroline overheard; and Caroline herself rushing to his aid, reviving the sick man, staying beside him, devoting herself from that time onward to caring for him, amusing him, and aiding him in his work.

"And all this," added the Duke, "with a devotedness, a frankness, a forgetfulness of self, unequalled in all my experience. This Caroline, you see, is a woman of rare worth, and I have sought in vain for a person who would suit my brother better in point of age, character, modesty, or congenial tastes. I do not find one anywhere. You know I have desired to have him make a more brilliant match. Well, now that he is safe from serious embarrassment, thanks to this angel here who has restored us all to freedom and dignity; now that I have seen the persistence and strength of my brother's love for a person who is, more than all others, the sincere friend he needs; and, lastly, now that Diana understands all this better than I and exhorts me to believe in love-matches, I have, dear mother, only one thing to say, which is, that we must find Caroline again, and you must cheerfully give her your blessing as the best friend you ever had, except my wife, and the best daughter you can wish beside her."

"O my children!" cried the Marchioness, "you make me so happy. I have hardly lived since this calumny. Urbain's grief, the absence of this child who was dear to me, the fear of setting at variance two brothers so perfectly united, if I acknowledged what I supposed to be true, what I am so glad find false. We must hasten after the Marquis, after Caroline; but where, for Heaven's sake? You know where your brother is; but he,—does he know where she is?"

"No, he set out without knowing," replied the Duchess; "but Madame Heudebert knows."

"Write her, dear mother; tell her the truth, and she will tell Caroline."

"Yes, yes, I am going to write," said the Marchioness; "but how can I let poor Urbain know at once?"

"I will take charge of that," said the Duke. "I would go myself, if the Duchess could go with me, but to leave her for three days,—on my word, it is too soon!"

"Fie!" cried the Duchess; "as soon as the honeymoon is over do you mean to be running off without me in that way, light-hearted and light-footed too? Ah! how mistaken you are, you charming man! I shall keep you in order, with all your inconstancy."

"And pray how will you do it, then?" asked the Duke, looking at her fondly.

"By loving you always more and more. We shall see whether you grow weary of it."

While the Duke was caressing the golden hair of his wife, the Marchioness was writing to Camille with a youthful sprightliness which was certainly remarkable. "Here, my children," said she, "is this right?" The Duchess read, "My dear Madame Heudebert, bring Caroline back to us, and let me embrace you both. She has been the victim of a horrible slander; I know all. I weep for having believed in the fall of an angel. May she forgive me! Let her come back; let her be my daughter always and never leave me again. There are two of us who cannot live without her."

"That is delightful! It is kind and just like you," said the Duchess, sealing up the note; and the Duke rang while his mother was writing the address.

The message being despatched, she said to them, "Why can't you both go after the Marquis! Is he so very far off!"

"Twelve hours by post, at the very most," replied the Duke.

"And I cannot know where he is?"

"I ought not to tell you; but I'm convinced he will now have no more secrets from you. Happiness induces confidence."

"My son," returned the Marchioness, "you alarm me seriously. Perhaps your brother is here sick, and you are hiding it from me, as you did at Séval. He is worse even; you make me believe he is away because he is n't able to be up."

"No, no!" cried Diana, laughing; "he is n't here, he is n't sick. He is abroad, he is travelling, he is sad, perhaps; but he is going to be happy now, and he did n't start without some hope of mollifying you."

The Duke solemnly assured his mother that his wife was telling the truth. "Well, my children," resumed the Marchioness, still uneasy, "I wish I could know you were with him. How shall I say it?—He has never been ill but that I have suspected it or at least felt a peculiar uneasiness. I was conscious of this at Séval, exactly at the period when he was so ill without my knowledge. I see that what you describe coincides with a fearful night which I passed then. Well, to-day, this morning, I was all alone, and I had what I may call a waking dream. I saw the Marquis pale, wrapped in something white, a shroud, perhaps, and I heard in my ear his voice, his own voice, saying, 'Mother.'"

"Heavens! what fancies you torment yourself with!" said the Duke.

"I don't torment myself willingly; and I let my presentiments comfort me, for I want to tell you the whole. For an hour past I have known that my son is well; but he has been in danger to-day. He has suffered,—or it may have been an accident. Remember now the day and the hour."

"There! you must go," said the Duchess to her husband. "I don't believe a word of all this, but we must reassure your mother."

"You shall go with him," said the Marchioness. "I don't want my gloomy notions, which, after all, are perhaps morbid and nothing else, to give you the first annoyance of your married life."

"And leave you alone with these ideas!"

"They will all vanish as soon as I see you going after him."

The Marchioness insisted. The Duchess ordered a light trunk; and two hours afterward she was travelling by post with her husband through Tulle and Aurillac, on the way to Le Puy.

The Duchess knew the secret of her brother-in-law; she was ignorant of the mother's name, but aware of the existence of the child. The Marquis had authorized the Duke to have no secrets from his wife.

At six in the morning they reached Polignac. The first face which attracted Diana's notice was that of Didier. She was impressed, as Caroline had been, with a sudden impulse of tenderness toward this dear little creature, who captivated all hearts. While she was looking at him and petting him, the Duke inquired for the pretended M. Bernyer. "My dear," said he to his wife, coming back, "my mother was right; some accident has happened to my brother. He went away yesterday morning for a few hours' ramble over the mountain, but has not returned yet. The people here are uneasy about him."

"Do they know where he went?"

"Yes, it is beyond Le Puy. The post will carry us so far, and I can leave you there. I shall take a horse and a guide, for there is no road passable for carriages."

"We will take two horses," said the Duchess. "I'm not tired a bit; let us start."

An hour after the intrepid Diana, lighter than a bird, was galloping up the slope of the Gâgne and laughing at her husband's anxiety about her. At nine o'clock in the morning they were swiftly passing through Lantriac, to the great wonderment of the townspeople, alighting soon at the Peyraque-Lanion domicile to the equally great disgust of the village innkeeper.

The family were at table in the little workshop. The wanderers had returned the night before after some slight detention, but without accident. The Marquis, weary but not sick, had accepted the hospitality of Peyraque's son, who lived near by. Caroline had slept delightfully in her little room. She was helping Justine to wait upon "the men of the house," that is, the Marquis and the two Peyraques. Radiant with happiness she went back and forth, now waiting on the rest, and now seating herself opposite M. de Villemer, who let her have her own way, watching her with delight, as if to say, "I permit this now, but how I shall repay all these attentions, by and by!"

What an outburst of joy and surprise filled Peyraque's house at the appearance of the travellers! The two brothers gave each other a long hugging. Diana embraced Caroline, calling her "sister."

They spent an hour talking over everything by snatches, extravagantly, without comprehending one another, without feeling sure they were not all dreaming. The Duke was almost famished and found Justine's dishes excellent, for she prepared another plentiful breakfast, while Caroline assisted her, laughing and weeping at the same time. Diana was in a wildly venturesome mood, and wanted to undertake seasoning the dishes, to her husband's great dismay. At last they seriously resumed their respective explanations and recitals. The Marquis began by sending off a courier to Le Puy with a letter for his mother, whose anxiety and strange presentiments they had mentioned the first thing.

They shed no tears on quitting the Peyraques, for these good people had promised to come to the wedding. The next day they had reached Mauveroche again with Didier, whom the Marquis placed in his mother's lap. She had been prepared for this by her son's letter. She loaded the child with caresses, and, restoring him to Caroline's arms, she said, "My daughter, you accept, then, the task of making us all happy? Take my blessing a thousand times over, and if you would keep me here a long while, never leave me again. I have done you much harm, my poor angel; but God has not allowed it to last long, for I should have died from it sooner than you."

THE MARQUIS AND HIS WIFE passed the rest of the bright season at Mauveroche, and a few autumnal days at Séval. This place was very dear to them; and, in spite of the pleasure at meeting their relatives again in Paris, it was not without an effort that they tore themselves away from a nook consecrated by such memories.

The marriage of the Marquis astounded no one; some approved, others disdainfully predicted that he would repent this eccentricity, that he would be forsaken by all reasonable people, that his life was a ruin, a failure. The Marchioness came near suffering a little from these remarks. Madame d'Arglade pursued Diana, Caroline, and their husbands with her hatred; but everything fell before the revolution of February, and people had to think of other matters. The Marchioness was terribly frightened, and thought it expedient to seek refuge at Séval, where she was happy in spite of herself. The Marquis, just as his anonymous book was about to appear, postponed its publication to a more quiet period. He was unwilling to strike the sufferers of the day. Blest with love and family joys, he is not impatient for glory.

The old Marchioness is now no more. Feeble in body and far too active in mind, her days have been numbered. She passed away in the midst of her children and grandchildren, blessing them all without knowing she was leaving them, conscious of bodily infirmities, but preserving her intellectual force and natural kindliness to the last, and laying plans, as most invalids do, for the next year.

The Duke is growing quite fleshy in his prosperity; but is still good-humored, handsome, and active enough. He lives in great luxury, but without extravagance; referring everything to his wife, who governs him, and keeps him on his good behavior, with rare tact and admirable judgment, notwithstanding the indulgent spoiling of her fondness for him. We would not assert that he has never thought of deceiving her; but she has contrived to counteract his fancies without letting him suspect it, and her triumph, which still endures, proves once more that there are sometimes wit and power enough in the brain of a girl of sixteen to settle the destiny, and that in the best possible way, of a professed profligate. The Duke, still wonderfully good-natured and somewhat weak, finds more delight than one would think in giving over his skilfully planned treacheries toward the fair sex, and in going to sleep, without further remorse, on the pillow of comfortable propriety.

The Marquis and the new Marchioness de Villemer now pass eight months of the year at Séval, always occupied—we cannot say with one another, because they are so united that they think together and answer each other before the question is asked, but—with the education of their children, who are all sprightly and intelligent. M. de G—is dead. Madame de G—has been forgotten. Didier is formally recognized by the Marquis as one of his children. Caroline no longer remembers that she is not his mother.

Madame Heudebert is established at Séval. All her children are brought up under the united care of the Marquis and Caroline. The sons of the Duke, petted more, are not so intelligent or so strong; but they are amiable and full of precocious graces. The Duke is an excellent father, and is astonished, though quite needlessly, to find that his children are already so large.

The Peyraques have been loaded with gifts. Last year Urbain and Caroline went back to visit them, and, this time, they climbed, under a fine sunrise, the silvery peak of Mézenc. They also wanted to see once more the poor cabin where, in spite of the Marquis and his liberality, nothing is changed for the better; but the father has bought land and thinks himself wealthy. Caroline seated herself with pleasure by the miserable hearth, where she had seen at her feet, for the first time, the man with whom she would have willingly shared a hut in the Cévennes, and forgetfulness of the whole world.

THE END

A Note About the Author

George Sand (1804–1876), born Armandine Aurore Lucille Dupin, was a French novelist who was active during Europe's Romantic era. Raised by her grandmother, Sand spent her childhood studying nature and philosophy. Her early literary projects were collaborations with Jules Sandeau, who co-wrote articles they jointly signed as J. Sand. When making her solo debut, Armandine adopted the pen name George Sand, to appear on her work. Her first novel, *Indiana* was published in 1832, followed by *Valentine* and *Jacques*. During her career, Sand was considered one of the most popular writers of her time.

A Note from the Publisher

Spanning many genres, from non-fiction essays to literature classics to children's books and lyric poetry, Mint Edition books showcase the master works of our time in a modern new package. The text is freshly typeset, is clean and easy to read, and features a new note about the author in each volume. Many books also include exclusive new introductory material. Every book boasts a striking new cover, which makes it as appropriate for collecting as it is for gift giving. Mint Edition books are only printed when a reader orders them, so natural resources are not wasted. We're proud that our books are never manufactured in excess and exist only in the exact quantity they need to be read and enjoyed.

bookfinity™

Discover more of your favorite classics with Bookfinity™.

- Track your reading with custom book lists.
- Get great book recommendations for your personalized Reader Type.
- Add reviews for your favorite books.
- AND MUCH MORE!

Visit **bookfinity.com** and take the fun Reader Type quiz to get started.

Enjoy our classic and modern companion pairings!

Classic & Modern